Kiamichi Journey

Book Three

of the

Kiamichi Survival Series

C.A. Henry

Kiamichi Journey: Book Three of the Kiamichi Survival Series
Copyright 2017 by Carol A. Henry Madding

Cover Art by Hristo Argirov Kovatliev
Editing by Hope Springs Editing

Acknowledgements

My sincere thanks to Dr. Nancé Hicks, who helped me with the scenes that required medical expertise. Any mistakes in those scenes are mine, not hers.

Many thanks to Mark Davis from Bob Hurley Ford in Tulsa, who helped with information about the Jeep, and kept after me to hurry up and write.

I greatly appreciate my beta readers, Kimberly "K-Slay" Slayton, Nancé Hicks, Jinnie Lettkeman, and Jennifer Murray. I don't know what I would do without these wonderful ladies.

A big thank you to Reggie Murray for his suggestions about the Masonic Order.

Dedication

To Jack,
the man who still thinks I can learn to do math.

Without you, I would never have become a teacher or a writer. Thank you for having faith in me, and for being a sounding board for all my crazy ideas. You are a great blessing in my life.

Contents

Chapter One – October 30
Pueblo, Colorado

Silence filled the cavernous RUBB BVE hangar where two helicopters sat like birds perched on a roost. The pilots and mechanics had left for the day, lowering the folding Heli-Door and locking up. Nothing moved for several minutes in the eerie silence. Then a shadow seemed to materialize next to a supply cabinet; the shape stood motionless for a few seconds, then darted over to the nearest chopper, got in, and after a brief time, emerged and returned to the spot near the cabinet.

Half an hour later, when the sky had gone fully dark, the figure slipped over to the small rear door of the hangar. The door creaked slightly as it opened a thin crack. The shadow peeked out, then widened the gap just enough to slide through into the night.

Sergeant Manny Lopez passed behind another hangar and strode purposefully to the perimeter fencing. He approached a guard who was patrolling the fence line.

"Agent Slayton, any activity?" he demanded.

"No, Sergeant. It's all quiet tonight, so far," the solidly built young man answered.

"Well, keep your eyes open. Sometimes when it's real quiet, that's when trouble starts."

"Will do, Sarge."

***

David Martin knelt and moved a box of flower vases aside, then reached into his pack, pulling out two small bags containing first aid supplies. As he started to put them in a space at the back of the cabinet, he noticed several MREs that he didn't remember having.

"Hey, bro," he called softly.

Price turned to look at him. "What? Something wrong?"

David frowned. "You forgot to tell me you had these extra MREs. When did you swipe them from the mess hall?"

"Huh? What MREs? We had fifteen last time I counted, but they're stored in the next cabinet to the left, doofus."

"Well, there are seven, right here in this cabinet. I don't imagine they sprouted legs and moved themselves."

"*I* didn't do it," Price protested. "Check the other cabinet. Dang, I hope nobody found our stuff. I want to be gone from here in a week or so, and we'll need all that food."

The brothers, who looked so similar that many people mistook them for twins, were planning to escape from NERC, the National Emergency Recovery Corps. Conscripted at gunpoint to serve in the new agency, they were working for a branch of FEMA that had been established to deal with the problems associated with the recent economic collapse. At first, the Martin brothers didn't mind their duties, which consisted of distributing food and water in the Pueblo, Colorado area, but when the duties gradually changed to forcing people into an internment camp, they decided that leaving would be an escape rather than a desertion.

Recently, Price had pointed out to David that with most of the area's remaining residents already in the camp, they probably would be reassigned to another city soon, possibly one even further away from their parents. This idea frightened them both, and they redoubled their efforts to gather enough supplies to survive the trip from Pueblo to Kanichi Springs, Oklahoma, where their family had taken refuge. They had to be careful not to take so much at one time that the losses were noticeable, while still gathering sufficient amounts for the trip. It was a balancing act that made both of them nervous.

David stood and stretched the kinks out of his back, then stepped to the left and opened the door under the florist's worktable. Quickly counting the packaged meals, he shook his head in confusion.

"There's still fifteen in this side. Did you get more and forget that you stashed them?"

"No, David,' Price replied, exasperated. "I would remember a good haul like that, and I would have told you. You sure *you* didn't do it?"

"Positive. If I didn't do it and you didn't do it, who did? We need to move our cache, in case whoever it is comes back."

"Move it where? We'd never get all this moved out without someone seeing us, and there's not anywhere nearby where it would be any safer. Maybe we should put it somewhere else in here, like in that walk-in cooler with all those dead flowers."

"Yeah, maybe. This is creepy. Who could be adding to our supplies? We've been super careful to make sure we weren't followed when we've come here. I think we need to move up our departure plans, and just go."

"Yeah, I think so, too. There are plenty of other things we could use on our little trip, but if we wait much longer, we may lose the chance to escape. We still have to figure out a way to load all this stuff into the kayaks, and we have to steal the kayaks before we can do that."

"Kayaks?" A disapproving murmur came softly from the back room of the flower shop. David and Price froze, recognizing the familiar voice. They looked at each other, and their shoulders drooped in defeat.

Sergeant Lopez stepped into the work area. His silent scrutiny and his scowl were indications of his displeasure.

"Uh, Sarge, we can expl---," David began, but Sarge cut him off with a slash of his hand.

"*Kayaks*? You gotta be kidding me. Canoes will work better. We could carry more supplies in canoes, and there are plenty at the rental place to choose from, but why go west of town to get them, then have to backtrack right through town on the river, where anyone could see us? Besides, their kayaks are all bright blue and yellow, and would stand out too much."

"We? Did you say '*we*'?" Price asked, stunned.

"Yes, that's what I said. I have news, so let's step into the storage room where we won't be seen through those front windows if any other NERC personnel happen by."

3

Price glanced at David, who shrugged, and they followed the sergeant into the back. Rolls of floral ribbons in a myriad of colors, cases of green Styrofoam, and other supplies for making flower arrangements lined the walls. Sarge fingered a length of purple ribbon that lay on a shelf, then turned to the brothers.

"I became aware several weeks ago that you two were up to something. My first clue was the fact that you stand outside your tent in the evenings, with David pretending to smoke, but I've never seen you light up any other time or place. So, I started watching more closely, and noticed that you seem to inhale, but when you exhale, no smoke comes out your nostrils or mouth. You're faking it, so I figured that the two of you must be out there for some other reason, like to keep your conversation private, and I started to wonder why. That's when I began to follow you.

"You've been stealing food out of the mess hall, and I examined those first aid kits you delivered to the motor pool and the internment camp the other day. Each one of them was missing a few items, so I put it all together. I saw you come from this part of town a couple of times, and since I knew that I had assigned a different sector to you, I had to ask myself why you were hanging around over here. You did a good enough job of keeping your plans secret from the average Joe on the street, but I gotta tell ya, you'd never fool anyone with experience in covert ops. Did I ever tell you what I did before the collapse?" Sarge's eyes had a wicked gleam as he stared at the two young men.

"No, Sarge, I don't believe you did," David commented.

"I did a couple of tours in Iraq. You may have heard of the Army Rangers. We rescued prisoners of war, and at least once, it made the news around the world. Then I went to Afghanistan for a year. Longest year of my life in the worst place I've ever been. I was home on leave when things went south, and was ready to join my family in Mexico when NERC decided they needed people with military experience to ride herd on you conscripts."

Sarge paused, and shook his head, frowning. "I never wanted this job. I had other plans, but I wasn't given a choice, any more than you were. You two are the smartest of the 'recruits' I've worked with, so when I realized you what you were doing, I

4

decided that we would all have a better chance of making it out of here if we joined forces. I'm going with you, and we're taking canoes, but not from Pueblo. I have some contributions to make to the venture, and I also have access to information that you don't have."

Sarge gave them a hard look, then continued. "Our work here is almost finished. NERC plans, uh, just *happened* to come into my possession before the lieutenant saw them." He grinned slyly, then continued, his voice gruff.

"They're going to leave fifteen guards, some cooks, and a few other people here to maintain the camp, and ship the rest to Idaho and Utah. Your names were on the list to be transferred. There's a lot of preppers up there, and the so-called government wants them rounded up, their supplies confiscated.

"Most of those folks are armed, and they know how to shoot. Many of them have military backgrounds, and personally, I wouldn't want to get into it with them on their home turf, even if I had a beef with them, which I *don't*. I happen to agree with them that the government got too big, too invasive, and started walking all over the Constitution. I refuse to fight against my fellow Americans, so I need to get outta here, and soon."

"Sarge, we'd love to have you join us, but we're going to Oklahoma. I seem to remember someone telling me you're from New Mexico, and that's not exactly in the right direction." Price gave the sergeant a questioning look. "Unless you don't mind going our way, this won't work."

"It really doesn't matter to me which way we go. Yes, I'm from Albuquerque, but my parents and siblings left just before the collapse. They went to Mexico for an extended visit with my father's family, and hopefully, they're safe in the mountains. I can't let myself think about that too much, because there's nothing I can do to help them right now. There's nobody left for me in New Mexico. If this mess ever ends, I'll find my folks, but for now, I just need to get out of NERC and find a safe place to wait it out.

"And I want you to start thinking of me as a friend and partner instead of as a superior. Until we leave, when other NERC personnel are around, treat me like 'Sarge', but when we're alone, and after we leave, I'm just Rian, your companion. You have to stop calling me 'Sarge' because they'll be looking for us, and anyone we encounter might remember if they hear you refer to me like that."

"You mean we'll be equals on this trip? You aren't going to boss us around like you've been doing for months?" David asked skeptically.

"That is exactly what I mean. I've watched you two, and I know that you have skills and knowledge that will come in handy. I realize that I'm horning in on your plans, and I don't expect to be in charge, but you should know that I do have some training and experience that you don't have. I could travel alone and I might even make it somewhere safe, but all it takes is one injury, one sickness, or one night of sleeping a bit too soundly, and a loner could die out there.

"With three of us, we can help each other, and watch each other's backs, too. And I'm not insisting that I join you. I'm asking. I'm sorry if it sounded like you don't have a choice in this. Just say the word, and I'll leave you to it, but I hope you'll allow me to travel with you."

Price and David looked at each other, and as they had done for years, communicated without words.

"We think having you with us would be great, Sarge." Price stuck his hand out and Sarge shook it, then grasped David's hand.

"So, about the news I mentioned earlier. The thermal-imaging equipment that was installed on the chopper doesn't work. It seems that a small memory chip 'fell out' in transit. Well, I kinda helped it fall out, if I'm being honest," Sarge smirked. "It'll take a few more weeks for a replacement chip to be sent, but we don't have that much time. The move to Utah and Idaho that I told you about is scheduled to begin next week."

"So, we have until next week to disappear?" David asked.

"No. We're leaving this afternoon."

"What?!" The younger men looked incredulous.

"An opportunity has dropped into our laps, and we'd be fools not to take advantage of it. Two NERC agents, a male and a female who have been, uh, *fraternizing*, deserted sometime during

6

the night. The lieutenant discovered that they were gone about an hour ago. I've been watching them, too, and figured that they were about to run.

"Last night, I did a tent check, and saw that they weren't around, but I sort of neglected to report them missing. Then I made sure I was in the vicinity when Sergeant Malone reported to the lieutenant that they didn't show up for roll call this morning. The LT needed someone to go after them, and I just happened to volunteer. He told me to pick out a couple of my best agents and go get those deserters, so we have a perfect excuse to be gone. They probably won't even miss us for at least three days, and since they're sure that the couple went due south, when they start searching for us, that's where they'll look first. We'll be a few hundred miles to the east by then.

"I hope you'll let me guide you through this initial portion of our escape. I've planned it all out, and you haven't had time to process it all. I'm not trying to be bossy, but if you agree, I'll be in charge temporarily, at least until we're away from town."

"It's okay with me," David replied, and Price nodded.

"Great. Feel free to ask questions or make suggestions, but here's what I think we should do…."

***

Sarge left through the back door of the little shop, and walked down the alley to the Jeep J8 five-door light-duty he'd picked up from the motor pool earlier. He had explained his strategy for their escape to the other two men, and they agreed that it was their best chance for getting away safely. Everything they did from that point until they were away from Pueblo was intended to deceive other NERC personnel, making them believe that they were on their way to capture the deserters.

As Sergeant Lopez came around the block, the Martins appeared, strolling along the sidewalk like two tourists. He pulled over, acting like he hadn't seen them just minutes earlier, and told them to get into the Jeep. They hopped in, and Sarge pretended to be filling them in on their assignment. He drove directly to the camp where NERC agents slept, and stopped in front of their tent, waiting for them in the vehicle.

David and Price entered the tent and were glad to find it empty. Four other agents shared the space with them, and it was a relief not to have company as they prepared packs for their supposed trip south. The less contact they had with other NERC agents, the fewer questions they would have to answer.

Sarge told them to just leave anything that might raise suspicions if someone noticed that it was missing, and only take what would be necessary for the mission they were pretending to be on, but Price had a small photo of their family which he had taped to one of the tent poles, and he slipped it into his pocket as they turned to leave.

As soon as they were back in the Jeep, Sarge drove to the motor pool, and ordered six cans full of diesel loaded in the back.

"Goin' after those no-good deserters, Sergeant?" one of the mechanics asked.

"Yes. We think they're headed south, but we'll need extra fuel, since we aren't totally sure they went that way." Sarge frowned. "We'll be back for more if we don't find them, and we'll keep hunting until we catch them and bring them in."

"Well, good luck to ya. There's no better man to send than you, Sergeant. I almost feel sorry for those two, once ya catch up to 'em."

"We have a lesson to teach, both to them and to all our agents. Desertion should be a hanging offense, in my opinion, but I just follow orders."

Sarge had David take the wheel, and moved over to the front passenger seat. They stopped off at the mess tent next, where they picked up boxes of MREs and several gallon jugs of water that they were entitled to for their trip to catch the fugitives. Their last stop was the armory, a building that NERC had appropriated to store and secure weapons. They checked out rifles and handguns, and a few boxes of ammo for each. Sarge signed the paperwork, chatting calmly with the duty officer and promising to return the guns when they got back.

Once they were back in the Jeep, Sarge gave the others a slight smile. "See, having those two run was a lucky thing for us, since we can now travel and eat on NERC's dime, at least for a while. I wish the lovebirds had waited a few more days, but still, this has helped us a lot."

They headed south, and once they were at the outskirts of town, hid the Jeep and settled in to wait.

"Sarge? What did you say your name is?" David asked.

"Rian, with an 'i'."

"That doesn't sound very Mexican," Price interjected.

"It's not. It's Irish. My father's family is from Mexico. He was born in El Paso, so he's an American citizen. He was a heck of a pitcher, and got a baseball scholarship. He graduated from the University of New Mexico, then decided to stay and open his own business in Albuquerque. He met my mother, who's Irish, and they had five kids, each with one name that's Irish and one that's Hispanic. I'm Rian Manuel Lopez, and have always been called Manny, but I want to use Rian now, because if NERC gets around to asking questions of anyone we encounter on this trip, 'Manny' is a common name in Mexico and might give us away. You'll notice that I have brownish-red strands in my hair, and my eyes are not as dark as most Mexicans, and neither is my skin. Maybe I can avoid anyone connecting me with the missing Mexican sergeant. That's my hope, anyway.

"Let's go over the next steps in the plan while we wait We'll stay here until everyone will either be on guard duty or at the mess hall this evening. Then we'll swing around the outer edge of the city, park the Jeep somewhere out of sight, and go on foot to the florist shop. It's fairly close to the eastern edge of town, so we should be able to get away without attracting much notice. David, you'll guard the Jeep, while Price and I will go retrieve the supplies.

"We'll set out immediately and put as many miles behind us as we can stand, taking turns driving. It's vital that we get as far away as possible before they start to suspect that we aren't where we're supposed to be. We'll make camp where we can conceal the Jeep and get some rest, then do it all again, until the fuel runs out, hopefully timing it so we're near a town and the river before we have to abandon the Jeep. We all need to be listening constantly for the sounds of vehicles or helicopters, and be ready to hide if we hear anything that's not natural, although in this country, hiding a Jeep may be a problem. We have to stay alert. We'll relax when we get where we're going. By the way, where *are* we going, specifically?"

"Price, you tell him. You talked to Jen about it more than I did."

"Well, we're from Tulsa, but our folks decided that with things getting so bad there, it was time to bug out. There were gangs of thugs looting and burning, and they were getting close to our neighborhood. Our older sister, Jennifer, has this friend who inherited a big hunting lodge in southeastern Oklahoma, near a little town called Kanichi Springs. She said the lodge is out of thick logs, with bulletproof windows, and had some sort of secret passageway into hidden caves where there are lots of supplies stored. The friend's name is Erin, and the uncle who left her the lodge was Ernest Miller, who wrote survival manuals and novels about societal collapse. I guess you might say he was an expert on survival and prepping, and he practiced what he preached."

"Really? *The* Ernest Miller? He was an expert, alright. I've read a couple of his books. His survival stories made the rounds when I was deployed, and were real popular with the troops. So, you haven't seen this lodge yourselves?"

"Nope. We were on Highway 75, headed south out of Tulsa, when we got stopped at a roadblock and forced into NERC. Our parents were allowed to continue their trip, and Jen was already at the lodge. We've spoken with them a few times on the radio, and they got there just fine. Well, actually, their car was stolen with all their baggage and guns, and even cell phones, and they had to finish the journey on foot, but they're okay.

"Evidently, there's quite a large group at the lodge now. We think there's even a nurse living nearby. If I'm remembering correctly, her name is Amber or Angie – something like that. We don't say things that would give away too much information on the radio, but by using references that only our family would understand, we're pretty sure they have a bunch of people, maybe twenty-five or more, staying there now. We've known Erin for years, and also two other friends of Jen's. Sarah was a teacher, and Val was about to open her own accounting office right before the collapse. She had just passed her CPA test when things started downhill. Erin edited books, and Jen sold cars at a big Ford dealership across from the Pepsi plant in Tulsa. They've all been friends for a long time."

"I'm not very familiar with Oklahoma. Never been there, in fact. All I know about Oklahoma is it's flat, treeless, and has a lot of Native Americans." Rian commented.

"Flat? Ha! The western part of the state has areas that are pretty flat, except where it *isn't*," Price smirked. "There are mesas and canyons, and some pretty big hills, and there's the Wichita Mountains in the southwest, but most of the eastern part of the state is rolling hills and small mountains. It has lots of trees, too – oak, hickory, pine, pecan. Erin's lodge is in the Kiamichi Mountains, and there are other mountains, too, like the Ouachitas and the Arbuckles. There are also lots of beautiful lakes. I've always wondered why so many people think Oklahoma is all flat." He shook his head. "Nothing could be further from the truth."

"Are you sure you know the way to this lodge?" Rian asked.

"We've been on vacation in that area, but never actually visited Kanichi Springs. We kinda have a general idea of the location, somewhere east of the turnpike and not far from McAlester. Jen said there's a sign for the exit, and to just stay on that road, which goes right through the middle of town. We figure that once we get there, we'll just ask folks where the lodge is. We know the lodge is a few miles north of the town, and if we have to, we'll search for it on foot," David assured him.

"Well, we have a long trip before we have to worry about that, I guess. We have to cross a chunk of Kansas before we even get to Oklahoma, and if this place is in the southeast part of the state, we'll be crossing a lot of Oklahoma, too " Rian commented. "Did you both remember to bring civilian clothes to change into? We'll do that when we stop and make camp."

"Yeah, we've got civvies. What will we do with our uniforms?" David asked.

"They might be handy to have, just as a change of clothes, but they'll also be a danger to us, marking us as NERC if we're wearing them, and deserters if we aren't. Lots of people don't like anything to do with FEMA, and we are going to have to be careful, since NERC will be looking for us." Sarge paused, tilting his head thoughtfully. "Maybe we can take off all the patches, and mix up uniform pieces with civilian pieces, but ... well, I'm still leery about it."

"We could do that, and dirt-dye the uniforms," Price suggested.

Rian raised an eyebrow. "Dirt-dye?"

"Yeah, dirt-dye. We could do it in the river, or anywhere we find dirt and water. The dirt will stain the cloth, changing the color from light khaki green to a dull mud color. It would work better if we could do it in red dirt, but it'll work okay, I hope, in the dirt around here.

David rotated his head, stretching to get the kinks out. "How will we travel when we run out of fuel?"

Rian grinned. "That's when we take to the river. Somewhere along the way, we'll liberate some canoes, or a raft, or maybe a small boat. The river will be up somewhat, due to all the rain, so we should be able to float some kind of craft. Maybe we'll find a marina on a lake, with some canoes or even paddle boats. We'll see when the time comes, and we'll go as far as we can by water."

"Then we'll probably be leaving the river at Muskogee, and making the rest of the trip on foot," David commented. "The river turns east just past Muskogee and goes into Arkansas, but we need to go south from Muskogee. And we have no idea how many locks and dams there are between here and the Kerr Reservoir. We may be on foot earlier than we planned. We'll have to get across some lakes, and find a way to portage whatever boats we have around the dams."

Price looked toward the sun, then added, "Looks like it's about time to move out. Let's go, and may God keep us safe."

Chapter Two – October 30
Southeastern Colorado

David took up a position where he could see the approaches to the spot where they hid the Jeep, and the other two slipped off toward the flower shop. They were almost there when they heard voices. Rian signaled Price to take cover in an alley, and they waited.

The sounds of people tiptoeing on concrete and the murmur of low voices drifted toward them, then three figures came around the corner. Price peered at them as they passed the alleyway. Two boys and a girl, and all three looked starved and scared. Price grasped Rian's arm, and whispered, "Go along with whatever I say."

He stepped out behind the trio and cleared his throat. The teens stopped abruptly, then slowly turned to see who was there.

"I thought I told you to get somewhere safe and stay off the streets," he said in a soft, menacing voice.

"Uh, yeah, but we need food. Please don't shoot us," the older boy begged.

Rian stepped out and stood beside Price. "What seems to be the problem here, Agent Martin?"

"Sergeant, these young people have been warned to stay off the streets, but have defied my instructions."

"Well," Rian narrowed his eyes and stared at the three teenagers. "I am ordering you to go immediately to the NERC encampment and turn yourselves in," he commanded in his best drill sergeant voice. "We're on an important mission and don't have time to escort you, but if I see you on the streets again, you will be arrested and sent to the detention center in Denver where we incarcerate dissidents. Go now, and report to the camp right away."

His tone was so pompous and melodramatic that Price had a hard time keeping a straight face, but somehow he managed it as they watched the young folks run down the street.

"You think they'll actually turn themselves in?" Price asked.

"Not a chance. Care to tell me what that was all about? You've obviously encountered those kids before."

"Yeah, I have. A while back, when we were clearing that plumbing supply place, I found them in an office. They begged me not to take them to the camp, and I let them go."

"Disobeyed orders, huh? Weren't you worried about what would happen if any officers found out?"

"I was only worried about one, this mean Mexican sergeant who is tough as a boot and has no mercy for slackers. All the agents are scared to death of him," Price replied with a grin.

"Enough of your lip, kid. Let's go; we've got work to do."

They got their supplies loaded into some shopping bags that were left in the shop, then Rian led Price out the back door and into the alleyway. Price carried three bags in his right hand, and Rian carried three in his left, and each carried a handgun. Rian crossed over to another door, and signaled for Price to wait, then set his bags down and entered the building. About three minutes passed, as Price waited near a dumpster that smelled like rotting vegetation and sewage. The night's darkness had deepened, but there was enough light from the quarter moon to enable them to get around.

Rian returned, a large military-style pack strapped on his broad back. He gathered his other bags and cocked his head in the direction of the Jeep.

"What's that?" Price nodded toward the backpack.

"My stash. You weren't the only ones who've been planning for a while. I have a little food, more ammo, knives, and a few other items that will come in handy. Now, let's get a move on, and maintain silence until we're back at the Jeep."

They quietly made their way back, stopping at every corner to peek around it and listen to make sure they wouldn't run into anyone else.

"Okay, I guess we're ready. We need to slip out of town as quietly as possible, and hope nobody sees us. The two who aren't driving should slump down and stay out of sight as much as

14

possible, until we're out in the country. That way, anyone who sees us will tell NERC that they saw one guy. It might buy us some time. I'd rather not be seen at all, and besides, anyone who does see us is probably not going to volunteer to tell NERC anything, since they're obviously hiding from them to keep from being forced into the camp."

"I'll drive," David offered. "Too many people might recognize you, Sar—uh, Rian. You're better known around here than we are."

Several pairs of eyes watched the Jeep at various points on its journey out of Pueblo. Those who saw it were people who stayed concealed during the day, and came out at night to search for food, and none of them ever mentioned the Jeep to anyone associated with NERC.

***

David stayed behind the wheel through the suburbs of Pueblo and as soon as they were out of town, they stopped to change out of their NERC uniforms. David suggested stuffing the uniforms behind the fuel cans until they could take the patches off. They continued, seeing no one in the towns of Fowler and Manzanola as they sped down US 50, headed southeast.

"The next town we'll come to is Rocky Ford. It was famous for the watermelons and cantaloupes that they grew there. They had a festival every year featuring melons, with seed-spitting and cantaloupe-eating contests. If I remember correctly, the population was just over 4,000 before the collapse," Rian explained.

"How do you know that?" Price raised an eyebrow. "You sound like a tour guide or a Chamber of Commerce website."

"I found one of those tourist welcome centers -- you know, the ones with all the brochures -- and grabbed any that were for towns along the way. I like to know what to expect. If we're going to try to avoid population centers, we need to know where the bigger towns are."

"So, do we avoid Rocky Ford?" David asked.

"I wish we could, but we'd have to go way around. I have a feeling that most of the population has stayed right there. It's an agricultural community, and there was a seed company or two there, so I imagine the people have some gardening skills that would keep the community fed. I just don't know how friendly they'll be to strangers." Rian shook his head. "It might be best not to press our luck so early in our trip."

"There it is. Looks like a nice little town, what we can see of it, and the buildings look pretty old. On the river and with a railroad, too; I'm surprised it stayed little," David added. "So, which way should we go? Who's my navigator, anyway?"

"I guess I am, at least for this leg of our journey. I wish we could get off the highway, but then again, it's faster and probably better on our mileage than taking off on side roads. The map I have isn't as detailed as I'd like. US 50 goes right through a lot of towns and runs alongside the river for quite a ways. I don't think we can avoid going right down Main Street."

The town of Rocky Ford showed little sign that the nation's economy had collapsed. Windows in the shops were intact and there was no sign that looters had set any fires. Downtown Rocky Ford was charming; buildings and homes from the early 1900s, as well as lovely, mature trees, lined the streets. Leaves from the trees skittered across the pavement, and faint, flickering lights could be seen in some of the houses.

David took his foot off the accelerator, then braked. A group of men had moved out in front of them, some carrying lanterns and others with rifles at their sides. They looked non-threatening, but ready. As the Jeep stopped, one of them stepped up to the driver's side and greeted the newcomers, raising the lantern so he could see their faces.

"Hello. We haven't seen many strangers in town lately, and under the circumstances, I hope you don't mind that we're being mighty careful about our town. Where you headed?" The tall, slender man had the look of someone who spent most of his time outdoors. About forty years old, he was deeply tanned and his hands were calloused.

"We're just passing through. We mean you no harm and we aren't up to anything. We're just trying to get home to Missouri," David offered.

"Where'd you come from? This looks like a government vehicle. Did you steal it?"

"Pueblo. In a manner of speaking, yes, we stole it. Is that a problem?" Rian interjected.

"Not as long as you didn't steal it in our town. We have enough to do without borrowing problems from elsewhere. So far we've managed to stay below the radar of FEMA, and we like it that way."

"You familiar with NERC?" Rian asked.

"Yessir, and we got no use for them."

"Well, I can tell you that they are pulling out of Pueblo, except for about fifteen guards, and moving on. They're too shorthanded in this area to give much thought to little towns, but once they get some other areas subdued, they'll probably be back to give you some attention. That's what they've done in other states, anyway. If you know of anyone with a ham radio, you might give Idaho and Utah a heads-up." Rian looked the other man right in the eye. "We'll keep driving, and I hope you'll forget that you ever saw us."

The man narrowed his eyes, then gave a nod and a slight smile. "Yeah, you keep going, and don't worry about folks here talking to any government types. Don't tell me if I'm right, but I think you might know a lot more about this NERC organization than you let on. Rocky Ford is a town full of independent types, and we wouldn't like being forced to work for them, either.

The man patted the roof of the Jeep. "Have a safe trip. I wish you luck, and by the way, you might want to avoid going through downtown Las Animas. We heard that they have some problems over there and aren't welcoming strangers, even if they're 'just passing through.'"

"Thanks. I hope we can come back to your town for a visit someday. It looks like a nice place."

"It is, if we can keep it that way. I hope you get where you're going." The man gestured for his companions to let them pass, and David drove cautiously past them and out of town.

"Whew! I was a little nervous there for a minute," Price rubbed the back of his neck. "Good job, bro, telling them we were headed for Missouri."

"Why did you bring up NERC, Sa—I mean, Rian? Why give them any clue who we are?" David demanded.

"Sometimes, you just have to take a chance on folks. Knowing what I know about the town, I figured they wouldn't like government interference in their lives. I knew NERC hadn't been there, but I figured they'd heard about the camp in Pueblo. I got the impression that guy was pretty intelligent and would figure it out anyway after seeing the Jeep, so I decided to be upfront with him. Occasionally, just being bluntly honest with people, even if you've done something wrong, will get them to trust you, but if you try to lie and they see through it, you've blown your chance. I bet he guessed that we were running from NERC as soon as he saw the Jeep, and that remark he make about being forced to work for NERC confirmed it. He knows, but those people will keep their mouths shut."

"I hope you're right," Price sighed. "I sure wish the Jeep was a different color. This drab green kinda screams 'government issue'."

"Yeah, it does, but this shade of green will be a lot easier to conceal than bright yellow, red, or white." Rian grinned. "Besides, we'll run out of fuel all too soon, and it won't matter what color it is when we leave it behind."

David accelerated as they reached the edge of town, and glancing at Rian, asked, "So, Mr. Tour Guide, what's next?"

"There's a tiny burg coming up pretty quickly, called Swink. It had about 700 people pre-collapse, and I would bet that most of them are now in Rocky Ford or La Junta."

They passed through Swink without slowing down. Just as Rian had guessed, the town seemed deserted, with only one faint flicker of light in a window above an abandoned store.

"La Junta is even closer to Swink than Swink is to Rocky Ford. Lucky for us, the highway is right on the north edge of town, and still runs parallel to the river, so we won't be driving through the main part of the city at all," Rian explained.

"How big a town is it?" David shifted in his seat, and glanced over at Rian.

"About 8,000 back when, but who knows today? It's pretty much high prairie around here. I guess whether people stayed or not depends on the availability of food, but I bet a lot of people stayed. Be ready to take evasive measures if we see a hostile-looking roadblock."

"Evasive measures? I'm not trained for that! My driving experience is limited to fighting rush hour in Tulsa, so I don't know what to do." David had a slightly desperate look on his face.

"If you're not comfortable with it, stop and I'll drive. I forgot for a minute that you two aren't military."

David started to pull over, then realized that there was no need to get off the road. They hadn't seen another moving vehicle since they left Pueblo. He stopped and switched places with Rian.

"Get your weapons ready, but keep them down unless we need them. And hang on if I have to do some fancy driving. The ride could get rough," Rian warned. "Hopefully, we'll be able to see any problems before we're right up on them."

The highway came into La Junta from the northwest, made a long, wide curve to the northeast, then went straight east for a short distance before curving again toward the northeast. Just as they entered the straight section, they saw the moon-lit silhouettes of several armed people standing around two pickups, one blocking each side of the four-lane highway.

"Hang on!" Rian yelled as he hit the brakes, then made a right turn on two wheels onto Lincoln Avenue. He floored the gas pedal, went a few blocks, and hit the brakes, turning left on 4th Street. They raced straight down 4th until it ended across from a locked gate into what appeared to be a nicely maintained housing project. Jerking the wheel to the left, Rian sped through the turn onto Smithland Avenue. Figuring that the people from the roadblock would be racing to catch them coming back to US 50, he swung right on 3rd Street and followed it, blowing through the four-way stop at Highway 109. David caught a brief glimpse of two old men standing in front of Boss Hogg's Saloon, smoking cigars.

Rian had studied maps of the towns along their route, but didn't remember that Highway 50 turned slightly southeast, merging with the street they were on. Three of the people at the roadblock had jumped into one of the pickups and were speeding down the highway, trying to cut them off. By the time Rian realized that the two roads were about to converge, one of the occupants of the truck was standing in the bed, using the cab as a rest as he took aim at the Jeep. His first bullet went high, but the next one pinged the left side of the rear bumper.

"David! Put your window down and see if you can give them second thoughts to worry about. Price, scoot over to my side and do the same!" Rian swerved around an island and onto the highway, pedal to the floor, and focused on the road, praying that there wasn't another roadblock up ahead.

Price fired at the windshield of the pickup, but missed with his first shot. His next shot also went wide.

David's first shot took out the passenger side mirror, and his second hit the grill. The third time he fired, he saw someone in the passenger seat slump over.

Price fired at the shooter braced against the cab and saw him jerk, but remain standing. He fired again, and the man fell back into the bed of the truck.

"Did you hit him?" David yelled.

"I think so, or maybe he just lost his balance. I don't see him getting back up, though."

Rian looked in the mirror and narrowed his eyes. "Is it my imagination, or are they dropping back?"

"I think so. Yeah, they're slowing down. Whew! That was kinda exciting, and not in a good way," David answered.

"You guys okay?" Rian glanced over at David. "Any injuries?"

"Uh," Price gasped, "I'm hit. Just a graze, I think, but man, that burns!"

"Put some pressure on it and we'll stop down the road a bit, first place I can find to get off the highway. You gonna be okay?" Rian asked.

"Yeah. Yeah, I think so."

Rian drove on until he spotted a dirt road that went north from Highway 50. There were a few scraggly trees visible up that road, so he turned and found a spot to park where the trees gave them at least partial cover.

David and Rian both jumped out of the Jeep. Rian darted around to the back to get their first aid supplies, and David helped his brother take off his shirt.

"Well, you were wrong. It's a bit more than a graze, and it sure has bled a lot," David remarked. "I think it may need stitches."

"Let me take a look," Rian insisted. "Looks like that idiot was shooting a .22. That's lucky for you, Price. It went through. I'll need to clean it up, but I doubt that small a caliber left any fibers from your shirt in there. It's gonna hurt, buddy, but it's gotta be done. I'm sure glad we've got some clean water to use."

Chapter Three – October 30
Southeastern Oklahoma

Sergeant Higgins glared at the four guards who stood at attention in front of his desk at the Stigler NERC camp.

"You had one job to do. One! Now, two of you have knots on your heads and two of the prisoners are missing. Care to explain how *that* happened?"

"Uh, well, Sarge, we were just patrolling the perimeter fence, like you said, and then we woke up on the ground. We never saw nothin'." The young guard rubbed the side of his head, where a lump was clearly visible.

"That's right, you saw nothing. That's because *you weren't paying attention!* How many times have I told you to keep your eyes open and your mouth closed? You two are as worthless as teats on a boar hog." Sergeant Higgins shook his head, narrowing his eyes at the two. "You're on half rations for two weeks, and latrine duty for a month. Now get out of my sight!"

The four guards turned to leave, but the sergeant snapped, "Not you, Gleason and Sutterfield. *You* stay."

He waited a few moments, obviously deep in thought.

"I know you were on the other side of the camp when this happened. You're not in trouble, but I need to ask you some questions. Did either of you see anything this evening, anything at all, that might be helpful? I don't believe our prisoners escaped without help from the outside."

Sutterfield glanced at Gleason, and nodded. "Yeah. That woman who escaped with the kid was talking to another woman just a little while before we discovered Andersen and Mullins on the ground, out cold. They seemed to know each other."

"Find that woman and bring her to me. And make it snappy."

Thirty minutes later, Sergeant Higgins sat behind his desk, glaring at the woman his men had brought to him. She was calm, but curious as to why she had been summoned to the office.

"It has come to my attention that you were seen talking to a woman and a young boy this evening. Those two are now fugitives, having escaped from the camp. How do you know them, and where would they have gone?" The sergeant gave her a stern look, trying to intimidate her into revealing something he could use.

"I met her years ago. I was a nurse in the neo-natal unit when the boy was born. I hadn't seen or heard from her since then, probably nine or ten years, but I recognized her and went over to say hello."

"Where is she from? Does she have relatives in this area?" he demanded.

"I think I remember that she lived in Wilburton when her son was born, but I'm not sure about that. And I have no idea if she has any other family. I just took care of her baby while she was in the hospital. That's all I know."

***

"It's a good thing that we're having a mild fall. It gets a tad chilly in these caves. How long do you think we should stay in here?" Jen asked.

Erin shrugged, pushing her long curls back from her face. "I wish I knew. I'm not even totally sure it's necessary, but if NERC comes looking for Dana and Tucker, we'd better not be where they can find us. The caves are going to be hard on the old folks and the little ones when winter gets here. There's a draft from outside when the wind blows."

Tanner entered the long cavern, carrying a box of food, and set it down near their small fire, smiling at his grandmother and patting her on the shoulder. They had decided to use the cave to the west of the lodge, which they had nicknamed "the sleeping cavern", for their main dwelling, since the cache cavern was full. The northern "cabana cavern" had the pool, but Erin thought the additional moisture in the air might aggravate the achy joints of the older members of the group.

Jen motioned for Tanner to join her and Erin. "Tanner, what do you think? Should we stay in the caves for the long haul, or is there a point when it'll be safe to move back into the lodge?"

"I think NERC will come looking, and when they don't find anyone, they'll give up and leave us be. Maybe we should stay a couple of weeks after they come, just to be sure, but I don't think they have the time or the personnel to keep coming back here. They'll conclude that Dana and Tucker went somewhere else, and that it's a waste of manpower to keep checking back to see if they've returned to the lodge. That's just my opinion, though. I could be wrong."

"I'm a little worried about the coolness and the smoke from the fire affecting the elderly people and the kids." Erin frowned. "Charlie and your grandmother are feeling the effects, even though they never complain. Their arthritis is bothering them some, I can tell."

"Yes, I've noticed that, too. I think that within another day or two, the lodge will get a visit from NERC, and I think they'll come loaded for bear, but after that, I doubt they'll come back. If they do, it won't be more than one more time, I hope," Tanner assured them.

"Well, I think that even if we do move back into the lodge, we should leave most of our supplies in the caves, and only take what we absolutely need into the lodge. That way, if we have to hide out again in a hurry, it'll save us a lot of time. And we should also let the housecleaning go for a while. A spotless home is a dead giveaway that somebody has been living there." Erin glanced over at Julia and the cook fire. "Maybe we should do the food prep in here, too, so the lodge won't smell like a hot meal."

"Yeah, you're probably right. Say, has anyone heard any news on the radios lately?" Jen asked.

Tanner grinned. "As a matter of fact, we have. Gus's repeater on the mountain works great from the north cave entrance, and we talked to Ken just a little while ago. Folks in town are doing fine. A couple of the men went hunting and each of them got a deer. Ken sneaked out with Terri and Lydia and went to the creek to fish. They got a freezer full of meat in Ernie's basement, and are

24

sharing with the folks who are staying in the basement at Lydia's shop. I'm so glad Ernie put solar panels on his house and the lodge.

"Speaking of Lydia's, Ken said they shifted some shelving and supplies around to disguise the door to the stairs even better than it was, and now it's really hard to tell it's there. They're sleeping in the tunnel on mattresses they scavenged from some houses, and they've even contributed some canned veggies to Ken's bunch. They found some food in one of the houses, hidden under a bed. When they lifted the mattress, they found cases of green beans, corn, and other vegetables."

"Must have been a sale on canned goods at the grocery. How are they cooking?" Erin asked.

"You remember that Gus's shop was damaged badly by the tornado, but did you know that the front section of the empty shop next door is intact? The back was pretty smashed in, but there's a solid wall between the front section and the back that wasn't damaged at all. The windows were boarded up, and the damage in the front was minimal. The men cleared the rubble away, opening up the stairs from the tunnel, so they can get out at that end if they need an escape hatch."

"They found a charcoal grill on the patio of an abandoned house, and they're using it for cooking, but with aged wood instead of charcoal. And they're doing it in that old empty store. They went around to every house with a fireplace, and gathered all the wood they could find. The smoke isn't as bad as it would be if they used green wood, and since they cook in the front of building, it doesn't drift down into the tunnel where they spend most of their time."

"What about the ham radio? Any news from outside our area?" Erin shook her head. "I almost hate to ask that. Seems like everything we hear from out there is bad news."

"Mac talked to some guy near Oklahoma City. He said things have quieted down, but it's because the good folks are hiding and the gangs have reached some sort of truce. He said it's the calm before the storm, most likely." Tanner grinned. "There actually was some happier news. A fellow from Missouri said that NERC's camp near Kansas City is closed. They just divided the food up so everyone got some, and opened the gates. Then the

NERC agents changed into civilian clothes and scattered in all directions. I guess they finally got sick of being told to do things that are un-American."

"I hope word of that gets around to all the NERC camps. Maybe it'll give the other agents the courage to do the same," Jen grinned.

"Yeah, me, too," Tanner nodded. "The only other news I've heard was about diseases. Those are still a big problem in most of the major cities, from what Mac said. He talked to folks who had talked to other folks, so it's all hearsay, but there were reports of diseases like cholera and dysentery in several large population centers, especially LA and New York. New Orleans, too."

"Do you think we'll ever get past this? Will we ever see 'normal' again?" Jen sighed. "We have it good here, compared to so many people. I just wish we could go to a movie, visit a museum, work at our jobs, and worry about paying our bills again. I want America back, like she was before."

"Ah, well, sorry for that," she grimaced. "I really try to stay positive, but sometimes it does get to me. I need to focus on helping this group stay safe and happy, not dwelling on what used to be."

***

"Anybody seen Gus?" Vince asked, loud enough for everyone in the cavern to hear him.

"He was here earlier, sitting alone with that *look* on his face. You know, that one he gets when he's pondering the great mechanical mysteries of the universe." Sarah pointed to the cave that led due west. "Then he went that way."

"Thanks," Vince said as he hurried in the direction that Sarah indicated.

He found Gus near the cave entrance. BJ and Frances were on guard duty, but Gus didn't join in their conversation. Instead, he stared at the wires and the doorbell button on the cave wall.

"I can see the wheels turning from here, Gus, and I have a feeling it means more work to do." Vince stepped over beside Gus and stared at the wires, too. "What great project have you cooked up this time?"

"I'm an idiot. I should have done it to start with, and we'd all be safer. Why didn't I see it before?"

"See what? Okay, Gus. We all know that as far as rigging ways to make things work around here, you're our resident genius. So what is it you think you missed?" Vince moved around to stand in front of Gus, getting between him and the wires to break the old man's stare.

Gus snapped out of his trance-like state. "We disconnected the warning bells in the lodge. What we should have done then was hook them up in the sleeping cavern. The radios don't work well in these crooked caves, so we don't have a warning system if the guards at any of the cave entrances need help.

"We just took the doorbells down and rolled up the wires. It's all piled up in the cache cavern. All we have to do is a little splicing to make the wire from the north entrance long enough to reach the sleeping cavern, and figure out a way to mount them on the wall. I'm pretty sure all three bells have a volume control on the back. We'll turn them down some, since the setting we had them on would be too loud in the cavern, and then I think we'll be all set. Sorry that I keep coming up with jobs for you boys."

"Don't be. We've all been looking around for things to do. I even offered to help with the cooking, but Frances and Julia ran me off. It's kinda boring in here, now that we can't really do all the things we did when we were in the lodge. I'm so desperate for activity, I'd even be happy to split wood. I'll see who wants to help, and we'll get right on it. You better come supervise."

"Aw, you guys don't need me," Gus muttered.

Vince gave him an incredulous look. "You gotta be kidding! We'd be in big trouble without you. I could list all the ideas and projects you've come up with, all the problems you've solved, but just remember this: none of the rest of us figured out ways to use the radios from the lodge, or how to grow more food, and none of us would have ever thought of doorbells as a warning system. You're one of the most valuable members of our little family. Is something wrong? You seem pretty down."

"Just achy and stiff lately, and I been having a little chest pain. I'm out of my medicine. Gettin' old."

"Chest pain?! Why didn't you say so? Did you forget that we have all of Richie's medicines? And a nurse just a radio call away? Come on, we're gonna see what we can do to make you feel better."

Vince led Gus slowly through the cave, and asked Tanner to contact Angie to find out what Gus should take for chest pains. He helped Gus get seated near the fire, then pulled Erin aside and explained the problem.

"I had a feeling there was something going on with him. He's been quieter than usual," Erin murmured.

"Staying here in these caverns is hard on him, and on Julia, Talako and Charlie, too," Vince whispered.

"I wish NERC would hurry up and get it over with, if they're going to come around again. Camping out in caves is okay for some of us, but it's going to be drafty in here when the winter winds start blowing. With three entrances, there's not much we can do to block the cold."

"Yes, and that's just one more reason we need to keep Gus healthy. Not only is he our friend, he's also our go-to guy for finding solutions to problems. But maybe we've been leaning on him too much, and the stress is adding to his problems," Vince wondered.

"Maybe." Erin shook her head. "But I don't know a way around it. Sitting on his butt doing nothing, having nothing to think about – that's not healthy, either. Gus has always had work to do. I can't see him lazing around. I think feeling useful is better than feeling like a burden."

Tanner stalked into the cavern just then, and joined Erin and Vince. "Angie said Gus should carry around a little bottle of nitroglycerin tablets, and take one when the pain starts in his chest. She's got a drug reference book and she's going to look up some arthritis medications and check for which one would be best for him and the other older folks, and she said that we should keep an eye on all of them and let her know of any problems. We've got nitro, right?"

28

"I assume so. I'd think any pharmacy would have that, and we have a pharmacy, thanks to Richie." Erin swallowed hard. "I sure miss him. He was such a good man," She blinked rapidly a few times, trying to keep her tears from falling.

"I know, honey. I miss him, too. We all do. Now, let's go look for that nitro."

"It shouldn't be hard to find. Richie was so organized, even his bugout was well planned. He showed me how the drugs are arranged in those clever boxes he used. I just hope he had plenty of it."

Vince put a hand on Tanner's arm. "I'm going to round up a couple of the guys and start on a project that Gus just thought up. We'll have the doorbells set up in here in no time."

Tanner grinned. "Now, why didn't I think of that?"

Vince grinned back. "'Cause you're not as smart as Gus."

Chapter Four – October 30-31
Southeastern Colorado

Rian glanced back at Price. "You doing okay back there?"

"I guess. It hurts, but I just keep reminding myself how much worse it could have been," Price groaned.

"We need to find some place to hide out for a few hours. I don't want to head into Las Animas in the dark. In fact, I don't want to go into that town at all if we can help it. I know we need to get some miles behind us, but with one driving, and one with a bum arm, I don't think tangling with the problems that guy told us about in Las Animas is a good idea." Rian yawned. "It's been a long couple of days for me. I was out most of last night, doing tent checks, and adding to my supplies, and then all day, running around taking care of last minute preps. I'm beat."

"Yeah, that's what happens when you get old," David teased.

"I'll show you 'old', kid," Rian warned. "I wish we had time to sleep through the night. What do you think? Should we hit Las Animas right at dawn, or should we go now? Or try to barrel our way through in broad daylight?"

Price and David looked at each other.

"We think dawn is best. People are the least awake at that time; even if they're up, they're groggy, and if there's a roadblock, maybe we'll catch them dozing off." David raised an eyebrow. "Is that logical?"

"Logical is often relative. In this case, it's logical if it works. I do think it's a plan, though. It'll allow us to rest a bit, eat something, and hopefully approach the town alert and ready. By the way, you two do that often?"

"Do what?" the Martins said almost simultaneously.

"That. And read each other's minds. I've noticed it several times. You look at each other, then one of you speaks for both."

"Hmmm, I guess we do. We just know each other so well, and think so much alike, that we seem mentally linked."

"Yep. He's an open book to me. So where do we go for the night? We aren't very concealed here," Price asked.

"We'll drive up this road a little way, see if there is anything to park behind. If not, at least we'll be further away from the highway," Rian explained.

Slowly making their way up the dirt road, they finally spotted a larger clump of trees. Rian carefully backed the Jeep into the cluster, ready to pull out in a hurry if necessary.

"David, would you mind taking first watch? Just wake me up in a couple of hours, and I'll be good to go," Rian requested.

"Sure. I'm not all that tired, since I wasn't out running around getting into things like you were last night."

"We should eat something first, then we should fill the tank. I think it would be a good idea to top it off every chance we get. We may have to make a longer run for it at some point, and a full tank seems like a good idea," Price interjected.

"Bro, only you would think of food first after the day we've had, and with a bullet hole in your arm, no less." David chuckled. "Rian, I know it's hard to believe, but Price is still growing, and has the appetite to prove it."

"Really?" Rian glanced at them skeptically as he opened the back of the Jeep and dug out some MREs. "How old are you, anyway?"

"He's barely twenty. I turned twenty-one five weeks ago, and he just had a birthday last week. We're only eleven months apart."

"Man. What have I saddled myself with? Practically teeny boppers. So, what were you studying before the collapse? I saw in your files that you were students."

Price sighed. "We had big plans. We're both good with computers, and we wanted to go into business together. Computer repairs, setting up networks in schools and businesses, and in our spare time, games. We have some great ideas for gaming, but I guess those dreams are on hold indefinitely. We took every computer class we could fit into our schedules, even more than required for our computer science degrees."

"Dad was really supportive, even though it meant our tuition costs were higher. He let us take as many courses a semester as we could handle and still keep our grades up," David added. "Mom had some doubts about the gaming part, but she came around when we showed her how much money could be made."

"And did you? Keep your grades up, I mean."

"We both had 4.0 GPAs when they closed classes. The last two semesters, we both got some pretty good scholarships because of our grades. Dad picked up the rest of the costs, like our apartment and groceries. He bought our textbooks, too. I just had two semesters to go, and Price could have finished in a year and a half, if he took some summer classes."

"That's great. Maybe someday you'll be able to finish up and start that business. I hope so." Rian stared off into the distance. "I was trying to decide whether to get out of the military or stay in the full twenty, but that decision was taken out of my hands. NERC got hold of me, and they swore that my time with them would count toward my retirement. I acted like I believed that crap, but I knew it would never happen. I witnessed too many instances of lying from those bureaucrats in the short time I was with them."

"What would you have done if you had gotten out?" Price asked.

"I saved most of my pay for the ten years I put in, so I have – uh, *had* – a nice nest egg. I thought about several possibilities, but I don't know. I just don't know. About the only thing I'm sure of is that I've spent too much of my life in the desert, first in New Mexico, then in the Middle East. I had this idea that I would like to live somewhere where there are trees, and it actually rains."

"Sarge – oops! I mean Rian, did you go to college? How old are you?"

"I'm thirty-three, and yes. I have a B.S. in, of all things, computer science."

"Cool!" Both Martins spoke at the same time.

They continued to talk, getting better acquainted, while they ate and filled the fuel tank.

"So tell me more about the people we're trying to get to," Rian requested.

32

"Well," David replied, "Our sister is a little bitty thing, but she doesn't take anything off anybody. She's one of the top salespeople at the dealership, and she carries a Glock that's almost as big as she is." He grinned. "Yep, Sis is feisty. Dad teases her that 'dynamite comes in small packages'."

"Erin is like a second sister to us," Price added. "She's really smart, and pretty, too. She's an orphan; her parents were killed at an air show when a stunt her dad was trying didn't pan out. She's rich, I guess. She inherited a lot from her parents and her uncle, but she's the furthest thing from a snob you can imagine.

"Sarah's tall, probably a little over six foot, and looks like a model, but she's a brainiac about science. Teaches --- no, *taught* --- at an expensive prep school in Tulsa. She's the quiet one of the bunch, until it comes to botany and biology. Then she's a real talker."

David chuckled. "Yeah, Sarah can talk your ear off about science. And then there's Valerie. She's a poor little rich girl whose parents gave her everything except their time. She's travelled all over Europe, even been to Asia and Australia, but recently, was mainly focused on becoming a CPA. Why anyone would want to sit and crunch numbers all day is beyond me, but she was determined.

"She's just a few inches taller than Jen, and was a little, uh, *plump,* the last time we saw her, but her face is drop-dead gorgeous. Long platinum blond hair, which Jen said she cut really short right before the collapse. I imagine she's slimmed down some since she can't go to restaurants anymore. Everyone is skinnier these days. Val's okay, but not my favorite of Jen's friends. She always struck me as being a bit of a snob, and spoiled, too."

"I wonder how's she's adjusting to life without all the fancy stores in Tulsa," Price grinned. "She shopped at Utica Square a lot, and wouldn't be caught dead in a Walmart."

"Utica Square?" Rian looked confused.

"It's the shopping center where all the rich folks liked to buy their clothes. Very ritzy and high-priced," David explained.

"You know, I can't help but wonder what happened to the wealthy people," Rian mused. "I bet most of them didn't make it, unless they had a bunker somewhere. And I was thinking the other day about museums and zoos. Where would they secure all the artwork and artifacts? Who's feeding the animals, or did they just let them die? Or maybe in some places, they turned them loose. That's a scary thought."

David finished pouring diesel into the tank. "Do you think we should save the empty cans, or throw them away? We only emptied one this time."

Rian looked thoughtful. "Well, we could toss them and have a little more room in back, but they don't weigh much, and we might get lucky and find some diesel somewhere. I'd say we keep them. I'd rather do that than need them later and not have them."

Then Price tried to get comfortable in the back seat, and Rian dozed, sitting up in the front passenger seat, while David leaned against the Jeep when he wasn't pacing. He estimated the time, and let Rian sleep what seemed like about four hours before waking him.

Rian slowly surveyed the area, noting a coyote slinking past in the moonlight. "Try to get some sleep, David. You let me sleep longer than two hours, didn't you?"

"Yeah, a little, but hey, you pulled an all-nighter, and you're old, too."

"Can we stop with the age jokes, please? We need to leave before the sun is up. I'll wake you as soon as I see a hint of light in the east."

A little over an hour later, Rian shook David, and at the same time, told Price, "Rise and shine, sleepyhead. You feel any better?"

"My arm hurts like the dickens, but I did sleep some."

"We need to take a quick look at this map, and a brochure I found about tourist attractions in Las Animas. Maybe we can find a way to get past them without going through town." Rian spread the map on the hood of the Jeep and turned on a small flashlight.

"Aren't you worried about somebody seeing the light?" Price asked.

"Not really. Those folks in La Junta aren't going to waste their gas looking for us, especially now that they know we shoot back. It's pretty deserted out here, and besides, we've got to see the map to know what we're headed into.

"Okay. Here's Highway 50. It looks like we could cut through this area on the west edge of town. This street goes for a few blocks, then we can jog to the east again, and meet up with Bent Avenue. It runs north for a while, then turns east, becoming Highway 50."

"We'll be on the wrong side of the river," Price protested.

"At this point, are there right and wrong sides? What this *will* do is get us out of town the fastest way, and into the agricultural flatlands of Kansas quicker. Highway 50 doesn't go straight east. It jogs north, so maybe we need to jog with it. If we go straight, the road narrows down to two lanes, and goes right through Lamar, which is bigger than any of the towns we've seen since leaving Pueblo. If we get over into Kansas, north of the river, there won't be any towns for a long way."

"Yeah, but it'll take us several miles north, and we need to go southeast. Where'd you get these maps, anyway? They don't look like the ones you could buy at a convenience store," David asked.

"I sorta liberated them from NERC. They're less colorful, but more detailed than tourist maps, and they show the topography, which in this case, is mostly flat. They also have more insets of towns. The whole back of the map is little maps of towns. The commercial maps you can buy only have insets for a few of the biggest cities in a state. I thought we'd need to know more about the towns, since we'll be going through a lot of them." Rian pointed back at the map.

"But look at this. That two-lane road goes east, then curves to the southeast. That might actually be better. I don't know, but I hate the thought of going through Las Animas with only one shooter available."

"Rian, I can shoot. I'm actually left-handed, and the injury is to my right arm. If I sit in the front passenger seat, and David takes the back, we'll both be able to shoot better than we did back there. It was really awkward trying to shoot left-handed out that back window, so I switched hands, which is probably why it took multiple shots to hit what I was aiming for." Price moved his right arm around a little. "See, it's not that sore. Yeah, it hurts, but we need me to help out if we get in a bind."

Rian glanced at David, who nodded and added, "I'm pretty much ambidextrous. I can do a lot of things with either hand, but I shoot a little better right-handed."

"Okay, how about this?" Rian suggested. "You two switch places, I'll drive, and we'll see what things look like as we get into the edge of town. We'll just play it by ear, since there's no way to know for sure which way would be better, and what we find there might make the decision for us."

"That's okay by me," David replied, and Price nodded.

"I'm going to jot down two sets of directions, one for going north and one for south. If we have to evade trouble, I'll need a navigator, unless you're busy shooting bad guys." Rian printed street and highway names and 'right' or 'left' for each route, with Price holding a flashlight on the paper.

"Okay, let's go. And make sure the extra mags are where you can get to them in a hurry."

Back on Highway 50 a few minutes later, Rian drove the few miles to the outskirts of Las Animas. They saw no human activity as they approached the town, just one mangy, starving dog walking along the shoulder. The poor mutt didn't even look up when they passed.

"Okay. Get ready, and keep an eye on things. Use clock positions, with 12:00 being straight ahead, and yell out if you see anything."

***

Just after they got into town and crossed Cottonwood Avenue, Rian spotted a pile of junk blocking the road a couple of blocks up ahead. He thought he could make out two men standing behind the heap, but couldn't be sure there weren't more.

"Heads up! Looks like we go north whether we want to or not. They've got the road blocked ahead. Hold tight!" he warned, and turned the wheel hard to the left, onto Poplar Avenue.

They saw another two men carrying some chairs out of a big building with a sign that read "Community Center". They took them toward the street, ready to add to a pile they had evidently just started to block Poplar. Two rifles leaned against the wall of the building, and the men dropped the chairs, running to grab their weapons.

"Discourage them from shooting at us!" Rian yelled, but the two brothers were already leaning out to take a few warning shots. The two townsmen scrambled back to the pile and ducked.

"If that hadn't been so scary, it would have been hilarious," Price chuckled. "Did you see the looks on their faces? I bet that bald guy needs to change his pants."

"Don't get too cocky, bro. Rian, best laid plans, huh? We're already off the two routes you lined out for us." David spoke as he alertly scanned the area. "We need to go east a bit more. Going south is out."

Rian instinctively turned right onto Fifth, and went a few blocks to Carson Avenue and turned left, went one block to First Street, and whipped back onto Highway 50, which had made a ninety-degree turn to the north about six blocks behind them. Glancing in his rearview mirror, he could see a roadblock on the highway at what he guessed was Third Street.

"They set their blockades up in odd places. It doesn't make sense even on the west side, where the road curves and you couldn't really see it until you were close. Why did they leave a couple of streets that people could turn down and avoid getting stopped? On this straight stretch, I don't understand their reasoning at all. I'm just glad they didn't put it at First Street, or we would have been in trouble."

Rian accelerated, then slowed a little when the highway turned east again, and drove seventy miles an hour for a few minutes before speaking again.

"Well, we made it past Las Animas. We should have it pretty easy for a while, since there's not much around for the next forty or so miles. We'll pass through a little place called Kreybill in about eight miles. I don't think it's even incorporated. It's what they call a 'populated place' so I don't imagine it's very big at all, if there's even anybody left.

"We'll go near, but not through, a few other little dots on the map. I don't know anything about them, except that some of them aren't right on the road. Eventually, Highway 50 joins up with 287 and turns south. We'll need to make some decisions before then."

***

After passing through Kreybill, which was apparently deserted, they crossed the bridge past the northern tip of John Martin Reservoir, and were surprised that nobody had set up a roadblock on the bridge.

"Bridges are choke points," Rian explained. "I dreaded crossing them when I was in Iraq. They liked to set up IEDs on bridges, and I lost a few buddies. I would have thought that someone would have set up on this bridge to catch travelers and take their supplies, but I guess the area is so sparsely populated that nobody thought to do that."

They continued for about fifteen miles, then Rian pulled over and stopped the Jeep.

"I need a break, just to pee and stretch my legs," he explained.

"I'm getting hungry. We didn't have time to eat this morning, so we should grab a bite while we can," Price suggested.

"You and food. All you think about is eating," David muttered.

"He's right, David," Rian commented. "We should try to eat and sleep when we can. Now, let's discuss our next move. We had a full tank of diesel, and six five-gallon cans, too. That's fifty-two gallons of fuel. I got friendly with one of the mechanics and he told me that this Jeep will get about twenty-two miles to the gallon, so how far will the fuel we have take us?"

David leaned down and did the math by writing the numbers in the dirt with his finger. "That's 1,144 miles! Kanichi Springs isn't that far, so we have enough fuel to drive all the way. Awesome!"

"Well, that's not taking into consideration Rian's crazy driving. I guess as long as our luck holds, we should have enough. I hadn't even considered that we might be able to drive the whole way. I've been wracking my brain about where we could get canoes or a boat. So, I guess we don't have to stay so close to the river, do we?"

Price gave him a mock frown. "And here I was, looking forward to being on the water."

Rian gave him a puzzled look. "I thought you were afraid of water. At least, that's what I heard around camp."

"Nah. That's just what we told the other agents. We figured that when they discovered we were gone, they'd never guess we'd travel by river, so they'd waste time looking for us on dry land. That was back when we thought we'd be traveling all the way from Pueblo to Muskogee by kayak.

"I'm not afraid of water at all. In fact, I was on the swim team in high school, then I was a lifeguard at NSU, and before that, at a community pool in Tulsa. We're both certified divers, too. Got all our own equipment. Or we did, before all this," Price replied.

"That was good thinking, making them believe you were afraid," Rian admitted. "Of course, now that we didn't go by water, it's a moot point. Well, let's look at the map again, and see if we can avoid any towns now that we don't have to stay so close to the river.

Chapter Five – November 3-4
Southeastern Oklahoma

Staring out into the dusky twilight, Vince watched as a doe stepped daintily out of sight. He sighed, then turned as he heard movement behind him.

Shane grinned. "I almost managed to sneak up on you, buddy. How's it goin'?"

"Fine," Vince answered without enthusiasm.

"Something's bothering you, Vince." Shane held up a hand to forestall a denial. "Don't bother trying to tell me otherwise. I haven't known you long, but we've been through a few – uh, *experiences* -- together, and I know you plenty well enough to tell when you're stewing on something. Out with it. Maybe it'll help to talk."

Vince scowled at him, shrugged, and turned back to the north opening to the caves. His mood showed: the usually upright posture had become slumped shoulders and a lowered head; an apparent loss of the ability to smile and an overall depressed demeanor added up to a definite Something Is Wrong.

Shane stepped closer. "Vince, I'm your friend, no matter what. We have a bond now, as brothers-in-arms, or co-survivors of the ninja-zombie apocalypse. I know that most men hold their emotions in, but I learned a long time ago that sometimes, it's good to have a friend who will listen and not judge. If you need a friend, I'm here."

"I thought you were some kinda tough guy. What's with all this girly emotional crap, anyway?" Vince growled.

"Hey, now. I *am* pretty tough, if I do say so myself. I just know that there are things that can be made better by talking it out with someone. I'm not pressuring you to talk to me. I'm just offering, and if you don't want to talk right now, tell me what I can do to help you."

Vince was silent for several moments, his jaw clenched and a frown marring his handsome face. It looked like every muscle in his body was coiled tight, then he took a long, deep breath, and seemed, from Shane's perspective, to shrink in on himself.

"I'm not ready to talk about it in depth. Erin is the only one who has a clue about this, and you better not let on to *anybody*, or we'll be seeing if you're as tough as you think you are." Vince glanced around to see how Shane took the threat.

Shane raised both hands in surrender. "I think you know I'm not one to blab secrets. If not, you're even dumber than you look."

Vince's mouth tried to smile, but failed. He nodded, and turned back, resuming his stare into the forest.

"Before Richie died, before I felt like I was really a part of this group, I...well, I...." He swallowed. "I noticed that Lydia is a fine woman, inside and out. I was half in love with her when I realized her partiality to Richie. Because I liked Richie, respected him, I backed off from letting my feelings show."

"Wow, man. I never guessed. You hid it well."

Vince continued as if he hadn't heard the remark. "Then Richie died. I lost a friend, too, you know. He was a great guy, honest, smart, and he really pulled his weight around here. I got to feeling guilty about caring for Lydia. It ate on me, like I was somehow to blame for Richie's death, even though I know I wasn't. I never wished anything bad on him, I swear.

"But then she stayed in town. I was going to bide my time, let her grieve, even grieve with her, and just be there for her, but she didn't come home. She's in town and I'm here, and I can't even be a friend to her."

Shane hung his head and stared at the cave floor. He'd had no idea that Vince had feelings for Lydia, and no idea what to say, but he tried anyway.

"She's a beautiful woman, and I can sure see why you'd fall for her. But think of it from her point of view. She watched a man she loved die in a horrible way, on the table where we usually took our meals. It had to be terrible for her to think about coming back to the lodge after that."

"Don't you think I know that?" Vince demanded. "I understand all too well, but I *miss* her. I miss hearing her laugh. I haven't seen her sweet smile in weeks. And I'm beginning to realize that I love her. It's more than an attraction to a pretty face. I *love* her. She's part of me, even if I'm not part of her, and I can't do a thing about it."

"So, what do you think would help you cope with it? What could make you feel better?"

"I need to go to town and help out there, or I need to bring her back here, if she'll come. But she's not where I am in this. She loved Richie, and I'd be trespassing on her grief. It's not fair to her for me to intrude, so I don't see a solution."

"Let me think about this. Maybe I can come up with something."

"Yeah. Good luck with that." Vince withdrew into his shell of depression again, and Shane knew that the moment of sharing was over.

***

Erin repacked the plastic tub and put it back on the stack, then gathered the items she had selected and turned to leave, only to find Shane blocking her way. She jumped back, dropping the multi-packs of socks she'd been carrying.

"Good grief, Shane! Will you stop doing that? We all know you can move around as silently as Tanner or Talako, so you don't need to keep proving it!" she scolded.

"Sorry. I really wasn't trying to prove anything. I was just practicing. It's how I keep my skills honed. I really am sorry." He gave her a rueful smile. "I need to talk to you, privately, if you've got a minute."

"Okay. Let's step over to the other side of the cavern, behind that stack of tubs. We won't be interrupted there," she replied, glancing at him quizzically. "Is this about Vince? Did you find out anything?"

"Yeah, he opened up some, but threatened bodily harm if I told anyone. But since you're the one who put me up to talking to him, I guess telling you is okay. He told me you already knew some of it."

"It's Lydia, isn't it?" At Shane's nod, Erin frowned. "How bad does he have it?"

"Bad. He's in love with her, but feels like he can't do anything about it. Why didn't you warn me?"

"It wasn't my secret to tell. I figured if he told you himself, we could talk about it without either of us breaking his confidence. Did he say what he wants to do about it?"

"No. He thinks there's nothing he *can* do, except just stay here and let her have time to heal. Do you think Lydia and Richie were in love so deeply that she'll never get over losing him?"

"She had just realized that she loved him. She told me so. I think it was something that developed slowly over time for her, and it was real, but new. It hadn't had time to blossom fully, and I think -- but I could be wrong -- that she's mourning the loss of the love almost as much as she's mourning the loss of the man. She went through hell with her ex-husband, and I don't believe she ever dreamed she'd let herself love again. And with losing Richie, she may be doubly shy about letting herself care for a man a third time. Poor Vince. I wish I knew what to do to help him."

"Let's talk about that. What would you say to a wee expedition, just me and Vince, to take supplies to Ken's group? They have to be running low on stuff. We could fill a couple of big packs, and go on foot through the woods. It would help them, and give Vince a chance to see how she's doing."

"I think that's a great idea, but let's wait a couple of days, and we'll hope that Vince won't catch on that you and I have talked about this. Meanwhile, I'll arrange for Ken to get back with us by radio and give Charlie or Mac a list of what they need most. That'll throw Vince off the scent even more."

"Anybody ever tell you you'd make a great spy? You're devious, Erin," Shane said admiringly.

She grinned. "Sometimes being devious is a good thing."

***

Three days later, the group members who weren't on guard duty sat around on the floor of the cabana cavern, eating venison stew for lunch. Frances and Julia had developed a few tricks for

43

cooking with canned and freeze-dried foods, and their efforts had made meal time enjoyable. It wasn't exactly five-star cuisine, but it tasted good and was nutritious.

Charlie came shuffling in from the west cavern, the one where most of them slept. *He looks better, healthier than he did when I first met him*, Erin thought. Maybe it was the regular, if rationed, meals, or maybe it was being part of a group who needed him, but Charlie seemed to thrive in spite of the hardships they had endured. *He's happy. That's what it is*, Erin realized.

"Hey, ever'body. I jist heard from Ken. He said things are goin' okay with the folks in town, but they do need sum things. I got a list here. I guess somebody'll have to take it to 'em. Charlie looked expectantly at Erin.

"Uh, well, we sure can't send anybody in a vehicle, with the possibility of NERC being in the area. We'll need to take it on foot, I guess." She looked around, as if considering who to ask. "Shane, how about you? Get someone to go with you, and stay back in the trees as much as possible?"

Shane kept a straight face with difficulty. "Sure. I'll go. I'm going nuts hanging out in here, and the exercise will do me good." He glanced over at Vince. "Hey, pal, you wanna go with me?"

Vince looked at him, eyes slightly narrowed, then glanced at Erin, who was studiously focused on her stew. Suspicion flashed briefly across his face, then his desire to see Lydia took control, and he agreed. "Sure. I'll go. We better camo up for this. When do we leave?"

"Tomorrow morning, I think. We'll need to get the packs loaded, and it's too late today to do that and get there before dark."

Charlie spoke up again. "Most of the things on the list ain't heavy. It's little stuff like matches or lighters, salt, pepper. It's important, but ain't gonna weigh ya down."

"We'll get it all together for you, and you can load the packs. There should be plenty of room, so we'll send some extras, too. Make sure your radios are on the chargers this afternoon. A full charge should last until you get back," Erin suggested.

After lunch, Sarah, Erin, and Jen took the list to the cache cavern. Ken had requested seasonings for their food, matches, candles, and a few health items, like decongestant and cough syrup. Some of the townspeople were still in the tunnel under Main Street, and Erin guessed that they might be developing respiratory problems from breathing the dust and mold down there. She threw in some aspirin, a package of dust masks, dehydrated garlic and onion, and a few bags of rice and noodles, and one of hard candy, just for a treat.

Vince and Shane brought their packs in and loaded up what the girls had picked out. They'd decided to leave through the north entrance, even though it would make the trip a little longer. Using that cave would put them deeper into the woods where they could swing around the mountain and the lodge, staying out of sight from the road longer, and avoiding the open area of the front yard.

After eating a light meal, the two men bedded down early, planning to be up and on their way as soon as there was enough light to see.

Erin and Jen tiptoed past the sleeping men, and headed out to the west cave for guard duty. They paused for a few seconds, staring at the people they had come to love, those slumbering forms that lay on variously sized mattresses on the cavern floor. Then they slipped away quietly, not talking until they were out of earshot.

"You've got it bad, don't you?" Erin asked her best friend.

"Yeah, but a lot of good it does me. Shane hasn't said a thing or made any kind of move to tell me that he feels the same way. I thought for a while that maybe he did, but not anymore."

"Something has changed, that's for sure. It...well...it seems like he's almost avoiding you. I don't get it. He was so protective of you, then a while before we moved into the caves, he closed off, sticking with the guys all the time and not even hanging out in the caverns with us after meals. Men are just weird, ya know?"

"Yeah. Well, two can play that game. It's not like we're in normal circumstances and can have anything resembling a regular romance. I can move on, too. I can, and I will. Starting now, I am done with Shane. Not that it matters. There's nobody else around, but I don't need a man to be complete. I just thought...oh, never

45

mind what I thought. As of now, I am going to consciously remind myself not to be anything more than a friend to Shane. My little infatuation is over."

"Sweetie, I wish I could tell you it'll be that easy, but the truth is, it won't, especially living in such close quarters. How are you going to break yourself of loving Shane?"

"I'm going to start concentrating on his bad habits, the way he annoys people with his stupid jokes and his tough-guy attitude, his aloofness and lack of emotion. I'm going to constantly remind myself of how much this hurts, and I'll build a wall that he'll never break through. And I'm going to stop looking at his broad shoulders, muscles, and how that lock of hair falls on his forehead no matter how many times he pushes it back. I'm going to quit noticing how gentle he is with the children, or how *right* he looks with a kid on his lap." Jen's voice got husky. "How can I be in love with someone who hasn't given me any reason to think the feelings are mutual? I *will* get over him. I *swear* I will."

***

Vince and Shane nodded to Ian and BJ, who were on guard duty, and stepped out of the caves into a dawn that was misty and gray. They had gotten permission to take Sheba, one of the German shepherds that Tanner had trained. Shane had a special rapport with her, and she needed some real-world practice.

The profound quiet was broken only by the occasional sound of water droplets hitting the leaves on the ground. The air smelled clean and there was a tiny hint of a breeze.

"Let's swing by and check on the McNeil's place since we're this close," Shane suggested.

Vince agreed, and they separated, traveling parallel routes northeast. The house came into view. They waited for several minutes, but nothing moved. Sheba stood quietly, completely relaxed. Shane signaled Vince to cover him, and made his way to the back door. It was unlocked, just as Talako had left it. The old gentleman had figured that bad guys were going to get in even if it was locked, but at least if it was unlocked, they wouldn't break the door down or smash the windows.

He sent Sheba in with the signal to clear the house. She came back with a wagging tail, so Shane peeked in, then entered, took a quick look around, and came back out and rejoined Vince.

"Doesn't look like anyone has been there. Being back off the road like this, hidden in the trees, nobody probably even noticed it was here. The driveway is pretty overgrown, too."

"Okay, now can we go to town? It'll be good to be able to report to Julia and Talako that the house is still standing, but I guess I'm a little impatient to get moving."

"A little?" Shane asked with a grin. "Ya think? I guess if I was in your shoes, I'd feel the same way."

"I thought for a while that you kinda liked Jennifer."

"I did....I do, but that's different." Shane looked a trifle embarrassed.

"How is it different? Oh, wait. I know – she isn't grief-stricken over another guy who you considered a friend, and she's right there with you, instead of living in another place where you can't even see her," Vince said sarcastically. "You acted like she hung the moon. Now, suddenly I don't see any signs that there's a romance brewing. What gives?"

"Hey, I have my reasons for cooling it."

"Shane, I would have sworn a few weeks ago that you would gladly die for that girl, and now, you don't even look at her if you can help it. You don't talk to her or tease her anymore, but I've seen the shattered look on her face when you are all chatty with the others. So, what's your problem?"

"Are you blind? Her *parents* are there. Her brothers are missing. We're in crowded quarters with no privacy, so what else do you expect me to do? Grab her and kiss her speechless in front of everyone?" Stepping over a rotting log, Shane turned to look Vince right in the eye. "I'm crazy about her, and keeping my hands off her is driving me nuts! She's beautiful, and feisty, and fun-sized, and I'm so much in love with her, I can't think straight. So I decided that the only way I could survive living with her and *all those other people* in a *cave* was to avoid her, not talk to her, and certainly not look at her."

He paused to take a deep breath. "It's so hard. I even asked Ian to change up the duty roster so I would be able to focus on guarding the caves. I can't think straight when she's around."

Vince stared at Shane's reddened face. "You've been hiding it well, but I can't help but think that you're making a big mistake. Ignore her long enough, and she might just write you off, buddy. You've hurt her, Shane, and I don't like it. She's like a little sister to me. In the short time I've known her, I've grown very fond of her, and of Erin, Sarah, and Val. Like any big brother, I don't like seeing Jen hurt."

"So, what would you do? You've moped around ever since Lydia stayed in town, and if I hadn't arranged this trip, you'd still be an old grump. What would you do in my place. Huh? Got an answer for that?" Shane spat furiously.

Vince stared at him, then said calmly, "I'd find ways to let her know I cared, and I'd find a way to talk to her. I'd be close by to offer help if she needed anything, and I'd make sure I got along with her parents, too. I'd treat them with respect and let them know my intentions are honorable, which yours had *better* be, my friend. And I'd stake my claim before someone else treated her better and won her from me."

"I can't marry her. I have no way of taking care of a wife until this is all over with," Shane protested.

"*You* are an idiot. You know that, don't you? There's no 'taking care' of a wife these days. Things have changed. Men and women have to work together to survive, and that's what we're already doing. When this collapse ends, if it ever does, then we'll worry about breadwinners and working wives. For now, we just do the best we can, and grab onto love wherever we find it, and be thankful we have each other. This group is our family. I have more people to care about right now than I've ever had. There's nobody in the group I wouldn't fight to protect."

"So, you're saying that I'm trying to impose old standards on a new reality. I see that, but still…if we did get married, we would be just like Tanner and Erin. No privacy, weighed down by the circumstances, struggling to survive," Shane argued.

"And just exactly how is that different from what you have right now? None of us has any privacy, all of us have responsibilities to the group, and we're all working to survive. At least you'd have Jen in your life, knowing that someday, maybe things will be better. You'd have what private moments you could sneak in. Wouldn't being able to just hug her and tell her how you feel be better than constantly struggling to ignore her? Man, you've set yourself up to be miserable, and it isn't necessary. No, things wouldn't be perfect, but they'd be better than this!"

Just as Vince's words left his mouth, he hunkered down behind a boulder and signaled Shane to take cover. They had almost reached the road, and once they stopped talking, could hear the sound of a motor coming their way. Shane kept his hand on the back of Sheba's neck, and signaled for her to be silent.

Both men watched as a truck pulled in the driveway to the lodge. It was about a hundred yards away, but they could see that it was a NERC truck. Four men got out of the back, and an older, heavyset man stepped out of the front passenger seat, and all of them headed for the lodge. Two broke off and went around to the patio. The one who had been in the front signaled the others to spread out, then he went up the steps and pounded on the door.

After just a few seconds, he tried the handle, and the door swung open. He made a beckoning motion with his hand, and two agents followed him into the lodge. Shane and Vince took the opportunity to move in a little closer, taking cover behind rocks and trees.

A few minutes passed, then all five NERC agents came out the front door, the others having entered through the unlocked back door. The man who seemed to be the leader started talking in a rather loud voice.

"Either they didn't come back here, or they just haven't made it yet. We'll check back in a few days and see if they show up. Okay, load up. Let's go to town and see if we can't round up some stragglers."

Shane and Vince waited until they were gone, then got on the radio and contacted Ken.

"Hey, brother, we just had a NERC truck at the lodge, and overheard them say they're coming to town. Better get everyone out of sight quick. I'd guess they'll be there within five minutes," Shane warned.

"Oh, no! We have two groups of three each outside right now. One is on the way to the river to fish, and one is checking traps at the edge of the forest. I have no way to contact them," Ken replied, urgency in his voice.

"They didn't take radios? Does anyone have a motor scooter or some other way to get out there in a hurry and tell them to hide?" Shane insisted.

"We don't have extra radios. Wait. Hold on." Ken was gone for several seconds, then came back. "I think we have a bicycle. We'll have to hurry! Get back to you later!"

Ken sent a young man named Connor to warn the trappers first, since they were closest to town. The skinny, red-haired teenager raced out to the northeast edge of town where the pavement ended, and continued down a dirt track that led toward the woods, legs pumping hard. He found the trio, and told them to stay hidden, then pedaled as fast as he could toward the east, where another group would be checking some limb-lines they had set the evening before. Nearing the trees that lined the banks, he saw the fishermen and gestured for them to take cover at the same time he heard the sound of a truck approaching town from the north.

Knowing that he was in plain sight, Connor took a dive for the ground, laying the bike and himself over, crashing flat and motionless in the high grass. He froze, afraid to even peek out to see if he had been spotted.

Minutes passed. He heard truck doors slam, then heard what sounded like orders shouted by an authoritative voice. He thought the next noise was a door being kicked in, and it was repeated a few times over the next several minutes.

Connor lay there, wondering what was happening, but knowing that risking a look could get him taken away from his family. He consciously slowed his breathing, forcing himself not to panic, and waited.

It seemed like hours passed, but in reality, it was less than forty-five minutes before Connor heard the truck start. He listened, and was pretty sure it was moving away from him, but knowing that taking a risk could be disastrous, he and the three fishermen didn't move until the sound died completely away.

***

After Ken abruptly cut them off, Shane changed channels and got Ian, who was still on duty at the north cave entrance. Explaining what they had witnessed, Shane told him that he had already alerted Ken, and said that he and Vince would continue their trip, but take it a little slower than planned.

"Well, that was interesting," Vince remarked, as Shane clipped his radio back on his belt.

"Yeah. Now I'm going to worry until we get to town and see if everyone is okay, but we can't hurry, because the last thing we need is to get careless and run into NERC ourselves."

"Let's get across the road while we can, then move a little further into the trees," Vince suggested. "I bet they'll leave town on the road that goes to the turnpike, but we can't be sure of that, so we need to use extra caution. Do you think we should warn the Fosters and their group? They're still camping back behind their house."

"Nah. Ian said he would put the word out. Mr. Gibbs and his family are still with the Fosters, too, so we'll let Ian take care of that."

Moving slowly from tree to tree, and staying at least fifteen yards apart, Vince, Shane, and Sheba made their way stealthily toward Kanichi Springs. About half a mile from the outskirts of the little community, they heard a truck engine again, and took cover. The NERC truck passed their hidden positions in the forest, and sped away.

With that danger past, the trio hurried the rest of the way to Ernie's house. Entering, they went to the bookcase that hid the doorway to the basement and gave the secret knock that Tanner and Ken had decided on. They could hear latches being pulled on the other side of the shelving, then Ken's smiling face appeared.

"Come in, come in!" he encouraged. "You're just in time for a cup of tea. Tell us all your news, and what you've heard from the outside."

***

"How are you, Lydia?" Vince asked as he helped her sort through the supplies from the backpacks.

"I'm doing okay. It feels good to be with people who need me. I've been helping teach the younger kids to read, and I help the ladies with the cooking. Just staying busy."

"Do you…do you think you'll come back to the lodge soon? We miss you." Vince couldn't quite meet her eyes, and hadn't intended to be so blunt, but the words just popped out.

"I've been thinking about it. There are too many mouths to feed here, and I miss everyone, especially Erin. Have you heard anything from Jen's brothers lately?" Lydia placed a box of candles on a shelf and turned to look at Vince.

"No. Their last message made it clear, at least to BJ and Frances, that they were planning something, but we haven't heard a word in quite some time. I suspect that they're on their way, but who knows? Colorado is a long way from here, and winter is coming. All we can do is hope for the best."

"And pray," Lydia added. "They're smart boys, from what Erin told me. She said they loved to hike and camp out, so hopefully they have some skills that'll be useful. I can't imagine what the rest of their family is going through."

Chapter Six – November 4
Southeastern Colorado and Southwestern Kansas

"This place is as flat as a pancake, and it's boring, too. Nothing around anywhere except farmland, with no crops to speak of. We haven't seen so much as a house in miles," Rian complained.

"Actually, it's flatter. Some geology classes at one of the universities did some sort of satellite measurements on Kansas, and the same type of scan on some pancakes. Western Kansas really is *flatter* than a pancake, but don't knock it. Being bored is better than being shot at," Price reminded him.

"Yeah, yeah. I guess. Speaking of getting shot at, how's the arm this morning?"

"David changed the bandage and it looks okay. No sign of infection," Price answered. "I'll be glad when it heals up, though. It's getting stiff from not moving it."

"Well, let it heal a little more before you start trying to work that stiffness out," Rian urged. "We've been taking it easy for a few days to let you rest, but at the pace we're going, it'll take us way too much time to finish this trip, and who knows how long the quiet will last. Eventually, we'll get into more populated areas. That's when we'll need you to help out more."

They had stopped early each night to allow all of them time to rest. The MRE supply was still plentiful, but soon, it might be necessary to do a little fishing or hunting to supplement their meals. The weather was cool, especially after the sun went down; there had been light rain for three days, but it finally let up and the sun was shining.

Highway 50 was a straight shot and they passed only few tiny towns. They hadn't encountered any significant trouble in any of them, since Rian had suggested that they make it obvious that they were alert and armed. The few people they saw just stared as the Jeep drove past.

Two nights ago, they had turned off onto Highway 96, passing the Big Timbers Museum, and stopping a few miles east.

David parked the Jeep behind a cluster of trees, where it wasn't visible from the road. They were able to relax more than they had since deciding to leave Pueblo, and Price even felt up to taking a turn at guard duty, so Rian and David got more sleep than usual.

The decision to get off Highway 50 for a while was an easy one. It allowed them to bypass Lamar, a town that none of them had ever seen before. Rian's map showed 50 turning south and going almost into the center of Lamar before taking a turn back to the east. None of the men wanted to be in an unfamiliar town, trying to find their way in possibly hostile territory.

If they somehow missed that turn, the road continued south as Highway 287/385, and according to the map, would take them far out of their way. Instead, they opted to avoid the town altogether, deciding to stay on 96 until they could turn south on what the map said was Kaw Road.

That meant crossing the Arkansas River again, then passing through the little community of Granada, where they would turn east on Highway 50. Soon after, they would cross the Arkansas yet again, as the river curved to the southeast.

The trip had been relatively uneventful since their encounters with armed locals in La Junta and Las Animas. Price felt some animosity toward La Junta, for obvious reasons.

"That town must be a magnet for jerks. I can't believe they shot at us just for passing through. Chasing us out of town sure wasn't very friendly. What a dump of an excuse for a town," he complained.

"Hey, I bet that most of the people of La Junta are good folks. We just ran into a few who were trying to run the show. Maybe the rest of the people just want to live in peace, but it's obvious that a gang has taken control. I feel sorry for anyone who has to live there now. Don't judge everyone by the actions of those few," David chided. "They were trying to block off the town for a reason, and I doubt they had the welfare of the townspeople in mind."

"Yeah, I guess you're right. It didn't really look like a bad town, but I'm the one who got shot, remember?"

"Oh, quit whining. I think you hit the guy who shot you, so you got even. Are we about ready to start looking for a place to spend the night?"

***

Randy "Rat-tail" Hawkins and his buddies, "Catfish" Malone and Archie Grayson had known each other their whole lives, and had gotten into trouble together almost that long. Of the three, Archie was the only one to graduate from high school, and he barely made it. His daddy bet him ten dollars that he wouldn't finish, and Archie stayed in just to spite the old man. He bought beer and cigarettes with the ten bucks, and shared with his two pals.

At almost thirty years old, they were known in the area for being lazy, sneaky, and sly. Most folks figured that the only reasons they hadn't wound up in prison were that they were too scared to pull any really big jobs and the fact that they only burglarized homes and businesses when there was nobody around.

Unlike more populous areas, southwestern Kansas was home to large ranches and farms, and very few of the homes scattered across the plains were equipped with security cameras. The trio of petty criminals knew which houses to avoid. They stole small items, mostly; however, one time Catfish had given in to temptation and hauled away a television that was almost too big to fit in the ramshackle mobile home he lived in.

Since the collapse, they were reduced to stealing food just to survive. They had run out of gas to use in the ratty pickup that Archie inherited from his grandpa, so they were pretty much restricted to staying close to home. Rat-tail and Catfish had moved in with Archie, just for the sake of convenience, and right after that, they pulled their last job using the truck. With the gas gauge sitting on "E", they drove to a little country store, pulled neckerchiefs over their faces, and committed armed robbery. Rat-tail pointed an old revolver at the clerk while Catfish and Archie loaded all the beer that was left into the bed of the truck.

The clerk, a middle-aged woman, recognized all three of them immediately, but had the presence of mind to pretend otherwise. She had already decided that she wouldn't be coming back to work anyway, and had made up her mind that anything left in the store would go home with her. Surprisingly, there was some food left, because most of the people in the area never considered looting an acceptable practice. Most of them had their gardens, their livestock, and their hunting rifles, and saw no need to steal the junk food and soft drinks that made up most of the stock at the little store.

But Maddie, the clerk, figured that it was better than nothing, which was exactly what she had at home. She had almost a quarter of a tank of gas in her beat-up Chevy Citation, and she planned to load up all the chips, candy, and sodas she could from the store, and never come back. The theft of the beer was disappointing, because it might have helped her convince her neighbor, Sammy Lawrence, to overlook the extra pounds she carried in spite of the near-starvation diet the collapse had forced on her. She'd had a thing for Sammy for years, but he had never taken any of her rather broad hints. *Oh, well*, she thought, *maybe he likes Cheetos.*

Back at the trailer, Rat-tail scratched his privates, belched, and reached for another beer. They had no way to keep it cold, but even warm, it was better than nothing. Archie was outside, trying to cook up some rabbit over a small campfire. He wasn't a very good cook, but he was the best they had, so the job was his.

Rat-tail stood, stretched, and joined his friends, his footsteps leaving tracks in the moist dirt that made up the yard. They sat on a bench cobbled together from a few pieces of scrap lumber and some concrete blocks.

"I been thinkin' it's 'bout time we think up sum new tactics, boys," Rat-tail announced.

"Like wot?" Catfish demanded.

"Like mebbe goin' down to th' highway and seein' if they's any traffic we can stop. If'n they got gas, they prolly got other things, too."

"How we gonna get 'em tuh stop?" Archie wanted to know.

"We shoot at 'em, dummy. Ammo is 'bout th' only thang we got lots of, so we might's well use it."

"Okay. Count me in. I'm gettin' plumb tired o' rabbit. When do we leave?"

"Right away sounds good, don't it? Ain't nuthin' to do 'round here 'cept eat that rabbit. We better put on our camo so's we don't stand out."

"Let's just mosey on down th' road to th' highway, and we'll jist wait and see if'n anybody comes along. Might git lucky and find us a woman, while we're at it," Archie suggested.

Rat-tail smirked. "Yeah, one that can cook better'n you."

"You can take over th' cookin' anytime ya want, Rat-tail. No, on second thought, never mind. Ah'd rather do th' cookin' muhself than have to eat yer cookin'."

***

Rat-tail lay on his belly in the high grass on the south side of Highway 96, while Archie and Catfish lay on the north side, just east of Hickok Road. They all had hunting rifles, and Rat-tail had the revolver. He had hopes that they would find more handguns when they stopped vehicles, since he had the only one, and it was old.

The day was at least dry, although a few clouds were starting to gather in the west. The ground was soaked, and moisture seeped through their camo coveralls, chilling them, but they were determined to wait for a vehicle to come by. Hours passed, and Rat-tail could see that his two friends had dozed off.

The sound came so gradually that it didn't register at first. A low hum, one that he hadn't heard in a while.

"Hey, wake up, ya idjits!" he called.

Catfish stirred first, then punched Archie in the shoulder to wake him. "Here it comes: *payday!*" Catfish told his sleepy pal.

Rat-tail stood up, and stepped out into the middle of the road, rifle pointed toward the car, but not yet brought up to his shoulder. He figured that just the sight of an armed man would scare whoever was driving into stopping.

Catfish and Archie decided that what Rat-tail was doing was pretty cool, so they stood, too, but stayed close to the edge of the road. Nobody had ever accused any of them of being overly bright.

David was driving, but Rian saw the men first. "Heads up!" he shouted, and rolled his window down. He heaved himself up to sit on the edge of the window, upper body out of the car, and fired a couple of shots over the head of the man in the road.

Price leaned out the back window and aimed at the two men on the shoulder, who quickly realized that their prey was not going to meekly stop and surrender, so they dropped back to the damp ground, and began to return fire.

Rat-tail shot twice toward the Jeep. David slammed on the brakes about fifty yards from the shooters, and spun the Jeep broadside across the road, then piled out to fire at their attackers from behind it. Rian and Price followed him, putting all three of them in a much safer position than their opponents, one of whom seemed to think he was bulletproof, and two who were trying to take cover in the weeds and grass that hadn't been mowed by the highway department in almost a year.

Catfish decided that he needed to take the offensive, so he jumped up and darted north, hoping he could curve around to the west and flank the strangers. His hope was futile. David saw what he was trying to do, and took him down with a shot that entered his left side, breaking a rib and puncturing both lungs, before tearing a jagged hole in his right side.

Archie scooted back away from the road, and tried to bury his whole body by pressing himself hard into the mud. He lay as flat and still as he could, afraid to even raise up enough to shoot.

Rian waited, watching the man who was standing on the center line. The guy was shooting a bolt-action rifle, and Rian timed it perfectly, rising from behind the Jeep and shooting him in the head before he could jack another round. The man stood there for a few seconds, already dead, before gravity took over. The body slowly crumpled to the pavement.

Archie was terrified, but finally risked a glance up to see why the shooting had stopped. When he raised his head, Price shot at the spot where the grass moved. Archie yelped in pain as the bullet struck his shoulder joint, shattering bones and exiting from his back. He continued to scream for a time, then the screams became whimpers.

Rifle at the ready, Rian scurried over, following the sounds until he located the wounded man writhing in the mud. He grabbed the man's rifle and threw it as far as he could, watching it land in a muddy field that bordered the road. He looked the man in the eyes.

"Well, I guess your days of whatever it is you thought you were doing are over. What *were* you morons thinking?" Rian demanded.

Archie could barely speak through the pain. "We jist wanted food, and guns, mebbe some gas."

"What you wanted and what you got are two different things. You're probably going to die from that wound. You know that, don't you? There's no doctor, no hospital anymore, and you've got it full of dirt and debris, rolling around in the muck like you have. Even if you don't bleed out, infection will set in, and you'll die slow." Rian shook his head before continuing.

"We weren't doing you any harm, you fool. We were just passing through, minding our own business, and now your friends are dead and you're dying. I should just let you suffer, but I'm not a monster. Do you want to end your suffering or take your chances out here alone?"

"There ain't no reason fer me to keep on livin'. Ah got nobody to help me, so jest end it. Jest put me down, and Ah'll be mighty grateful."

"I'm not the one who's going to do it. I noticed that your friend had a pistol; I'm going to leave it with you. One bullet only. You can do the job yourself, if you've got the guts. We'll be on our way, and you can decide for yourself how your life will end. I hope God is merciful to you. You better make your peace with Him before you go."

Rian stalked out to the middle of the highway, and dragged the body over to the side. He retrieved the revolver and made sure there was only one shell left in it, then went back to the wounded man, and placed the gun in his uninjured hand.

"Remember, you only have one shot. If you use it to try to get one of us, you'll be the one to suffer most, because we'll leave you to die in agony. And you better pray before you end your own sorry existence, because hell is waiting for you."

Without saying another word, Rian turned and walked away, returning to the Jeep. As he reached for the door handle, he heard a shot, but he didn't slow down. He got in, buckled his seat belt, and nodded at David, who was once more behind the wheel.

Price swallowed hard. "What happened?"

"I gave him a choice," Rian answered softly. "He took it."

David started the Jeep, backing it up and turning toward the east once again. He accelerated, but moments later, noticed steam coming from under the hood.

Rian saw it at about the same time. "Blast it all! They must have hit the radiator. Keep driving. There's nothing we can do about it, so we might as well get as far as we can before we're on foot. Price, looks like you're going to get to travel on the river after all."

Price grimaced. "I'd really rather travel in the comfort of this Jeep, if I had a choice. It's a good thing we aren't far from the river, but we may not find any type of boat to use. Who knows if anyone around here has one? Of all the rotten luck, to have fuel, but a vehicle that won't run, and be in the middle of nowhere and need a boat."

Vince talked Lydia into walking the short distance to her shop so they could check on the people living in the tunnel off her basement. Shane caught a look from Vince, and hastily made excuses to stay for a visit with Ken.

Cutting through back yards and staying off the streets just in case the NERC truck came back, Vince felt a little tongue-tied. He was usually articulate, but his words had never mattered so much to him, so he kept the conversation light, asking about the children and how everyone was getting along.

Lydia answered, her demeanor cheerful. She seemed to have recovered, at least on the surface, from Richie's death, but Vince knew that if Richie was mentioned, she would become sad again, so he carefully avoided the subject.

They entered the shop through the broken front door, stepped carefully through the debris scattered everywhere, and entered the equally cluttered back room. Vince nodded approvingly at the way the boxes were arranged in such a way as to seem careless, yet completely hiding the door behind them.

Using Vince's flashlight, they went carefully down the steps and across the basement to a second door, another one that was hidden by boxes. Entering the tunnel, they were greeted by a group of townspeople who had taken refuge there. Vince shared some items from his pack with them, and sat down for a short visit. A little girl, about three years old, stood near him, twisting a strand of her dirty hair around her finger. When he sat, the child stepped over to him, and without a word, climbed into his lap, leaning against him as though he was a long-lost friend. Vince simply put his arm around her, and continued talking with the adults.

Lydia watched him from across the tunnel, the sight warming her heart. *He looks so natural, holding a child. What a good man he is. After what he went through with his sister and nephew, he could have become hard, cold...but he didn't. He still cares about others.*

Vince noticed the look on Lydia's face, and smiled at her. He had no idea what she was thinking, but her expression was soft and sort of wistful. *Maybe there's hope*, he thought. *Maybe.*

Back at Ernie's, Shane had accompanied Ken and Terri upstairs so they could talk privately. He gave them a brief summary of Vince's feelings for Lydia, and asked how she was really doing.

"I talk to her more than anyone, and she told me that she has decided to do what Richie told her to do, be happy. He loved her so much, and I know she loved him, but they had barely acknowledged it when he died," Terri explained. "I know she's stopped crying all the time, and she's made a conscious effort to put the bad memories of how he died behind her, but it hasn't been very long, so she's still hurting. She's just trying so hard not to grieve that I worry sometimes that it will sneak up on her and hit her again."

"Well, Vince is letting it eat at him, He feels guilty about having feelings for her, because he thought of Richie as a friend, but he's got it bad for Lydia. He wants to either come stay in town, or get her to come back to the lodge, but he doesn't want to push her. Any advice on that?"

"I think he is going to have to be patient. Lydia isn't ready for another romance yet, but I believe, that given time, she'll open up to that possibility. She isn't going to get over losing Richie in just a few weeks," Ken reminded him. "She needs longer than that. If he truly loves her, he'll have to wait."

"Yeah, that's what I figured. I guess if you need anything, he'll be one of the people making deliveries from now on. I wouldn't even dare try to tell him he can't see her, but I'll encourage him to be patient. Thanks for your insights. This is a delicate situation for them both, and I just don't want to see either one of them hurt, if we can help it."

After catching them up on the latest news, Vince and Lydia said their farewells to the tunnel group, and Vince handed the little girl back to her mother, kissing her on the forehead as he did. Then he helped Lydia up the stairs and out of the looted store.

"Someday, I want to reopen my store, and make it better than ever," she told him. "I loved owning my own business, but seeing this mess just makes me mad. It would be bad enough if the storm had done this, but it didn't. Those looters just demolished my shop, and what in the world did I have here that would interest a bunch of convicts?"

"They just liked to destroy things, I think. So, when this is over, if it ever is, you plan to stay in Kanichi Springs?" Vince inquired, not daring to look at her.

"Yes, I do. This is home. I knew it from the first time I drove down the street, and I feel it even more strongly now, after going through what we've endured. I have real friends here, and I plan to stay, no matter what. How about you?"

"I have nothing in McAlester to go home to, except bad memories. I feel like the group at the lodge is my family now, and I'd do anything for any of them. Honestly, that's how I feel. They didn't have to take me in, but everyone there just welcomed me and made me a part of the group without hesitation. When this ends, I'll stay close, maybe even here in town. I'm not sure exactly where I'll find a new place to live, but it will be around here, and I know I won't be going back to McAlester. I don't have anyone there anymore who cares what I do."

"I guess when it's over, most of the people at the lodge will go back to their homes, if they have one left. Erin and Tanner won't know what to do with all that space, after all their friends and family leave."

"True. Can you imagine starting out your married life with a literal houseful of people? They're two of the most unselfish people I've ever known. I wish I was half as kind and giving as they are."

"Vince, you *are* kind, and brave, too. I think *you* were blessed when Ian brought you to the lodge, and all of *us* were blessed at the same time. You're a good addition to the group, and you've pulled your weight."

Vince stopped and looked at her. "Thank you for saying that. I've tried to contribute in whatever way I can, because no matter what I do, I will never be able to repay Erin for allowing me to stay. I was…well, I was…coming apart that day, after…."

"Shhhh." Lydia patted his arm. "you don't have to talk about that. Losing people you love – well, I understand."

Walking on in silence, they arrived back at Ernie's house; he guided her up the steps, and held the door for her. Shane was waiting, ready to return to the lodge, and Vince said goodbye to everyone. He smiled at Lydia, then walked away.

Shane led the way, allowing Vince time to sort through his thoughts. They moved quickly, staying in shadows when possible, and hurrying across streets. Once they reached the trees, Shane slowed so Vince could catch up with him.

"Well, it looked like they're doing okay, considering. This collapse has been an effective weight-loss program, if nothing else. Ken sure is thin these days," Shane commented.

"Yes, I suspect he's taking the bare minimum of food for himself, to make sure the children get enough. That's the kind of guy he is, I guess."

"Well, I am going to suggest that we start hunting and fishing more, and making regular trips into town to take them meat. They're getting some rabbits and fish, and an occasional deer, but I'd feel better if I knew they weren't on the verge of starving." Shane glanced at Vince, grinning. "I think you should volunteer to head that effort up. That way you'll have a perfect excuse for frequent trips to town."

"I would do it even without the lure of seeing Lydia, you know. I hate seeing those children so thin. I held a little girl when we went to the tunnel; I thought she was maybe three, but her mom told me she's almost five. I could feel her bones. Lack of food is stunting their growth, Shane.

"They *need* us to bring more food. I can't stand to see children going hungry, so some time before next summer, I'm going to come to town and search some houses and see if there's another canner we can use. If Erin and the gals had two canners, they could put up a lot more veggies next summer."

"That's a great idea. We'll search for Mason jars, too. And hope that NERC doesn't come around while we have stuff growing in all those planters out front."

Vince sighed. "Yeah, that's a problem. We need to get Gus and Charlie thinking on that one. Maybe they can figure out a way to…I don't know, maybe camouflage the garden, or something,"

"So, how did things go with Lydia?"

"Good, I think. I know she likes me as a friend, and respects me. That's a start, at least. And I caught her with a funny look on her face once, when I had that little girl on my lap."

"Funny how?" Shane wondered.

"Sort of, well, *soft*. It vanished almost as soon as I glanced at her, but I didn't imagine it. I think I might have a chance, if I don't blow it by moving too fast. I can be a very patient man when I need to be."

Chapter Eight – November 5
Southwestern Kansas and Western Oklahoma

Steam continued to waft out from under the hood of the Jeep, as David drove east on Highway 96. In only a couple of minutes, they saw a sign for Kaw Road, the one they thought they wanted to take south so they could avoid towns and hopefully get back on Highway 50. David turned, nursing the wounded vehicle along, and hoping the engine wouldn't overheat before they got to the river.

Only about three miles down Kaw Road, the temperature gauge pegged out, and the Jeep was finished. David let it coast off the road into the grass, and the three just sat there staring out the windows, each thinking of what they faced, and whether they would ever make it to the lodge.

Rian suddenly straightened, unfastened his seatbelt, and turned to look at his two companions. "Well, we'd best get on with it. We'll go on foot until we find some type of water transport, but we have a long journey ahead, so let's go. Pack all the food you can in your packs, and grab as much water as you can carry. Fill your pockets with ammo, too."

Price glanced at David, then nodded to Rian. "Is there something handy that I can pad my shoulder with? The strap on my pack is going to rub on my wound."

"Okay, change of plans. Price, you pack up mostly food. Those MREs don't weigh as much as water. We'll work it out. There's an old tee of mine back there you can wrap around the strap of your pack. If it gets to hurting, try carrying it on one shoulder for a while, or I'll carry both yours and mine."

They sorted through their supplies, and each drank a whole bottle of water before they set out. Some things had to be left behind, but it couldn't be helped.

"I hate to leave this Jeep here," David frowned. "I'm embarrassed to admit it, but I've gotten kind of attached to it, since it's been our home-away-from-home for several days. I'm gonna miss it. Somebody's going to find it and get the diesel and what we couldn't carry. I just hope it's not somebody like those guys back there."

"Yeah, well, when this is over and you two are filthy rich from designing computer games, you can send somebody after it and have it restored. Let's go. We need to find some kind of shelter for the night. Those clouds look and smell like rain." Rian got his pack situated comfortably on his back and grabbed his rifle. "Let's get a move on."

They walked for a few miles, with Price alternating between carrying his pack on his back, one shoulder, or with one hand. He kept up without complaining, something that surprised his older brother.

David glanced over at him, and asked, "You doin' okay? Shoulder hurt much?"

Price grimaced and said, "It's okay. Should we be thinking about stopping to eat and rest, or should we move on?"

"I say we try to cover as much ground as we can. We haven't made as much progress as we should."

"Let's keep going. We have a few hours, I hope, before the weather does whatever it's going to do," Rian agreed.

Walking at a steady pace, watching around them for signs of people, they continued down the road, covering a few more miles while trying to avoid mud puddles left by the days of intermittent rain.

The sky got grayer, then darker, and the wind picked up slightly. Rian kept an eye on the clouds, worry creasing his forehead.

"We need to find a barn or a shed or something, and soon. Look over there." He pointed to the southwest. "That's rain, and it's coming this way. I also saw some lightning flash just now. We don't need to be caught out in a storm. Step it up."

Five minutes later, David spotted an old homestead a short distance off the road. The house and barn had obviously burned sometime in the distant past, but he saw a slight hump in the backyard with a turbine vent spinning on top.

"Hey, there's an old storm cellar! Probably full of spiders, but it beats getting struck by lightning or soaked to the skin. Come on!"

The door creaked and groaned when they opened it, but the inside was relatively clean, considering. A few cobwebs seemed to float on the air that they'd stirred up, but they saw no other signs of eight-legged inhabitants. Someone had made a wide wooden bench that went around three sides of the shelter, and the floor was dry. It was a large commercially produced shelter that looked fairly new, probably eight feet across and twelve feet in length. Rian got a candle out of his pack and lit it.

"This'll work. Good job spotting it, David. I didn't even notice it. It looks like it would hold a fairly large family. Let's pile the packs over by the stairs, and have a bite to eat. Then we can each have a whole side of the bench to sleep on." Rian dropped his pack and rubbed his neck, then began digging around in the MREs.

"I've got beef stew, chicken chunks, and a 'rib-shaped barbeque pork patty'," he said, making quotation-mark gestures with his fingers.

Price pulled his pack off and opened it. "Here's hash browns with bacon, chili and macaroni, spaghetti with beef and sauce, and lemon pepper tuna. Yummy."

"Just toss me one," David said. "They all sound equally gross."

"Hey, this is fine cuisine, son. You should have tasted the ones we had when I was in Sand Land. They've improved some since then."

"I'm glad I didn't have the opportunity to try them," David grinned. "We're both pretty spoiled. Our mom is a fantastic cook, so this is pretty much slop in comparison. But I guess we should be glad we have these lovely entrees. A lot of people would kill for them."

"Yeah, they would," Price agreed. "But Mom's turkey and dressing is awesome, and she makes a mean chicken-fried steak. Her pies are out of this world, too. I'm going to pretend I'm eating her cooking while I try to force this stuff down. I think I'll try the lemon pepper tuna. Can't be any worse than the rubber-chicken stew I had last night."

While they ate, the storm arrived, complete with thunder, which made conversation nearly impossible. The turbine spun wildly, and a few drops of water splashed on the bench below it, but they felt secure in the underground lair. Once they were all finished eating, they made themselves as comfortable as possible on the benches, and tried to sleep. By the time the storm moved on, Price and David were snoring softly and Rian was getting drowsy and hoping for a better day tomorrow.

***

Price woke first, and as quietly as possible, rummaged through the MREs, finding those that would do for breakfast. He grabbed three bottles of water and woke the others.

"Rise and shine, boys! I can see light through the turbine. I think it's gonna be a sunny day for a change. Let's eat a bite and take care of our morning – uh – *business*. I'm getting eager to look for alternate transportation."

David and Rian reluctantly and stiffly rose, stretching and yawning. They ate their meal, and each finished off a bottle of water before David cautiously raised the door and looked out.

"Coast is clear. And the sun is definitely shining. Let's go one at a time over in the weeds for our private needs, and the others can stand guard." David exited the shelter, ready to be first to find a spot to relieve himself.

Once all three had taken care of the basic necessities, they went back down to get their packs and rifles, then climbed out of the cozy shelter, ready to get on their way. Rian pulled the map out and studied it for a moment, then turned his gaze to the south. The road seemed to stretch forever before them, but they knew from looking at the map that Highway 50 wasn't far. The problem was, now that they were on foot, a major highway could be a death trap, and they all knew it.

"It's time for a new game plan. We need to avoid the main roads, just in case. There may be more bad guys out looking for an easy target, and next time, we might not be as lucky. Also, it's possible that NERC may have started searching for us. I seriously doubt that they've figured out yet that we didn't go after the deserters, but we can't take the chance. I think we might need to angle over and get closer to the river, instead of sticking to our plan to travel on Highway 50. That was a good idea when we had the Jeep, but we have to do things differently now."

"Yeah, but look at this," Price insisted, pointing to the map. "The river turns more north, and there are more big towns that way. If we go south, we could meet up with the Cimarron River. It goes through a few towns, too, but we'd miss Wichita, which is a pretty big city. The Cimarron feeds into Lake Keystone just like the Arkansas does, and either way, we have to decide what to do when we get to Tulsa."

"I agree," David added. "There's no point in going through any towns we can avoid. Most of what I've seen of the Cimarron is pretty isolated. When we get there, I think we might need to wait until the wee hours of the morning to tackle Tulsa. I'd really like to go by the house and see if any of our stuff is still there. We could use some clothes, for one thing." He pointed to a spot on the map. "We lived about here, on the southwest side, almost in Jenks. It isn't far out of the way, and might be worth it, if the house is still there."

"Okay, sounds good to me," Rian agreed. "Keep your eyes moving. There's not much cover anywhere around here, just flat fields. Listen, too. If we hear any mechanical sounds, such as cars or helicopters, we need to make ourselves as invisible as we can, and quick."

The trio plodded onward, turning slightly east on a dirt track, and slogging through mud that constantly tried to suck their boots off their feet. It was rough going, but the sunshine felt good on their faces. The only sounds they heard were their own footsteps and birds chirping.

There was a brisk breeze from the south and with the warmth of the sun, things began to dry out a bit. The path they took was packed down hard, making it much easier to walk on than the fields would be. After a few hours of walking, they could see nothing but more of the same scenery they had passed through all day.

"I think we've made good progress today. How about when we get to the next road, we stop and eat a bite? I'm getting hungry, and I *know* Price is hungry," David joked.

"Sounds good," Rian agreed, picking up the pace a bit.

Finally reaching a stand of young trees, they stopped for a brief rest and to drink a little water.

"Tell me more about this place we're going, and the people there," Rian requested.

"Well, as we said, we never actually saw the lodge, except pictures that Jen showed us on her phone. It's big, on the side of Oklahoma's version of a mountain, and made out of thick logs. Jen told us that the upstairs is set up like a bunkhouse. It has room for a bunch of people. We know that Erin got married to a guy from the town. Jen said he trains police dogs and is super tall. We really don't know much about the rest of them, except Jen and Erin's other two friends, since we were all being careful what we said on the radio, even how many there are. No telling who might have been listening in." David looked at Price, who shrugged.

Rian gave them a questioning look. "Are you sure there'll be room for one more? They have no idea I'm coming, and I hate to butt in where I'm not wanted."

"When we tell them how much you've helped us, you'll be welcome. If not, we'll just go into town and find an empty house to move into, but I'm pretty sure, knowing Erin, that she'll want you to stay. She's really nice," Price explained.

"I wish I knew a way to contact my family. They're probably worried about me," Rian sighed.

"There's a ham radio guy at the lodge. I think his name is Mac, and we'll ask him to see if he can get someone in Mexico to get word to your folks. Where in Mexico are they?" David asked.

"Monterrey. It was one of the better places in Mexico to live. My brother married the daughter of one of the vice presidents of BMW *de Mexico*. There are lots of big, well-known companies there, so it's much more prosperous than most of the country. Unfortunately, it went from being one of Mexico's safest cities to having trouble with the drug cartels. Since about 2011, it isn't quite as safe as it used to be."

"I wonder how much Mexico was affected by the collapse. It's hard to understand how this has impacted other countries, when we don't get any news," Price complained.

Rian smiled. "My family probably won't be in the city anymore if things got bad. My uncle works in the national park near Monterrey, and has a nice cabin in the mountains. There are caves there, and my grandparents own land that's close to my uncle's, but even more isolated. I choose to believe that they've gone there until it's over.

"And I agree with you. It's impossible to know what's going on five miles from here, much less in other countries. I think Mexico is probably hurting, since all the companies that are there need customers to buy their products, and the United States was where most of those customers were. But the rural areas may be okay. People there know how to grow food. At least, I hope that's the case."

"Well, we better get back on our feet and put some miles behind us," David added. "I wonder if we'll even know when we cross into Oklahoma, since we're avoiding main roads."

"Maybe we need to veer more southeast. You know, the North Canadian River is just south of the Cimarron, and it goes to Lake Eufaula, really close to Kanichi Springs," Price suggested.

"And right through the metro area of Oklahoma City. No thanks. That's miles of heavily populated territory, with bridges and overpasses everywhere. Besides, we wouldn't be able to swing by the house if we go that way. At least we know our way around Tulsa and will only be on the west and south side of town"

"You're right, bro. I was just speaking before I thought it out. Never mind."

Chapter Nine – November 7-8
Southeastern Oklahoma

"Ken, I need to speak with you privately, please," Ted Isbell said when he found the preacher on the street near Ernie's house. Ted was a young father who was staying in the tunnel with his wife and two children, aged four and six.

Ken led him around behind one of the houses, and looked at him quizzically. "What's on your mind, Ted?"

"Well, Ginger and I have been talking, and we've pretty much decided that we'd be better off if we just went to a camp. Sissy has a cough, and keeping Junior quiet down in that tunnel is hard. Kids need to run and play. They need sunshine, and I think the dust and dampness down there is the cause of Sissy's coughing. I just wanted to tell you, and assure you that we won't tell anyone about the folks here."

"And how will you keep your kids from mentioning the tunnel? Little kids don't understand the danger or the need for secrecy. They're too little not to slip and give us all away. I wish you would reconsider this. I think it'll put all the rest of us in jeopardy." Ken shook his head. "You can move your family in with us, or find another house, one with a basement where you can hide if NERC comes back."

"Our kids don't know where you're hiding out, and neither do we, so we can't give you away. You've kept your hideout secret, so I guess you never trusted us. The other folks in the tunnel will just have to find a new place to stay. I want out, and Ginger agrees, so for the sake of the kids, we're going," Ted insisted.

"We never trusted you because you never helped the group. You've never *earned* any trust. And now, you've proven that we were right to keep our secrets, since you'd risk the capture of people who don't want to go to a camp, when you could stay here. You'd force all of them to relocate away from the safest place in town! After all that Erin and we have done for you? She sent medicine, and food, clothes, and blankets. You lived at the church, and ate our food. Lydia let you use the tunnel, and we've helped you for months, and you would do this to us? Your kids are both chatterboxes, and you know it. They'll tell everything they know and bring NERC down on us with a vengeance."

"I'll make sure they don't tell."

"Yeah, right. Like that's going to work. I'm going to be honest with you, Ted. I don't think you've even begun to pull your weight around here, and neither has Ginger. You've taken our supplies, and not helped one bit with gathering more food. Ginger doesn't help with the cooking or teaching the kids, and *you've* been asked to fish or hunt several times, and always had some excuse to say no. Neither one of you has helped with searching the empty houses for anything we can use.

"You sat around all day, complaining about how unfairly life's been treating you, and forget to be thankful to the Lord for keeping you from being victims of the gang or the storm or hunger. You didn't even help defend the town from the gang, when we needed everyone to stop them. Your own family was endangered by those thugs, but you stayed hidden with the old folks and the kids.

"I can't stop you from going, but I can certainly stop you from coming back. If you change your mind about the NERC camp, don't come back here and expect *any* help from us. I believe in Christian charity, but I don't believe in taking food out of the mouths of those who contribute in order to give it to those who won't help."

Ted glared at him. "You can't tell us where we can go. We have a house here, and the right to come back! And we want some food to take on the road with us. We'll have to find the NERC camp, or a NERC truck out looking for folks, so it may take a while. You gotta give us some food. You wouldn't send children out there without food!"

"We owe you nothing. And you *rented* that house. You don't own any property here, and haven't paid any rent in a long time. No, we *won't* give you food or anything else. And do *not* try to return. I mean it, Ted. You won't be welcome. I wish you luck, but I won't help you do this. I think you're making a huge mistake, giving up what you have here for life as a prisoner living in a tent.

Mac heard that they take people to another camp and force them to work on farms. Even the little kids have to work. Your kids will get some exercise and sunshine, alright, as *slave laborers*. You better think on this before you start out, because once you go, you're *gone*."

Ted clinched his fists and took a step closer, obviously angry, then turned and stomped off. Ken took a deep breath and let it out with a *whoosh*, staring at his feet and wondering if he had done the right thing.

Lord, forgive me if I didn't do Your will. I just get so tired of trying to help people who won't help themselves, and who gripe all the time about all the things others do for their benefit. Nothing was ever good enough for Ted and Ginger, yet they did nothing to contribute to the group. Please watch over them if they decide to leave, and keep them safe. In all things, Thy will be done.

Terri came through the door and put her arms around her husband. "Ken, what's wrong? I can tell something has upset you."

"Ted came by. He said that he plans to take his family and find a NERC camp, because they think they'll be better off than they are here. I mentioned that his kids never stop talking and will tell NERC about the tunnel. He said they won't, so I told him that if they leave, they can't come back. He got mad, so I let him have it. I'm *sick* of the way he and Ginger sat on their backsides and never did a lick of work, but were never satisfied with what others provided and shared with them."

"I agree with what you're saying, Ken. I've tried and tried to get along with Ginger, but she's one of those women who's competitive with other women, no matter what. She has to one-up anyone about anything, whether it's clothes, jewelry, how smart her kids are, or what kind of car she drove. It's not like they really had much to brag about, but she always looked down her nose at any good fortune that someone else had.

"More recently, I've had to do a lot of praying to keep from resenting her," Terri admitted. "No, that's not honest; I've had to work hard to keep from *hating* her. She seemed to think that the other women in the tunnel were there to serve her, and I've seen some of them in tears because of her unkind words. She treated them and me like servants. She was a disruptive influence on the group. And Ted? I've never seen a lazier man. Makes me wonder how he kept his job. I can't say I'm sorry to see them go, but you're right about the tunnel. It won't be a secret for long. The kids aren't the only ones who have big mouths. Ginger tells everything she knows and then some. She's a terrible gossip, and she likes attention, so I have no doubt that we'd better see what we can do to get everyone out of that tunnel, and soon."

***

Ted struggled to get his anger under control, but only because he wanted to appear calm to the people in the tunnel. The other men had taken advantage of the sunny day to fish, check traps, or hunt, in an effort to keep everyone fed. The only ones still in the tunnel were women and children, and two of the women were across the street cooking in the old building next door to the mechanic shop.

Ted grabbed a couple of shopping bags from Lydia's store, then descended the stairs to the basement and made his way to the tunnel. He pulled his wife aside and whispered in her ear for well over a minute. At one point, she leaned back to stare at him, then nodded, and listened some more.

He handed her the bags, and walked over to the women who sat with the children, teaching them simple arithmetic. He stood between them and Ginger, who moved over to the stash of food and began filling the bags.

"Hey, what are you doing?" one of the young mothers exclaimed, leaning to see around Ted.

"Just sit there and shut up. We're leaving, and we're taking our share of the food with us. If you try to stop us, you're going to get hurt," Ted snarled, with his hands fisted at his sides.

"*Your share?* You two haven't contributed a thing since you joined our group. You're *stealing*, you jerk, taking food out of the mouths of all of *us*, the people who provided that food. You're nothing but a thief, Ted, and you, too, Ginger. A *real* man would be out there hunting, not threatening a bunch of women and children."

"Shut your mouth, stupid. I won't warn you again. We're going to the NERC camp, and we just might tell them about this place. I'm sure there'll be some kind of reward for turning you all in." Ted gave them a sly smile.

"Well, I say good riddance. We'll be better off without you mooches and your complaining," another woman said.

Ted took a step toward her, raising his fist threateningly. "I said to *shut up*," he growled.

Ginger had loaded both bags with as much canned food as they would hold, which was almost everything, and called her children to come with her. She led them up the stairs while Ted stood guard over the others, then called down to him that they were ready; he shook his fist toward the women, and snapped, "Don't call out or try to stop us. You and your brats will be sorry if you do."

***

"Do you think we're going the right way, Ted?" Ginger was breathless from trying to keep up with her husband's angry strides.

"I have no idea. Did you ever hear any talk about where this NERC camp is?"

"You know I didn't listen to those silly cows. All they talked about was getting the food cooked or teaching those kids, bragging about how intelligent their little ones were. Stupid women. Anyone could see that their kids were nowhere near as smart as ours."

"You should have been listening. You never know when someone will say something that might be useful. I guess we'll just head toward the turnpike and hope a NERC truck comes along soon."

"Sissy doesn't need to be out in the cold. Her cough seems to be getting worse, Ted. How long will it take to get to the turnpike?"

"You sure ask some dumb questions. I've never walked it before, so how would I know? I guess there'll be some kind of shelter along the way, maybe an abandoned house or a nice barn. We'll find something."

Sissy's cough was indeed getting worse, and she was feverish, so Ted picked her up and carried her. Ginger carried the two heavy bags of canned goods, while Junior walked along beside his dad. He insisted that he was too big to have to hold hands anymore.

They trudged along the shoulder of the road in the near-silence, each lost in thoughts of times past and what the future might hold.

Late that afternoon, they saw the overgrown remains of a dirt driveway or road. It was hard to tell which, but Ted turned down it, glancing over his shoulder to make sure Ginger followed. She was past exhausted, since this was the first real physical effort she had made in months. All that time sitting around wallowing in self-pity had resulted in a zombie-like state from just walking and carrying bags.

They followed the track for about two hundred yards, and saw a small clearing around a shack and a storage shed, with piles of junk scattered around. Ted signaled for Ginger to take Sissy and Junior behind a boulder, and once they were hidden, he continued toward the shack.

When Ted got close, the front door opened so hard that it slammed into the wall, and a man stepped out onto the porch, carrying a shotgun. He was filthy and had a long, scraggly beard that held what looked like the remnants of past meals, and when he grinned, the rotten state of his few remaining teeth was obvious. From the drooping, flapping folds of skin on his face and arms, he had once been very obese.

"What're ya doing on muh property? Ah ain't puttin' out no welcome mat, stranger."

"We need a place to stay for the night, and wondered if we could bed down in your shed."

"*We*? Who ya got with ya? A woman?" the man asked.

"Uh, just my wife."

Ted barely finished the words when the shotgun blast knocked him down, most of his face missing. Ginger peeked out from behind the huge rock to see what had happened. Seeing Ted's mangled head, she cried out in horror. At the sound of her scream, the man jumped off the porch and ran at the boulder. He took in the sight of Ginger hunkered down with two kids, and laughed.

"Well, now. Ain't you a purty thang?" he said to Ginger. "Ah always did like me a redhead." He grabbed Junior's arm and shook him, them gestured at Ginger and Sissy with the shotgun. "You just git on up to th' house, missy. I'm gonna take good care of ya, doncha worry 'bout that none."

Ginger was tempted to resist, but the sight of the gun and remembering what had happened to Ted changed her mind. The man walked behind them and directed them toward the shed. He told Ginger to open the door, then he shoved both children inside and clicked the big padlock that had been hanging on the hasp.

"Now, ya better listen close, woman. Yer gonna do what Ah say, or them kids is gonna suffer fer it. Ah figger cookin' and sech is woman's work, and so is making a man happy. You're gonna make me *real* happy, any time Ah want it, or Ah'm gonna start out by cuttin' fingers and toes off them worthless kids. Ya hear me? Ya best be getting in the house and gettin' them clothes off. Ah'm eager to get happy."

Ginger stared at him, aghast. "I'd never let a pig like you touch me. I'd rather die!"

The man's eyes narrowed as he shoved her against the shed wall. "Ah ain't gonna *let* ya die. Ah'm just gonna make ya wish ya was dead." He backhanded her, knocking her to the ground, then, unzipping his grimy pants, he was on her. He raped her, pinching her hard and slapping her face repeatedly, laughing as her children screamed out, "Mommy! Mommy!" from inside the shed.

When he was finished, he stood and looked down at her bruised body. "Ya best git this through yer head. If'n ya want those kids to git any food or water, ya have ta do what Ah say. If'n ya don't, they can go hungry. Don't matter to me if'n they starve. Now, git in th' house and fix me some supper. And after supper, yer gonna make me happy ag'in."

***

Ginger trudged into the rat-infested shack, but the filth barely registered. She was in shock, wondering how in the world things could have gone so wrong so quickly. There wasn't a clean pot or dish anywhere, so she took the least crusty pan, and asked where she could find some water. The man pointed out the back door, so she took the pot and went outside, locating an old handpump. She scraped at the pot with a spatula, getting most of the dried food off, then rinsed it and filled it about half full of clean water.

The man brought in the bags of food that she and Ted had taken, and left them on the peeling plastic counter, along with a bag of jerky he had. Ginger chose a can of green beans and one of carrots, and made a pot of what might pass for soup. Her cooking skills were certainly not five-star, but she managed to find some salt and some garlic powder to season the meal, and it was edible.

The man ate with all the finesse of a starving hog. Ginger couldn't even force herself to watch him, and was unable to bring herself to eat. He ate almost all of the food, leaving only a few bites each for the children, which he took to them, not allowing her to even see them.

"Git that kitchen cleaned up now," he said, as he looked through the dirty dishes and collected the sharp knives. "Ah ain't gonna give ya a chance to use muh own knives ag'in' me. If'n ya need one fer cookin', Ah'll let ya use it, but Ah'll be sitting here with muh gun, watchin' so's ya don't get no funny ideas."

Chapter Ten – November 9-10
Southeastern Oklahoma

BJ and Jen neared the north cave entrance, ready to relieve Shane and Val. BJ watched his daughter as they approached, wondering why she was acting so oddly. She greeted Val, nodded at Shane without meeting his eyes, then turned toward Val again, her back to Shane, and as she scratched Blitz behind the ears, began telling her all about the delicious meal that Frances and Julia had prepared.

"It's scrumptious. I don't know how those two make such great meals without modern conveniences."

Val glanced at Shane, who just turned and walked away. He had decided after talking to Vince that he would tell Jen how he felt, but she had been giving him a wide berth lately, avoiding him to the point of rudeness. She wouldn't even look at him, much less speak to him, and he was thoroughly confused. *I will never understand women*, he decided. *Here I am, ready to put my heart out there, and suddenly, she won't give me the time of day. She acts like she hates me, and I think her buddies are helping her avoid me.*

As they walked together through the cave, Shane glanced over at Val and found her staring at him. He stopped suddenly, convinced that enough was enough.

"Okay. I give up. Can you *please* tell me what I should do?"

"About what?" Val asked with feigned innocence.

"Oh, here we go. Right. I get it. You're her friend, so I'm the enemy now."

Val sighed. "Shane, you're not the enemy. I just have a loyalty to Jen that precedes, and *supercedes,* my friendship with you."

"I'm not trying to hurt her!" Shane almost shouted.

Val's eyebrows shot up. "Really? Could have fooled me. Of course, I sleep next to her, over on the women's side of the cavern, and I'm the one who hears her crying at night. I don't understand what's going on with you two, except that my friend is hurting, and I think *you're* the cause. So, unless you can give me a very good reason for the way you've been acting, I don't plan to discuss any of this with you."

"I'm a man, and therefore a fool. How's that for a reason?" Shane replied, with a disgusted frown.

"It's a start," Val chuckled. "Seriously, what in the world is going on with you?"

"I just tried to stay away from her because, well, because I didn't think it would be the right time to tell her I love her. I can't romance her in a cave! Or with her parents and everyone else looking on. I thought it would be better to be distant, but I know now that I was wrong. Just when I decided to tell her how I feel and beg for forgiveness, she turned all cold on me. She won't even acknowledge my existence."

Val's eyes narrowed. "When did you make that decision?"

"Well, Vince and I talked when we went to town. He pointed out all the flaws in my thinking, and told me I was an idiot to make myself so miserable when the circumstances we're living in aren't going to change whether I'm happy or not. Does that even make sense?"

"Yeah, sort of. Vince is a smart man. The timing sure could have been better. Jen told me that the day you were gone, she and Erin had a long talk, and she decided that she wouldn't waste any more time on you, because you were so cold to her. Meanwhile, you're talking to Vince and deciding not to be cold anymore. You two seem to be at cross-purposes. You were pushing her away, and now you want her back. She wanted you, but now she's determined to get over you because you convinced her that you don't care. That's why she's acting like the Ice Queen."

"Well, crap. I don't know what to do, which is nothing unusual lately. How can I convince her that I'm crazy about her if she won't listen to me?"

"I have an idea."

***

Erin shoved a plastic tub back onto a stack and turned to Jen. "Hey, could you do me a favor? I need some denim to make long pants for the children, and I think it got moved to the little cavern – you know, the one that dead ends. Could you go see if you can find it? There are two or three colors of denim in the boxes, and I don't care which one you get. I promised to help Julia with something, or I'd go myself."

"Sure. Be right back." Jen set off to toward the cave where their excess supplies had been moved. It was small, and only had a small opening to the outside, which Charlie and Gus had managed to block off so the cold wind wouldn't come through. She used her flashlight to read the labels on the end of the tubs, and found several that said "Fabric" on the far side of the cavern.

Stretching to her tip-toe height of 5'5", she pulled the top tub down and opened it, looking through the folded lengths of cloth for some denim. Not finding any in that tub, she reached up and pulled down another one.

"There you are," she murmured as she pulled out a bulky, folded length of the fabric.. She put the lid on the tub, then large hands came around and grasped it, and a deep voice said, "Let me help you with that."

Shane. Jen stiffened, said a curt "thanks", and turned to leave, but he put a gentle hand on her shoulder and said, "Please wait."

She stopped, but didn't turn around. "What do you want, Shane? I can't think of anything that we have to talk about."

"How about this? I'm a moron, and I'm sorry I've treated you like I have, and I can't stand to let another hour go by without telling you that I fell in love with you the moment I saw you, and I just keep falling deeper. It scared me, and I acted like an ass."

Jen turned slowly, a look of hope mingled with distrust on her face. "Why?"

"Why did I act like that?" At Jen's nod, he shook his head. "I had this dumb idea that I needed to be able to provide for you, to give you a home. Vince helped me see that our situation doesn't lend itself to that sort of life anymore. I thought that with all of us living in caves, and no privacy, it would be easier on both of us not to even try to build a relationship, but I can't stop feeling what I feel. I can't stop wanting you, loving you. I *need* you, Jen."

Jen tilted her head slightly, staring at his face. She saw desperation, love, remorse, and fear in his eyes. "I gave up on you. I thought you cared, then stopped for some reason, and it hurt. You put me through hell, Shane."

"I know, and the really stupid part is, I made myself miserable, too. I made both of us unhappy, and I can't express how sorry I am. I love you. I want you to be my wife, and whatever the future brings, I want us to be together … if you'll have me."

"A year ago, I'd have been tempted to make you suffer a little. I'd have stayed cool for a while, and kept you dangling. But I've learned that life is too short to play games." She looked deeply into his eyes. "I love you, too, and yes, of course I'll marry you, you big oaf."

Shane whooped, arms raised in victory, then swept Jen up, spun her around, and kissed her. The kiss quickly became passionate, and when they both were breathless, Jen put her small hand on his cheek, and whispered. "And now *I* have a question. Just how many of our friends were in on this little 'chance meeting'?"

"Several, and I have a feeling they've been waiting just around the corner, listening to see if you forgave me."

"Well, I'm sure they already heard plenty, so give me another of those kisses."

Chapter Eleven – November 12
Northwestern Oklahoma

"Are we lost yet?" Price joked. They had plodded along for miles, cutting across fields and trying to keep pointed mostly in the right direction, but the maps weren't helpful since they hadn't seen a road sign in hours.

"I think so," Rian shot back. "I gave up on trying to navigate with any accuracy a long time ago. If we don't know where we are, that sounds lost to me."

"Nah," David insisted. "We're going east, I think, and sometimes we go south, so we'll find something recognizable in a few days. Man, can you imagine living out here? There's nothing but fields and an occasional house, most of which we've managed to avoid getting too close to. I'd go nuts if I had to spend much time here."

"I read once that pioneers who settled this area sometimes went absolutely stark-raving crazy, because it's just so empty and open. They would scream and run around wild-eyed, not even able to talk coherently." Rian looked around, shaking his head. "I don't know if it's true, but I can certainly see how it would be possible."

"It took a lot of mental toughness to stay here and raise a crop year after year. Can you imagine what a wildfire would do if it got going in the wheat stubble?" David grimaced. "And tornadoes – they have a lot of those. You'd be able to see it coming, but have nowhere to hide unless you had a shelter or a basement."

"I don't think we're in Kansas anymore," Price quipped in a girlish voice. David picked up a dirt clod and threw it at him.

They had bypassed a little community called Cimarron the day before, and thought they might be getting near the Cimarron River, but the map showed that the town wasn't even on the river of the same name. Having no idea how many miles they had walked, they were getting discouraged at what they perceived as a lack of progress. The sun was high in the sky, but the wind was chilly enough that they all had their hoodies zipped up.

Every plan, every route they had decided on had had to be changed due to events beyond their control. Under normal circumstances, the trip would have gone much more smoothly, but losing the Jeep had been a setback that truly wreaked havoc with every aspect of their travels.

"I know it doesn't do any good, but my mind keeps wanting to say 'if only *this,* or if only *that* hadn't happened'." Rian spat on the ground. "We need to keep going, because if we don't get a move on, we'll be caught out here in when the weather gets really cold. It's already too cool to be outside at night, and in a couple of weeks, we could be in serious trouble."

"I think we should look for an abandoned homestead. Maybe we could scavenge some blankets or even sleeping bags. I'd give a lot for some insulated coveralls and wool socks," David moaned.

"Have you always been a dreamer? We can look, but I doubt we'll find much. I'd be happy to find a nice tent or even a tarp. If we don't have some sort of shelter we can take with us, we may have to hole up for the winter somewhere," Rian added.

"That would be a disaster. We don't have nearly enough food to last until spring, and we don't have any camo to wear if we want to deer hunt. We simply don't have a choice. We have to keep moving and get to the lodge before it gets so cold we can't go on." Price actually sounded serious for a change. "I try to joke about it, but frankly, I'm getting a little worried."

"It'll be okay, bro. Somehow, we'll get through this."

***

Later that day, they finally found a river that they figured had to be the Cimarron. Turning to follow the course of the river, they knew that if they weren't already in Oklahoma, they were close. The river's turns took it out of Kansas into the Oklahoma panhandle, then back into Kansas just south of Sitka before it turned back toward the southeast and Oklahoma once again. As the map promised, it then went in a fairly straight shot to Waynoka, Orienta, Okeane, and Kingfisher before turning northeast briefly near Guthrie.

86

About dusk, they crossed Highway 283, and Rian took another look at the maps, knowing at last where they were.

"We're in Oklahoma, but this is about where the river goes back into Kansas. I think we should cut through going east, or slightly southeast, so we'll run into the river again without going out of our way. But for right now, maybe we should be looking for a place to stay the night."

"Rian, we agree," David replied, speaking for both himself and his brother.

"There you go again, doing that mental telepathy thing. Okay, it's getting dark already. We better hurry."

Increasing their pace, they searched for a barn or even a shed for shelter from the wind, but all they found was an old flatbed truck parked beside some rows of junky antique farm equipment. Under the bed of the truck, they would at least be protected from any dew or precipitation in the night, so they quickly ate yet another meal of fine military cuisine. Rian took first watch, so David and Price settled in for a cold rest.

David was on watch when the first rays of light lit the eastern sky. He blinked, hardly believing his eyes; a young girl, maybe ten or eleven years old, was sitting on the ground about fifty yards away. Her shoulders slumped, and even though she faced away from him, David thought she was crying.

"Hey," he whispered, shaking Rian and Price. "Wake up, but be quiet. You gotta see this."

The two sleepyheads crawled out and stood on the other side of the truck from the girl, and David pointed, still speaking very quietly.

"Where'd she come from? I never heard a single noise of anyone around, but when it started to get light, there she was. Something about this creeps me out."

"Let's just stay really still and wait until the light gets a little better. I don't like this, either. You think she's alone?" Rian had learned long ago to question things that seemed a bit off.

"There's not a house or anything in sight, so I doubt it. The hair on the back of my neck is standing up, and my Spidey-sense is on high alert," Price murmured.

"Spread out a little, but keep an eye on all this junk equipment. If she has friends, that's where they'll be," Rian cautioned.

The three young men crouched low and moved silently back, away from the girl, staying concealed as much as they could. The light gradually increased, and the girl turned her head a bit, peeking out of the corner of her eye to see where the men were. That movement gave her away; she was definitely bait, but for whom or what, they had no idea.

Rian signaled the others to move even further back, but as he stepped around an old, rusted front-end loader, he glimpsed a figure with a handgun rushing around a partially dismantled tractor on his right. Turning quickly to face the threat, Rian caught his foot under the edge of the bucket; his momentum caused his leg to twist painfully. He got a shot off as he fell, and suddenly, all hell broke loose.

Price and David practically dove around the last piece of junk in the row, and came face to face with another man who was raising his rifle. David was a split second faster, killing the man with a shot to the chest and causing him to drop the rifle. Price jumped over and grabbed the weapon, just as the girl flung herself onto David's back and wrapped one arm around his neck, trying to choke him. The filthy fingernails of her other hand raked his cheek, barely missing his eye. David rammed himself and the girl backwards, slamming her hips violently against the wheel of yet another old tractor. She screamed in pain and let go of David's neck, falling against the brush hog that was attached to the tractor, and hitting her head on the gearbox. She went limp and still.

Rian shouted something unintelligible as his assailant clutched the hand that Rian's bullet had hit. The man had jerked violently, losing his grip on the gun and was looking frantically on the dimly lit ground, hoping to recover it. Rian fired another shot, this time striking the guy in the neck. He stumbled and fell on Rian's injured leg, causing him to cry out from the pain.

David and Price split up, hurrying down parallel rows toward Rian's position. A third man, smaller and stouter than the others, let Price pass, then stepped out behind him. He made a wild swing with a short, heavy metal pipe, but missed. The weight of the pipe and the force of the swing pulled the man off balance, and he stumbled to the ground. Looking up, he blinked at the two rifles pointed at his head.

"Rian! You okay? Where are you?" David yelled.

"Over here. Is that all of them?"

"We think so. You okay?" David shouted back.

"You better make sure of that! Don't relax until you *know*!" Rian's voice was full of pain.

David nodded at Price, then tipped his head toward the man. Price understood that he was to keep the man covered while David checked the rest of the small lot of old farm implements. The light was getting brighter by the minute, and he quickly cleared the area, noting that the man he had shot was dead. The one who lay across Rian's legs was bleeding out, and the blow to the girl's head had cracked her skull. She was gone.

David helped Rian get his legs free, and told him about the others. "We've got one alive, unfortunately. That puts us in a quandary. Hey, what's wrong?"

Rian shook his head. "I think my leg might be broken. I twisted it pretty bad. First thing we have to do is tie that guy up real tight, then I need you to play doctor. There's some paracord in my pack. It's gonna be one of those days."

Trying not to move the leg, David gently turned Rian's upper body so he could reach the pack. Rian clenched his teeth to keep from crying out.

"Sorry. Which pocket is it in?"

"The bottom one in the front," Rian answered.

"I'll be right back." David took the cord to Price and helped him hog-tie the man, who sneered at them without speaking.

"Okay. Now I need you to help me with Rian. He's hurt," David explained, and the brothers turned to go, but the man on the ground decided it was time to break his silence.

"You can't leave me here!" he almost shouted.

"Hey, just watch this," Price answered with a smirk, then he and David walked away.

"What happened to Rian?" Price wanted to know.

"Don't know, but he thinks his leg may be broken."

"Great. What'll we do now? He won't be able to walk, but we can't stay here. Obviously, this isn't a safe place."

"It might be safe now that this bunch is out of commission, but it doesn't have any real shelter from the cold. We have to move him somewhere better, so we'd best be thinking up a way to do that."

Rian was sitting up when they got back, feeling the lower part of his leg, manually examining it with his fingers through his jeans.

"I think the damage is just on the outside, right above the ankle. Broken fibula is my best guess. If I gotta be hurt, I would say that breaking a bone wasn't my best choice. If you'll maybe find something we can use as a splint, and figure out some kind of crutch I could use, we can get out of here."

David and Price split up to search for something they could use, and Price soon returned with some short metal rods. Following Rian's instructions, Price was able to tie the rods on either side of the lower leg. He used his knife to cut up Rian's old NERC shirt and used it to pad around the ankle where the rods touched it, and on each side of the knee.

David came back emptyhanded, but suggested that he might be able to find a forked tree limb that would make a decent crutch. They could see some trees off in the distance, but Rian didn't want anyone to go off alone, and the trees were in the wrong direction.

"Help me up. David, you can support me on that side. Price's shoulder is better, but I don't want to strain it. I'll just keep a hand on his good shoulder for balance. I can hobble over to those trees, and we'll stop for breakfast once we get there. Save what's left of that shirt and I'll use it to pad the top of the crutch."

"There's just one problem," Price reminded them.

"What's that?" Rian asked.

"Our prisoner. What are we going to do with him? He and his pals tried to kill us. It was premeditated, because they used the girl to distract us, and they were hiding, lying in wait. The others are dead, and I don't feel right about killing this guy, but we can't let him go to prey on others."

"Where is he?" Rian asked. "Take me to him."

David helped Rian get up and they slowly make their way over to where the man lay. Rian leaned against the tractor, and stared hard at the man.

"Why'd you attack us?"

The man sneered. "Why not? You have packs, so you've got something worth taking."

"Who was the girl?"

"She's dead?" At Rian's nod, the man continued. "She was our wife, you murdering SOB."

"Wife?! To all of you? She was a little kid!" Rian snapped.

"She was older than she looked, almost thirteen, and what business is that of yours, anyway?"

"You made it our business when you tried to kill us. We can't let you go. You know that, don't you? Scum like you would just do this again, and we can't allow that. You've got a few minutes to make peace with your Maker, then I promise I'll make it quick."

"You can't do that. No lawyer, no police, no judge, no trial. There ain't any law now, so you can't say I broke any laws." The man said it like he thought he had just won the argument.

"My friends arrested you, so they're the acting police. There's no prosecutor, so there's no need for a defense lawyer. This is your trial, and these two are the witnesses. I'm the judge, and I say guilty and you're sentenced to death."

David interrupted. "Death, for three counts of assault, three of attempted armed robbery, three of attempted murder, and three of murder. And God only knows how many counts of statutory rape of a child under thirteen."

"We didn't kill nobody!"

"Ah, but we're in Oklahoma, and state law here says that any death that occurs during the commission of a felony is murder, and any remaining persons who were helping commit that felony are equally guilty of those deaths, no matter what they were doing, even if it's just being a look-out. You attacked us, trying to kill us to steal our supplies. I'm pretty sure that qualifies as a felony. That's three counts of attempted murder and armed robbery. Your friends are all dead, and you're alive, so that's three counts of murder."

Rian's head jerked around in surprise. "How'd you know all that?"

"I took a class on street law my freshman year. Pretty interesting, actually. Anyway, it's really the law in this state, and since there's no justice system around to enforce it, I say we decide how we're going to execute this vermin."

David let that sink in, then reminded the man, "Besides, you just said there's no law anymore, so you're bought and paid for. Looks to me like you're the one who's tied up, so you don't get a voice in what happens. This is frontier justice, to protect the innocent from violent scum like you."

"If there was a tree, we could hang him, if we had a rope," Price muttered, not quite under his breath.

"Brother, you are on a roll lately with those one-liners, but cut it out, okay? This is serious."

"What if we just leave him here, tied up tight?" Price suggested.

"Nah, he might get loose. The whole idea of the death penalty is to stop repeat offenses. Besides, we need the paracord. I'd hate to waste it on a corpse." David could see from the corner of his eye the fear and desperation on the man's face. It was finally sinking in that they weren't going to let him live.

"We have quite a bit of ammo. We should just shoot him and be done with it. Quickest and most humane way, I guess, especially if we shoot him in the ear. His brain won't have time to register the pain," Rian said. "I'll do it. We need to get on the road, and talking isn't getting us where we need to go."

"Why should you be the one to do it? I'm not saying that I want to do it, because I'm still not totally convinced it's the right thing, but if we're going to do it, why you?" Price asked.

"Because I've killed before, and one more isn't going to keep me awake at night. And because I volunteered, so the only question remaining is do you want to stand there while I do it, or start walking?"

David and Price looked at each other, and both nodded, frowning. "We'll stay. You shouldn't have to do this alone," Price replied.

Rian didn't hesitate. He pulled his handgun out of the holster, and aimed it at the man's ear. Cringing in terror, the man closed his eyes tightly, hunched his shoulders, and moaned. Rian squeezed the trigger.

"Let's get this paracord off him. Never leave something behind if it might be needed later," Rian calmly instructed.

Chapter Twelve – November 12
Southeastern Oklahoma

Ginger had barely spoken a word since the first time the man raped her. She was his prisoner, even though she could have left many times when he was asleep or not paying attention, but she had no way to free the children from the storage shed, and she knew she could never leave without them. Even if she could escape and try to find help, the man might kill them as soon as he noticed that she was gone.

No, she thought, with what little sanity she still possessed, *I have to figure out another way. I'll wait for my chance, and I'll do whatever I need to do when the time comes. I can endure this – I* will *endure, for my kids.*

But then what? Ted said we couldn't go back to town, and I have no idea what to do to survive outside. That pig of a man is eating up our food so fast, if I don't do something soon, there won't be any left. I need a weapon. I gotta find something I can use to kill the pig, and it's gotta work the first time, because I don't think I'll get a chance to strike again. Maybe I can get him to relax a little so he isn't watching me so closely. Yeah, that's what I'll do.

The back door slammed, and the man walked in with a few sticks of firewood, which he dumped on the floor near the cook stove.

"Git in here an' fix me sum grub, woman. Ah'm hungry."

Moving more quickly than usual, Ginger hurried to do his bidding. "What's your name?" she asked softly.

"Why would you want muh name? Ain't none o' yer bizness."

"I just don't know what to call you. How about 'Mister'?"

"That'll do. You got a name?" he growled.

Something about the thought of her name coming out of his disgusting mouth made Ginger feel sick. She couldn't stand the thought of the name her parents had lovingly chosen being sullied by the nasty creature, so she gave him the name of a girl she hadn't liked in school.

"It's Brenda," she answered, and began preparing the meal.

As he had done each time she placed food in front of him, Mister ate almost all of it, leaving only a little for her and the kids. He always took the few leftover bites out to the shed to feed the children, and she wasn't allowed outside when the shed door was unlocked. Occasionally, he did allow her to stand outside the door and talk to them, even though she couldn't see them.

They were cold and hungry, and Sissy's cough was terrible, but she knew she'd never be able to convince the man to let them come into the shack, where it was at least warmer. As for her own health, Ginger knew that if she didn't eat, she wouldn't have the strength to kill him and get her children to safety, so she had been hiding little bits of food as she cooked, and ate them when he went outside. *If only I could sneak some to the children. They'll need some extra nourishment, too. I'll have to carry Sissy, but Junior has to walk. I can't carry him.*

The man came back in, shoved the empty pot into her hands, and said, "Well, now, *Brenda*. Put that pot tuh soak and get them clothes off. Ah ain't waiting while you warsh 'em dishes. Hurry up, now, and git on that bed."

Ginger obeyed, but only because she knew he would beat her again if she resisted. He had also threatened to hurt the children if she didn't do as he said, but it was all she could do to lie still and let him use her body. *Thank God,* she thought, *he's never tried to kiss me. I couldn't bear for that mouth to touch mine. He's so filthy, and those rotten teeth....* She tried to concentrate on ways to kill him and how great it would be to escape with the kids, thinking of anything besides the grunting, rutting beast and what he was doing to her.

Chapter Thirteen – November 12
Southeastern Oklahoma

"Can this day get any grayer?" Will quietly asked, as he and Brian stood guard at the north cave entrance.

Brian chuckled. "No, but I think it might get wetter and colder. This was the kind of weather that made my business tough this time of year."

"Do you miss it? Building houses, I mean. I kinda miss the contact I used to have with all the farmers and ranchers. Tractors are okay, but the part of the business that I liked was the good, honest folks who came in to find equipment they could use to earn a living."

Brian looked thoughtful. "I do miss it, now that I think about it. There was something satisfying about starting with a bare piece of land and helping a family create a place they could call home. We also built workshops, buildings for businesses, and barns. I bet some of those barns housed some of your tractors."

"Yeah, I wouldn't doubt it. Were some of your clients hard to please? I know a couple of old coots who were difficult, to say the least, when it came to making a deal on a tractor. They wanted top-of-the-line brand new equipment at used prices. I learned early on to just stand firm on my best offer, and they could take it or leave it."

"I know what you mean. I had this one couple who kept changing their minds on what they wanted. Their house started out small, kinda plain, then they came into some unexpected money. That little house was almost halfway finished when they decided to add on a formal dining room and a big library-slash-office. Then they came back a few years later and added on six more rooms. But that old gal was a bargain hunter. She took my estimated cost for all the fixtures and flooring and such, and came in way under budget on almost everything. She could sure pinch a penny." Brian smiled at the recollection. "Her husband and I pulled a fast one on her, though. I don't think she ever forgave me."

"What did you do? Come on, 'fess up," Will urged.

"She wanted the dining room in front, near the bar in the kitchen, so they could serve buffet-style. She went to town to pick out ceiling fans, and while she was gone, we switched it. Moved the library to the front, and put the dining room in the back. When she got home, the wall was in place and I'd already started the built-in bookcases, so it was too late to change it. He wanted to sit at his desk and look out the big window so he could see fish jumping in the pond. She didn't want his desk to be visible from the front door, because she said it was the first thing people would notice and it would always be a piled-up mess. She was right. Every time I've been there since they moved in, it was junky."

Will grinned, then sobered. "I hated that I had to close up. All my employees were left without a job, but I guess that was true just about everywhere. I only had seven guys and two gals working at the dealership, but I still feel like I let them down somehow." Will sighed. "I guess I shouldn't let myself feel responsible, since it wasn't my doing, but they were my people, you know?"

"I understand. I had three crews, and most of them had families. Our business just died. We didn't have fuel to get to the jobsites or to run the equipment. I'm just thankful that I got to come here. I don't have a house to go home to anymore. But I have an idea of how I can partially repay everyone for letting me join the group."

"How's that?" Will asked.

"Well, I know that with NERC hanging around, we'll have to do something about all those big planters out front. We can't grow stuff out there, or the NERC guys will know there's somebody living here. I've got a plan to solve that problem. I came up with it last night, and I just need to talk to Gus and Charlie about it to see if they think it will work."

The two men were so busy talking that they didn't notice that Ranger had stiffened. He was staring intently out at the forest, hackles raised.

"I know they've been trying to come up with some answers to that problem, so let's see if we can't have a little meeting and hash it out. Our relief should be here in just a bit. I want in on this, Brick. Sounds like a chance to get outside for a change."

"Nobody has called me that since the collapse. My crews gave me that nickname because I encouraged people to build with brick or metal, with metal roofs, in case of fire. Feel free to call me that anytime. I've kinda missed it"

"I think part of why they called you that is you're a solid kind of guy."

Brian laughed. "Or else I've got a very hard head."

Ranger gave a soft "woof."

"Listen!" Will hissed, holding up a hand to silence his friend.

They could hear someone, or something, moving toward them from the east side of the cave. Will signaled for Brian to wait, and peeked around the edge of the rock wall at the entrance.

"Noah? Come in here, quick." Will whispered, pulling the young man into the cave.

"Wow, I had no idea there was a cave here."

"You haven't seen anything yet, my friend. We don't hang around outside the entrances, in case someone might be around. What caused you to come, anyway?"

"Erin said to come around the mountain if I got lonely or needed help. I was just about out of firewood, and it's getting colder, plus I couldn't have a fire at all during the day because of the smoke. I'm getting really tired of fish at almost every meal, too. If it's okay, I'd like to stay here through the winter."

"I'm sure it'll be fine. You've been a good neighbor, and you've certainly earned your place here, as far as I'm concerned. What you did for our Gina...." Will started to choke up, remembering how Noah had saved his daughter from a bear.

"Here, Noah. Let me introduce you to Ranger." Brian took Noah's hand, letting the dog sniff it, and said, "Friend, Ranger. Friend." Ranger's tail wagged and he gave Noah a doggy grin.

"Well, if Erin doesn't agree, I'll go back, but I sure hope I can stay. I promise to earn my keep. I took cooking classes in high school, and even a few lessons from a friend who specialized in preparing wild game. I can stand guard, or be a go-fer, or whatever is needed. I can even help with the kids. I had a lot of cousins who were little, and I even know how to change a diaper."

"Here comes our relief. You're in luck. It's Erin and Tanner, so you can ask her yourself," Brian offered.

"Ask me what?" Erin smiled.

"If I can stay with you guys at least until spring. I'm about out of wood and food, and well, I was lonely. I'll work hard at anything you need me to do, I swear."

"Noah, what did I tell you about that? You're welcome here for as long as you want. You're part of our group and have been for a while. I told you to come when you got tired of your own company, and I meant it. We'll let Will and Brian take you through and show you where to stow your pack. You get settled in and meet everyone, and we'll get Ian to add you to the watch list. There's always work to do, and I'm sure you'll find your niche in the group in no time."

Noah's eyes filled with tears. "Thank you so much. I was a little afraid you'd changed your mind."

"Hey, none of that, now," Tanner reassured him. "When you know her better, you'll realize that this hardheaded woman seldom changes her mind."

While the others tried to stifle their laughter, Erin punched Tanner lightly on the shoulder. "Careful, or I might *change my mind* about asking Frances to try making you a birthday cake."

Chapter Fourteen – November 13
Northwestern Oklahoma

After walking away from the body of the man they'd executed, Rian, David, and Price kept up as fast a pace as they could with Rian's injured leg, hobbling and lurching across the almost barren landscape. The brothers were on either side of him, holding him up as he hopped on one foot.

None of them had anything to say for over two hours; their thoughts were on what had happened, but each of them wrestled in his heart whether they had done the right thing, but it was the only thing they could have done.

"Any idea where we are?" David asked.

"Nope, and I don't think it matters much, as long as we're moving this direction. We'll find the Cimarron again eventually. That river isn't going anywhere," Rian assured him.

"Is anybody besides me getting hungry? We kinda missed our breakfast," Price rubbed his tummy. "I think my stomach is shrinking from hunger."

"See what I mean, Rian? He's got a hollow leg. Food is number one on Price's mind. He'd rather eat than do anything else."

"Well, in this case he's right. We need to eat a bite. Maybe we can get by with only eating twice today, which'll make our food last longer. Let's find a good spot for a break and see what scrumptious, tasty treats we have left. Besides, I need to rest this leg."

They kept going for almost an hour, and gave up on finding a spot with any cover.

"Let's just find a dry spot and sit down. There's not a house, a shed, or a tree anywhere without going too far in the wrong direction. I need to rest a bit," Rian suggested.

"Anybody got chili and macaroni? I've got a pork patty I'll trade for it," Price joked.

"I want chicken. Not that I really want it, but I figure the sooner we eat it all, the sooner we won't have any more of it to eat," David quipped. "How *do* they make it so tough?"

"I have no idea, but they do it well," Rian answered. "Okay, how are we on water?"

"We're low. Got enough for today and tomorrow morning, and then we'd better be finding some. We have LifeStraws, but how can we use them to refill the reservoirs in our packs and those empty bottles we saved?"

"Ah, that's a good question and I have the answer. I found a Sawyer Squeeze water filtration system at headquarters, and liberated it from the office supply cabinet. We'll be able to take river water and get all the clean drinking water we need, once we get to the Cimarron. It's a good system. I'll have to show you how to use it, but it's pretty simple, and versatile, too. It filters out all kinds of bacteria and such. I just wish I could have found more than one," Rian explained.

"Cool. I know I speak for both of us when I say that we're glad you invited yourself to join our little party," Price teased.

"I'm glad, too. You two wouldn't have lasted a day without me, so I've earned a star in my crown for helping the helpless," Rian shot back.

"Ow. That stung," David moaned. "We need to get on the road – well actually, *off* any roads, and get on with it. I sure hope we find that river soon. Then we just have to find something that floats, but at least the river'll be a milestone for us so we know we're making progress."

They dug a small hole with Rian's folding shovel and buried the wrappers from their meals. Rian had taught them not to leave an evidence lying around, because someone might come along and see it, then track them by the direction of any footprints they left.

The ground was getting drier and more solid by the hour, making it easier to walk across fields and avoid the roads, what few roads there were. They continued their erratic pace for a few more hours, then noticed a dark line at the eastern horizon.

"Is that what I think it is?" David asked.

"If you think it's the top of a line of trees, I think you're right. And trees grow along streams of water out here. I think that just might be the river." Rian turned on some speed, doing a slightly faster limp and pulling David along with him; he was excited to finally have a destination in sight. Price hurried to keep up.

It was, indeed, the river. The band of trees didn't extend very far, leaving the banks of the red stream mostly bare. The river was up due to the frequent rains upstream. The men turned and followed along hoping that soon they'd be able float and paddle their way to the Tulsa area.

***

A woman and a teenage girl hunkered down behind the trees, hoping the undergrowth would provide enough cover to conceal their presence. They heard the men talking, saying something about Lake Keystone and canoes. They could see that two of the men were fairly young, and one was a bit older, and they all seemed to be excited about the river.

The woman was afraid; she and her daughter had been run out of their home by a family of vicious people, a man and his wife and their two twenty-something kids, who simply threw them out and locked the doors after warning them not to come back. The now-homeless woman was a widow, her husband having died when a tractor he was working on fell and crushed him two years earlier. She was a trained horticulturalist with the college degree to prove it, and spent her time filling their basement with veggies and fruits that she had grown and canned. She had been so sure that that she and her girl, who was fifteen, would be able to survive, until those horrible people shoved their way into the house.

Now they were cold and hungry, and desperate for help, but too scared to step forward and ask these strangers for something to eat. They just hid, and listened.

"It's going to be getting dark in about an hour, and we've put in a long day." Rian yawned. "How about we just camp here tonight? In the morning, we can refill our water containers, and we'll be all set to head out."

Price looked at David, then said, "Sounds good to us."

David looked around the small grove of trees. "I think I'll see if I can find a branch that will do for a crutch. We'll make better time that way. I need to borrow your hatchet, Rian."

He returned soon with a stout branch from a tree. Price helped him get Rian into a standing position so they could measure the length, then David cut it and began smoothing the Y-shaped top. When that was done to his satisfaction, he wrapped the remainder of Rian's NERC shirt around the top for padding, and announced that it was ready.

Rian took a quick turn around their little camp, and smiled. "This is great, but I think I would be more stable on the uneven ground if I had two."

David scowled at him, then chuckled, and went to find wood that would made another crutch. Both times he had gone in search of wood, the two women who watched from nearby breathed a sigh of relief when he went in the opposite direction.

They took turns going over into some bushes to relieve themselves, then picked out which MREs to complain about. Soon, David and Rian were resting, while Price sat against a tree, listening for movement and occasionally taking a turn around the immediate area.

Price woke Rian when it was time for his guard duty, then Rian woke David a few hours later. All of them knew to move around the area at random intervals. This accomplished two things: it helped them stay awake, and it gave them a better overall picture of the situation. It also gave Rian a chance to practice using his makeshift crutches.

Near daybreak, while he was making the rounds, David tripped and almost fell over something lying across his path. He yelped, jerking around to see what it was. *Whatever* it was began scuttling backwards away from him, and he realized suddenly that it was a girl.

"Hey, hey! Settle down. Where'd you come from?" he asked.

Something moved to his left, and he swung his rifle in that direction, and at the same time, shouted, "Price, Rian!! Get over here!"

The woman could see the rifle in the dim morning light, and raised her hands over her head. "Lila, get your hands up. We're caught, so don't make any sudden moves."

Rian and Price ran up, and Rian used his flashlight to further illuminate the scene.

"Please don't hurt us. We were here when you arrived, and saw you eat, heard you talking about the lake and canoes. We're unarmed. Please don't shoot," the woman said.

"Who are you, and why are you out here alone?" David demanded.

The woman drew a ragged breath. "My name is Peggy Wilson and this is my daughter, Lila. We lived in a house just a few miles from here, downriver, until some people came and kicked us out. That was three days ago, I think. We don't have *anything*, no food, no winter clothes, only one empty water bottle and a cigarette lighter."

"Who were the people who kicked you out? Did you know them?" Rian asked.

"We knew *of* them, just by reputation. They're a family who lived in a hovel near Waynoka. Pretty much worthless, if you ask me. They lived off welfare and what they could steal. Mean as snakes, too. Their boy used to bother Lila after school. He was a dropout, but hung around waiting for her to come out to catch the school bus. He wouldn't leave her alone, always trying to touch her or kiss her. She finally told the principal, and they ran him off, but he'd stand across the street and stare at her, rubbing his crotch and grinning."

"Go on," Rian urged.

"When things went bad, the school closed and I started teaching Lila practical things at home, like gardening and canning. That boy didn't see her for a long time, then one day, there he was, standing out at the end of our driveway, watching us. The next day, his daddy came, and demanded food. I wouldn't open the door, but he yelled through it that they wanted food and they'd be back.

104

"About a week after that, the whole family came, and caught us not paying attention. They pushed their way inside, and that boy wanted to take Lila right then, but his mamma apparently still had at least a little decency, because she slapped him and told him she didn't raise a rapist. The dad wanted to let him have Lila, but the mom must wear the pants in that family, because she stood her ground with both of them. They took the jackets we were wearing and just tossed the two of us out the door, then locked it, with that man hollering that we better not come back, or he'd give Lila to his boy."

Lila stood quietly, head down, as she listened to her mother tell their story, but she looked up at her mom's last words and said, "We wanted to come out. We wanted to ask you for help, but we were afraid. Can you help us?"

"What do you have in mind? Do you have relatives who would take you in?" David asked.

"What I really want is too much to ask," Peggy said bitterly. "I want my home back, and those filthy people gone. I'll settle for a little food, though. We thought we might make it to Kansas, where my late husband's people are, but it's just too far on foot in this cold. Would you think about letting us tag along with you as far as Waynoka? We have friends there."

"Do you know anywhere we could find a raft, a canoe, or even a small boat? We want to travel on the river as far as Tulsa." Rian glanced at his two companions. "Let us discuss this, while you eat. And don't gobble it," he warned, "if it's been three days since you ate. Eat slowly or it might not stay down."

He gestured for David and Price to follow him. They went back to their packs, and grabbing two MREs at random, Rian went back closer to the women and tossed the packets to them before returning to talk quietly with the brothers.

"What do you think?" he asked.

"If they had a gun, they could have taken us by surprise any time. I think they're telling the truth." David tilted his head to the side. "I'd like to help them."

"Me, too," Price agreed. "Nobody's that good at acting. I wonder what kind of weapons the people who took over their house have. I'd kinda like to see them get their home back."

Rian pursed his lips and muttered, "It's just one thing after another with you two."

David and Price laughed, and David said, "Get real, buddy. You wanna help them, too. We need a lot more information before we decide for sure, but this world would be impossible to live in if good people didn't help out when there's a need. Come on, let's go visit with them a little more."

Sitting down near the woman and her daughter, Rian explained that they would like to help, but needed some answers before they could make a plan. When the women finished their food, he asked them to draw a diagram in the dirt, showing the location of the river, their house, any outbuildings, and whatever other information might be useful.

Peggy found a stick and cleared off a flat area in front of her. She drew a curved line that was the river, then added other important items as she described them.

"Our barn is here, and the drive goes between it and the house. There's some grain storage silos behind the house, about thirty yards, I would guess. The henhouse is attached to the back of the barn. There's a propane tank over on the other side of the house. The front door is here, and the back door is here," she explained as she pointed to each shape in her drawing.

"Mom, don't forget the entrance to the basement," Lila reminded.

"Good thinking, sweetie. There's a door in the kitchen that goes down to the basement, right about here, and there's also an outside door behind the house, like you'd see on a tornado shelter. We seldom use it, but it's always a good idea to have an escape route if a tornado tears the house up and the other exit is blocked. That door has a combination lock on it when it's not tornado season. So, we have a way in that they can't open."

"Were those people armed?" David asked.

"The father had a big knife, like my husband used to gut deer. I didn't see any guns of any kind, did you, Lila?"

106

Lila shook her head. "They just used the fact they are bigger than us to push us around. Four against two, just how they like it," she said bitterly.

"But my husband had a rifle, a shotgun, and a pistol, which they may have found, but I doubt they found the extra ammo for them. Oh, how I wish I had given in when he wanted to teach us how to use guns! I didn't like them and refused to have anything to do with shooting, but if I had only known how, maybe we could have defended ourselves."

"Or made them mad enough to go find some guns of their own and come back. If you'd killed or wounded one or two of them, they probably wouldn't have just walked away. With only two of you, you couldn't have guarded the place twenty-four hours a day. Do you think you'll be safe there if we clear them out for you? Do you have any friends who would come out to help you in exchange for getting to eat? Someone you can trust, preferably with their own guns?" Rian suggested.

"Mom," Lila interjected, "we could ask the Robertsons. There's seven of them, and they all know how to shoot. They'd help with the gardening, too, I'm sure. We have plenty of food, and room for all of them if some sleep in the basement."

Peggy nodded, and turning to the men, explained, "The Robertsons are our nearest neighbors. We should have gone to them instead of trying to get to Kansas, but we didn't want to be a burden. Larry lost his wife about four years back, and he has four sons and two daughters. The youngest is fifteen, like Lila, and the oldest are twins in their early twenties. They'd be wonderful, and I'm sure they'd come if we asked them. Their house had some damage from the recent storms and needs a new roof, so winter in a warm, dry house may be all the incentive they need. We know them from church, and they're good folks."

"Where do they live from here?" Rian asked, obviously thinking hard.

"They're between here and our house. Oh, that's really perfect, isn't it? We can go by there and get them to help us, then they can come stay at our house!" Lila exclaimed.

"Do they have guns? Would they be willing to take part in what amounts to an attack to recover your home?" Rian looked at Peggy, and continued. "We're outnumbered, and we could sure use some more people on our side."

"Larry was in the Marine Corps. He served in Afghanistan and some other places; his boys won a sharpshooting contest last year. They all hunt, even the girls, and they have quite a few guns."

Peggy paused, glancing hesitantly at Lila. "You didn't know this, honey, but Larry asked me out back in the spring, right before the collapse. We dated some in high school, then he enlisted, and I went to college, then later married your dad. Are you okay with them coming to live with us knowing that Larry and I have a history?"

"Oh, Mom." Lila rolled her eyes. "Do you think I'm blind? I figured out Larry had a thing for you at least a year ago. He's really nice. Good looking, too," she teased. "You've mourned Daddy long enough. I know you'll always miss him, and so will I, but it's okay to move on and live your life. I think it would be great to have some brothers and sisters, so if you two get together, fine. If not, that's okay, too. We'll just all be friends, like always. I want you to be happy," she whispered as she leaned over to hug her mother.

"Okay, then," Rian agreed. "We'd like to offer our assistance. Let's get over to your friends' house and see if they're interested, and we'll make a plan on how to take your house back from the bad guys. By the way, I'm Rian, and these two are David and Price. We're just passing through, trying to get home."

"Well, I think that maybe Larry's family can help you with that. I'm pretty sure that his kids still have some canoes, and I would bet that he'd be willing to let you have a couple of them. The older boys don't use theirs much lately, and if I'm not mistaken, they're just hanging in the barn gathering dust."

***

Larry seemed happy to see Peggy and Lila, but his eyes narrowed when he noticed three strangers standing behind them.

In spite of his distrust, he invited all of them to sit on the big porch and told one of his daughters to bring them some tea.

"We have a hand pump on the well, and tea is about the only thing we have to offer you. Sorry," he apologized. Looking at Peggy, he asked, "What brings you to visit us?"

"Larry, we should have kept in touch better, but Lila and I were afraid to leave our farm. These men helped us, and are going to help us more. This is Rian, and those two are David and Price. I'm sorry," she admitted, "but I'm still not sure which is which. It's been an upsetting few days."

The brothers clarified the confusion, then motioned for Peggy to continue her tale. She explained how she and Lila had been driven out of their home, and Larry almost exploded in anger.

"Those rotten, no-good...!" He made a visible effort to control his anger, taking a long breath and letting it out slowly, his teeth clenched. "So, what are you going to do now? You know you're welcome to stay here, but we've got some roof problems."

"Actually, I was hoping that you and your family would come live with us." Peggy smiled at the confusion that flashed across Larry's face, then saw understanding dawn as he realized what she was saying.

"I get it. You guys are going to help us get Peggy's house back, aren't you? Wait. Let's get the rest of my kids out here." he suggested. The youngest girl, Faith, who had been sitting with Lila and listening, ran to call her siblings to join them on the porch.

"Well, we're certainly hoping to get Peggy's home back. We're only traveling through, but don't like the thought of two sweet ladies being homeless, hungry, and cold, and we offered to help them, but having your bunch along would sure improve our odds," David agreed. "Rian here is an Army Ranger, and we understand that you're a Marine. We know that people like you two never really stop being warriors, but we think Rian has a broken fibula, so he's not entirely mobile, and he's going to have to stay back some, and Peggy and Lila can't shoot, so we could sure use some extra guns."

Larry grinned, and looked around at his family. "Ya'll up to a little action? Peggy's been our friend for a long time, and I can't see letting scum take their house and supplies. What do you say?"

Every one of Larry's kids grinned, nodded, or both.

"Dad, you raised us to stand up for what's right and to help our neighbors. You know we don't hold with letting the bad guys win. We're all ready to help," Alex, the oldest, said.

"Well, Peggy has also offered to let us move in with her and Lila. We have enough gas in the truck to take our supplies and clothes, if we can get everything in two or three trips. We'd all be safer if we joined forces, plus I don't see how we can repair that roof without lumber and shingles. Any objections to moving to the Wilson farm?"

Again, the agreement was unanimous.

"Okay. Now we need to figure out how we're going to do this," Rian said. He then explained the situation, what weapons they thought the bad guys might have, and how they might be able to clear the house while minimizing the risk to themselves.

"I think that plan will work. At least, it sounds good, but you know how plans are, soldier," Larry told Rian. "Let's get you all settled in and fed, and we'll talk some more over dinner."

Chapter Fifteen – November 14
Northwestern Oklahoma

About an hour before daylight the next day, Operation Home Free began. Larry's oldest daughter, Carla, came up with the name, and everyone thought it fit their goal perfectly.

Peggy, Lila, and Larry's youngest two, Eddie and Faith, would stay at the Robertson home. Eddie and Faith both had shotguns, and would guard the house.

Price and David were checking their rifles when Price's head suddenly went up, and he said, "I get it! It just hit me."

David looked at him like he was crazy, and asked, "Get what, bro? You been smoking wacky tobaccy?"

'No. It just dawned on me about the names. They're alphabetical."

"Huh?" David looked thoroughly confused.

"Larry's kids' names, bro. They're in alphabetical order. Alex, Ben, Carla, Denny, Eddie, and Faith. How cool is that?"

"It's cool, but you get excited about the weirdest stuff. Sometimes I wonder about you," David replied, shaking his head. "Hurry up. It's time to go."

Those who were participating in the recovery effort gathered their weapons and gear. Larry hugged Eddie and Faith, telling them, "Hold down the fort. I love you, and we'll be back soon." He grasped Peggy's hand, looked into her eyes for several seconds, then smiled and nodded, and left with the others.

There was a full moon to help them see as they moved quietly down the road toward the Wilson homestead. Rian had his rifle slung on his back, and used both crutches, with David on one side and Price on the other in case he stumbled.

When they got close to the farm, the group split up. Rian, Denny, and Carla slipped around and into the big barn. Rian took up a position at a window on the lower level, and Carla climbed up to the hayloft, quietly opening the double doors and setting up her little sniper's nest. Price sneaked over behind the storage shed, which was next to the grain silos. From there, he could maneuver around quite a bit if necessary. His shoulder wound hadn't bothered him in a couple of days, other than a tiny twinge if he raised his arm too high.

Denny would provide the distraction that they hoped would lure at least two of what he called "the zombies" out into the open. He sneaked through the barn behind Rian and Carla, crossing the entire length of the building to a door that allowed access to the henhouse.

David hunkered down behind a few big round bales of wheat straw that sat in a row along the driveway. Larry, Alex, and Ben crept under the windows of the house and waited at the corner near the locked outside door to the basement. Peggy had given them the combination to the lock, 6-20-26, and all three had memorized it.

Just as the sun cleared the horizon, Denny literally jumped into the henhouse, startling the chickens. He waved his arms, shooing them off their roosts, and causing quite a ruckus of clucking and wings flapping. Most of the birds fled from the intruder, dashing out into the chicken run, still squawking and trying to fly away.

The back door of the house opened, and the father and son came running out to see what was disturbing the birds, which they considered to be their personal food source. Both were armed, evidently having found Peggy's husband's guns. David yelled, "Hey, there!" at them, and they spun around to fire into the straw bales.

As soon as they heard the first of the chickens' frightened clucks, Larry and his two older sons rounded the corner of the house, and Larry dialed the combination of the lock on the cellar door as quickly as he could. They opened the door just as the shooting started, and the loud reports of guns covered the squeak of the hinges as they lifted the metal door and entered the basement.

As soon as David drew the zombies' fire, Rian, Price, and Carla opened up on the two men. The younger one went down with Carla's first shot, which hit him in the right temple. Rian's shot hit

112

the father in the thigh; Price's grazed across his back, lodging next to the shoulder blade, but the man kept coming, firing until Rian shot him a second and a third time, hitting him in the chest and the throat. The man finally dropped, and silence fell over the farm.

Inside the house, the mother and daughter heard the shooting, and grabbing sharp knives from a drawer, squatted down behind the counter in the kitchen. Larry's team cleared the basement and came up the stairs, trying not to make a sound. The door at the top of the steps was open, and they could see into the kitchen, but not where the women were hidden. Larry came through the door first, and the mother leapt at him, trying desperately to stab him with a large chef's knife. He blocked her lunge by slamming the butt of his rifle into her arm, causing her to drop the knife. As it skittered across the tile floor, the daughter came up screaming, slashing the air with a steak knife, but Ben shot her before she reached his father.

Alex rammed the barrel of his rifle into the mother's ribs, and snarled, "Don't move. I'll drop you where you stand."

Furious as seeing her daughter shot, she ignored the warning, diving to retrieve her blade, and coming back up faster than any of the men expected, but Alex made good on his threat, and shot her in the heart. She was dead before she hit the floor.

Larry leaned down, and checked for a pulse on the daughter's neck. It was very weak; she was obviously bleeding out. He looked over at the mother's glassy eyes, and knew she was gone.

"We need to clean this mess up before Peggy comes home. I don't want her to have to see all this blood on her kitchen floor," Larry mumbled, and his sons immediately moved to help him drag the bodies outside.

They dumped the dead women with their menfolk and the team that had been outside came in and helped with the cleanup.

"What'll we do with the bodies?" Denny asked. He was shaken by the carnage, but told himself that it had been necessary.

"When we come back with our first load of supplies, once we get it unloaded, we'll use the truck to take them off somewhere and dump them. I really don't want the younger kids to see them,

113

or Peggy, either," Larry answered. "We'll talk them into waiting until the last trip to come here."

Rian slapped Larry on the back and said, "Marine, ya done good. We couldn't have done it without you and your family."

Larry looked him in the eye. "No, *we* owe *you*. You didn't have to do this, but you three put yourselves in danger for people you just met. Peggy and Lila are our friends, and now, so are you. If you're ever back this way, we'd be proud to have you for a visit. If there's anything we can do for you now, just name it."

Rian, David, and Price all grinned, and Price said, "Well, now that you mention it...."

Chapter Sixteen – November 14
Northwestern Oklahoma

Peggy was thrilled to see the group walking back toward the Robertson farm. She and Lila quickly counted heads, but noticed that two members of the team were missing. Panic grabbed at them, and they ran out of the house to see if someone was hurt.

"Where are the others? Rian and Alex? Were they injured?" Peggy cried.

Larry chuckled and reassured her. "No, no, they're fine. We all are. They just stayed behind to watch the place. Rian's leg was hurting some, and he didn't feel up to making the hike back here, and Alex is keeping him company."

"So, what happened? Are the zombies gone?" Lila asked.

"The plan worked exactly as we hoped it would, and that *has* to be a first. The bad guys shot first, and we shot last. The women stayed in the house, but attacked us with knives, and well...they won't be bothering anyone, ever again," Larry explained. "It's over, and we'll take care of the bodies when we go back with the truck."

"Well, we're glad that everything turned out like it did." Peggy sounded relieved, and smiled up at Larry. "I'm so glad you'll be joining forces with us. Neither one of us has been able to sleep much lately. We'll all benefit from this."

She turned to the Martins. "And David, Price – thank you. I don't know what we would have done without you. We weren't thinking clearly, or we'd have asked Larry for help sooner. It's just hard to figure things out when you're cold, scared, and exhausted. We'll never forget you."

"Do you know a ham radio operator around here, one that has a power source? There's one at the lodge where we're going, and we'd sure like to keep up with you and how you're doing." David leaned closer to Peggy's ear. "I think Price has developed a thing for Carla, if you want to know the truth," he said in a stage whisper.

Price heard him, and slugged him in the arm. Everyone laughed, except Carla, who blushed.

With all of them pitching in at the house, loading Larry's truck and trailer with food, clothes, and other supplies, the job went quickly. Larry had his girls grab family albums and a few heirloom items, as well. They got the mattresses off the beds, and every sheet, blanket, and quilt they had, plus towels, camping gear, and a big box of seeds that Carla had saved from their summer garden.

Larry, Ben, Price, and David took the truck to Peggy's to unload, then assisted in disposing of the dead, which they dumped in a muddy ditch about two miles away. They didn't much care if wild animals ate them; those people certainly hadn't cared about Peggy and Lila, so they didn't deserve any consideration, either.

With some of them sitting on the canoes, there was room for all of them to pile onto the trailer for the second trip, and soon, they had things organized at Peggy's house, and she asked everyone to come to the living room.

"I want all of you Robertsons to understand something. This is *your* home now, as much as it is ours. We're together for the duration, and I hope we'll all work as a team to help each other to not only to survive, but to thrive.

"Lila and I welcome each of you to this house, because without you, we wouldn't have this roof over our heads. To our new friends, I say again, *thank you.* You're welcome to stay until you're rested, and our prayers will go with you when you leave us.

"I think this calls for a celebration. We're going to eat well tonight, and if I can persuade Larry to pop the corks, we'll even have a glass of wine to toast our new friends. I have a few bottles in the basement that I was saving for a special occasion, and this is *very* special."

***

Feeling stuffed from eating a homecooked dinner that seemed like a feast after living on very little for days, most of the group went to their respective beds. Lila moved into her mother's room, which made space in her room for Carla and Faith. All the male Robertsons would be sleeping on mattresses they had placed on the floor in the big basement family room. They hoped that they could get by for one night without standing guard, because everyone had put in a hard day.

Larry and his boys had already decided that one of their first projects would be to build an outhouse. Peggy and Lila had been able to get by with bringing in a few buckets of water from the pond each day and pouring it as needed in the toilet, but with seven additional people, that wouldn't be practical anymore. Larry also had ideas about solar-heated water for bathing, and several other possibilities that would improve their quality of life.

David, Rian, and Price settled down in the living room. Rian got the sofa, because getting down and back up from the floor wasn't feasible with his leg. It was the first chance the three of them had found to talk all day.

"Do we leave in the morning?" Price asked.

David looked at Rian, shrugged, and extended his hand palm up, as though to say, "It's up to you."

"I think that after a restful night, I, for one, will be ready to head out. Since Ben and Alex have insisted on giving us their canoes, we'll just need to get them to the river, and be on our way."

David nodded. "The longer we stay, the harder it will be to leave these fine people and good food. And the closer it will be to real winter weather. I vote we go."

"I figured you'd say that," Price complained. "I find a pretty, smart gal who can shoot, fish, and cook, and you want me to leave before I get a chance to get to know her."

"Brother, be realistic. Are you willing to stay here without me and Rian, and not see our parents or Jen again, at least for a long time? Or do you think Carla would leave her family and go with us to the lodge? The longer you have to get to know her, the more it'll hurt when we leave. It's better to go now, before you really fall for her."

"I know. I just have a feeling that she's one of a kind, but I see your point. Tomorrow morning, it is. Goodnight."

Morning came with a few clouds, but lots of sunshine and wind. After breakfast, Peggy handed David a camping pot with a folding handle, a bag of hard candy and one of pasta, some deer jerky she'd made, and baggies full of dehydrated onions, carrots, celery, and potatoes.

Larry gave them two packs of coconut-flavored emergency food bars. "Those have three thousand calories in a whole bar, so one of them will keep you going strong for a day, if you eat part of it in the morning and the rest later in the afternoon. With what Peggy gave you, you can make soup when it's safe to have a fire. When you have to keep moving, those bars can be eaten on the go.

"Good luck, and God bless. We'll try to find a ham operator and let your family know you're okay. When you get there, please let us know. We'll be praying for you every day."

"We appreciate that." David smiled. "There is one other thing you can do for us."

"What's that?" Larry asked.

"Teach Peggy and Lila to shoot. We'll feel better knowing they won't be helpless ever again."

"Consider it done. I already planned to begin their training right after I get the boys started digging a hole for the outhouse."

After hugs and handshakes all around, the Wilsons and all the Robertsons except Alex and Ben watched their new friends load their gear into the back of the truck. The twins drove the truck to a spot close to the river and helped get the canoes into the water, then assisted the travelers in getting their packs situated, and the canoes launched into the muddy river.

"Safe travels!" Alex called to them, then he and his twin stared after them until they were out of sight.

"One, two, three, four, five." Ginger slowly counted all the cans of vegetables that were left from the two bags that she and Ted had taken from the people of Kanichi Springs. Her mind jumped from one thing to another, sometimes so fast she couldn't understand any of it, and she had begun talking to herself, sometimes in her head, but increasingly, muttering out loud. She asked herself questions and answered them, and she talked to people who were real, but not present, like Ken and Terri. She said, *I'm sorry* over and over inside her head, apologizing to those who lived in the tunnel, especially when she realized that their food was now feeding the pig who had been raping her at least once a day since he'd killed Ted.

Ted. My Husband. He's dead now. He wasn't a bad man, but he did some pretty bad things, like stealing money from work, and telling me to take that food from the people in the tunnel. They helped us, but I stole their food. Ted died. It's my punishment for stealing from them and their children. Children! Where are my children? Oh, that's right. They're in their little house in the backyard. That pig-man feeds them, but only a little. He's mean. I wish he was dead.

Ginger's mind retained only enough sanity for her to realize in a very vague way that she was insane. The terrible things that had happened since she and Ted left Kanichi Springs with the children had been too much for her fragile psychological state. She couldn't face it all, so her brain had devolved to a child-like state. When she spoke aloud, which was seldom, she sounded like a little lost girl, and she knew somehow that she wasn't mentally living in the real world. She had retreated into a state of being where her brain refused to accept anything around her as real. It was all a dream, and that was the only way she knew to cope.

Mister, the man who held her children captive, was a brute. He wasn't intelligent at all, but he was in control. Ginger knew somewhere in her sick mind that she had to change that somehow, or her children would die.

I would kill myself if it wasn't for the children, she thought in one of her more lucid moments. *But if I did, he wouldn't feed them anymore. He might cut them up, like he said. Cut them up and...and eat them? Would he eat children? Yes. Yes, I think he would, when the food runs out. Oh! It's almost out already!*

I'm crazy now. Isn't that funny, that I'm crazy and I know I'm crazy? I always thought crazy people didn't know it, but I know. Crazy people can still think. They can still plan, and I've got to plan how to help the children.

***

Ginger had found that the only way she could endure the beatings and being raped by Mister was to go somewhere else inside her head until it was over, pretending that it was happening to another woman, not her, because *she* wasn't really there.

He was an angry man, always looking for something to use as an excuse to hit her or yank her hair. She tried to avoid making him mad, but he mostly stayed mad, so she retreated into her own world, and talked to herself more and more.

He came into the kitchen and heard her mumbling something. He grabbed a handful of her hair, and pulled her across the room, shoving her down on a chair. Then he leaned in so close that she could smell the rot of his teeth.

"Shut up! Ah'm sick of hearin' yer voice. Mutterin' all th' time, talkin' constantly. Just. Shut. Up!!" He yelled, slapping her so hard that she tumbled off the chair and lay on the filthy floor.

"Now, git up and git them dishes warshed, then cook me sum grub," he snarled, and went out the door.

Ginger got up slowly, and did as he ordered. He'd be back in an hour or two, she knew. She had no idea where he went every day, but he had a habit of disappearing for a while every afternoon.

Ginger got the dishes cleaned up as well as anyone could with cold water and no detergent, then figured out what she could cook that wouldn't require close supervision. The voice in her head had told her to find a weapon while he was out, that there had to be *something* she could use to kill the pig.

A quick but thorough search of the house yielded nothing that Ginger thought of as certain to accomplish his death. For every possible weapon, there was too great a chance of failure, and she knew that failing would mean the death of one or both of her children. He had hidden the sharp knives entirely too well.

Then she heard him returning. By the time he entered the kitchen with an armload of firewood, she was back, stirring the soup that simmered on the antique wood-burning cook-stove. He dumped the load on the floor, as he always did, and one of the chunks of wood bounced a bit, hitting Ginger's ankle.

She started to cry out, but stifled the cry, knowing it would anger him. *Ouch!* she thought. *That really hurt. Hurt! Really hurt.*

***

That night, Ginger made herself stay awake. She was glad that Mister didn't make her sleep in his bed. No, once he was through with her, he pushed her out, and she usually slept on the ratty sofa in the front room.

She sat there, thinking that the answer was right in front of her, but not knowing what to do. She rose and went to the shabby kitchen to get a sip of water out of the pitcher she'd left on the counter. When she turned around, she stubbed her toe on a piece of the wood that remained on the floor. *That hurt!* And then she knew.

Picking up the heavy log, which was about twenty inches long and three inches in diameter, she held it in her hands, turning it and examining the bark as though it was a fascinating work of art. It had a sharp stub on one end, where a smaller branch had broken off. She tiptoed over to the open bedroom door. She could hear Mister's snores, and knew he was sound asleep. One tiny step at a time, she approached the bed, watching her feet carefully so she wouldn't trip and make even the slightest noise.

She stood over him, watching his loose, floppy lips vibrate every time he exhaled. She could see his flabby arms and stomach, and the nasty boxers he wore. His odor was almost overpowering, but she refused to allow it to distract her.

Turning the log so the sharp stub was pointed downward, she raised it as high as she could, and with all her strength, slammed it down on his head, again and again. She hit him until his head was unrecognizable as anything human. She kept on, pounding his shoulder and arms, then his legs, working her way down the already dead body, hitting him over and over, until her strength gave out.

She looked at him. *Closer, closer, closer,* the voice urged. *Is he breathing? No? Ah. The pig is dead. He's dead at last.*

Locating the dirty jeans he had apparently been wearing for months, she dug in the pocket and found the key to the storage shed. She went back to the living room and placed the key on a table, then laid down on the sofa and fell into a deep, dreamless sleep.

***

Late the next morning, Ginger woke, but lay there, wondering why she felt more at peace than she had in a long time. *Why is it so quiet? Mister must be angry because I slept late, but why didn't he come in here and hit me?* She got up, and when she didn't find Mister in the kitchen, she went to the bedroom door and peeked in. His blood-splattered body lay on the disgusting, stained mattress, his battered head on the pillow.

Oh. Now I remember. He died, so now I can get the children and leave. We're free to go, her mind said in a sing-song voice. *Free to go, free to go.*

Ginger looked around the bedroom for anything she might want to take, but found nothing. She walked into the dingy bathroom, and caught sight of herself in the mirror. Smeared brown blood speckled her face and arms, and big blotches of dried blood covered her clothing. She stared at the face in the mirror. *Is that me? I'm not pretty anymore. Ted said he loved me because I was pretty. He won't love me now. No. Ted died. The pig died. But the children might be scared if they see me like this. I need to wash my face and arms.*

She darted out to the pump, and filled a bucket that Mister kept nearby. The water was icy cold, but she scrubbed at her face and hands, rubbing her arms, even using her fingernails to scrape the blood off. When she finished, her skin was an angry red with deep scratches, some that were beginning to ooze fresh blood.

That's better. Now I can get the kids out of their little house and we can go. Go where? Back to town, I guess. They didn't mean it. I know they'll let us come back.

She went back inside, grabbed the key, dumped the three remaining cans of food into one of the bags, and ran out to the shed. It took three tries to get the key into the lock, but she opened it, and called sweetly to the kids, "Junior. Sissy. Come out and see me." She looked in and smiled at them, but never noticed that her kids were covered in feces and dried urine.

Junior rose from the corner where he had huddled when he heard the key in the lock. Sissy lay on her side on the dirt floor, every breath labored. Her face was very hot, and she coughed even in her sleep.

"Mamma?" Junior whispered. "Mamma? Is it really you?"

"Yes, baby, it's me, and we're free to go. Free to go. Wake up, Sissy. We're going on a trip. Hurry now, and get ready."

Junior knew something wasn't right, but he was still very glad to see his mother.

"Sissy? Wake up now, right this minute," she sang.

"Mamma, she won't wake up," Junior insisted. "She sleeps almost all the time. You'll have to carry her. I can carry the bag."

"You're such a good boy. Hold the door open for me, you hear?"

Ginger bent down and lifted Sissy. She grinned at Junior, and walked jauntily toward the highway, not bothering to see if Junior followed.

***

Ginger carried Sissy until she got tired, then they stopped for a brief rest. Junior was so hungry he felt sick, but hunger had become a way of life. Still, maybe his mother had some food he could eat.

"I'm hungry, Mamma. May I have something to eat?" he asked timidly.

"You can have whatever you want, Junior. See what's in the bag, and pick one."

The bag contained one can of pork and beans, one of corn, and one pears. Junior noticed that the cans the beans and corn were in required an opener, and he guessed correctly that they didn't have one, so he chose the pears, which had a pop-top. Ginger grinned as she opened it for him, and he used his dirty fingers to eat the fruit, then drank the juice, wiping his mouth with the sleeve of his filthy shirt.

When he was finished, Ginger picked Sissy up again, and resumed her walking. She walked as fast as she could, but the whole time, the voices in her head were arguing with her.

I'm a fool to go back. They'll never take us in. Yes, they will, if you ask real nice. You'd be better off dead. I'm not well, but Sissy is really sick. Who can help her? There's nobody to help. Leave her behind, and save Junior and yourself. No. Save her. Must save her. Find help, that's what I have to do, and help is in town.

The voices wouldn't be quiet, no matter what Ginger did, so she just kept walking. Then she looked up the road and saw that they were almost back to Kanichi Springs. Mister must have lived closer to town than she'd thought.

She stopped. No matter what, she couldn't go into the town. Her shame at having stolen food from hungry children wouldn't allow her to go back.

"Junior, come here, honey, and pay close attention to what I tell you. I'm too tired to go on, but you can see the town right up there, can't you?"

At his nod, she continued. "I want you to go get that preacher man, and tell him that your daddy died, and Sissy is real sick. Tell him to come here and help us, because I can't carry her anymore. Can you remember that?"

"Yes, Mamma. Find the preacher and tell him to come get Sissy because she's sick and Daddy's dead. I can remember that."

"Good boy. Now you go on, and do what I told you. We'll be right here when the preacher comes for us."

Junior hurried away, almost running down the road, eager to help his sister and mother. When he was too far away to see what she was doing, Ginger took a stick and found a large patch of bare ground where she could write in the moist dirt with a little stick she'd found.

Almost thirty minutes later, Ken and two other men came, rushing to help the sick child. They found her alone, lying on the shoulder of the road, barely breathing. Looking around for Ginger, Ken noticed the writing on the ground.

Preacher – I'm not going to come back. I got someplace to go where Mister will never find me. Please take care of my kids. Goodbye.

Ken showed the message to the other men, and they talked about what it might mean on the way back to town. Ken used his radio to alert Angie, and he knew that help was on the way, but where in the world was the mother of these children, and what had she done? Who was Mister? There were no answers to the questions he had.

Angie told Terri what to do to help the little girl's breathing, and promised to get there as quickly as possible on foot. The danger of driving on the roads was too great with NERC possibly in the area again, and besides, it would take too long for someone from the lodge to go to the McNeil's and get a vehicle, stop by to get Angie, then drive to town.

When Angie got there, Sissy was barely alive, and in spite of Terri's best efforts, the child passed away without waking.

Ken talked to Junior, and asked him what had happened, and the boy told him what he knew, which was only that a man shot his daddy, then locked him and Sissy in a shed.

"Mamma was acting real funny today. We didn't see her when we were in the shed, just the really ugly man who killed Daddy and said he would kill us, too, if we made any noise. Then Mamma came today and took us out of the shed. She said she and Sissy would wait for you, but where is she? Where did she go?"

The boy was confused and heartbroken, and Ken suspected that none of them would ever know the whole story.

Chapter Eighteen – November 15-17
Northwestern Oklahoma

"This is barren country, David. There's nowhere for us to take cover if someone spots us on the river and decides they want to use us for target practice," Rian said softly as he and David paddled their canoe downstream.

Price was slightly behind them in the second canoe, but he heard the comment. "You're right, but what can we do about it? You aren't up to walking all day every day, and it'd be the same way, moving across the fields. There's nothing to hide behind out there, either."

"True. It just feels like we're sitting ducks on this river. I always think of rivers as being lined with trees and other vegetation, I guess. It's weird for a river not to have something growing along it."

"There are plants and trees on this river, just not thick and green. And not solid, either," David interjected. "This was prairie land that farmers and ranchers turned into, well, farms and ranches. It's flat and windy, and I don't really know why there aren't majestic oaks and tall willows and stately elms everywhere, but this is just how it is, but pretty soon, there'll be trees."

"This is actually how I picture all of Oklahoma, flat and boring. You two have tried to convince me that it isn't, but so far, I'm not believin' it," Rian joked. "All of Oklahoma that I've seen so far has been pretty flat, just like Kansas. I guess you're going to try to tell me that all of Kansas isn't flat, too."

"Yep. The west is very different in the eastern part of the state. You'll see soon enough. In the next day or two, in fact, we'll be getting to the Cross Timbers and seeing a lot more hills and wooded areas," Price insisted.

"The cross timbers?" Rian asked.

"Yeah. It's a wide band of forest that stretches north and south from somewhere up north all the way down through Texas."

"I'll believe it when I see it," Rian replied. "I need to take a look at the maps and see if I can tell which town we'll pass next, and it would probably be good to get out and stretch our legs."

"There's a sandy area up ahead that looks like a good place to stop."

They rowed over to the bank, and Price hopped out to pull the canoes up onto the sand. He and David helped Rian get out, and Price handed him his crutches.

"I'm going to climb up that little bank and take a look around," David told them. "Take care of your business and I'll be right back."

He scrambled up the small slope and scanned the area, but saw nothing except a house in the far distance. From what he could tell, there was nobody around at all, which he considered a good thing, since they'd had a bit too much excitement recently, every time they were around people.

Rian was standing, stretching the muscles in his legs and checking out how much it hurt to put weight on his foot. Price was enjoying a piece of the candy they'd been given. It was quiet, except for the slight noise created by a breeze and the gentle sounds made by frogs.

"Did you know that back in the late 40s, three guys decided to go from Pueblo all the way to the Gulf of Mexico in canoes? They went down the Arkansas to the Mississippi, and on south from there. I think they went through five states, stopping in all the towns along the way." Price seemed proud of this obscure piece of knowledge.

"Where'd you hear that?" Rian asked.

"I took a class called 'Geography of the United States' last semester. The professor told us all sorts of stuff like that. There's a book about those guys, too. They got more famous the further they went, and people started watching for them to come to their towns. Mayors put them up in their own homes, or in hotels, and took them out to the best restaurants. Sometimes, they even got to see movies for free. The professor said that the only town where they were treated badly was Muskogee. One of their canoes was stolen there.

"Of course, that was before they built dams to control flooding, so they didn't have lakes to cross. And there weren't any locks, either, so they just got on the river and didn't have to worry about portage around any obstacles. Most people don't even know that today, barges can come up from the Gulf all the way to the Port of Catoosa, north of Tulsa."

Rian looked skeptical. "You're kidding, right? A navigable river in Oklahoma? Sorry, I'm not buying it."

David barked out a laugh. "It's true, Rian. Really. You can take a boat or even a huge barge all the way from Catoosa to the mouth of the Mississippi. No lie, man."

"Whatever. Hey, you guys come over here. I need to show you this Sawyer water system." Before they left Peggy's, they'd gotten plenty of water for a few days, but it would run out soon.

"This bag is the one we'll use to get dirty water from the river or some other source. You fill it, then screw on the filter, and squeeze the clean water into this other bag. You sure don't want to get the bags mixed up. See, they're different. The filter will also screw onto regular water bottles, or you can drink right from the filter."

"Wow, that's cool. How long will the filter last?" David asked.

"Well, if you always remember to clean it by back-flushing, it'll last a really long time," Rian assured them, demonstrating the technique. "This one is new, too. It was still in the box when I found it. I just left the box there so they wouldn't notice it was gone."

"Well, we better get going. Did you get a look at a map, Rian?" Price raised an eyebrow.

"No. I forgot. Let's do that, then we'll head out."

David got the maps out of the canoe and they all sat on the sandbar to study them.

"There's this little community here called Orienta." Rian pointed. "I don't know if we passed it or not, but it doesn't look like there are many towns actually on the river for a long way. That's good for us, since it will hopefully mean that we won't be getting shot at for a while. Let's see. We'll be going under quite a

129

few bridges. Maybe we'll be able to get a better idea of our progress if we see a highway sign somewhere, but we'll have to be careful. Bridges can be dangerous. To be honest, I have no idea where we are, other than on the river."

"If the river didn't have so many oxbows and turns in every conceivable direction, we'd probably be a lot further along, but it can't be helped. This is the easiest method of travel for us, and right now, easy sounds pretty good." David looked at his companions. "What will we do when we get to the lake? Keystone is big, and has lots of arms. If we get off course, we could be lost for a long time."

"We know that area well enough to recognize certain landmarks, like the marinas and Vallarta's. We'll be able to recognize Mannford from quite a distance, since it's up on top of a hill," Price said confidently. "We just have to take it one step at a time and hope we don't run into any more trouble."

"What's Vallarta's?" Rian asked.

"It's a Mexican restaurant. Good food and the best margaritas this side of the Red River," Price bragged.

"And you know this how? Both of you were underage before the collapse."

Price and David just looked at him, grinning. "We heard it from friends," Price answered.

"Yeah, right." Rian shook his head, eyes twinkling with suppressed laughter.

David's hope for a quiet passage held true for a few days. Covering many more miles than they realized, the trio floated and paddled the Cimarron across parts of several counties. They saw very few people, and those few were mostly trying to catch some fish in the river. They would watch silently as the young men went by. One or two waved half-heartedly; none were aggressive. David mentioned later that he thought they were all just worn out by the new reality of working every day to stay alive.

The days started to blend into one another, making it hard to keep any kind of measure of time. They were sure that by now, NERC officials had realized that they were missing, but whether any search was happening was simply a matter of conjecture.

"You know," Price said, having one his out-of-nowhere random thoughts, "NERC may think we went after that couple, and either were killed, or decided to join them. Or they may have figured out that we left, too. I bet there was an argument or two about us when we didn't come back."

"Probably so. But I seriously doubt that they'd search very far outside Pueblo for us. Most likely, they just put out an alert to all the camps to be on the lookout for us." Rian grinned. "I just happen to know that there are three camps in Oklahoma, and only one of them is near where we're going.

"I thought the location of the camps was need-to-know only. How'd...never mind. You sneaked a peek at something at headquarters, didn't you? You sure had us fooled," David accused.

Rian's grin grew larger. "Me? Ha. I bet you two thought I was a real by-the-book, hardnosed sergeant who would never even think about doing half of what we've done."

"Actually, everyone in the camp thought that, not just us. So, where are the camps in our fair state?" David asked.

"There's one near Fort Sill, down by a town called Lawton. Not right in town, but east several miles. And there's one near a town that starts with a *V*, some woman's name."

"Vera?" Price guessed. "Or Velma?"

"Vivian?" David offered, then thought for a few seconds. "Vian? Vinita?"

"Yeah, that's it! Vinita. And then there's one that I remember as being in between a couple of lakes, in the eastern part of the state. I just remember that it's sort of south of Muskogee. I think it started with an *S*, but I'm not sure."

Price gave Rian an exaggerated look of astonishment. "You not only don't *know* something, you *admit not knowing?*"

"Hey, I had a lot of information to absorb, and I didn't know where we were headed at the time, or I'd have paid more attention to that area." Rian shrugged. "I just had the idea you two would head back to the Tulsa area. I had no idea the lodge even existed. The only reason I even checked on camp locations was in case the authorities have been told to watch for three guys, complete with descriptions of all of us."

"And maybe not just FEMA and its divisions, huh?" David speculated. "Maybe any Guard units or police who are still active. We do look a little different now; at least Price and I do, since we don't shave anymore. Rian, you don't have a very heavy beard, so maybe we need to think about some way to change your appearance."

"All of us needed a haircut even before we left Pueblo. We're getting downright shaggy now. Do we still want to try to check our old house in Tulsa? Maybe going there isn't such a good idea," Price said, worried.

"We'll decide that for sure when we get there and have a chance to see what the situation is," Rian suggested. "We don't have to make any definite plans about that now."

With that, they lapsed into silence, concentrating on maneuvering the canoes through a series of oxbow curves. Price glanced over and caught Rian's eye, then pointed to the banks and mouthed, "Trees. Told you so."

Rain grinned and nodded, having already noticed that the banks of the river were more heavily wooded and steeper the further east they went. The water was still high and moving swiftly, making the use of oars unnecessary except as a way to steer.

That evening, they made camp in a grove of trees, having pulled the canoes completely out of the water and hidden them in the weeds. They saw no sign of other humans, and decided that it might be safe to have a small fire in a Dakota hole. David used Rian's shovel to dig the main hole, then used a knife and his hand to finish, while Price gathered some small pieces of aged wood that would burn without creating too much smoke.

Price filtered some water with the Sawyer, and helped David make a pot of soup, using some of the jerky Peggy had given them. David seasoned it with salt and pepper from an MRE, plus some of the onions, and celery from Peggy's bounty. He added some dehydrated potatoes and carrots, and soon, Rian and David were teasing Price because they could hear his stomach growling from several feet away.

Standing watch had become routine. This night proved to be uneventful, and all three were rested when morning came. They checked out the area once more, and made sure the Dakota hole was filled in, then pulled the canoes back down the short slope to the river, and set out, hoping for another calm day.

***

The next evening, just as Rian was taking a turn about their latest camp and the brothers were about to fall asleep, the quiet was shattered by a loud scream. David and Price jumped up, startled, and saw that Rian was holding out a warning hand, and looking to the northeast.

Another scream, this time trailing off to a whimper, and they could tell it was human, not animal, and that it was coming from the trees just a short distance downriver.

Rian turned to his friends, who had grabbed their rifles and joined him at the edge of the tree line. "What do you want to do about this?" he whispered.

"Go check it out, see what's going on," Price muttered to David. "*Without* being seen," he added.

David nodded. "Rian, you stay here and guard our stuff. We'll work our way closer, but stay in the trees, and see if there's anything we can do."

"Okay," Rian reluctantly agreed. "But please be careful. It could be a trap. Maybe somebody smelled our food cooking, or the smoke from our fire. Don't start something if there's any chance you won't win."

David and Price slipped away into the darkness, and moments later, Rian heard a shout. *David's voice, and he sounded mad*, Rian thought. Then he heard a shot, and a woman's voice, crying.

He didn't dare leave their camp. Everything they had – their packs, their food, the canoes – was there. So, he waited.

Minutes passed, and his apprehension grew, then he heard rustling sounds, and David followed Price into the clearing. Price was carrying a skinny young woman, who was obviously injured. He winced when he set her down; the shoulder wound reminding him that he was wasn't totally healed.

"What happened?" Rian asked quietly.

"Let's check out her wound, then we'll see if she can tell us what took place before we got there," David pleaded.

She looked about sixteen years old, except for her face, which made Rian think she must be in her mid-twenties. Blood covered the sleeve of the jacket she wore, and a cut in the fabric made it evident that the wound was caused by a knife. David helped her pull the sleeve off, and it was apparent that the blade had gone into the muscle just below the elbow.

Price stood guard while Rian and David cleaned the arm with water, then an alcohol wipe. Their patient was conscious, but silent, until Rian asked her if she thought she could bear the pain for him to stitch the one-inch gash closed.

"I've been through worse, so please get it over with, and thank you for helping me," she said through clenched teeth.

"What happened out there?" Rian asked.

"We were trying to get to my brother's house. *We,* as in me and my friend, Joey. A guy was over there, lurking in the woods, and when we went by, he jumped out and stabbed Joey in the back. We didn't do anything to him!" she sobbed. "He killed Joey, I guess to get our packs. It's so stupid. He wasted his time. Even if you hadn't been here and he'd gotten both packs, he wouldn't have gotten much of anything, because we already ate all our food.

"We never even saw the guy, never suspected anyone was around. He seemed to be high or something, because he grabbed Joey's pack and was going through it, just ignoring me like he forgot I was there. When he saw that the pack was pretty much empty, he got mad and came after me. I should have run, but I was too scared to move. I froze."

"That could happen to anyone. Is the guy dead?" Rian asked.

"Yes, thanks to your friends. I think he would have killed me, too, without a doubt. I'm so glad you were here. How'd you learn to do that?" she asked, tipping her head toward the neat row of sutures.

Rian finished, then tied off the last suture, and taped a bandage over the stitches before answering. "I was in the Army,

134

and we all got some training in basic first aid. I got a little extra, just a couple of classes beyond what the others got."

"Oh. Well, you did a good job. I could have done it for someone else, but not on myself, since I would only have one hand to use. I had just finished medical school at OU when the embargo was announced. They closed everything in the medical school even before the rest of the university shut down. I don't know why, and I don't know if I'll ever get to finish now. There was some important paperwork in the office that I needed."

"Maybe you'll get to go back someday."

"I was so excited to be starting my residency," she replied, obviously distressed.

"Are you hungry? Do you think you could eat something?" Rian said, in an effort to change the subject."

"I guess. We hadn't eaten all day. I'd appreciate anything you can spare."

David got her an MRE and while she ate, introduced himself and the others. She nodded, and said, "I'm Bree. Joey and I grew up together, right next door. My parents have a farm on the river, between Okeane and Hennessey, and my brother lives there with them. That's where we were going, too. We thought we'd be there in just a couple of days, so we didn't bring much in the way of supplies."

"Our story is pretty much the same. We're trying to get to our parents and sister, and have a friend tagging along," David explained. "Do you know how far we are from Keystone Lake? We're not really familiar with this area, and there isn't a good way to keep track of how far we've come on the river."

"You're travelling *on* the river? You've got a boat?" she asked, surprised.

"Canoes, actually. Why? Is that unusual?"

"Yes, it is. A lot of the time, there are large parts of the river that are too low to float much of anything. I guess all the rain lately has changed that. Where you headed?"

David's natural tendency to keep their destination private took over and he said, "Tulsa. We came from Kansas. The lie rolled off his tongue without effort. "So, you never saw that guy before?" he said, changing the subject.

"No. Is it just me, or does this seem like a strange place to lie in wait for someone to come by? He could have been there for days without a soul getting near him. Like I said, I think he was on something. Or maybe he was nuts."

David nodded. "Well, we're sorry about your friend. We could bury him, I suppose, in the morning."

"Yes, please. I'd feel better knowing he wasn't just left lying on the ground. Joey was a good guy. We drifted apart after high school, but he came back to Enid for a visit - that's where we grew up - and he was still there when the embargo started. I was at OU, but came home when they shut classes down. Things got bad in a hurry, but we still hung around Enid, hoping the situation would improve. Joey kept me safe and stuck by me. Finally, we decided to try to make it to my parents' farm."

"Well, try to get some rest now. We'll take care of your friend tomorrow, then help you get where you're going. One of us will be on guard all night, so you don't have to worry about a thing."

***

Using the little folding shovel, Price and David got a fairly decent grave dug. The looser dirt near the river made the job less arduous than they expected, and none of them mentioned to Bree that the body might wash out if there was a heavy rain or the river flooded. She didn't need to know that.

She said a few words about her friend and cried a little, then they filled the grave and loaded their packs into the canoes. They were all quiet, each lost in thoughts of what they had lost and how their lives had changed.

Finally, Rian broke the silence. "How will we know where to let you off? Will you recognize anything on the riverbank that will tell you we're near your brother's farm?"

"Oh, yeah, I forgot to tell you. We came to the river a lot, just to relax or fish. We had a little area that we used near a deep pool, and Dad tied a rope on a tree so we could swing out and drop into the water. It'll be on the east side of the river, and it's easy to spot," Bree told them.

About ten minutes later, she suddenly cried out, "There it is! There's the rope, so my parents' house is not far at all. Can we pull out over there? You can just let me out." She pointed to a sand bar.

"We're going to make sure you get to the house, and that your family is still there," David insisted. "Our mom would disown us if we left a lady without seeing her safely to the door," he said, giving his best bow and causing her to smile, considering that he was still seated in the canoe. He and Price jumped out and helped her and Rian. They pulled the canoes up onto the sand and got them secured.

Rian stood on one foot and lifted his crutches out to the side, giving Bree a wry grin. "I'll say goodbye here, as I'm stuck being the guy who stays behind to guard the canoes. I hope everything gets better for you."

"Thank you, Rian. Have a safe trip."

David and Price helped her up the slope, scrambling for footholds in the loose sand. At the top, they peered through the trees, and Price asked, "Are you sure this is the right place? I don't see a house. Is it further than you thought?"

Bree ran to the edge of the tree line, panic showing on her face. "It's gone. Oh, no, Lord. The house is *gone*."

Checking the area carefully for signs of anyone lurking around, David turned to his brother and murmured, "Stay here with Bree. I'll go check it out. I think I see the remains of a house that's burned down."

"Okay, if you say so. I don't like this."

"You got a better idea?"

"Well, no. Just be careful."

"Price, I will. I promise."

David ran toward a tractor that sat out near where Bree had indicated the house should be. From there, he could see that the house had indeed burned, and most of the debris left from the fire had fallen into the basement. He turned, and signaled his intentions to Price, then sprinted toward the blackened ruins.

There was no way to know how the fire had started, but David climbed carefully down into the hole, stepping over charred furnishings and rafters. There he found human remains, burned beyond recognition even if he had known them forever. Two bodies lay together in the corner, and the other was a few yards away. *Oh, these poor people. Poor Bree. We can't let her see this. What will she do now?* David's brain raced from one thought to another, too fast for him to focus on anything.

He moved closer, trying to find something, anything, that might help identify the bodies. On one, he found a wide, silver cuff bracelet, partially melted by the heat. He removed it and put it in his pocket. Across the basement, a larger body had a clinched hand with some kind of blackened chain hanging from it. David pulled on the chain, and the hand literally fell apart, revealing a pocket watch. He took that, too, then climbed out of the hole and headed back toward the trees where Bree and Price waited.

Bree could tell that something was terribly wrong by the look on his face and the black, sooty smudges on his clothes.

"I'm so sorry, Bree," he said quietly. "The house burned down to the basement. That's why we couldn't see much from here."

"My family!? What about my family?" she cried, grabbing the front of David's hoodie and shaking him.

David felt like a deer staring into headlights. He didn't want the words to come from him, but he had no choice. "I…I found three bodies, so badly charred that I couldn't tell their genders, but…one was wearing this." He pulled the bracelet out, holding it in his open palm.

Bree stared, then reached out with a shaking hand and took the silver cuff, holding it up and turning it over. "This was my mother's. I gave it to her for Mother's Day two years ago," she muttered, almost too softly to hear.

She looked up into David's eyes. "Was…was that all?"

He shook his head, and handed her the watch. "This was clutched in the hand of one of the others".

She opened the watch. Inside was a tiny picture of a whitetail buck. Her knees buckled, and she would have fallen if David hadn't grabbed her arms to steady her.

Tears flowed down her face. "This was my grandfather's watch. He left it to my brother, who carried it every day, no matter what."

David held her while she wept, then gently turned her and guided her back to the canoes, his arm around her bony shoulders.

"You can't stay here, Bree. There's nothing left, no shelter, no food. Do you have anyone you could stay with?"

She shook her head. "I have other family, but they live in Iowa. It's too far to even consider going there. I don't know anyone around here, except to say hello to if I see them."

David looked at Rian, a question in his eyes. At Rian's slight nod, David turned to Price, who immediately gave him a sad smile and a nod.

"Would you like to go with us? We have a large group of people who are working together to stay safe. If you'll agree to help out, I'm sure they'd allow you to stay."

Bree stared at him, then looked at the other two men. "Are you serious? You really mean it?"

"Yes. We can't promise five-star accommodations, but you'd be a lot safer than you are here."

"I…I don't know what to say. Why are you doing this? You don't even know me."

"There's too much bad happening, and we just want to try to do good. We wouldn't be able to live with ourselves if we abandoned you. We don't have to know you to want to help," Rian said.

Tears streamed down Bree's cheeks. "I guess that's really my only option. I didn't think I had *any* options, and now you offer me a place to be safe. I didn't think good people still existed. Yes, I'll go, and thank you, for everything," she sobbed. "I'd be dead right now if not for you. This is just too much for me to take in. Could I be alone for a while?"

David's voice was full of sympathy. "Sure. Don't wander far, though. But first, what do you want to do about your family?

We could bury them for you, but I really don't think you want to remember them the way they are now."

"They're all in the basement? Are they together?"

"Two are. I assume that's your parents, and one is about five yards away. Why do you ask?" David asked.

"If they were together, we could just bury them in the basement. There's a frontend loader on the tractor, and there's probably some diesel in the tank. I know how to use it, if none of you do, and we could just scrape enough soil on them to cover them."

"Are you sure that's enough for you? We could dig graves. There's probably a full-sized shovel somewhere."

"It'll be fine. I don't believe my family is in that basement. Just the physical shells where they lived their lives. Their spirits are gone, and while I appreciate the effort to show respect to their remains, I think it would be okay to just cover them. It's too hard to dig a deep grave around here. And I'm smart enough to know what you didn't say about Joey's body. It really doesn't matter, because they're all with Jesus now."

"Okay, if you're sure. We really should go soon. And we're sorry about your family. Really sorry."

Bree went to the edge of the woods and scanned the farm. Her mind remembered the happy times she'd had here with her family: the holiday dinners, the flag football games, the quiet times when they just sat on the front porch and talked. Her heart hurt unbearably, and she cried for a few minutes, then David and Price followed her to the homestead, where the men carefully moved her brother's body over to the corner where her parents lay, and she used the tractor to push dirt into the gaping hole, being careful not to look down at the bodies.

Chapter Nineteen – November 17
Southeastern Oklahoma

The day was almost blindingly sunny; it was one of those fall mornings that seemed as though summer was unwillingly to let go. Sarah and Ian were on guard duty at the west cave entrance, and were having a hard time staying awake.

"I'm going to step outside for a little air, and I'll take a look around while I'm out there. You wanna go?" Ian asked.

"Yeah. We just have to stay within sight of the cave, so we aren't neglecting our duties. Let's take a look and see if the world has changed while we've been cooped up in here."

Major was with them, curled up in a furry ball and sound asleep. Ian nudged the big dog with his toe, and said, "Hey, wake up. Guard."

Major obediently went to the entrance and sat, alert for any unusual sounds or smells. He was completely relaxed, so Ian knew that stepping out was safe, but he still peeked out cautiously before exiting.

Sarah came out a few seconds later, stretching and yawning, while squinting at the brightness. It was cool out, but still warmer than just inside the cave. The breeze rustled the leaves, which were beginning to fall, and they could hear birds nearby.

"This is my favorite time of year," Ian commented, reaching over to grasp Sarah's hand. "I'm not really sure why, but I love fall. Maybe it's because hunting season opens."

"My favorite season is spring, when there are lots of baby critters being born. I know it's trite, but I enjoy the rebirth of plants, and seeing calves and foals playing in pastures. Spring is full of hope, plus it means that school will be out soon and we teachers can recharge our batteries. Summer isn't for the students. It's definitely for teachers."

Major suddenly gave a soft, "woof." His head was the only part of him that was outside the cave, but they could see that he was alert and his hackles were up. Ian gave him the signal to be silent, then he and Sarah listened.

A faint rumbling could be heard in the distance, getting louder, until they knew it was a vehicle of some type. It sounded large, and the first thought in both of their minds was "NERC."

"Inside, and push the button!" Sarah urged. "Hurry!"

"Where are you going?" Ian demanded.

"I'm in camo, and I'm going to sneak around and hide where I can see what they do. Don't worry. I won't get caught," she assured him.

"No way. I'll go instead."

"You're wearing a white shirt, doofus. Now quit wasting time and go ring the bell!"

Ian reluctantly did as Sarah instructed. *Bossy woman. She'd make a great drill instructor.*

Sarah went up the hill and to the south, moving stealthily from tree to tree, and found a rock to crouch behind where she could see the front yard. The truck pulled in, and it was definitely a NERC truck. Five men and one woman got out and checked the lodge, then scanned the area for signs of habitation. *Man, it's a good thing we stopped cleaning house. It must really look abandoned, if they gave up that easily.*

The agents moved around in the yard, looking for anything suspicious, and two wandered over near where Sarah was hiding. Sarah could hear the whispered words of the two.

"This is dumb. I heard Sarge tell him that if we didn't find that woman and kid this time, we'd quit checking on this place. There's nobody here, hasn't been for a long while. Waste of time and gas, if you ask me."

The woman agreed. "We should just leave when we get the chance. This whole thing is creepy, making people go to the camp when they don't want to. I can see setting up camps for those who *want* help, but it should be voluntary."

"You mean it?" the man whispered.

"Mean what? That we shouldn't have mandatory camps?"

"No. That we should leave. I've been thinking about it for a while. There are lots of directions we could go, and they'd never find us. I'm sick of 'guarding' citizens who are, for all intents and purposes, prisoners of their own government. It's not right." The man looked intently into the woman's eyes. "I'm ready to get out, if you're serious."

"Bill and Cinda are leaning that way, too. We'd have a better chance with more people, don't you think?"

"Yeah. We'll talk more later," The man warned, seeing that the others were gathering near the truck.

One of the men yelled at them from across the yard, "This place is empty. Let's go."

They all climbed into the truck, and left, turning toward town.

Sarah waited until they were out of sight, then hurried back to the cave. Four other members of the group were there, carrying rifles, and Tanner had brought Moxie, as well. She knew that the other entrances were similarly defended, each with at least three extra guards, and an extra dog, even if one of the dogs was little Moxie, who was still a pup. Tanner generally kept her with him, so he could take advantage of training opportunities such as this.

"We need to warn Ken. They headed his way," she huffed, trying to catch her breath.

"Already done," Tanner grinned. "We contacted them immediately and they're taking precautions. Seems they set up a new protocol after the last time NERC came around. Those who are going to fish at the river don't cross the pasture anymore. They go north into the trees, then east, staying out of sight from town, and come back the same way. They're a lot more careful moving around outside than they were.

"Today, they didn't have anybody out to hunt or fish yet. They were just getting ready to go when I got them on the radio. Ken sent that young man to warn the people in the tunnel. Connor. Yeah, I think that's his name. Good kid. I wish they could spare him for some training from Shane. He's got leadership qualities that we need to be developing. Ken says he's smart and also good with his hands."

"Well, I heard something interesting out there," Sarah said. "I know I took a slight risk, but I overheard two of the NERCs talking about how they won't be looking for Dana and Tucker after today. Their sergeant figures they didn't come back here. And then they started making plans to leave NERC because they don't agree with what they're doing, namely locking innocent people up in camps."

"Well, I guess the idea of liberty isn't totally dead. I wish we could help them escape, but we don't dare," Ian remarked. "We have too much to lose."

"Does this mean we can move back into the lodge?" Val asked.

"We'll have to talk about that. I think it would be good to put the little ones and the older folks back in there, at least to sleep. We could put a couple of guards on the doors, with a dog or two, and it should be okay. But that's not my decision. We all need to discuss it before we decide," Tanner insisted.

"Of course," Vince agreed. "But it'd be better for your grandparents, and Charlie and Gus. It's too cool in the caves, and it's a little damp, as well, at least near the pool."

"I wish we had eyes in town. With all the town folk in hiding, we really don't know what NERC is up to. Probably more of the same, just looking for people, but who knows?" Ian ran a hand through his shaggy hair. "Wouldn't it be nice if we could live like we did before Dana and Tucker got caught?"

"Yes, it would. And while I'm thinking about it, you need a haircut," Sarah said dryly. "And so do most of the men. Charlie's braid is halfway down his back now."

"We've got scissors. You volunteering?" Ian shot back.

"Ha! I can't cut hair, but surely someone around here can."

***

Ken secured the last bolt on the back of the bookcase that hid their basement hideout. All of them were present, plus Junior, who was staying there so Ken could try to subtly do some gentle counselling with the boy. Losing his whole family in such a short time had made the boy withdraw from everyone except Ken and Terri.

144

One thing that Ken wanted to accomplish with the boy was to reverse the sense of entitlement that had ultimately resulted in the death of his father and the disappearance of his mother. If they had been willing to help their group by working, and had stayed instead of trying to go where they thought they would be given more food without working for it, they might still be together. Ken felt that Junior was young enough that he could be taught the value of work and helping others. At least, he hoped so.

The members of the group in the tunnel were also all accounted for. The charcoal grill they were using for cooking had still been hot from breakfast, so they ran two rods through the handles and carried it down into the basement with them, hoping that the smell of smoke would dissipate before any NERC agents smelled it.

The big white truck came into town from the north, cruising slowly down Main Street. The young man who was in charge for the day had the idea that since they'd searched the houses and found no one, today they would take a look at some of the other buildings in town. He just didn't quite believe that every single person in the whole town was gone.

They stopped in front of what had been the diner and got out of the truck. The damage from a tornado was obvious, but something about it bothered the young man. He stood in the street, staring until he realized what it was. Someone had cleared enough debris out of the street to let a car drive through. Everywhere else, broken pieces of glass, brick, wood, and metal were scattered all over the ground, but one narrow, crooked lane down the street was cleared.

He motioned for the others to join him. "Notice anything?" he asked, making a wide sweep of the town with his arm. "Tell me what's wrong with his picture."

The other agents stared hard, each hoping that someone else would answer the question. Finally, the young woman said, "Someone cleared part of the street."

"And why would anyone go to all that trouble if they were going to leave? I think maybe we've been fooled and there's someone here, hiding and probably laughing at us because we haven't found them."

"Maybe not," the young woman speculated. "Maybe they cleared it out so they *could* leave. Maybe they had a little gas and left in a pickup or a van or something."

"Or maybe they're still here. We'll go in pairs, but first, we'll check the school out together."

He led them around to the school that had once been the pride of the town. Most of the windows and the glass front doors were shattered, so they had no difficulty getting in. In the lobby, they found a pile of textbooks that had been partially burned. The roof must have sustained some damage, because the floor was wet in places. They checked every room: the cafeteria, the gym, the offices. The vending machines had been broken into and the cafeteria pantry stripped bare.

Then their leader took them back to Main Street. "Okay, work your way down to the end and we'll meet there. Both sides of the streets. Check every building for any sign of people being around lately. The storm wasn't that long ago, and we may have missed a lot of people because Sarge said to only search the houses. This time, we'll look in the stores and other businesses; if you find any indication that there are people here, don't raise an alarm. Be quiet, and come get the rest of us."

They cleared the diner, Richie's drugstore, and the shops across the street, even those that were mostly rubble, looking for anywhere that people might hide, and any clue that there could even be people around at all. They peeked into the back of Gus's shop, seeing the mobile home imbedded in the wall. Then two of them, the same two that Sarah had heard talking, stepped into the shop next door to Gus's.

The woman breathed in a few times, and looked at her partner, who had become a very good friend. "You smell something?" she asked.

He gave a series of little sniffs. "Yeah. Smoke, and something else, maybe."

"Look," she pointed. "The ceiling has a big area right above us that's darker, like someone has had a fire right about here," she gestured to the cleared area in the middle of the floor.

"We better go tell the others," he replied.

"No. Let's look around a little more first. We might find out something useful, if we're really going to try to get away from all this. Check out that back room, while I take a closer look in here."

The young man scrambled carefully over the remains of the back wall, which had fallen in and knocked down some of the dividing wall in the process; then he noticed a small area that had been cleared in the corner. He moved around to see behind a section of wall that was leaning at an angle against the side wall, and saw a doorway.

Glancing down, he could clearly see shoeprints in the crumbly dirt on the floor. He moved back over where his partner could see him, and frantically gestured for her to come.

Holding a finger to his lips, he led her to the doorway, which was at the top of some very dark stairs. Raising his eyebrows, he silently asked her if she wanted to check it out. She nodded, and got a penlight out of her pocket.

They stepped carefully, if not quite silently, down the stairs, finding a basement, which was mostly empty. Shining the light around the cavernous space, she noticed what looked like another door in the opposite corner. She touched her partner's arm and pointed. He led the way to the door, and placed his ear against it, listening intently. Not a sound.

He looked at her and shrugged as if to say, "what now?" and she made a twisting motion near the doorknob. He looked skeptical, but took a deep breath and opened the door. The tiny light shone on brick walls on either side, but couldn't reach the end of the long, narrow passageway.

A slight scraping sound came to their ears, then a shushing sound, then silence, but the two NERC agents suddenly knew that their leader had been right. This was the hiding place for whoever was still in the town.

"We're coming in. There are more agents outside, so don't do anything you'll regret," the male agent warned.

A light suddenly illuminated the tunnel, and they could see several anxious faces peering back at them. Men, women, and children stared with a mixture of fear, anger, and resignation at the two agents of a government that could no longer be trusted.

"Is this all of you?" The female agent seemed to be counting heads.

"Yes," a male voice answered.

"We're from the National Emergency Recovery Corps," she continued.

"We know who you are, and why you're here," the man growled. "You're here to take us to an internment camp and make us into slaves."

"Well, that's one way of looking at it. Look, we don't like what we're being forced to do, either. We certainly didn't volunteer to work for NERC. They 'drafted' us into service with no warning," the male agent said. "How long have you been down here?"

"Since NERC started sending trucks here to round us up. We're getting along just fine, and we don't need the government butting into our lives. We hunt and fish, and some of the ladies had veggies put up before the collapse. We don't need you *or* your camps."

The two agents looked at each other, and something seemed to pass between them.

"We've got a proposition for you. We've been talking about leaving NERC, deserting, if you want to get technical. We aren't going to tell anyone we found this place or saw you folks down here. But if we can escape and make it this far, is there somewhere we could hide out? Some other secret place where we could live until all this blows over?" The man looked at the dirty, thin people, and hoped they would say yes.

"There are several empty houses and buildings around town. Maybe some cabins in the woods. We don't know about hiding places, but if you can convince NERC that you didn't find anything, maybe we could be looking for a place you could use," the group's unofficial spokesman replied.

"There may be four of us. We aren't sure yet, but we don't expect you to feed us or anything. We'll do our part. A lot depends on our being able to get away in the first place. If we get caught, they'll separate us and send us far away from here. But we'll do our best, and we won't say a word," the woman promised.

"We better go, or they'll come looking for us. Take care, and maybe we'll see you soon."

The two NERC agents turned and left, going upstairs and quickly down the alley, skipping a couple of buildings before entering the one on the end, in order to make the others think that they'd been searching the whole time.

Coming out the front door of the last building, the pair crossed the street and checked in with their leader, who told them to see if there were any businesses located on side streets. They went around behind the buildings they had just searched, and found the daycare center. The front door had already been forced, so they entered, looked around a little, and took the opportunity to talk privately.

"I hope this doesn't come back to bite us later. We're now accomplices of those people, and we have to try to protect their secret, because now it's our secret, too." The woman took a deep breath and let it out in a whoosh.

"That's okay. Only you and I know about them. Nobody else even suspects, so all we have to do is be careful what we say. I don't think we should even tell Cinda or Bill, at least not until we're almost here. I want to trust them, but these days, who knows? Let's just keep it to ourselves, okay?"

"Yeah. Do you think we should even try to get Cinda or Bill to come with us?"

"Well, it's a risk. I'm pretty sure they're getting tired of not being able to 'fraternize'; heck, they're in love, but NERC doesn't acknowledge that we're humans with feelings. How about if you kinda sound Cinda out about how she feels, and maybe she'll say something about Bill's thoughts on the subject. I'll talk to Bill a little, see if I can get him to say something that indicates a desire to get out, and maybe he'll say something about whether Cinda is willing.

"That way, we'll know if they've talked about it between the two of them. We can pretend that we haven't been talking to each other, that I don't know how you feel and vice versa. We won't mention Kanichi Springs or any other specific destination, and see if they have any better alternatives. What do you think?"

"I like it. We'll have to be very careful how and where we approach them about this. I think I'll try to lead Cinda into bringing it up herself, by commiserating with her about not being able to spend time with Bill. I really am sympathetic to them."

"So am I. And I'm really sympathetic about you and the guy you love."

"Really? Then why aren't you kissing me?"

Chapter Twenty – November 18-19
Northeastern Oklahoma

David confidently steered the canoe around a sandbar and Bree glanced back, feeling a little guilty for not helping. When the three men had left Peggy's, they only had three paddles, so Bree was left to sit idly and let David do all the work.

She was feeling sad, but hopeful, knowing that she was starting a new chapter of her life, one without the love and protection of her family, but with three new friends who had proven that they were willing to help her.

She had much to think about as she rode in the canoe. She had no idea where they were going, and no idea if she would really be welcomed, but she did have skills that could benefit this group of strangers she was headed toward. She could cook and sew, knew her way around a garden, and perhaps most importantly, she was a doctor.

She had knowledge, although that knowledge was of a type of medicine that depended on modern diagnostic equipment, surgical techniques, and medications that she would not have access to. It would be quite an adjustment for her to try to help people without utilizing all the things she was trained to use, but she was willing to learn. She just hoped it would be enough.

She would always miss her parents and her dear brother. She would also miss Joey, but while he was a good friend, she had grown uncomfortable with his obvious desire to be more. She hadn't felt any romantic interest in him, but he had been pushing her to begin a physical relationship that went against her core beliefs.

Besides, with the world so crazy, she didn't want to get involved with anyone, and certainly not Joey. He had been fun and loyal to his friends, but he never stuck with a job and he didn't like children. Both of those were deal-breakers for her. She had gotten the distinct impression from something he said that Joey thought she would marry him and support him with the money she made as a doctor. That hadn't set well, either.

The day was sunny and not terribly cool; the wind was blowing some, but the banks of the river kept them sheltered to some extent. The river continued its curvy path across Oklahoma. They'd passed a couple of small communities, and seen a few people, but none had done more than wave, and most didn't even do that.

Late in the afternoon, Bree saw the head and shoulders of a man peering at them from the high bank. The rest of him was concealed by tall grass and weeds. She started to wave, but just as she began to raise her arm, the man stood suddenly and shot three rounds at them. Bree screamed as the canoe started to drift sideways in the current.

Turning back toward David, she saw him gripping his stomach. Blood poured from between his fingers. Rian and Price had immediately begun shooting at the man, who dropped down out of sight. They had no idea if he was hit or merely hiding.

"Bree, grab the paddle!" David hissed. She rose slightly and turned, almost upsetting the canoe, but regained her equilibrium, got a good grip on the paddle, and began racing frantically toward an oxbow turn.

Price was doing the same, while Rian kept his rifle trained on the bank, wondering if the shooter was racing to catch them downstream. That's when he noticed the water in the bottom of the canoe.

"Price, yell at David, get his attention. Signal for them to stop on the opposite side from the shooter." Price did as Rian ordered, not resenting the commanding tone in the least. He knew that the rest of them were in over their heads, but Rian was the natural leader in a situation like this.

Bree beached their craft, helped David get out, and pulled the canoe up behind some cattails faster than anyone would have guessed she could move. David stumbled over into a small cluster of trees and plopped down, still holding his arm across his abdomen. Price assisted Rian with his crutches, then grabbed up their rifles and covered the retreat.

When Rian got to the trees, Bree was already kneeling beside David, pulling his shirt off to examine the wound. The bullet had grazed him from right to left across his abdomen. It was bleeding freely, and Bree's first thought was that if she had some supplies, she could stop the bleeding and help her friend. She folded the shirt, and told David to press it against the wound.

"Do you have any first aid supplies?" she asked calmly.

"Yeah, a few in our packs, and a kit, too, but they're in the canoe. Until we know where that shooter is, we can't go get the kit," Rian answered.

Price leaned over his brother, staring at the blood. "Rian, I'm going after him. We're trapped here until we know he's down, and *I'm going*. The water is pretty shallow along here; I'll wade over and hunt him down. Cover me." Price took off his hoodie and threw it to Bree. "Use this if you need to."

"Price, are you sure? I can put some weight on my foot now, and I can go," Rian insisted.

"No. I've got this," and Price slipped away, moving carefully through the brush and tall weeds. Bree grabbed the hoodie and folded it into a pad, then pressed it against David's bleeding injury.

Price slid into the water, holding his rifle high, and managed to cross without incident. Rian kept his rifle raised, scanning the bank for any movement, but he saw nothing. Then Price was on the other side, quietly making his way to the top of the bank.

He found a clump of some kind of tall grass, and slowly raised his head beside it. He waited, moving nothing except his eyes. The wind died down a little, and he noticed that one area of grass continued to move when the rest went still. He locked his eyes on that spot, and soon caught a glimpse of dingy white. He continued to survey the area, but saw nothing to cause him to think that the man wasn't alone.

Aiming carefully at that patch of white, he quickly shot three times, moving just a tad to the right with each shot. The white spot jerked upward a little, and Price fired twice more.

Keeping his eyes just to the left of where he had last seen movement, Price stayed still for several minutes. The silence was broken at last by a moan, then nothing.

Ducking down and moving to his left several yards. Price lifted his head just enough to see the area where he thought the man was. Nothing moved, so Price went even further around the curved bank. This time, when he lifted his head, he could see his target. He scanned the area once again, but saw no sign of movement.

The man lay face down in the dirt, motionless. Price let his rifle hang by the strap and pulled out his handgun, then crept up the slope until he could stand. Never letting the man out of his sight, he approached. The ground was soaked with blood; Price kicked the man in the side and got no reaction. He used his boot to shove the man over, and saw that his shots had been accurate. Four large splotches of blood were slowly blending into one huge blot along the man's left side.

Price spat at the man, then whispered, *"That's* what you get for ambushing innocent people, and for *shooting my brother!"*

He picked up the rifle the man had used, and scrambling down the sandy slope, waded back across the river, placing the extra rifle in one of the canoes for Bree and grabbing the first aid box.

Bree worked on David for a long time. The graze wasn't deep, but she feared that the stitches might pull out if he used those muscles. In just the short time she had known him, she had already learned that he and his brother used their bodies hard. She flushed the gash thoroughly with water that Rian had run through the Sawyer, then sutured it carefully, wishing she had 3.0 sutures instead of 6.0, but knowing she was lucky to have anything at all. She found a little packet of antibiotic cream in the kit, and spread that along the ugly line, all the while lecturing David on being very careful not to put excessive strain on the stitches. He just glared at her, teeth clenched and face red.

"I'm sorry, but you're going to have a scar across those six-pack abs. I could have done a much better job in a hospital, but I did the best I could under the circumstances."

David sighed. He knew she had done as much as could be expected. He gave her a little smile, then turned his head toward his brother.

"Well?" he demanded, as Price sat down beside him.

"Done. *Over*done, actually. Multiple shots to multiple vital organs, in a nice neat row, just like those stitches Bree put across your belly. He won't be ambushing anyone else," Price told him.

"Good. Scum like that deserve their fate."

"Bree," Price began, looking embarrassed. "Would you be offended if I take my jeans off? They're wet. I've got on some decent boxers."

Bree gave a little laugh. "Of course not. It won't bother me at all. Hang them over that limb over there and maybe they'll be dry by morning."

Rian had been sitting against a tree, close enough to assist Bree if needed. He'd watched her making the neat, even stitches, admiring the quick, confident way she worked.

"I can't remember the name of that stitch. What's it called?"

"This is a horizontal mattress suture. It's good for injuries like this, because you put it back further away from the wound, four to eight millimeters back. I tried to do about seven mil, because I really needed 3.0 sutures, but all we have is 6.0. That's thinner, so it's more likely to tear out; that's why I moved back further. The problem with this type of suture is that if it's too tight, it can make an unsightly, puckered scar. I think I did okay in that regard. See how the flesh isn't bunched up?"

Rian examined the long line of sutures. "Yeah. I think it looks great. He'll have a nice scar he can lie about to all the ladies."

David's eyebrow shot up. "Stop talking about me like I'm not here." Everyone grinned.

Rian looked around the little clearing they were in, and decided that enough was enough.

"It's been a while since we took the time to really rest. I think we should just set up camp right here. I know it's way early, but this is as good a place as we're likely to find, and we've all been through a lot. All of us are injured, even though Price's shoulder seems to be doing okay. I can't get around with any speed, and now David is hurt. Bree, you've had a terrible couple of days. Even though your physical injury isn't serious, your emotional trauma has been about as bad as it gets.

"We all need a break, even for just half a day. I say we stay here, try to relax, and get some sleep. We can even take turns napping for the rest of the afternoon, so long as at least one of us is awake and watching for trouble. What do you think?" Rian looked at his friends questioningly.

Bree immediately nodded, and both the Martins looked relieved.

Rian cleared his throat before continuing. "We do have another problem. There's a bullet hole in one of the canoes and it was taking on water. We need to find some way to patch the hole tonight."

"If we had some kind of glue, we could whittle a piece of wood from a tree and glue it over the hole," Price said.

"But we don't have any glue, do we?" Rian returned.

"My brother always kept some wood glue in his barn. Maybe we could find an abandoned farm. They'd have some type of glue or caulk or whatever. Maybe even some nails," Bree suggested. "Price and I could go."

"I don't like the idea, but I don't see an alternative," Rian complained. "Just stay out of sight as much as possible and be very careful. Don't go too far, either. You need to be back before dark, whether you find any glue or not. I'll stay here and guard our invalid."

David threw a pebble at him.

Price and Bree left immediately, staying near the edge of the trees and looking for a house or barn where they might find something to use in repairing the canoe. They didn't want to leave the cover of the woods and cross a pasture until they had a destination in sight.

An hour later, Bree came back, followed by Price. They were both grinning.

"Success!" Bree raised both arms like they'd just made a touchdown.

"You found something?" David asked excitedly.

"Yep," Bree said proudly. "We checked two farms, but the first one was totally empty. Not too far past that place, we found an old barn. It looked like there used to be a mobile home parked there. There was a pad and some PVC pipes sticking up, but no house. Anyway, in the barn, we found part of a bottle of Gorilla Glue. *And...*we found a small piece of wood that should do the trick."

"That's great. Let's get that patch on the canoe taken care of, so it'll have all night to dry."

By the time they had the canoe repaired, it was early evening. David ran a bead of the glue around the outside of the wooden patch, hoping it would serve as caulking to keep water from seeping under it. They saved the leftover glue, just in case.

"We've put in a long day. I'm beat," Bree sighed.

Rian tilted his head to the side and looked at her. "You are a very accomplished young woman, but can you shoot?"

She laughed softly. "I wish you could have seen the ten-point buck I took last year with my bow. Lung and heart shot. Dropped him dead. I rifle hunt, too. Hogs, deer, turkeys. I'm not so good with a shotgun, though; doves and quail are too fast for me and I never seem to lead quite enough. Yes, I can shoot, and just as importantly, I *will* shoot, if necessary. I assume you're asking if I can stand guard, because without David, I'm needed."

David scowled, and muttered, "I'm fine."

Ignoring him, Rian continued addressing Bree. "Right. Do you think you're up to it?"

"Sure. I'll be happy to, tonight and any other time. I hope I'll be considered a full member of this team, expected to do my share. I'm no moocher."

Rian smiled. "No, you're certainly not. I couldn't have done nearly as neat a job on those sutures. I'm not very familiar with that technique, but I can see how it would be less likely to tear out. You did a good job."

"Yes, and with a grumpy patient, that isn't always easy," she teased.

David tried to glare at her, but couldn't resist the chuckles coming from the others. He fought the grin, but it escaped, so he gave in and joined the laughter.

"Okay, now. Who's hungry?" Price asked.

"You are. That's one of life's absolute certainties, like death and taxes," David joked.

"Are taxes still considered a certainty? WE sure haven't been paying any lately," Bree added.

"True. Do we still have any of the food Peggy gave us? Maybe enough for some soup?" Rian suggested.

"Yeah, I think so," David answered. "Somebody else will have to dig the Dakota hole. My doctor won't let me do it."

"I'll do it," Bree volunteered, and immediately went to get the little shovel.

Rian, Price and David stared after her, astonished. "She shoots, she hunts, she sews, she cooks, she can handle a canoe, she's calm under pressure, *and* she knows what a Dakota hole is?" Price mumbled.

***

Bree not only made a decent Dakota hole, she cooked the soup, and without being told, filled in the hole, smothering the fire so it wouldn't continue smoking. David fell asleep soon after they ate, and Price took first watch. They'd agreed that Rian would also take a turn guarding them; even though he had a hard time getting around with the makeshift crutches, his vision and hearing were excellent and his military training made up for his slight handicap. Bree would have the last watch, giving her several uninterrupted hours of rest before she had to get up.

The night passed without incident. When David woke up, Bree and Price already had MREs picked out for breakfast, and everything else was loaded in the canoes. Rian had taken over from Bree on guard duty, since he couldn't get down to the canoes very easily.

"How do you feel this morning?" Bree asked, kneeling beside her patient. "Much pain?"

"It's bearable. I'll be okay to travel," David assured her.

"I'll be your 'designated driver' today. Ah! No arguing!" she declared, holding up a hand to silence him as he opened his mouth to protest. "The muscles of the abdomen are used more than people realize for paddling a canoe. Your pain level tonight would show you just what 'unbearable' means if you try to do too much. Doctor's orders!"

"Yes, ma'am," David muttered, frowning. "You done much canoeing?"

"Don't forget: I grew up on the river. Dad used to haul our kayaks upriver several miles and let us out. We'd take a picnic lunch, and spend the day floating. Some of our friends had canoes, and a couple of times, we used a neighbor's little aluminum boat, but I'm not familiar with this part of the river, because it's downstream from home."

She rose, and called Price over. "It's time for us to help the walking wounded into his canoe," she told him. Turning her head and using her best professional voice, she warned, "David, don't even think about trying to be a he-man. I want you to let us do most of the work. Getting up from the ground is one really good way to cause yourself a lot more pain. So just help a little with your legs, and let us do the lifting."

David's lip twitched as he held back a grin. "For such a little gal, you sure are bossy," he complained.

"Yep. Get used to it," she returned, not missing a beat.

Chapter Twenty-One – November 21
Southeastern Oklahoma

Clint knocked softly on the back door of Ernie's house. He'd been staying alone in the basement of a home near the edge of town, one that the NERC agents had been careless in searching. When they looked through all the houses in the area, he had hidden behind an old washing machine in the corner of the basement, and when NERC came, they only came about halfway down the stairs, looked around, and left. They'd never come back to that house.

When he didn't get an answer to his knock, Clint tapped again, this time a little louder. Finally, he tried the knob, and discovering that it was unlocked, he entered. It was his first time inside the house, but Ken, feeling that the younger man had earned their trust, had told him about the bookcase full of cookbooks in the kitchen. Clint crossed the room and gave the secret knock. Soon, he could hear bolts being drawn back, and then Terri pushed the bookcase aside and beckoned him to come in.

"It's so good to see you, Clint. How are you? Getting lonely yet?" Terri knew that the young man didn't feel comfortable about being completely accepted into the group.

His former association with a gang of convicts, even though he was an unwilling gang member, still caused him considerable embarrassment. He couldn't understand how the citizens of the town could just forgive him, even though they repeatedly pointed to his cooperation in helping stop the gang, and his later efforts to warn them that NERC was in the area rounding up people. *They* felt he had earned a place in the community, but *he* still believed that getting drawn into the gang was unforgivable.

"I'm doing okay, but running a little short on food. I've been thinking, and I'd like to talk to you and Ken together, if that's okay," he said quietly.

"Sure. Ken's out right now, checking on the other families, but he should be back pretty soon. Come have a snack while we wait for him."

About fifteen minutes later, Ken came back, and Clint asked if they could go upstairs to talk privately. Terri looked at Ken and shrugged, then nodded.

They sat around Ernie's old kitchen table, and Ken regarded the former college student with concern.

"You've lost a lot of weight, Clint. Aren't we sending enough food your way?" Ken asked, worried.

"I'm okay. Everyone has been so nice, but I hate to ask for anything. I feel like I'm taking food out of the mouths of those who let me stay here." Clint looked away for a moment, then continued. "I would like to join one of the groups, if it's okay with everyone. I think if I did, I could be more useful.

"I could help fish and trap, maybe even work growing food next summer. Living alone seems kind of a waste, and I don't feel like I contribute much, for sure not as much as I use up. Do you think one of the groups would accept me?"

Ken was shocked at the lack of confidence Clint exhibited. The young man had pushed himself to the point of collapse to save the people of Kanichi Springs from the labor camps, and he'd given Erin's group valuable information that helped them destroy the Simmons Gang. But now, he seemed lost and unsure.

"I think you've been alone too long, son. Of course, I'm sure you can join this group or the one in the tunnel. I'd be *very* surprised if Erin's group out at the lodge turned you away. You don't seem to understand how grateful we all are to you for what you did for us. You're welcome to stay here as long as you want."

"But...I was with the gang," Clint reminded them.

Terri patted his arm. "You were, but you were trying to get out. They were ready to abuse you, and had already threatened you. It's not like you were actively trying to participate in their crimes. We've forgiven you, not that we think there was much to forgive. Now, *you* need to forgive yourself. Sometimes that's the hardest thing to do."

"But which group do you think I could fit in with best? Where can I do the most good?" Clint wondered.

"Do you feel that you could maybe relate to a young boy who lost his family recently? He's gotten withdrawn and too quiet. He needs a friend, someone to look up to. I've been working with him, doing some counseling, but I think he'd open up better to a younger man. What do you say, Clint? Would you be willing to help him?"

"Yeah. I can understand how he feels. I have no way of finding out if my family is even still alive, so in way, I've lost them. It's a terrible feeling to be alone in the world. Yes. I'd like to try to help. Is he here, or in the tunnel?" Clint looked more animated than he had in a long time.

"He's here. I need to tell you a little about the family. They were staying in the tunnel, but decided to leave and go to a NERC camp. They thought they'd be better off there. Evidently, they didn't get far. Junior saw his father's body after a man shot him in the head with a shotgun. Then he and his sister were locked up in a shed. The mother was taken away by the man who shot the dad, but somehow, she got away and got the kids out of the shed.

"They were almost back to town, but the little girl was really sick. The mom sent Junior ahead to get help, but when we got there, she was gone. The little girl was unconscious, lying at the side of the road. She died a few hours later. We have no idea what happened to the mother. She just disappeared." Ken watched emotions play across Clint's face. "Are you still interested?"

"Oh, man. That poor kid. I've been feeling sorry for myself, but he's been through a lot more. Yes, I want to try to help him, Ken."

"Okay. He talks his grief out with me. That's not really what I'd like for you to do. I think he needs someone who will teach him things, and show him how to help others, and just listen when he wants to talk. Tell him stories about your childhood, and try to cheer him up. Tell him about what a real man does to help others. That's why I thought you would be good. You have a kind, generous heart and are willing to sacrifice for others. He…well, he didn't have a strong male role model in his dad. I have my hands full with other responsibilities, so if you could kinda be a pal and a good example to him, I think it would do him a world of good."

"When can I move in? Are you sure there's room here, or would you want us to go to the tunnel?"

"Oh, no. Not the tunnel. It would probably bring back too many memories for him, and some of the people there may still have hard feelings toward his parents. I think here is better," Ken explained. "Right now is fine. You don't have a lot to bring, so just go get your pack, and we'll get you settled. I would suggest being friendly, but let Junior come to you. I have a good feeling about this."

***

Mac and Charlie hurried into the sleeping cavern, both of them a little excited. They'd been listening to Mac's ham radio, and they had news.

"Okay, spill it. We can see that you know something," Erin laughed. "Have a seat, and tell us everything."

"Well," Mac began, "we just listened, like usual, but we heard that a few more NERC camps have shut down. One in Idaho was just getting started. The NERC people had it all set up and were ready to start hunting down people who didn't come in willingly, but folks in that region of the country didn't take kindly to the idea. They staged a huge raid on the camp and made off with all the supplies stored there. Food, water purifiers, medical supplies, blankets, everything.

"A guy up there told us all about it, and he sure sounded legit. Then there was one in Utah, near the Wyoming line. The NERC agents themselves took off with the supplies and used them to barter for safe passage to who-knows-where. Anyway, it seems that conscripting young Americans to put other Americans in camps isn't going well."

"Wow." Tanner grinned. "What else did you hear?"

Charlie shifted to get more comfortable. "They's this rumor, an' thet's all it is right now, thet the embargo might be lifted. Ain't no tellin' if it's true, but we heard tell that OPEC is meetin' about it. I guess we'll see."

"And," Mac added, "in some of the bigger cities, the National Guard has restored order. The gangs killed each other off, then the Guard moved in. That doesn't mean all our problems will go away, but it's a start, if it's true. The only major cities that are still in total chaos are supposedly Los Angeles, Chicago, New York, Seattle, and Houston. Even Atlanta has been secured."

"Yep, and sum folks told us that they seen people tryin' to start up biznesses, like sellin' seeds and doin' repairs on clothin'."

"I hope it's all true," Erin sighed. "It would sure be nice to get back to living our lives without constant fear. In any case, I think we can ease up on our restrictions about going outside."

"It'll be a long time before we have the services that we took for granted before, even if all of this is true. So many have died, from sickness, starvation, and violence. I guess a lot of criminals managed to get out of prison. It'll take a while to get everything going again, so don't get too excited that things will miraculously turn around overnight," Talako warned. "You know I usually try to see the bright side, but there's been a lot of damage done, and it won't surprise me if this is a lull before more trouble."

"That's true. You're almost always the optimistic one, so I guess if you say not to get our hopes up too high, we should listen," Tanner said. "I can easily imagine more unrest as various levels of government duke it out over who has jurisdiction. We haven't heard much at all about the president or congress lately, just bureaucracies. Who's in charge now? I can't help wondering how many state governments even exist anymore."

"Exactly my point," Talako insisted. "We have no idea who's running things, if anybody. But I do think that NERC is about to implode. If they had made it voluntary to live in a camp and work in exchange for food and shelter, it might have been successful, but forcing people into camps who didn't want or need help was doomed to failure."

"Well, I just know that when things do get better, there's going to be a real need for mechanics, and I don't have a shop anymore. I'm going to be thinking about which empty building in town could be converted into 'Two Guys Auto Garage'. That's the new name I picked for my business, and my young friend Micah is going to be my apprentice and heir."

Micah beamed. "Really, Gus? Awesome!"

***

"I talked to Ken on the radio today," Tanner told Erin as they stood watch at the north cave entrance. Blitz and Moxie lay side by side; Moxie slept, but Blitz was watching Erin's every move.

"How are they? Do our more frequent trips to deliver supplies help?"

"Yeah. He was pretty enthusiastic about it. I think putting Vince in charge of getting that organized was a great idea. He's not as depressed as he was, and I don't think it's just that he gets to see Lydia more often. I think it's partly because he now has a real sense of purpose."

"Did you ask Ken about that little boy? Junior? Any news there?"

Tanner rubbed the back of his neck. "He seems to be doing okay, considering what he went through. Ken said that Clint came to stay at Ernie's and he's agreed to try to be a sort of big brother to the kid. Teach him stuff, and talk to him. Ken is doing the counseling, but he was excited to have a younger man take an interest in the boy. Ken and Terri's kids are also trying to befriend him."

"I can't help wondering what happened to the mother. Did she just leave on her own, or did someone abduct her? Somehow, I have the feeling that she sent the boy into town so she could disappear. Maybe she was too humiliated to face all the people in the tunnel." Erin shook her head. "They stole almost all the food, so maybe she figured she wasn't welcome anymore."

Tanner nodded. "According to Ken and Terri, she wasn't. The folks in the tunnel still aren't ready to forgive that family. Ken told Clint to keep the boy away from there because some people are still angry."

"That's ridiculous. The children didn't have anything to do with the parents' decision. Blaming that little boy – well, it's just petty, especially after all he's lost."

"I've been meaning to ask you something. Do you think we should try to have some type of Thanksgiving celebration this year? Does anyone even know what day it is? I haven't been keeping up, but I know it's got to be soon, if it hasn't already passed." Tanner grinned. "We could try to get a wild hog or turkey. Actually, I think it would take two turkeys with this bunch."

"I'll ask around among the adults, but let's keep it quiet around the kids in case we decide to pass on this one," Erin suggested. "If they don't remember it, they won't be disappointed. I have a feeling that they won't forget Christmas. When it gets cold, one of them will remember and then what will we do? We don't have any way to do gifts."

"On a different note, my curiosity is getting the best of me, Tanner admitted. "Tucker and Zeke mentioned the narrow cave again. I made them promise not to try to explore it, but I'm not sure they'll be able to resist. What would you say to trying to take a look, just to see what's there?"

"There's no way you're going through that passageway, big guy. It's too narrow for *me* to get through, and you'd never fit."

"But Jen would. She could take the boys, if Dana and John agree, and they could just ease through to see if there's any danger. That should satisfy the boys, and give the parents a little peace of mind, unless they find something dangerous. If they do, we'll just get busy and seal it off."

"You really want to know what's in there, don't you? I guess we could ask Jen, but if she's not willing…."

"You gotta be kidding. Jen will jump at the chance to do something different. She's an adventurous gal, and I'd bet you ten back rubs she says yes immediately."

"Ten back rubs, huh? I'll take that bet. I'm not sure about the boys going, though."

"We shouldn't send anyone alone, and no other adults are small enough."

"Tanner. Think about it. Noah has gotten really thin, and he's not super tall. I bet he'd do it."

"Great idea."

When Vince and Val relieved them, Tanner and Erin hurried to the sleeping cavern to see if Jen and Noah were there. Jen was, but thought that Noah was in the cabana cavern helping watch the kids.

"Come with us, Jen, and we'll tell you both our idea at the same time," Erin urged.

Noah was carrying Wyatt on his back and making monster noises at Gina, Isabelle, and Kyra, who squealed in delight. He handed the little boy off to his mother, and obeyed Tanner's gesture to come talk. They stepped over where the kids wouldn't hear them.

"Jen, Noah, we've been talking about something, and want to bounce it off you. You know the little side passage off the west cave? We know that Zeke and Tucker have talked about exploring it, and that's a worry to my sister. Micah may have considered going through it, too. I'm really curious about what's in there, and we were wondering if you two might be interested in seeing."

"Why us?" Noah asked, puzzled.

"Because Tanner is way too big and I'm afraid he'd get stuck in there," Erin teased, poking Tanner in the ribs. "You're the thinnest of the adults in the group. We need to know if it's safe, and if it isn't, we need to seal it off so the kids won't try to play explorer. I wanted to let the two boys go with you, but we aren't going to say anything to them until we have permission from Dana and John."

"I'm game if Jen is. We'll need good flashlights, and extra batteries, but it sounds like it needs to be done," Noah agreed.

Jen looked hesitant. "I'm not sure I want to."

Erin gave Tanner a triumphant glance, but he was focused on Jen.

"Why not? I figured you'd jump at the chance for an adventure."

"I would, except…I think Shane will have strong objections, and well, I don't want him upset. We just made up."

167

"Ask him instead of telling him. He'll say it's okay," Tanner assured her.

"I'll try that. And unless he has strong reasons against it, I'll go."

Erin's face fell, but a huge grin spread across Tanner's face.

***

Jen took Tanner's advice, and Shane readily agreed that the cave should be checked out. He asked for a promise from Jen that she would be extra careful and stay with Noah at all times, and tuck an extra light in her pocket. She gave him a solemn vow that she would do all three.

Dana and John were both firmly against the boys joining the first expedition into the uncharted areas of the cave system, so it was decided that Jen and Noah would go while the boys were doing math lessons in the cabana cavern.

There was no reason to delay, and the only preparation was making sure the flashlights worked. Erin, Tanner and Shane would hang around near the opening and pretend to be chatting if any of the children happened by. They had no way of knowing if the cave had an outside opening so Tanner decided to send Blitz though first, just in case there were any animals holed up in there.

When Tanner gave Blitz the command to clear the cave, the big dog looked at him as though to say, "Boss, are you crazy?" but Tanner pushed him a little and showed him that he could make it through.

Noah had to duck to keep from cracking his head, but Jen slipped easily around the jagged rock that stuck out into the passage. Their voices faded out, and the others waited.

Suddenly, they heard Noah's voice, but the words were indistinguishable. Jen's voice replied, sounding excited, and Blitz gave a happy bark. Then several minutes of silence passed before they heard the two returning.

"And?" Erin demanded, as soon as they squeezed back out.

"Oh, Erin! It's wonderful! I'm so glad we went, and now we have to figure out a way to use it."

"Use what?" Tanner asked. "Start from the beginning, please, and tell us what you found."

Noah and Jen grinned at each other, and Jen gestured for Noah to do the honors.

"After we got past that pointy rock right there, the whole thing opens up. I could walk upright without bumping, and there's room for any of us to get through. It goes in about twenty yards, and there's a huge cavern. It's so high, our lights couldn't reach the ceiling, and even bigger than the cache cavern. The floor is sandy and mostly flat, and best of all, for some reason, it's warmer in there. Why would that be?"

"I have no idea," Tanner looked bewildered. "So, are you saying that if this rock right here wasn't sticking out into the passage, any of us could go in there?"

"Yes! That's exactly what we're saying. We all thought the whole cave was narrow, but only this tiny bit is mostly blocked, and only by the pointed bulge of this rock." Jen beamed at them. "If we could knock this bump off somehow, we'd have a warmer place for the older folks and kids to sleep."

"Is there any other outlet? More caves going off from this one?" Erin asked.

"Nope. There are a couple of what I would call alcoves. Kinda like it started to be a cave, but changed its mind. There's no way in or out except right here," Noah frowned. "That's not good, is it?"

"No, but it's not a big problem. We have guards at all the outer openings and the alarm system set up. If anybody gets this far, we've got huge problems anyway," Tanner replied.

"How do we get rid of the rock that's blocking the way through?" Jen pointed to the problem.

"We go to our resident experts, our Fix-It Guys. Let's get Gus and Charlie in here. Vince and Mac, too. They seem to have some good ideas occasionally."

Jen said softly, "Did we ever mention what my dad got his degree in?"

The others shook their heads, and she continued. "Geology. He used to do field work, but later got an office job so he'd be home more. He knows a lot about stuff like this."

***

BJ studied the rock, and had Jen go through and look at the other side after pointing out what she should look for. They talked around the pointed stone, checking the placement of cracks, and the size and shape.

Gus, Vince, and Charlie watched and asked questions, but this was clearly BJ's area of expertise. When Jen emerged, BJ turned to the others and grinned.

"I think we can knock off enough of this wall to make the passage accessible. You've been calling this a rock, and it is, but it's really a part of the rock wall. It sticks out quite a bit, but it has some cracks I think we can use to our advantage."

"What tools do we need?" Gus asked.

"A chisel or some other type of wedge, and something to hit it with. I think it's a one-man job, though," BJ warned. "There's no telling just how much we'll need to chip away at it before it breaks off, and when it does, it could crush a foot or break a leg, so we don't need extra people standing around. It could fall and roll, and I can't say for sure in what direction. Let me think on that just a bit. We don't have the safety equipment we need, but maybe we can rig something up. We can't let ourselves get in a hurry with this, or someone could be badly hurt.

"We also need to decide what to do with the chunk that falls off. It will weigh a lot, and we can't leave it. It'll be in the way whichever direction it falls. How will we get it out?"

"Worst case scenario, we break the big rock into little rocks, I guess," Gus offered. "Sure be a lot of work, though."

"Well, if we have to, we will." BJ admitted. "But the safety issue is paramount. We may need to at least control the way it falls. The types of injuries that could occur would be crippling."

***

170

Gus sat on the cavern floor with Charlie and BJ, thinking hard about how to safely remove the obstacle that prevented most of the group from getting to the new cavern.

Charlie rubbed his whiskered chin. "So, are ya lookin' fer sum way to control thet there rock?"

"I don't think that's an option," BJ said, shaking his head. "It's too heavy, too bulky, and the shape would make fashioning a sling to support it impossible. I think we need to go at this from the opposite direction."

Gus grinned. "We could build a scaffold out of strong lumber, and make a sling to hold the human who is going to chip away at those cracks. He'd be suspended above or level with the rock so it couldn't fall on him.

"We'll need some heavy canvas or something like that for the sling, plus some strong rope, and the scaffold. The biggest problem will be getting it built where the rock won't hit a leg of the scaffold and break it. But I have an idea."

Charlie gave him a narrow-eyed look. "So yer sayin' that instead o' keepin' the rock from fallin', you'll just make sure there ain't nobody fer it to fall on."

"Right. This way will be safer, because I'm not sure I would trust any device we came up with to hold the rock, and also easier, because nobody around here weighs nearly as much as that stone."

BJ stood up. "Okay, Gus. I'm going to leave it in your capable hands. I just hope we can find all the materials we need to build this contraption."

"What d'ya think causes it to be warm in that there cavern, BJ? What in tarnation could do that?" Charlie asked.

"I have a theory, but no way to prove it. The water from the spring in the cabana cavern is warm, and it's not far from the new cavern. The cavern may be sitting over a warm underground pool, fed by a hot spring, which could be what's warming the stone walls and floor."

"Well, whatever's causin' it, it'll be nice havin' a warm place to stay this winter. We'll hang us a quilt fer keepin' the warm air in, and be right cozy."

Chapter Twenty-Two – November 22-23
Central Oklahoma

"I'm certain that the next town we'll pass will be Guthrie. That means we'll be going under I-35," Rian told his companions.

"Uh-oh. Do we want to try to do that in broad daylight?" Price asked.

Bree looked puzzled. "Why not?"

Rian paddled up closer so he could explain. "A major highway always means a bridge. It doesn't really matter if you're crossing the bridge itself or going under it, it's a chokepoint where just a few people with guns can control who passes. Bridges are good places to get killed these days."

"Oh. I hadn't thought of that. Joey and I didn't have any problems coming south from Enid, but I can understand how that works. So, what do we do?"

"We could wait until it gets dark, but that's a long time from now. Or we could stop and let Price do a little recon. He could sneak up close and see if our way is clear to just float on by. If it isn't, we'll have to figure something else out."

"I like the second plan better, personally. It's really cold today, and I hate to sit around, knowing that every hour we delay, it's just going to be that much closer to winter." Bree shivered a little. "I don't do well in the cold."

Price glanced over at Rian. "Do we need to take a look at the map? Maybe we can figure out how close we are. I'd hate to come around a curve and have guns pointed at us because we didn't know the interstate was so close."

"Yeah," Rian responded, handing Price the paddle. "Here. Earn your keep for a change, and I'll take a look."

Rian got the map out, and traced the blue line that represented the river. "We went under Highway 81 already. That was the one early this morning, before the fog lifted. It looks like the river will make a swing toward the northeast for a short distance, and I don't see any big curves near the bridges. I wonder how far away we'll be able to see the first bridge. If there's someone on the bridge and we can see them, they can see us, too. We'll cross under Highway 77, then immediately after that, I-35. Man, two bridges really close together. I don't like it."

"Nope, I don't either. We definitely need to check it out before we get into the middle of a real problem." David looked worried. "I can still shoot, but if we have to scramble around or climb to keep from getting shot, I'm in trouble and so are you, Rian."

"Yeah, I know. Price, you up for this?" Rian asked.

"I am. How do we want to do this? Stop before the first bridge and let me check it out?"

"That sounds like the safest plan." Rian nodded thoughtfully. "It's really hard to tell on the map, but it looks as if the I-35 bridge is just east and quite a ways to the north of the 77 bridge. If we let you out on the east side, I think you'll be able to see both bridges better, without walking very far. You might need to trade shirts with me. That lemon yellow one you're wearing doesn't exactly blend in, and mine's at least a drab color."

"I knew we should have dirt-dyed some of our clothes," Price joked.

The two men switched shirts. Price caught the one that Rian tossed to him, and dramatically sniffed it, making an awful face as he did. Everyone laughed except Rian, but his eyes twinkled.

The terrain had definitely changed as they floated down the Cimarron. Flat, open bareness had given way to gently rolling hills and trees. Most of the leaves had already fallen, and the only green was the cedars.

Approaching the dreaded bridges had all four of them nervous. If they had known the truth, they would have been even more apprehensive; there were not *two* bridges. There were *five*, in rapid succession. The first was a railroad bridge, followed by the old highway bridge, which had been demolished, for the most part.

Next was the new Highway 77 bridge, then shortly after that, the I-35 bridges. The interstate was a four-lane divided highway, so there were actually two bridges that made up what appeared on the map to be only one.

173

They had intended to let Price go ahead on foot to check out the situation, but they'd come much further than they realized. Trying to follow a map when they had few useful landmarks was nearly impossible, especially on a zigzagging river. Rian had done the best he could as navigator, but suddenly, there was the unexpected railroad bridge, just ahead.

David back-paddled to slow the canoe, and gave Rian a questioning look. Rian shrugged.

"I thought we had at least another mile to go. It doesn't look like anyone is around, and that bridge isn't on the map. At least, I don't think it is. Let's go just past it and we'll stop to let Price out."

David and the others agreed, and they continued paddling. The river was still higher than usual, hiding the hazard that lay directly in their path.

Passing between the supports for the railroad bridge without incident, none of the four saw the broken, jagged remains of the old bridge hidden below several inches of muddy water. Short, stumpy ends of thick, steel reinforcing rods stuck up from the concrete footings, and it was not until David and Bree's canoe lurched and they heard the sound of aluminum tearing that they realized there was danger.

Water began gushing through the long slit in the front starboard side of the canoe, and it tilted at an odd angle. Price and Rian were able to avoid the same fate, and maneuvered carefully and slowly over to assist.

Bree was unbalanced by the cant of the little boat, and fell gracelessly into the river, but regained her usual calm and swam hard for the south shore. David remained in the canoe long enough to hand the supplies and packs to his brother. He decided that if he tried to step into the intact canoe, which was already heavily loaded, it might overturn, so he slid out and into the muddy water, following Bree to safety.

Price looked across the river, tracing in his mind where the old bridge had been, then cautiously allowed the surviving canoe to drift past a second set of old pilings, and turned toward the bank, where Bree and David stood, soaked and shivering. He tied the canoe to a tree, and helped Rian out, then turned to his brother.

"Let's get a fire going, and find something dry for you two to wear. We have to get you out of those wet clothes as fast as possible."

"What? No jokes, no smart remarks?" David stuttered.

"Not when you picked the coldest day so far to take a swim," Price shot back.

Rian was already looking for a spot to build a fire. The area was covered with brown grass, leaves, and sticks. He needed bare dirt for a fire, since it hadn't rained in a few days, and the wind was blowing. *Starting a wildfire isn't on the agenda,* he thought.

"Can you two make it down to the next bridge? It's right there," he pointed. "I don't see anyone around, and as much as I distrust bridges, it's our best choice under the circumstances. We could shelter underneath it, and have a fire without the danger of it getting away from us."

Bree and David gave jerky nods, and helped Rian climb a little slope to the flatter terrain. Price got into the canoe and paddled the short distance, retying it under the third bridge.

David dug into his pack and pulled out a long-sleeved tee shirt and some jeans. Price found a set of clothing for Bree. It would be way too big, but she hadn't brought any clothing with her when she set out for her brother's, thinking it would be a short journey to a place where she had plenty of clothing.

"You can roll the legs and sleeves up. We'll have to cut a piece of paracord for you to use for a belt," he explained as he handed her the items.

"Uh...There's nowhere for me to change. Will you guys turn your backs and promise to look elsewhere?"

All three men looked a tad embarrassed, but none of their faces were as red as Bree's. They turned, and she quickly stripped off the soaked clothes and donned dry ones.

"Let's get that fire going, bro," David said as he slapped Price on the back.

Before long, they had a nice blaze going, and Bree spread their wet clothing on the rocks to dry.

"Well, what do we do now?" Price asked. "Rian, you're not going to be able to travel very fast on those crutches. I know they must make you awfully sore under your arms. We have supplies to carry, and we're still quite a distance from Kanichi Springs, so what's the plan?"

"It would be closer to go cross-country than to follow the river. That means we can't go check the house in Tulsa," David complained.

"Can the canoe be repaired?" Bree wanted to know.

"It could, if we had the proper materials, but while Gorilla Glue might hold a bullet-sized patch, I don't see it holding on *that*," Rian answered, pointing to the canoe, still impaled on the steel rod. "We really should try to retrieve it before it breaks loose and drifts away."

David stood, and as he walked toward the surviving canoe, called over his shoulder, "C'mon, Price. Let's get 'er done."

"David," Bree warned, "don't you dare pull those stitches out."

The brothers got into the good canoe and paddled against the current to the damaged one. Freeing it with some difficulty, they tied a rope on it and towed it, half-full of water, to their new camp.

While David and Price were doing that, Bree combed her hair with her fingers, leaning just near enough to the fire to feel the heat. She glanced at Rian, and asked the question that was plaguing her.

"What will we do if we can't figure out a way to repair the canoe?"

"I don't know. Those canoes were old, but had been well cared for. I hated patching that aluminum canoe with a piece of wood, but it was all we had. This new hole is much larger and pretty jagged. It'll be a much bigger challenge to repair it, and there's not nearly enough glue left to even begin."

"So, we may be in trouble, huh?"

"I'd have to say yes, we are definitely in a world of trouble. I've managed to hobble around on flat surfaces, but the hills and vegetation around here will make it impossible for me to go very far in a day. And those crutches do hurt my underarms. I don't like to complain, but I can't take whole days of that."

About that time, David and Price pulled the good canoe up on the bank, then dragged the damaged one up behind it. They turned the canoe over to empty the muddy water and get a closer look at the gash. Satisfied, they sat down across the fire from Bree and Rian.

"I guess we need to make some decisions, don't we?" David said dryly.

"That's what Bree and I were just talking about. I can make it into Guthrie and try to manage on my own, or I'll find an abandoned farmhouse. You three go ahead, and don't worry about me," Rian offered.

All three of the others protested long and loud over that.

"*No way* are we leaving you behind!" Price insisted. "If it wasn't for you, we wouldn't have made it this far. You're going with us, or we're staying with you. That is *not* negotiable."

Bree and David nodded, never taking their eyes from Rian's.

"I'll just slow you down. I can't manage this type of terrain with crutches, not even the best of crutches, which these certainly aren't."

"Rian, you can't make us leave you, so don't waste your breath. We'll stay together, because that what friends do," David said. "I say we make camp right here under the bridge, even though it probably isn't even noon yet, and try to get some rest. Our clothes need to dry, and we need time to figure out what to do next."

Rian scowled, but nodded, and Bree got busy checking the various injuries they each had sustained in the past several days.

With the sun still high over the treetops, David and Bree sat and talked while Rian took first watch. Price decided to take a look around the immediate area and see if there were any houses or barns nearby. He was concerned about having a fire, but the bridge seemed to be helping keep the smoke dispersed.

He climbed the slope, and staying out of sight behind weeds and trees, he had a good view of a farm. The house was

177

across a huge meadow, and too far away for him to be able to tell if it was occupied. There was a barn and a few other outbuildings, but Price thought that the homestead was far enough away that anyone living there probably wouldn't notice them.

He checked the other side of the bridge, then stared across at the other side of the river, but saw no other structures. Reassured, he crept back down and rejoined his friends.

"There's not much around here, just a farmhouse back that way," he said, gesturing toward the slope behind them. "I didn't see anyone. Hopefully, we'll be safe staying here while we see about getting the canoe fixed."

The hours passed slowly, but with each of them resting when they weren't standing guard, the day finally ended. David took the watch when the sun went down, and the others made themselves as comfortable as possible for sleep.

Minutes after David woke Price for his turn on guard duty, a shout startled them all, causing all four to jump up and grab their rifles.

"Hello, the camp!" the male voice yelled again. "I'm coming in, nice and slow. Don't shoot me."

Seconds later, a tall, lanky man in jeans and boots, wearing a black Stetson and an NRA jacket, stepped into the meager light cast by the flames.

"Saw your fire and thought I'd check on who was under the bridge. Who are y'all, and where'd you come from?" the man asked in a pleasant manner.

"Don't try anything. We've got four rifles trained on you," Price warned.

"Well, that's not very friendly of you. I have seven trained on you. Just as a precaution, of course. We're kindly folks around here, but the current situation requires safety measures, you understand." The man suddenly raised his voice. "Boys, show these nice people I'm not lying."

Several other men stepped into view, all armed and looking serious, but not threatening.

"Now, please explain your presence at the edge of my farm."

Rian decided to speak when nobody else did. "We're just passing through, on our way east. Had a little trouble with one of the canoes, and two of us wound up in the river. The canoe was damaged by something under the water, and with four of us, we can't continue with only one canoe."

"Why can't you just walk to where you're going?" The man asked.

"I have a broken fibula, and my crutches are made from two tree limbs. I can't get around very well or very fast," Rian admitted.

"Thank you for your honesty. I watched your accident with the canoe earlier. I intended years ago to put a warning sign up to prevent that sort of thing, but we don't have much traffic on the river, and I just forgot. Sorry. We tried to get the engineers to remove all the pilings when they tore down the old bridge, but the state didn't want to spend the extra money."

"May I see your ring?" David said out of the blue, catching a glimpse of a familiar emblem.

The man gave him a strange look, but extended his hand. David saw that he'd been right.

"You're a Mason." David said.

"We all are. The Oklahoma Grand Lodge is in Guthrie, as is the Scottish Rite Temple. We're all 32nd Degree Masons. Why?"

David gestured toward Price, "This is my brother, and our dad is a Mason. He has a ring like that."

The strangers exchanged glances, and nodded. "And you need help," the first man stated.

"Any ideas on repairing a big gash in an aluminum canoe? We patched a little hole the other day with wood and Gorilla Glue, but this one is too big for that to work," David said.

"What caused the little hole?" the man wanted to know.

"A bullet," Rian replied.

The man nodded slowly, not surprised.

"I'm sure we can think of something. Come on up to the barn. You can sleep there the rest of tonight, out of the wind. Tomorrow, we'll see what we can do about your canoe. Are you hungry?"

"No. We just ate, thank you," Bree said quietly. "My dad was a Mason, too. Mom was Worthy Matron of her Eastern Star Chapter."

"Was?" the man asked gently.

"Yes. They and my brother died in a fire recently."

"The daughter of a Mason only has to ask for help from other Masons, you know. We take care of our own." He then took the opportunity to introduce his friends, gesturing to each as he said the name. "I'm Nick, and this is Bob, Guy, Colton, Mitch, Ron, Joe, and Stephen."

After Rian introduced himself and his fellow travelers, a few of the men helped David and Price pull the canoes further up so that they were hidden better. Bree gathered the damp clothing and the four friends grabbed their packs and supplies, then followed the strangers to the barn.

**

Sleeping in the loft on beds made of hay, the four friends got a good night's sleep. Rian woke first, puzzled by some faint sounds he heard. Soon, the others were sitting up, stretching, and yawning, and the sounds changed slightly, accompanied by a soft murmur of voices.

"What's that noise?" Bree asked.

"Don't know, but I know how to find out," Rian answered. "Let's go down and see what's going on."

They climbed down the ladder, dusted the hay off their clothing, and stepped outside to see five of the men they had met the previous night. Four of them were standing around the fifth, watching him do something to the canoe.

One of the men looked up and saw them. "Good mornin'! Did you sleep well?" he asked cheerfully.

Rian nodded, and Bree smiled, saying, "*I* sure did, even though these guys all snore." They immediately denied it, amid laughter from Bree and the other men.

"Well, we've just about got your canoe repaired," their host informed them. "The guys carried it up here about daybreak. Bob, here, owned a machine shop and did all sorts of work with metals before the collapse, so he had what was needed. Bob, you wanna explain what you're doing?"

"First, I tapped down the protrusions on the inside, then cut a patch out of a piece of aluminum that I had in my scrap pile. After that, I used my torch and a brazing rod. To put it in layman's terms, it's like soldering the patch on, but at a lower temperature. The brazing material has a much lower melting point than the aluminum. It's really a pretty simple job. I just lack a little bit on one end, and you're good to go. It's a little rough, but I can't smooth it out very well without electricity. It won't hurt anything for it to be a bit bumpy, though, and it'll hold, unless you run into any more pilings."

"It's awfully nice of you to help us like this," David told them. "We were worried about people shooting at us from the bridges, and never expected hospitality and help solving a major problem."

"Folks around here are generally good people. Guthrie's a friendly town. Oh, there's a few old grumps, and maybe a handful of troublemakers, but for the most part, it's a great place. If you're going to need help, this is the good place to need it," one of the other men said. "*Especially* if you're related to a Mason."

"Is there any way we can repay you? Any chores we could do for you?" Rian offered.

"Not a thing. We're just glad to help. There's some clean water in those buckets, if you want to wash up a little, and my wife has breakfast on the stove. Should be about ready, so just come on in when you've washed your hands."

They took their host's suggestion, washing their faces and hands, then entering the door he had indicated. A tall woman with auburn hair stood at the stove, turning bacon in a skillet.

"Welcome to our home. I'm Missy, and as soon as I take up this bacon, we'll eat. Just have a seat there at the table."

Soon, they were eating a wonderful home-cooked meal of scrambled eggs, bacon, and toast made with bread Missy had baked. She gestured toward a jar in the middle of the table.

"There's some peach preserves I put up last year. Help yourselves. And please pass the butter."

181

"This is delicious. Thank you so much for sharing it with us. We've been living on MREs and that does get old," Rian told her.

"We're happy to have you. The Lord has blessed us, and it's only right that we should help others. We have a few solar panels, just enough to keep a small refrigerator going, and we have a few pigs. The butter and milk are from our goats, and of course, our hens laid the eggs. We had a bumper crop of peaches last year, too."

"Well, we haven't eaten food this good in quite a while," Price said.

"Where are you headed?" Missy asked.

"A friend of our sister's has a lodge in the Kiamichis. Our parents are there," David answered.

"That part of the state is beautiful. We'll be praying that you get there safely," Missy assured them. "Times are hard, but if good people just work together, we can keep our humanity and survive all this. If you're ever back in this area, you know where we live."

As soon as they finished eating, Bree asked for a few minutes of privacy to change back into her own clothing, which she hoped was finally dry. She climbed into the loft and changed, then called down to her friends to come up and get their packs.

Nick and Missy walked with them to the river, while the other Masons carried the repaired canoe. Bree hugged Missy, and Missy handed her a cloth bag, smiling. "Just some things you might find useful," she whispered.

"We have a few people on the I-35 bridge, keeping it clear for you. Safe travels to you all," Nick said.

With thanks, good wishes, and handshakes all around, the four young people paddled their canoes away. Their new friends stood on the shore, watching until they were out of sight.

Once they were past the interstate, Bree opened the bag and looked inside. There were bags of peanuts, pecans, and raisins, plus dehydrated apricots, raspberries, blueberries, and apples. There was a box of tampons, a small box of teabags, some ponytail holders and barrettes, and a pink camo baseball cap.

"What's in there, Bree?" Price asked.

"Some tea, some fruit, and some girl stuff," she grinned, putting the cap proudly on her head.

Chapter Twenty-Three – November 24
Southeastern Oklahoma

"Hold that end steady while I nail this board," Vince instructed.

Shane and Ian held on tight, and soon the odd design of the scaffolding could be seen taking shape. Gus and BJ had debated long into the night over how to build it so it would hold a man up, yet fit in the space available, and hopefully not break or collapse if the big chunk of rock fell against one of the legs. It was an ungainly-looking contraption, but it was sturdy and, so far, seemed to be fitting together well. It was wider than most of them had envisioned it, but that width gave an extra margin of safety for those who would steady it.

BJ insisted that he should be the one to chip away at the cracks that would help them remove the stone. He reasoned that his size was a benefit, since he was slender and of average height. A few of the other men volunteered to do it, each offering various reasons why he would be a good choice.

In the end, it was agreed that BJ would do the honors, partly because of his lighter weight, but mostly because he so obviously knew how to work with the problem. Erin and Frances designed a sling, using a doubled-over tarp. BJ would lie on his stomach in the sling, with his head and arms free, and be lifted to the proper, safe level to do the job.

It took most of three days to finish the apparatus and test it, mostly because other duties couldn't be neglected, but at last, it was ready. BJ made sure that only those who were necessary personnel were present. He still worried about the stone rolling or sliding into someone and causing severe injuries. The biggest and strongest of the young men were there, at safe distance from the rock, bracing the legs and arms of the strange-looking device.

Tanner put on a pair of leather work gloves, and nodded at BJ, who was already lying in the sling on the floor of the cave. BJ gave him a raised thumb, and Tanner began pulling on the rope that ran from the sling and through a pulley bolted to the top of the scaffold.

Once BJ was lifted to the right height, Tanner wrapped the end of the rope around his waist and held on. BJ used a chisel and a hammer from Gus's toolbox, and began the tedious work of loosening the obstruction. He had predicted that it would take an hour or more, if they were lucky, but within thirty minutes, the chunk of rock fell. The men stood in silence, except BJ, who grinned and shouted "Woohoo!!"

Tanner lowered BJ carefully, since the stone was now under him, holding him just above the rock. The other men ran to help get BJ out of the sling and onto his feet, slapping him on the back and congratulating each other on their success.

Gus came around the corner, smiling at their enthusiasm. "Let's see this new sleeping place! I'm ready to be warm at night!"

After everyone had the chance to inspect the new cavern, BJ reminded them that they still had work to do. "We don't need to be climbing over that thing to get in and out. It's in the way, but we'll have to break it up into manageable pieces to move it. Nobody – and I mean *nobody* – is to be in the area without safety goggles. We only have two pairs of those. I nominate the strong, virile young gents, the ones who have been complaining about boredom, to get that done."

When the laughter finally died down, Vince and Shane agreed that they would do it, and Tanner volunteered himself and Ian to relieve them when they were ready for a break.

***

Junior sat on Ernie's front steps, tearing a brown leaf into tiny pieces and watching the wind blow them away. He was making progress in his grief, but sometimes, he got too quiet, drawing into his own mind and not speaking to anyone.

Clint came out the door and sat beside him. "Hey, buddy. It's nice to be able to come outside now, isn't it? Now that most of the danger from NERC is passed, we can enjoy the sunshine."

Junior didn't answer, so Clint kept talking. "I used to live in Texas with my mom and stepdad. I was at college, and tried to get home, but it didn't work out. I've lost my family, too. They may be alive, but I don't know where they are or how to find them."

Junior finally looked up. "What's 'college'?"

"Well, it's like school, but it's for people who already finished high school. I was learning how to work on the insides of computers, and how to write programs for them. That's what college is for, to help people learn how to do different jobs they want to do. What do you want to be when you grow up?"

"I don't know. Maybe a fireman."

"That's a good choice. What's your real name? Junior means you are named after your dad, I guess."

"Theodore James Isbell, Junior. Daddy was Ted," the boy explained.

"Ah. Ted's a nickname for Theodore. Do you like being called Junior?"

"No. I think it's a baby name. Mommy and Daddy always called my sister 'Sissy' and I didn't like it. Sissy's name was Maria Jeanette Isbell, but they never called her that. I wanted to be called James, but Mommy just laughed at me, and kept calling me Junior."

"Okay, James. I think that's a much more grown-up name than 'Junior'. I'll call you that, and try to help everyone else remember that you're James now."

"Really? It's okay to pick what people call me?" The boy looked uncertain.

"Sure. You get to make lots of choices in life, like what job to do, how to act, who to be friends with. I choose to be friends with you, if you want," Clint said.

"Cool. What other things can I choose?"

"Well, there are some very important things that a man has to decide. To be a good man, one who works hard and is honest and treats people like he wants to be treated, or to be a bad man, lazy or dishonest, one who lies and steals, or hurts people. I choose to try my best to be a good man."

"My daddy wasn't very good. He lied a lot, and he stole from people sometimes. I heard him tell his boss that he was sick, then he went to a football game somewhere. I saw him with a lot of money once, and Mommy hugged him and said it was okay to steal it because his boss owed them the extra, and then he and Mommy stole food. They were always sneaking around grabbing cans in the tunnel, then when we left, they took it all! Well, *almost* all."

"Well, just try to remember the good things your dad did, and decide that you'll be a good man. How old are you?"

"I'm six. I was supposed to be in first grade, but Mommy said the school closed."

"Six is the very best age to decide that you'll be a good man. You have to choose to work hard at whatever job you do, and be nice to people, not lie or steal, and always help others when you can. You'll make mistakes sometimes, but if you always keep trying, you'll be successful."

"Do you make mistakes?"

"Oh, yes. I've made some mistakes that were really stupid, but I think I made up for them, and I'll keep trying, no matter what. How about if we make a pact, a promise, to each other that we'll both be good men, and we'll help each other keep that promise."

"Yeah. That would be cool. We'll be the Good Guys."

***

"Ken, is it just me, or does it seem lately like time moves slowly, yet events move really fast?" Seeing the puzzled look on the preacher's face, Lydia smiled. "What I mean is, it seems like forever since the embargo and things started falling apart, but so many things have happened so quickly. Maybe that's why it seems like such a long time; our minds want to believe that more time has passed so we aren't overwhelmed by the constant turmoil.

"Oh, I'm not explaining this very well at all. I just have so much to think about, and so many feelings to sort through that I can't make sense of any of it."

"So, what's really bothering you, Lydia? What brought on this analysis of time and events?" Ken smiled gently. "What is it that really needs resolving?"

Lydia sat on the porch step and stared at Ken, who leaned against the railing. "How do you know that something is bothering me? Did you take mind-reading classes in college?"

Ken chuckled. "No. I just know that you've been through a lot, and that your natural inclination is to be a happy person, so when you're troubled, it shows. Terri and I have been concerned for you, but I knew that you would talk about it when you were ready."

"Well, I guess I'm ready. It hasn't been long since Richie died, and I loved him, but somehow, I can remember his sense of humor, things he did, and things that happened, but his face is getting vague in my memory. It bothers me that I can't picture him clearly in my mind. It's only been about nine weeks. I don't want to forget him, and yet I want to move on, find a way to be happy, and go on living.

"This collapse has made me look at life differently. The violent things that have happened, the whirlwind of changes coming so fast…well, I feel like I need to grab onto any happiness I can find and hang on, because life is so uncertain."

Ken smiled gently, then looked out at the remains of the town. "You mean like gangs and tornadoes and things like hunger, fear, love, and loss? Yes, the pace of life *has* changed. It's all different. Instead of jobs and weekends and routines, now we have to struggle to provide food and shelter. We thought life was hectic before, and now, somehow it isn't as *hectic*, but it's more *urgent*."

"Yes. That's exactly it. We aren't on a timeclock, but we're more aware of time, because our survival depends on using it well. And loss has to take a backseat to living, to moving forward. If I let myself wallow in the grief I feel over Richie's death, I would be no use to anyone, so instead, I've had to…I hate to say it like this, because it sounds so cold…get over it."

Ken nodded solemnly. "When I took classes in grief counseling, they talked about the stages of grief. I agree that some of us really go through those stages, but each stage takes a different tone and a different amount of time for each person. But not everyone goes through them; our circumstances can affect how we deal with loss. We've had so much to grieve over, that perhaps we've grown accustomed to losing the people and the things – like our homes and your business – that make up our personal worlds."

Lydia nodded. "Somehow, the tornado made it all real to me. This doesn't make sense even to me, but when Richie's store was hit, I knew he was really gone. Silly, but that's how I felt."

"Lydia, feelings are not right or wrong. They just *are*. You feel what you feel, and while you can adjust your attitude and decide to try to feel differently, there is nothing wrong with *feeling*. And when you decide to stop feeling a certain way, it's *okay*. I believe you'll always hold Richie in your heart. You'll always miss him, but there's nothing wrong with letting yourself experience joy again, even falling in love again. Richie would be the first to tell you not to grieve forever. There wasn't a selfish bone in his body, and he wouldn't mind if you decided to stop mourning and start rebuilding your life."

"Yes, that's true. The last thing he said was for me to be happy. I think it was a blessing, in the old-fashioned sense of wishing a person the best and giving permission for that person to do something. He was saying that I had his blessing to move on with my life, and he did it because he loved me."

"He did. And now, maybe you can make peace with the idea of tucking Richie deep into that corner of your heart, and opening the rest of it to whatever or whoever you need to live a full and satisfying life."

Rian unfolded the map and studied the route that the river would take. It didn't look too bad, except for all the bridges, until the river flowed into Lake Keystone. What they would find there was anyone's guess, but Rian knew that the portage around the dam would be difficult. He felt useless with his injured leg and the dismal excuse for crutches that he had.

"Looks like we'll pass near several towns. Pleasant Valley, Coyle, Goodnight, Vinco, and then, it looks like we'll go right through Cottingham, which I think is really small. After that, we'll bypass Ripley, Amabel, Cartoco, and a few others, and then we'll be traveling through the Wildlife Management Area for a while. We'll go past Cushing, then it looks like maybe right through Oilton, and not long after that, the river widens out, which means it will probably also be shallower. I hope it's deep enough to float us."

He cleared his throat, then continued. "After a sharp curve back to the west, we need to steer around a long, skinny peninsula, turn back toward the east, and then go south to the dam."

David used his paddle to slow down so Rian and Price could catch up. "There are marinas on the lake, and that means there may be other boats, although I would bet that the lake is way up, and roads to the marinas may be flooded. Lots of people have sailboats on Keystone. We'll go by some parks, too, I think, and some of them are up on top of the bluffs. If there's someone up there with a rifle, we'll be sitting ducks."

"So, do we hug the shore, or get out in the middle? Do we go at night, or in broad daylight?" Bree asked.

The four were silent for a moment, then Price spoke up. "There are bridges coming up past the lake that make me more nervous than crossing the lake. There's Sand Springs, then at least four more before we get out of the Tulsa area. Five, if you count Bixby, and I'm probably forgetting some.

"David, you've been set on going by the house, but I have to tell you that I'm not sold on that idea. By now, it's almost certainly been looted. Our stuff is gone, bro. I don't think it's worth risking our lives to go check on an empty house, since we don't know if it's even still standing."

David frowned. "You're probably right. I know it, but I just hoped…well, I wanted our gear. Hunting, fishing, diving. It might have come in handy, but let's just forget it."

"Whew, that's a relief," Bree said. "Rian and I would have had to wait on the river while you checked it out, and I wasn't looking forward to that. I kept wondering what we would do if you didn't come back. Keep waiting? For how long? No, I'm relieved you've changed your minds."

"Yeah," Price agreed. "The house is about two miles from the river, two miles through who knows what dangers? And for things that are most likely long gone."

"Okay, okay. I get it. I said you were right, so drop it. We need to decide about the lake."

"It looks on the map like the peninsula is really narrow. If it isn't too steep, maybe we could portage across it, Rian speculated. "That would save us a few miles on the lake and line us up pretty well with the dam."

"If there's a safe spot to pull the canoes out, and a place we can put in again, that'll work. We didn't spend a lot of time on Keystone, and don't know the lake well enough to say for sure," David added, "but I think there's a good chance that the neck of that peninsula is submerged, unless they left all the floodgates open on the dam."

"Well, I don't think there's any chance that we'll get there today, anyway. It's hard to guess our speed, but I sure we'll have plenty of time to think about it. I'm hungry. Is it time for lunch?" Price said, with a mischievous grin.

Bree dipped her fingers in the water and flicked it on him. "We had a big breakfast, and we need to conserve food. You're a greedy gut."

**

The river was straighter for a while, then began a series of sharp turns, twisting so many times that it was hard to tell what direction they were going. They passed two teenagers fishing on the bank; when the boys saw them coming, they ran.

They'd passed under a few bridges with no problems, and saw another one ahead. Rian signaled for them to pull over to a sandbar.

"I think we need to see what road that is, so we can figure out how far we are from the lake. We've been moving right along all day, and may have come further than we thought."

"I'll go," David volunteered. "Be right back."

He climbed up until his head was just above the level of the road, looking around carefully before showing himself. There was no sign of anyone, so he hurried north just a bit, where he could see a highway sign. Stepping past it, he glanced back, and saw the number, then returned to the canoes.

"It said that's Highway 99. So, where are we?"

Rian studied the map, using his finger to trace the river. "We're past Oilton already. That means that the river *doesn't* go through Oilton after all. It goes north of it, I guess. We're close, real close, to where the river spreads out, then joins the lake."

"The sun will be down in thirty minutes or so. Let's find a place to camp, and talk about what to do next." Bree arched her back, stretching the tight muscles. "I'm too tired to tackle whatever we run into on the lake."

"Okay. Sounds like a plan," Rian agreed. "I wish I had some regular crutches instead of these tree branches. Even with the padding tied around the tops, they kill my underarms."

"Buddy, we wish you did, too. If we have to take off on foot, it's gonna be rough on you, and after Muskogee, we'll for sure be on foot," Price replied. "How long does it take a broken fibula to heal enough to put weight on it?"

"I have no idea. Too bad we can't look it up on the internet," Rian said wryly.

Bree interrupted by loudly clearing her throat. "Did you forget that you have a doctor right here?" She gave them an arch look. "Hey, I admit it: I'm young and inexperienced. It usually

192

takes four to six weeks for a fibula to heal, and that's if you stay off it. I'd like to check it more closely. We'll need to take the splint off so I can do that."

"As soon as we make camp, we'll do it," Rian agreed. "Let's get past the bridge and find a spot out of sight from there, okay?"

David and Price pushed the canoes off the sandbar, got in, and continued a short distance down the river. They found a good spot about three hundred yards beyond the bridge.

While David and Price took care of securing the canoes and getting their packs up the slope, Bree helped Rian over to a log where he could sit. She untied the strips of fabric that held the metal bars against his leg, and then, in her most professional voice, told him to take off his jeans.

"How's the pain lately?" she asked.

"No pain. It really hasn't hurt in a couple of days."

"I'm going to see what I can feel, so relax your muscles as much as possible. It won't tell me much, but maybe it will tell me something. Let me know if it hurts. Don't try to be macho. I need to know."

Bree grasped the head of the fibula and manipulated it.

Rian sat, waiting until she finished, and when she looked up at him, he shrugged. "It doesn't hurt."

'Hmm. I'd give a lot for an x-ray of that leg. I wonder if it was even broken. I wish I had a lot more experience with this. I know that it's not good to put weight on it if it *was* broken, but what if it didn't actually break? I should have thought of this before."

She moved from his side to his feet. "I'm going to tap the distal end of the fibula, the lateral malleolus. Tell me if you feel anything at all, any change." She tapped, and he shook his head.

She took his foot, bending it slowly from side to side, then pulled his toes down, and pressed them back up. He responded with a shrug.

"This is not modern medicine. I hope you realize that. It's about as primitive as it can get, but I'm beginning to suspect that the fibula was never broken. If it was, it was no more than a hairline fracture. At least, that's my best guess. I think you may have sprained or pulled something. Whatever it is, it isn't causing you any pain now. A broken fibula would probably have hurt pretty badly with what I've just done to you."

"So, what does that mean?" Rian looked hopeful, but apprehensive at the same time.

"It means that I still can't know for sure, but I *think* it may be safe to try putting some weight on it. If you're willing, I have an idea that might tell us a little more."

Rian nodded. "I'm game."

David and Price had finished the chores for setting up camp and sat watching Bree's examination. She gestured for them to come over and help her.

"I want you to lift Rian to a standing position, and I'll hand him his crutches. Then, Rian, I want you to very slowly and carefully put just a tiny bit of weight on that foot. Put the whole foot on the ground first, not just the toes, and barely shift just a fraction of your weight to it. If you feel any pain, lift it back up. David, Price, you hold onto him and keep him balanced, so he doesn't have to worry about falling."

The brothers helped Rian to his feet and held him securely. He let Bree place the crutches under his arms. He took a deep breath and put the foot down for the first time since his accident. Holding back from fully standing on that foot was harder than he'd assumed, but he gingerly tested the leg.

"A little more, Rian. Does it hurt? Keep going," Bree encouraged.

To everyone's surprise, Rian put most of his weight on the leg before he felt any discomfort, and then, it was only a little soreness.

"I'm almost positive I'm right," Bree said quietly. "I think you got lucky and that fibula is just fine."

"That's great," Price interjected. "Now can we eat?"

Three pairs of eyes turned to stare at him, and when the laughter faded away, they ate.

"Man, this fruit is great. It sure was nice of Missy to give this to us," David said as he reached for another piece of dried apple.

"Don't eat too much at once," Bree warned. "Our systems aren't used to fruit anymore, and it could give you diarrhea."

"*That'*d be fun in a canoe," Price murmured dryly.

"We need to decide something about the lake. What are our options and what are the pros and cons of each?" Rian reminded them.

"Uh-oh. We haven't been keeping watch since we stopped. Did anyone besides me notice that?" David asked.

"Nope," Price replied. "I'm finished eating, so I'll stand up and keep an eye out, but I want to stay close enough to hear the discussion."

That discussion took over thirty minutes, covering every possible scenario that they could imagine. When a consensus was finally reached, the plan wasn't what any of them had really wanted; it was just the best they could do under the circumstances.

***

Night fell, and the moon was almost full. The canoes were loaded and ready to go, so after everyone took care of what Bree had taken to calling "personal matters", they set out. Traveling the river in the dark wasn't ideal by any means, but the fear of being seen on the lake in daylight had convinced them that it would be safer at night.

Luckily, the river was still up, although not as high as it had been. David and Bree ran aground on a sandbar almost immediately, but soon got back into the channel. The light from the moon helped a lot, except when they were on one of the many curves where trees blocked the moon's rays.

Gradually, the river widened, but somehow, they managed to stay afloat and moving most of the time. Shallow areas were impossible to see, and running up onto the sand became routine.

The trip took longer than they expected, but at last, they realized that they were on the lake. The narrow neck of the peninsula was somewhere ahead, and their biggest concern was the possibility of missing it and having to go the extra miles around.

Price had been on the peninsula once, several years earlier, on a fishing trip with friends, and thought he might be able to recognize the spot. A few small campfires were visible on the hills around the lake, and they wanted to get past the open water as quickly as possible.

"There!" Price hissed. "I'm almost positive that's the narrowest part of the neck, but it looks like it's totally under water."

"Woohoo! That'll simplify things a little," Rian cheered softly. "We won't even have to get out of the canoes."

From what they could tell in the dim light, pretty much the entire peninsula was submerged. The lake was still up several feet above normal levels due to heavy rains. That also meant that the floodgates were not fully open.

They could see a big bonfire on a hill. A large group was gathered around it, but fortunately, it was far across the lake and up high. Someone was playing a guitar, and several people were singing an off-key rendition of "Against the Wind." None of the people there were paying any attention to the lake. They were noisy and boisterous, and had evidently found some liquid refreshment somewhere, because most of them acted like they were drunk.

"Okay," David reminded them. "That big fire looks like it's in the state park, near the cabins. Keep your body as low as you can so you aren't silhouetted out there. The dam is over that way." He gestured to the south. "We have to cross open water. The alternative is miles of hugging the shoreline, with no guarantee that it will be any better than going the most direct route."

The wide expanse of water seemed daunting, and they couldn't quite make out the dam in the moonlight. It appeared only as a dark, flat expanse, and it was impossible to gauge with any accuracy how far away it was.

"Keep some distance between the canoes. One at a time will be less conspicuous than two together, and it'll make us smaller targets, as well. Rian and Price, you go first, and remember: fast, quiet, and keep your heads down."

The first canoe was in the middle of the open lake when the second started across. As though the clouds were in league with the travelers, one of them drifted across in front of the moon, hiding their passage in a cloak of darkness. Rian and Price made it almost to the dam without any trouble, but just as Bree and David were about to pass behind the hill near the bonfire, the cloud left the moon behind, and the light seemed to spotlight their canoe. Someone on the hill caught sight of them and yelled out, pointing. Several men suddenly darted in their direction, disappearing and reappearing as they ran through the woods toward the highway across the dam, calling encouragement to each other as they went.

"Hurry!" David called to Bree, who doubled her efforts to turn the canoe. Rian had heard the shouting, and looked back at the second canoe. David frantically waved at him to head toward the north end of the dam instead of the southern one.

Rian called loudly, "Price, reverse course! We've got company!" and Price, having already learned to trust Rian without question, managed to spin around on his seat and change direction in mere seconds.

"Did you notice any weapons in that group? I didn't see any when they were lit by the fire," Bree asked.

"Now that you mention it," David replied, "I didn't, but that doesn't mean they don't have any."

'No, but what if we let them know that we do?" Bree suggested.

"Can you get close without killing anybody? They're just a bunch of drunks, and while they may be a slight threat, I hate to kill them just for chasing us. They seem excited, rather than menacing. Hand me the paddle, and *don't argue*. I'm okay to paddle for a short distance."

Bree didn't answer. She just passed him the paddle, turned on her seat, and lifting her rifle, took careful aim, shooting twice right in front of the group of men who had just reached the highway. She pinged both shots off the guardrail that ran along the side of the road, and the pursuers skidded almost comically to a halt, some ducking, and others scrambling back into the trees.

"Well, that slowed them down. We may have to do it again if they regain their stupidity, but nobody fired back, so it's a fair bet they aren't armed," Bree gloated.

"Good job, doc," David acknowledged. "You really are a decent shot, and that was quick thinking, hitting the rail. It made enough noise to warn them off, and let them know there's a serious shooter out here."

"Thank you, sir. I *did* tell you that I can shoot."

"Yes, you did, but *now* I believe it," he teased.

"Here come Rian and Price, and I think another cloud is about to move across the moon, just in time to make our landing harder."

Bree peered ahead, noting that close to the dam, the hillside was covered in chunky tan rocks, probably to prevent erosion. To the left, though, was a flat area, so she directed David to try landing there. Price saw what they were doing, and followed them in.

As they were pulling the canoes onto dry land, the moon reappeared, casting enough light for them to see that they were at a small area set aside for fishing. Up a gradual slope, they could see a tiny parking lot.

"Let's go!" Rian urged. "I think I have to, just this once, ignore doctor's orders and help with the canoes. We need to move!"

"Put your packs on. It'll lighten the canoes. Just leave any loose stuff in there.," David added.

Toting the canoes as quickly as possible, they crossed the parking area, went up the short entrance drive, and hustled across the highway. Directly across from the driveway, they saw a closed gate, blocking the entry to the Corps of Engineers office. The gate was formed of thick pipes, but was low enough for an adult to climb over. Rian got there first, and rested his end of the canoe on the pipes while he clambered over; he then balanced the canoe while Price followed suit. David and Bree did the same.

Rushing forward, Price called out, "There's a ramp down to the water. We have to take it, because the only other way down is over a bunch of very large rocks. This way!" he yelled, as he pulled on the canoe, forcing Rian to veer to their left.

The ramp had a gradual slope, but was very long, with a 90° turn to the west. Glancing up, Bree saw that the drunks had decided to continue their pursuit. They were almost across the bridge.

"David!" she cried. "Stop!"

David looked up and saw the problem, and told Bree to prop her end of the canoe on the metal handrail that ran alongside the ramp. As soon as the canoe's weight was off, she grabbed the rifle, and shot in front of the men, once again hitting the railing on the bridge. The inebriated men dropped to the pavement, and Bree waited.

As soon as one of them started to rise, she repeated the shot, but just a bit closer. The man hadn't realized that the moon was slightly behind him and made his movements visible from where Bree stood.

She kept the rifle slung across her chest this time, and picked up the end of the canoe. Rian and Price were already down the ramp, waiting on a sidewalk that had been put in for people who wanted to fish or watch the bald eagles that nested in the area and often came to the dam to feast.

Bree was keeping an eye on the drunks, but all she could see was shadowy shapes as several men retreated across the dam. She sighed, glancing back longingly at the brown, corrugated-metal potty across the parking lot.

It disappeared from view as they descended the sloping ramp and joined their friends.

"You do realize that that's the first chance we've had in a long time to take a bathroom break that wasn't behind a bush," she moaned.

"You wanna run back up there and pee?" Price asked. "We'll wait."

"No, because I can't be sure all those guys are gone. I'll hold it until we stop again. What's coming up next on our grand adventure?" she replied, as she lowered her end of the canoe.

"We'll float past some mobile home parks and some industrial buildings, then we'll go under Highway 97. That'll be in Sand Springs. Not far past that, we'll start getting into Tulsa, which may be where the fun starts. I am *not* looking forward to that," David complained.

"I'm going to suggest that Rian and I trade places in the canoes," Bree stated with frown. "That way, we'll have a strong person to paddle each, freeing me up to shoot without making David strain his stitches." The others nodded and made the change.

They began paddling downstream, but it was hardly necessary. The high water below the dam was flowing swiftly. Evidently, someone had decided to leave a few of the floodgates partially open, just in case there was a lot of rain. That had been a smart move, because the torrential rains upstream could have caused the lake to come up so much that the water might have gone over the dam. It was a scenario that would give the Corps of Engineers nightmares.

"Tell us about what to expect, please," Bree asked Price.

He considered for a moment. "Oil refineries, which are almost certainly shut down. There's the River Parks, with a long stretch of bike and jogging trails, kiddy playgrounds, and picnic areas. Bridges, including a pedestrian bridge, I-244, I-44, 21st Street, 71st Street, and the Creek Turnpike, then one further downstream in Bixby. I've probably forgotten one or two. We aren't on the Cimarron anymore. Both it and the Arkansas flow into the lake, and once you're past the dam, it's called the Arkansas."

"We're back to the same old problem, then, aren't we? Whether to go at night, or during the day," Bree said as she shifted on the seat of the canoe. "We might as well get on with it, although I'd like to get some rest at some point. We've been going since yesterday morning, and it's going to be daylight before we know it."

"How about we try to find a place to get a good rest, and set out again later, just before the sun sets?" Price used his paddle to shove a drifting limb away. "We're all tired, and that means we won't be as alert as we need to be going through a populated area."

200

Rian and David had gotten far ahead, but when they noticed the distance between the canoes, Rian paddled over to the leeward side of a sandbar to wait. When the other canoe caught up, Rian made a beckoning motion.

"What's up?" Price asked.

"We were just talking, and we want to stop for a good rest, at least until the sun goes down," David told them.

Price and Bree looked at each other and started laughing.

David and Rian stared at them, then looked at each other and shrugged, wondering what was so funny.

Bree asked, "Which one of you came up with that idea?"

"He did," Rian said, pointing his thumb at David.

"That's what I figured. Price just said almost those exact same words to me. You two must have a mental link."

"They're mental, all right," Rian muttered, rolling his eyes.

"This looks like a good spot, if we can pull the canoes out of sight. I'm beat. I don't think I have the energy to keep going," David said, turning to his brother. "And I just remembered something. That 'Vision' project, or whatever it was called…didn't they build a couple of low-water dams in the Tulsa area? Can the canoes go over those?"

"Dang. I forgot about that," Price replied, disgusted . "They were supposed to put in one or two in Tulsa, and fix the existing one. First responders used to call that one 'the Drowning Machine' because the water going over it created a rolling effect, dragging people under. Folks *died* there."

David added, "I'm pretty sure it's right by some big oil storage tanks on the west side, and the park on the east.

"So, what do we do? You don't know if they ever did the improvements, and you aren't sure if there is more than one?" Rian sounded frustrated.

"We've been in Tahlequah, and only home for brief stays the past couple of years. We weren't exactly keeping up with what was going on in Tulsa," Price explained, feeling slightly defensive. "We both took summer classes, and when we were home, we were too busy having fun to care what construction projects they had going."

"Okay. Sorry. Maybe we need to think this through. Trying to avoid manmade hazards is going to make this more challenging than we thought. Doing it at night? I don't think I'm up for that." Rian shook his head.

"Well, one thing is for sure. We all need some rest, and maybe we'll be able to figure out all the options we have when we're not so exhausted," Bree said. "If we make decisions now, they probably won't be good ones. Let's see if we can rest until daybreak."

They made sure the canoes were securely hidden in the weeds, then ate a quick snack of fruit, refilled the water reservoirs in their packs, and decided that Rian would take first watch. The others got as comfortable as they could and were soon fast asleep.

***

Price had the last watch, and he let the others sleep until the sun was high over their heads. Bree woke first, and got out some MREs for their breakfast.

When Rian and David woke, she put her hands on her hips and frowned. "I hate to mention it, but there are only three MREs left in the box. Those, plus what's in the packs, are all we have. We might as well leave the box here. It's just taking up room in the canoe."

"Well, we all knew the food wouldn't last the whole trip. We need to do some fishing or trapping, I guess," Rian replied.

"So, what's the plan? Anyone have any suggestions?" Bree was rested, but apprehensive about the prospect of all the possible problems they could encounter in Tulsa.

"I think we should go as soon as we can, and use the scope on one of the rifles to check out the bridges from a distance." Rian grimaced. "If there's someone blocking the bridge, they're not going to ignore two canoes passing underneath. At least, I don't think they will."

"If we see something, what do we do? If *they* see *us*, they won't necessarily stay on the bridge, and they could send someone after us," Bree protested. "We're too easy a target."

"True," Rian interjected, thinking out loud. "Let's just hold on a minute and analyze this. Someone uses a scope and watches for bad guys, plus we all keep a constant eye out for possible places to land and take cover if necessary. The spotter will be in the lead canoe, and we'll stay within voice range of each other so we can communicate better. No more letting the canoes get so far apart that we can't hear warnings from each other.

"When we get to the low-water dam, we portage around it. I don't know if a canoe would get sucked under, but it isn't worth taking the chance."

"If I'm remembering correctly," David mused, "the low-water dam is under the pedestrian bridge, and they had a rule that people weren't to get within fifty yards or so, either upstream or down. We need to really stay alert so we don't get too close and get dragged over."

"Okay, let's get ready and get going," Price urged. "The sooner we get this over with, the happier I'll be."

They gathered the packs and shoved the canoes into the water, with Price paddling the lead canoe and Bree using the scope to check for trouble. The river seemed to be faster, possibly because it narrowed slightly, but they couldn't be sure.

Bree spoke in a moderate tone. "Looks good so far. There's some big buildings coming up, but nobody around." And later, "There's a couple of women at that trailer park, but they aren't paying attention to us."

Then they saw the first bridge. It was a long one, with bluffs visible on the south side, large homes seeming to hang on the edges. On the north, they could see some businesses, but few signs of life other than two older men fishing. Bree checked them out carefully, and saw no signs of any weapons, so she signaled to keep going.

They passed under the bridge with considerable speed, not wanting to linger, but knowing that the probability of running into trouble only increased the closer they got to Tulsa.

Chapter Twenty-Five -- November 25
Southeastern Oklahoma

Gus and Vince found Brian sitting on a boulder outside the north cave. He had a legal pad and was working on a sketch of some sort, with a row of numbers in the margin.

"Hey, Brick," Vince greeted him. "I see you're enjoying some freedom now that we can be outside again. You better not let Erin catch you out here alone. You know how she is about always going with a buddy or two. What's that you're working on?"

"I'm not alone." Brian grinned. "You're here, and the guards can see me from the cave entrance. Remember I told you I had an idea about how to hide the big planters? In the spring, when Erin does her gardening, those big containers with plants in them, sitting in the middle of the front yard, are going to tell anyone who comes around that someone's living nearby. Not only could strangers steal our food, they might also decide to search for whoever's growing it. No one has discovered the caves yet, but it wouldn't be good to have someone snooping around."

"Have you solved the problem? You said you had an idea," Gus asked.

"I think so. I was just about ready to come find you two so I could bounce it off you, but since you're here, I can just show you." He pointed at the drawing. "I found a nice clearing that gets plenty of sun, high up the mountain. I doubt that it's visible from anywhere except maybe a plane or a helicopter, and it's been a long time since we saw one of those."

"But how will we get the planters up there? Your Bobcat will leave tracks, and you'll have to maneuver through the trees." Gus scratched his head. "And how will you keep the wildlife out?"

"We'll have to move the fence, too. I know, that's a lot of work that we've already done once, but it's necessary. I plan to break one of Tanner's hard-and-fast rules: never go the same way and make a path for strangers to follow. I'll move the planters along a route I've already chosen.

"Yes, it'll leave a clear trail, but once they're all moved, we'll get everyone who can help to rake it out and spread leaves, twigs, and pine needles over it. This time of the year is best for that. There're plenty of leaves piled up around here that we can gather.

"The guys will move the fence and put it around the clearing, then we'll rake the front yard and use more leaves to cover the bare spots where the planters were. I'm pretty sure there's enough barbed wire left to make two more circuits around the new garden, so we'll have three total, which should keep bears out. I hope so, anyway."

"I don't know that it will, to be frank. Bears can be pretty crafty when food is involved," Gus commented.

"Well, Gus," Brick continued, "I'm going to suggest that one or two of the ladies try their hands at cutting hair, and we'll scatter what they cut off all around the clearing, plus we'll encourage the guys to pee around it. The human smells may help some. I sure hope we don't have to post guards."

"I really need a haircut," Vince complained. "I haven't had hair this long since...well, since forever. Long hair and working around convicts is a bad combination."

Brick grinned. "I can imagine. Dangerous, too. Anyway, I'm pretty sure there's enough hose to run through the cave and come out this entrance, and I think it'll reach the new garden. If not, we'll need to go to town to borrow some from the empty houses."

"Naw." Gus chuckled. "I picked up some hoses when I gathered up stuff from the old hardware store. They're in one of the caverns somewhere. And I have another idea. Just in case somebody comes through the forest, we can camouflage the planters and fencing."

"How are we going to manage that?" Vince asked.

Gus gave him a satisfied smile. "On that same trip to the hardware store, I grabbed whatever I thought might be useful, and I just happen to have several cans of spray paint. Brown, tan, green. In fact, I've got more than one shade of each. We can use small tree branches to break up straight lines, like the sides of planters and the fence posts. We'll hang vines or sticks from the wires. I don't think it'll take much. Then, unless someone walks right up to it, it won't be noticeable."

"Good thinking. I think it's pretty unlikely that anyone will walk up there. Most wanderers take the easiest, shortest route, and this definitely ain't it, but if someone got close, they might notice that something up there didn't look natural." Brick grinned. "I think we need to get started on this, and hopefully, it'll rain after we get through and help cover up all traces of the move."

***

That evening, as most of the group ate their meal, Brian asked Tanner and Erin to sit with him, Gus, and Vince. He showed them the plan he'd drawn out and the three men answered all their questions. Then Erin looked thoughtful for several moments.

"I like it, but I'd like to take a look at this clearing before we commit to it. You've done a good job of thinking this through and planning solutions. Let's go tomorrow and check it out before we break it to all the people who'll doing the bulk of the manual labor."

Tanner laughed. "The guys have been getting restless and bored again. This should cure that!"

***

The next morning, Brick took Erin, Tanner, and Vince up the slope to the spot he'd found. Moxie trotted along beside Tanner. It was on the west side of the mountain, almost halfway between two of the cave entrances, but considerably higher. Gus was busy helping Mac rewire something on the ham radio unit.

"I figured that being located here, the guards and dogs at the entrances would likely spot any intruders well before they got near the garden. It's doubtful that anyone would have a reason to go up there, but someone might wander by on the ledge above the spring, and they'd be in sight from one or the other entrance." Brian pointed toward the little pool down the slope. "I wish we had some type of pump that we could use to get water from there."

"I'll put that on my Amazon Wish List right away," Erin said wryly. "Yeah, that would be ideal, but I don't know anyone who would have one. I guess Uncle Ernie didn't think of everything after all."

"Maybe not, but he thought of *almost* everything. Have you checked the inventory list for something like that?" Tanner's lips pursed thoughtfully. "It kinda surprises me that he left it out."

"I don't recall seeing a pump on the list, but I'll look again when we get back. Now, Brian – or Brick, as I've been hearing Vince call you --show me how you plan to lay this out."

"I thought the gate should be about here," he explained, pointing to a spot near Tanner's feet. "That way, it'll be easier to get the hose in and out. We'll cut down those three saplings over there, and those two trees in the middle, to clear out enough space. We can use the bigger stuff we cut for firewood and the little stuff will work to help with the camouflage."

"I think this is a great spot. It'll get plenty of sun, but not too much. It isn't level, but we can put a chunk or two of the firewood under the pots and solve that problem." Erin looked all around the clearing. "Yes. I believe this'll work just fine. When do you want to start?"

"This afternoon would be great. It's a clear day, and we can't move stuff if it's been raining. The chances of getting stuck are too great, but we'll hope for rain when we're finished, so any tracks we miss when we rake will be smoothed out."

"Who wants to break it to the guys that we have to do all that work again?" Tanner groaned.

"Why, I figured that would be *you*, Tanner," Brick teased, then his face fell. "Oh. I just thought of something. My Bobcat runs on diesel, and it's gotta be just about empty after we used it to load and unload the planters, not to mention the graves we dug, There should be some in the tank behind my workshop, but how will we get it here?"

Erin looked resigned. "I guess we'll have to take the chance of using Tanner's pickup to go get it. Do you have fuel cans we can use?"

"Yeah. There's several in the shop," Brick assured her.

"Tanner, you want to get a few people and go to town? Brian should go, too, and maybe a couple of others -- all armed, of course."

"Of course. We'll take the back way, and cut across behind the church. Quick in, quick out. No extra stops this trip, unless you have something else you need for us to do."

"I can't think of anything. Let's get this going. What would you think of posting guards with radios near the roads, out a mile or so, when Brian starts moving planters? The Bobcat's noisy, and if there's anyone in the area, they might decide to come investigate." Erin sighed. "A nice thunderstorm would cover the noise, but cause other problems. I guess we can't have everything."

Chapter Twenty-Six – November 25
Tulsa

Gradually, the skyline of Tulsa came into view. Price, who still rode with Bree, could almost feel the tension rolling off her. Her head swiveled constantly, watching for anything the least bit threatening, but the few people they saw were some distance away and didn't seem to notice the canoes.

Rian paddled the second canoe, concentrating on keeping the distance between the two canoes closed. David decided that two scopes were better than one, and raised his rifle to join Bree in looking ahead.

The first bridges loomed in the distance. Interstate 244, which curved around the west and north sides of downtown, had been a major route for those traveling to Oklahoma City or Joplin, as well as one that got a lot of traffic from locals. There were actually three bridges in a row. Neither David nor Bree saw anyone on the bridges, but when they looked lower, they saw something that made their eyes widen.

Under the first bridge, dozens of ragged, hungry-looking people loitered. Some stood, others sat, and a few were wrapped in filthy blankets, sleeping. Their eyes were dull and almost lifeless, giving them the appearance of zombies, but without the blood dripping from their mouths.

Their eyes followed the canoes in a way that Bree, in particular, found to be both fascinating and creepy. Not one of them made a move to stop the canoes or harm the passengers. Price and Rian made sure they stayed as close to the middle of the river as possible, to put them out of range of any rocks or debris that might be thrown, but nothing happened.

Bree's heart had barely started to slow its frantic pace when another bridge appeared. It was narrower than the first one, but it also had people living under it. This time, some of them yelled, beckoning the travelers, and when the canoes didn't turn toward them, a few started throwing large rocks and chunks of wood at them. All the projectiles fell far short, but the threat was there. David turned as they cleared the bridge, watching to see if anyone tried chase down the bank after them.

Bree called out suddenly, and pointed. "There are people on that bridge! Looks like they have some sort of barricade on the west end. I saw at least two rifles."

David trained his scope on the approach to the area Bree indicated. Another group of people, armed with bats and clubs, were running toward the barricade, and as they got closer, they began to yell and wave their weapons over their heads.

The group behind the barricade watched intently, and didn't seem to notice the canoes at first. Suddenly, four shots rang out from the west end, and the attackers turned and ran.

David and Bree both looked up as they went under the bridge. The last sight they saw before the view was cut off by the bridge was faces staring down at them.

"They saw us! Paddle!" David yelled.

They emerged into the sunlight once more, and looking back, saw a few men standing there at the railing, watching them. One shook his fist, and shouted, "Just keep going, straight on out of town!"

David waved at him and nodded, and the four took a deep breath, wondering what else they would encounter before they left Tulsa behind.

"That was I-244, which along that stretch is also Highway 75, and crosses the river just west of downtown. The 21st Street bridge is next," David called out. "It's in an area with a lot of homes and some schools and businesses."

Bree's nerves were on edge. She was usually a calm, deliberate sort of person, but worrying about being the target of possible violence was wearing on her. She took several deep breaths, said a quick prayer, and focused on watching ahead through her scope.

The 21st Street bridge was narrower by quite a lot. It was blocked off on both ends by cars and pickups, but no guards stood watch. Bree let out a sigh of relief when they passed safely under it.

It seemed as if only minutes had passed before Bree noticed another bridge, and they could all hear the sound of falling water. Price yelled to get Rian's attention, and when Rian looked back, he frantically waved, signaling for him to land on the east side of the river.

Once both canoes were stopped on the sandy bank, they got out, grabbed their packs, and as quickly as they could, carried the canoes as far as possible past the low-water dam. They were prevented from going further on foot by scrubby plants that were too thick to walk through. *Besides,* Bree thought, *that looks like a good place for encountering snakes, if there are any out this late in the year.*

They lowered the canoes, pushing them partway into the water, and letting David and Bree get in. Rian and Price pushed them off, jumping in just before the river caught them in its current again.

The relief they felt at being past the "Drowning Machine" was palpable. There was a long stretch of river and they passed a handful of men fishing, but the men never glanced up.

"Next is the I-44 bridge, which is about three miles, I think. It's at about 51st Street. The car dealership where Jen worked is near there, and the Pepsi bottling plant. Both sides of the bridge have businesses, and both sides have some homes nearby. There may be some people on that bridge."

There were, indeed, people on the bridge. Guards stood with rifles at each end, but in the middle, several people were fishing. A couple of them waved and smiled when they noticed the canoes. The guards saw them, but were more focused on watching the highway. No one said a word or tried to stop them.

"Close it up, Rian!" Price called to the canoe that was lagging behind. Rian paddled faster, and soon caught up to within hearing distance.

David called out to them, "Next is an area known as Tulsa Hills. It's got a lot of restaurants and shopping, plus medical offices. There are houses back behind the shopping center; Jen's boss lived back there. I have no idea what to expect, so stay alert."

The 71st Street bridge was long; the only people they spotted were manning a blockade of the east end. One of them raised what looked like an AR15 and followed the canoes with the barrel until he couldn't see them anymore.

David looked a little angry. "I'm an *idiot*. I forgot a couple of bridges. There's the old bridge in Jenks, with the new one right beside it. I have no idea what we'll run into there. Jenks grew really fast, and the area around the bridges is restaurants and retail stores. A lot of people who live there are well off, but some aren't. Those bridges aren't far past the Creek Turnpike bridge. Dang, I wish this was over."

The Creek Turnpike bridge was unoccupied, strangely enough. The travelers would never learn an answer to the question of why nobody was around, but at that moment, they had no time to ponder it. They would be in Jenks shortly, and they had to stay alert.

The old bridge just stood there, but the new one had been blocked by cars parked sideways across the lanes. There was a manned barricade at each end, facing each other as though to keep their own townspeople from crossing. Most of the people were armed and not trying to hide the fact.

One man ran out, about a third of the way from the east side, and yelled down to them. "Keep moving if you know what's good for you. No strangers welcome here! Just keep going."

"So much for the town that prided itself on friendliness and handling problems without the threat of violence," David said dryly, as Rian pulled their canoe up even with Price and Bree's

"So, what's next?" Bree asked. "I've enjoyed about all of this I can stand."

"The river is going to start making big turns, but we still have the bridge in Bixby to go under," David called to her.

"We've been lucky so far, but don't let that lull you into thinking there's no danger," Rian warned. "Nothing is sure in this new world, except that when we least expect trouble, *splat!* It'll slap us right in the face."

Chapter Twenty-Seven – November 25-26
Northeastern Oklahoma

David and Rian followed the other canoe, staying close behind and slightly to the left. Their luck so far hadn't, as Rian predicted, caused them to relax or become less vigilant; on the contrary, it had made them even more nervous about the remaining bridges. Luck like they'd had couldn't hold, and they dreaded finding out just how it would change.

"Just think, Bree. If we had a car, we'd only be a couple of hours away from the end of this trip. But if we had a car, we probably wouldn't be *on* this trip in the first place," Price mused.

"Price, your feeble attempts at being a philosopher aren't quite making the cut. I wish we did have a car. I'd drive somewhere with hot running water and take a long shower. I feel grubby, and my clothes will probably stand up on their own when I take them off."

"Yeah, I hear ya. There's being dirty, then there's being nasty-dirty, and I think we're all way past that point. I can't even smell the stink anymore; my nose has gotten used to it, but I know it's still there."

They saw few people, and that made Price curious. "Where do you think all the people are? Everywhere we've been, people are scarce. They can't all have gone somewhere else."

Bree thought for a moment, then answered. "I think that a lot more people have seen us than we have seen. If I was in a city, I sure wouldn't be out and about if I could help it. I bet there are people in the buildings and in some of the houses. They probably only come out to find food. It's dangerous to be out where others can see you."

"How many do you think have died?" Price asked softly.

"Too many. Now stop talking and keep paddling."

The bridge in Bixby came into view, and it looked, at first glance, to be deserted. As they got closer, though, they could see men guarding the east end.

As soon as the men saw the canoes, that end of the bridge seemed to be lined with rifles pointed in their direction.

"Pull out!" one of the men shouted down at them. "Our side! Stop, and keep your hands where we can see them!" he ordered.

Rian looked at the others, nodded, and began paddling toward the east bank. They really had no choice but to obey.

The man scrambled down from the bridge and met them as they sat in the canoes, waiting. He looked them over, saw the rifles in the canoes, and nodded.

"You traveling through, or hoping to stay?" he demanded.

"We're on our way Muskogee to check on our parents," David answered before anyone else could. "We're not looking to cause any trouble, just trying to get home."

"Well, in that case, we may let you keep going. Just be sure you do. We're just checking, and not letting outsiders come in."

"How? Some of the other bridges aren't even guarded, except by homeless people who throw rocks."

"We aren't trying to guard the whole city, just our little part of it. We have people all around this area, and we're keeping the riffraff out. We don't need any more problems than we've already got."

"May we go now? I promise we aren't here to start trouble. We just need to go help our folks."

"You aren't all related. Who are you, really?"

Price looked the man right in the eye. "That's my brother, and this is my girlfriend. That other guy is a good friend of the family. He's an Army veteran, too, so don't be thinking he's here illegally."

The man looked at Rian. "Veteran, huh?" he said skeptically.

Rian responded quietly. "Army Ranger, Iraq and Afghanistan, two tours. Born in Texas. I was home on leave when things fell apart."

The man noted the lack of an accent that a recent immigrant would surely have, and could sense the truth when he heard it.

"Okay. Just don't try to stop along here anywhere. We got a former Marine sniper who won't take kindly to it if he sees you do anything suspicious. Good luck to you."

With that, the man turned and walked away.

"I don't like something about this," Rian muttered.

"What's the problem? They're letting us go." Bree gave him a look that said he was crazy.

"I don't know. Maybe I'm just paranoid, but things are going entirely too well, and something just seems off about this."

Price and David looked at each other, and then at Rian. "We agree that this is pretty much too good to be true." David insisted. "How are they guarding the 'area'? There are too many ways in and out of this neighborhood, too many places to hide, for them to be able to control who comes and goes. Something's fishy."

Bree's eyes grew large, and her voice was sharp. "You're all nuts. We should be glad we haven't been shot at or captured by some gang of thugs, but you guys can't see the good in this. You have to try to find something negative, something to worry about. What's the next bridge?"

"I'm not really sure. We'll be getting out of the Tulsa metro area and into the country for a while. I truly hope you're right, Little Miss Sunshine. I *truly* do, but I'm not going to let down my guard just because you think it's all gonna be okay."

Bree scowled at him, and they shoved the canoes off the sand and headed out, looking back to see a man with a rifle tracking them.

Not long after, the river made a sudden v-shaped turn from southeast to northeast, passing through farmland. A thick band of trees on the east side looked appealing as a spot to camp.

Rian patrolled the immediate area while the others ate, then David took the watch so Rian could eat. Bree discovered that she had left the bag Missy had given her in the canoe, and went to get it.

Rian and Price talked about the day and cleared the moldy leaves away so they could rest. David circled the camp once more, and returned, leaning against a tree nearby and watching the woods.

Rian got out the map, running his finger along the line that represented the river. "We're on a wide finger of land before the river curves again to the southeast. Then it angles off to due east briefly, and turns due south. I wonder how many miles we've gone so far."

Something clicked in David's brain. "Where's Bree?" he asked. "She go off to take care of 'personal matters'?"

Rian stared at him for a split second, then jumped up, grabbed his rifle, and ran through the trees. "C'mon! She should have been back a long time ago!"

Price and David caught up just as Rian stopped at the edge of the embankment. Bree was nowhere to be seen, and neither were the canoes.

David spun around and glared at his brother and Rian. "Why'd you let her go off by herself? Somebody's taken her!"

"Let's go!" Rian turned, ignoring the possibility of damage to his leg, and began running toward the east.

"Wait!" David called out. "What if they took her upstream?"

"You go that way, and I'll go downstream. Price, just pick one, and *hurry*!"

Price decided to go with David, since Rian probably didn't need him as much. Not bothering to grab their packs, and already carrying their rifles, they raced in opposite directions, hoping they'd be in time, hoping to rescue Bree and recover their canoes.

***

Bree squirmed, trying to change her uncomfortable position in the bottom of the canoe. Her hands were tied, as were her ankles, and she was gagged with a dirty rag that smelled of motor oil. She was furious, with herself for being so careless and with her abductors, one of whom was the bossy man from the bridge in Bixby.

She thought he had seemed like a decent enough fellow, since he let them pass, but she now knew that he'd been playing a

216

part. Whether the others at the bridge were involved, she had no idea.

When she'd reached down to get her bag from the canoe, an arm snaked around her waist and a hand covered her mouth; before she could put up any resistance, two men had her trussed up and helpless. They dumped her into the canoe and took off.

She hurt all over, and knew she would be bruised from the rough treatment, but she managed to put the aches out of her mind and focus on the conversation of the two men, who were laughing about how clever they'd been.

"You nailed it, buddy. They never expected us to follow them. Cutting across on bicycles, then on foot...smart plan, then the gal walked right into it."

"Yeah. I didn't expect that little bonus. I just wanted out of town and away from those fools. They think they can keep that area safe from marauders, but there's no way, and they weren't about to let us leave. Hendrix said that nobody could leave who knew their 'security setup'. Ha! Nothing secure about it. We'll be better off in Arkansas, and these canoes will get us there just fine."

The men were so busy talking that they weren't watching the river. The canoe Bree was in ran into a shallow area, grounding itself on the wet sand. The jolt when they stopped added to her bruises, but she forced herself to ignore the pain and keep listening; however, what she heard next was a real surprise.

The man who had talked to them at the bridge got out of the canoe and was trying to shove it back into the water when a shot rang out. His lifeless body fell lengthwise into the canoe, pinning Bree and blocking what little she had been able to see.

Another shot, then a third, and Bree heard splashing, a grunt, then silence. Fear would have paralyzed her if she hadn't already been unable to move.

With a heave, Rian lifted the body off the canoe, and dragged it across the sand. He returned, and gently lifted Bree to a sitting position. He untied the gag, then her wrists, and finally her ankles. He was wet all over, and began to shiver.

"Hey, doc. You okay?" he asked.

"Yeah, I guess so. Where's the other canoe?"

"Behind you. I had to swim out and get it after I shot the other scumbag. What happened?"

"I went to get the bag of fruit out of the canoe, and they jumped me. They were after the canoes, but called me 'a little bonus.' From what I could tell, they wanted out of Tulsa, but whoever was running things on that bridge wouldn't allow anyone to leave. They saw our canoes as a golden opportunity. Where are David and Price?"

"We didn't know for sure which way you went, so they took off upstream. I'm sure they'll be back when they don't see you on the river anywhere. You think you could paddle one of the canoes upstream to find them?"

"No, I don't think so, and I'm afraid if we go, we might miss them somehow. Can we just stay here and wait for them?"

Rian thought for a moment, then nodded. "I'll go up the bank and see if I can see them. I won't go far, I promise. Just wait here."

Rian picked up his rifle and climbed the steep bank. The farms there were fairly flat, but in the trees where they had stopped, it was hard to see very far. There was no sign of the brothers anywhere, so he called down to Bree that he would wait a while, then look again.

The fifth time he scoped the area, he saw movement in the distance. Two shapes gradually became David and Price, and Rian waved at them. They returned the wave, and began to run.

Chapter Twenty-Eight – November 26
Southeastern Oklahoma

Brian turned the Bobcat into the clearing and dropped off one of the planters. When he looked up, Val was waving frantically and motioning for him to cut the engine. Silence descended, and Val rushed over to him.

"Tanner says they've sighted some people coming from the north on our road. I hope that if they heard the Bobcat, they couldn't tell what direction the sound was coming from. We need to head that way, and fast!"

Brian grabbed his rifle and followed the people who had already started north, staying in the trees, ready to take cover.

Tanner and Shane had been on guard a little over a mile north of the lodge, hidden right at the edge of the trees. Vince and Sarah had taken the western approach, and Ian was with Jen on the road that led to Kanichi Springs.

Shane had spotted movement up the road, and told Tanner to radio the others. It looked like four people, all carrying packs and rifles; however, the rifles were all slung on their backs. *That's not too smart these days, but it'll make our job easier.*

"How do you want to handle this?" Shane asked. "Wait until they get closer? I think we can handle this bunch; there's only four of them."

"And two of us," Tanner reminded him.

"Yeah, but I'm worth five," Shane teased.

"We'll stop them, and try to stall until our people get here. A show of force may be enough to turn them around, without having to break any heads. We need to see if they're alone, or advance scouts for a larger group."

"True. And here I was, ready to practice some moves," Shane grinned.

"I think it's two men and two women." Tanner raised his rifle to look through the scope. "Yep. Looks like two couples., and they're holding hands."

They watched from the trees as the foursome approached. The couples seemed too casual, too carefree to Tanner, but maybe they hadn't seen what he had seen. The dangers of life during the collapse didn't seem to touch everyone, or else they were just too dumb to know that roads and a relaxed attitude were for people who wanted to die.

"I think I hear leaves crackling across the road. Yeah, look over there," Shane pointed. "That's our people. Just in time."

Tanner stepped out into the road, and it was a few seconds before the strangers noticed him. He just stared with a neutral expression, until one of them spoke first.

"Uh, we aren't trespassing, are we? We don't mean anyone any harm," one of the men said.

Tanner raked them with his gaze. "Looks like some of you are wearing parts of NERC uniforms. You deserters?"

"Yes, sir, we are. We just couldn't keep ignoring what we believe as Americans. Putting other Americans in camps is just wrong," the other man said as he stepped forward.

"Where you headed?" Tanner demanded.

"Kanichi Springs. There're some empty houses there and we thought we might hole up in one," the second man answered.

Sarah came out of the trees and crossed to where Tanner stood. She spoke only loud enough for him to hear. "Tanner, those two in the front are the two I heard talking about leaving NERC. I think other two are probably the Bill and Cinda I heard mentioned. They may be legit, but we can't take on any more responsibility for feeding people. How will they make it through the winter?"

Tanner glanced at her. "Good point. Where's Erin?"

Sarah gestured for Erin to join them. She came down from her spot in the trees with a questioning look.

"They want to stay in Kanichi Springs," Tanner explained. "But they don't seem to have much in the way of supplies. Ken and Terri have their hands full as it is, and I don't see how these folks will stay alive all winter."

Erin turned and looked the strangers over. "Why Kanichi Springs? You know anybody there?"

"No, not really," the first man said.

"Then why do you think you can survive there without food and access to water?" Erin's eyes narrowed.

Tanner stepped forward, looking at the two in the back. "Well, Bill and Cinda," he bluffed. "Did you know they're talking about you on the NERC radios? All four of you, mentioned by name, and they have plans for you once you're in custody."

"Now, listen here!" the one they thought must be Cinda snarled. "You'll let us pass and mind your own business, or we'll go back to NERC and tell them about you and your friends in the tunnel!"

Silence fell, then Tanner stepped toward them, eyes narrowed. "What did you say?" he asked in a deadly voice.

"Uh, she's just upset. We don't know anything. Nothing at all," the second man said, giving his girlfriend a dirty look. "We can hunt and fish, so we won't be needing any help from anyone."

"You wouldn't dare go back to NERC. We hear they're punishing deserters now with beatings and starvation rations. Then they send them to Idaho or Utah, where the civilians fight back. You won't get a chance to tell them anything once they catch you."

"You have no right to stop us! You don't own that town, and we need a place to stay!" the woman cried.

Tanner raised his voice. "Group! Cover them! If one of them tries anything, you know what to do." Then he pulled Erin, Sarah, and Shane back out of earshot.

"Well, what now?" he asked.

"We can't let them go to town. It's going to be nearly impossible to feed the people who are already there. These people may plan to provide their own food, but when they get snowed in and hungry, they'll take food from our friends," Shane replied.

"I agree. We need to get rid of them, but how?" Sarah shrugged. "We also need to talk to our friends in the tunnel. Why didn't they *tell* us they'd had visitors?"

Erin held up a hand. "I have an idea. It's risky, but I say we tie them up and blindfold them, put them in the back of one of the

221

pickups, and take them somewhere. Use the backroads, make lots of turns, and leave them out in the middle of nowhere. If they think they can live off the land, they're welcome to try, but not in Kanichi Springs. I didn't like that one woman's attitude, and I have a bad feeling she won't make a good neighbor."

Tanner glanced at Shane. "You remember that trip we took east, just into Arkansas? We can tell them that if we ever see them around here again, we'll kill them, and drop them off over that way."

"It's okay with me. We'll have them so turned around, they won't know what direction to go," Shane grinned. "And I vote we put a gag in that one gal's mouth."

Sarah wasn't happy with the plan. "I don't like the idea of anyone going very far from the lodge with only one vehicle. What if something happens, some kind of mechanical trouble?"

"Do we really want to risk two vehicles, though? Two will make more noise, draw more attention, and use more gas," Shane argued.

"Okay. One vehicle, but full packs with whatever gear necessary to make it back home if the truck breaks down. And only the most fit will be going," Tanner stated, looking at Erin for confirmation.

"Sounds good. Let's get these people trussed up. I don't want them to see any more group members, either. They know too much already, and don't need to have any clue how many of us there are."

"I'd like to take Vince and Shane, if that's agreeable. Ian, too, if you think we need four," Tanner suggested.

Erin grinned. "Good choices, and I'll leave the number up to you."

"We have time to get there if we leave now, but there's no way we can get back tonight. We can plan an overnighter, or wait until morning," Shane added.

"You guys need to figure that out. I know you're tired from working all morning, but I also hate to keep those four around any longer than we have to. Someone will have to guard them if you wait until morning." Erin obviously wasn't sure which was better. "As I said, you guys decide."

Tanner turned to his best friend. "Okay, Shane. First order of business, restrain them. That's going to be right up your alley."

***

They decided that Ian would stay at the lodge, because without him, they wouldn't have enough people to stand guard. A decision was also made to leave right away, dump the NERC deserters, then travel several miles back toward the lodge before stopping overnight. Where they stopped would be based on how much daylight was left, since driving with lights on would make them a target. They were sure they could find a suitable location to camp, and all three men were looking forward to another chance to get out of the caves for a while.

Shane and Tanner got the prisoners tied up and blindfolded, then several of the men helped load them into the bed of Tanner's pickup, laying them in like four logs. All four NERCs decided to loudly protest this treatment, so all four were quickly gagged. Erin and Jen went back to the cache cavern to gather what the guys would need.

"Here are your packs." Erin handed off the two she was carrying. "And these radios are all fully charged. They won't work until you get closer, but I'll feel better knowing you have them. We'll expect you back by lunchtime tomorrow, but I put in plenty of food in case something happens to delay you."

Tanner pulled her into his arms and kissed her. "We'll be careful. I have important people to come home to," he murmured, looking into her eyes.

Shane bent down and picked Jen up, bringing her petite body into a bear hug. He gave her a deep, hard kiss right in front of her father, and whispered, "I love you, Jen."

She held his face in her hands, and smiled. "You better come back in one piece, buster. I love you, too."

***

Tanner drove down twisting dirt roads, made U-turns, and tried to keep the NERCs in the back of the truck from being able to tell what general direction they were going. As a result, it took nearly twice as long to make the trip as it would have had they been able to travel in a direct path on paved roads.

Crossing into Arkansas, they looked for somewhere far from any homesteads to drop off their passengers. Angling southeast, Tanner took off onto some logging trails deep in the forest, and found a clearing where they could turn around. He drove the truck in tight circles, trying to further confuse their captives, and finally stopped. The three friends piled out, and unloaded their cargo, putting three of the captives together, and one across the clearing.

The woman they separated from the group was the quieter of the two women. Vince and Shane propped her against a pine tree in a sitting position. Tanner removed her blindfold and took the gag out of her mouth, then knelt in front of her.

"Listen very carefully. We're going to untie your hands and leave you here. You'll have to untie your own feet and then go help your friends. We're keeping your weapons, because we don't believe you can be trusted not to hurt others when you get hungry this winter, but we're leaving your packs.

"Let me be clear on this: if we *ever* see any of you near Kanichi Springs again, you will be shot on sight. There were a lot more people in the woods this morning than you saw, but they all saw *you*. Come back to our area, and we will assume you have the intent to harm us and our friends. Believe me when I say this, because if you come back, you're bought and paid for."

The woman glared at him. "What right do you have to tell anyone where they can live? We didn't harm you, and you're leaving us out here defenseless and with no way to hunt for food."

"What right did NERC have to harass us, making us leave our homes and hide out in the forest? What right do you have to move into someone else's home like it's yours? And you may think you can live on fish and venison, but when the weather gets cold and there's snow on the ground, you'll run out of food. That's when you'll become a real danger to us and our friends.

"*We* prepared for the future. *We* learned to grow our own food and preserve it, and we don't have enough to share, but you would expect us to. It was apparent from your friend's attitude that she thinks she's entitled to do as she pleases. If you want the truth, *she's* the reason you're out here. Threatening us with exposure to NERC was a serious tactical error. Good luck to you, but stay away from Kanichi Springs."

Tanner untied her hands, and jumped into the truck with his friends, driving away as fast as the dirt track would allow.

***

"We're probably far enough away from them now to start looking for a likely place to camp tonight," Vince suggested.

"Yeah, I know. I'm just keyed up pretty tight about this. I don't know if we did the right thing or not," Tanner admitted. "The only one of them that seemed to be a troublemaker was the one woman, but who knows if the others felt the same way? We may have really condemned them to death. But if we let them stay, how would we ever be able to relax around them?"

"We wouldn't. You know, we like to think of ourselves as good guys, but there are times when the lines get a little blurred," Shane added. "Erin has taken in almost everyone from the area. There's got to be a limit somewhere, and these folks were strangers who wanted to just move in. I see a difference in them and someone like Noah or Clint, who earned our trust and respect."

"That one woman, Cindy or Cinda – whatever – now *she* seemed to be one who thinks that she should get to do as she wants, no matter who gets stepped on," Vince said. "No, I wouldn't want her anywhere around, because she's trouble."

"There," Tanner interrupted, pointing to a faint trail into the trees. "Wanna see what's up there? I'm ready for some grub, even if it is an MRE."

"Go for it," Shane encouraged. "Let us out, and we'll brush up the weeds and smooth out our tracks, just in case."

Tanner stopped to let Vince and Shane get out, then continued until the track ended. There was barely room to turn the pickup around, but he managed to do it, putting it out of sight from the road, yet ready to take off if the need arose.

"Looks like a clear night," Vince commented, glancing at the sky as he and Shane rejoined Tanner.

Tanner nodded. "Yeah, but it's going to be cold. Erin put a tent and three sleeping bags in the back seat. We better get set up before dark."

Shane pulled the tent out and glanced at the label that was still attached. "Hey, this is brand new, and it's a pop-up. Nice."

"You think we need to stand guard tonight?" Vince asked.

"Yes, I do. We didn't see a soul after we entered this part of the forest, but that doesn't mean nobody saw us," Tanner insisted. "I'd hate to have to go back and face Jen if I let anything happen to Shane," he teased.

"Huh," Shane snorted. "I'll be protecting you because I couldn't stand to see Erin cry."

Vince grinned. "I don't have anyone committed to waiting for me at home, but there's been progress with Lydia."

"Really? Why do you say that?" Shane asked.

"Well, the last time I went to take supplies, I didn't have to ask her to walk down to the tunnel with me. She looked really happy to see me, and just got up and joined me when I started to leave Ernie's house. I think she's interested, but doesn't know it yet."

"I'm glad for you, Vince. She's a wonderful lady, and we're all hoping that you two get together," Tanner told him.

"Hey! *All*? Who else knows about this? I thought we were keeping it a secret." Vince looked embarrassed.

"Vince, people just figured it out. If you saw your face when you come back and give a report on the folks in town…well, I'll just say that you light up and are more enthusiastic when you talk about Lydia than you are when you talk about Ken and Terri or Chief Johnson's widow. I didn't tell anyone, I promise, but your face did," Shane assured him.

"Well, I guess I don't mind if people at the lodge know, but not people in town. Somebody might say something; I think she'd go right back into her shell if she felt rushed."

***

Shane took the last watch, practiced moving silently when he circled the camp, then leaned against a tree, being perfectly still, in between circuits. Just before sunup, he heard a rustling in the leaves, like something large was moving in their direction. As whatever it was got closer, he could hear a sniffing sound.

Erin had included three flashlights in their supplies, and one of them was large and powerful, really more of a spotlight. Shane slipped around the truck, putting it between himself and whatever was out there, and balancing the spotlight on the hood, pointed it toward the sounds he could still hear. Raising his rifle, he reached over and flipped the switch. A blinding beam illuminated an adult black bear, nosing and prodding the side of the tent where Vince and Tanner slept.

Shane took careful aim and pulled the trigger. The bear roared in anger, looking at Shane and rising to its full height. Shane shot again, and the bear scrambled away, crashing through the forest. Silence fell, then Shane heard the death moan.

"What the devil?" Tanner shouted as he emerged from the tent, rifle in hand. "Shane, what is it?"

Vince joined Tanner in staring at Shane. Both had been sound asleep when the light and the shooting started. Shane pointed toward the north.

"Bear," was all he said.

"Big one?" Vince asked.

"Yeah. Biggest one I've seen." Shane smiled. "He was sniffing around the tent, maybe looking for a meal before settling in for the winter. You guys must smell like breakfast."

"Well, I'm glad you interrupted his plans. We might as well stay up now. I'd never get back to sleep after being startled like that," Tanner griped. "That light has to be the brightest one ever created. If there's anyone around, between the light and the shots, they know we're here."

"Sorry. Seemed like a good idea at the time," Shane muttered. "The bear was really big, and it was actually touching the tent when I shot it."

"Okay. I'm just grouchy when I wake up to shots fired. Let's eat and pack up. It'll be daylight soon." Tanner dug into his pack and pulled out an MRE. "Ah, my favorite, 'Sole of Boot Stew'."

Vince cleared his throat. "Even eaten bear meat?"

Shane and Tanner looked at him, realization dawning. "Bear meat?" Shane grinned. "We better get him loaded up. We can butcher him back at the McNeil place."

By the time they finished eating and got the tent and sleeping bags packed up, there was enough light to track the bear. They found him about fifty yards north of their camp, and dragged him to the truck. Tanner handed Shane the keys, and raised an eyebrow at him.

"You get to take the wheel. That's for waking us up so rudely this morning."

"You'd rather I let a bear claw his way into the tent?" Shane joked. "I could have just jumped in the truck, and lived to tell everyone how bravely you died."

"Go on, doofus. Get us home in one piece," Tanner laughed. "I'd have liked to sleep a little longer, but being a meal for a bear isn't on my bucket list."

Chapter Twenty-Nine – November 26-27
Southeastern Oklahoma

Tanner, Vince, and Shane arrived back at the McNeil home and parked the pickup in the trees beyond the house. Talako had a large metal butchering table beside the storage shed, and they skinned and butchered the bear, saving the fat to render. After loading up as much as they could carry, they walked through the trees to the north cave entrance, surprised that there were no guards posted there. As they passed the cabana cavern, they could hear cries, moans, and calls, a cacophony of voices, all ringing with a sense of urgency.

Erin was waiting when they entered the cache cavern on the way to see what the ruckus was about. She stopped them, holding up a hand to forbid them from going further.

"You can't go into the sleeping cavern. Angie's orders. We've made it into a clinic and the sick are isolated there."

"Who's sick? What's going on? Tanner demanded.

"Angie isn't sure if it's a virus or food poisoning, but several people have vomiting and diarrhea. It's been awful. Just in case it's infectious, you need to stay away. We don't have enough healthy people to take care of standing guard now, and if *you* three get sick, we're going to be in real trouble."

"Jen! Where's Jen?" Shane insisted, as he tried to push past Erin. Tanner stopped him, pulling him back.

"Shane, Jen isn't sick, at least not yet, but she's been helping Angie. They're taking precautions; gloves, masks, protective tops, frequent washing up, but you *can't see* her. I'm sorry, but we need you to help with other things,"

Tanner looked very worried. "Tell us who all is sick."

"The children, all of them except Ford; BJ, Gus, Will, Ian, Sarah, Noah, Claire." Erin counted them off on her fingers, then looked into Tanner's face and added softly, "Rose, Dana, and your grandmother."

"I need to see them. I'll wear a mask, and not touch anyone or anything, but I *need* to see them," Tanner demanded.

"And I need to see Jen." Shane looked desperate.

"No, Shane. You can see her after her shift is over and she's had time to clean up, but you can't go in there. Tanner, please, don't. I know how you feel, but you shouldn't go in there. It's awful, and just about impossible not to touch vomit or worse."

"I'm going, Erin. I have to."

She looked at him for a long moment, then gave in. "Okay. We need to get you into some protective clothing. Angie has us using trash bags as tops, and so far, it's working to keep most of the projectile vomiting off our skin. You'll need the long gloves, and we'll tie old Walmart sacks on your feet. All of it has to be burned when you come out, and you can't touch anything until it's all off."

Erin cut holes in a bag for Tanner's head and arms, and helped him get ready. She tied the plastic bags over his boots, and told him again not to touch anything at all.

The stench in the cavern was almost unbearable, reeking of vomit and feces. Angie already had IV fluids dripping into the veins of four people, and was inserting a needle into Micah's arm.

When she finished, she turned to him, irritated, and said, "Who let you in here? I said *nobody* who wasn't already exposed to this could come in." She was clearly exhausted, but continued to berate Tanner as she worked, until he interrupted.

"I need to see my family. And I need to hear it from you how they're doing." Tanner spoke softly, but with determination.

Angie stopped to see to Gina and Isabelle, checking their pulses. She took a deep breath, visibly forcing herself to calm down. "Your sisters have stopped vomiting, and only have a little diarrhea now. Your grandmother...Tanner, she's not doing well. I'm about to run out of supplies, even though I stocked up on a lot of things before the collapse. I need to know what we're dealing with here, but I don't have time to figure it out. There are too many patients to take care of."

"Can I help? Tell me what to do, and after I see the rest of my family, I'll do it."

"Take a poll. Sick and not sick, ask everyone what they ate last night. We had two different choices for dinner. Ian caught several fish, but not enough for everyone, so we opened some chicken that the ladies canned. If all the sick people ate the same thing, and all of the not-sick ate the other, I think we'll have our answer. And if some of each group ate some of each food, we'll figure it's a virus, which will just have to run its course. I have no way to treat it other than trying to get fluids into those who become dehydrated. I'm pretty sure your nieces and nephews are on the mend. Your grandmother and sisters are over there." She gestured toward the far wall.

Tanner checked on his family, and found out that not touching them was much harder than he had imagined. He wanted so badly to hug his grandmother, who was barely conscious, but seemed aware of his presence. Rose and Dana were in much better shape, and were able to ask him about their children. He was glad to be able to give them encouraging news.

He went toward the opening to the cave and asked Erin to bring him a legal pad and a pencil. She ran to get them, and returned, laying them on the floor where he could pick them up without coming into contact with her. He drew a line across the page and labeled one section "Sick" and the other "Not Sick".

Since he was already in the Angie's makeshift clinic, he polled the people there first. Almost immediately, a pattern began to emerge. All of the children had eaten chicken, except, of course, Ford, who too little for solid foods. As he polled the adults, the trend continued. Rose and Dana had both eaten mostly fish, but also had a bite or two of chicken when they finished off what their children had not eaten.

He stepped to the cavern entrance and let Erin, who was wearing gloves, remove the protective items he wore, then he got busy locating and questioning those who hadn't gotten sick. All of them had eaten the fish. Tanner made a point of asking them if they had eaten even a little of the chicken, and none had.

He wrote each response on his list, then took it to the cavern entrance and laid it to down for Angie to pick up. She glanced over it, and knew immediately that the chicken was the problem.

She looked at Tanner, who was waiting for her opinion. "This explains why your sisters aren't quite as sick as the others. Tell Erin not to let anyone eat any more of that chicken. It won't even be okay to feed to the dogs. It's rare for a dog to get salmonella, which is what I suspect this is, but with dogs as valuable as these, we can't take the chance.

***

Tanner found Erin with Brian and Mac, trying to figure out how to guard the three cave entrances with the few people who were still upright. He pulled her aside and told her what he and Angie had discovered. Her face went white.

"Then it's my fault. I've made our friends sick," she said shakily.

"Erin, you can't blame yourself for this. Did you do the canning all by yourself, or did some of the others help?"

"The chicken was in the freezer. I bought it when it was on sale, and froze it, planning to can it later when I'd learned more about canning. Several of us helped with it. I don't remember exactly who, but it was a group effort. But Tanner, I taught them how to can, so it doesn't matter who did it. I'm responsible."

"No, you're not, not any more than a someone who taught a kid to drive is responsible when the kid doesn't obey the rules and has a wreck. People make mistakes, and someone made some type of mistake on this, but it could have been any of the ladies who helped. You can't take everything on yourself, sweetheart."

She stood there, and he took her into his arms, stroking her back and reassuring her, until she finally nodded.

"We are going to be short of meat soon, I'm afraid."

Tanner stared at her, then remembered. "Oh, no, we won't. Shane killed a black bear that was snooping around our camp. We just need to send someone to get the rest of it from my grandparents' house. We couldn't carry it all in our small packs, and needed our hands free in case of trouble."

"Great. There's some room in the freezer now, since we've eaten so much of our stash. What should we do with the rest of the chicken? Throw it away?" Erin wondered.

Tanner shook his head. "Yes. We probably need to bury it. Angie said it wasn't even fit for the dogs. They aren't always affected by the same things we are, and but they *are* important members of the group. We need to make very sure that nobody eats any, even accidently. How much of it is left?"

"Maybe twenty jars still in the cache cavern. That bear meat is going to make things a lot easier for getting through the winter. I'll have to learn how to cook it, but there's a book of wild game recipes in the cache cavern. The Lord works in mysterious ways, doesn't He? He provided meat before we even realized we needed it. I'll have to see about canning some of it, because I doubt it will all fit in the freezer. We'll have to boil the jars the chicken was in, to be sure they're safe to use. I'd say to throw them away, but we need all we have."

Tanner looked thoughtful. "What if we can find some jars in town? There may have been some ladies there who canned. Some of the guys were talking a while back about looking for another canner, too, and if there's a canner, there's probably jars."

"That'll help next year, but I think that in the meantime, we're going to have to cut down even further on serving sizes of the fruits and vegetables I canned, and it'll be months before we have fresh veggies again. All of us are losing weight, but maybe now we'll be able to continue to help our friends in town. Thank the Lord, we didn't send any of those jars of chicken to them."

"Would cooking it again at high heat kill the germs in it?" Tanner asked.

"I have no idea, but I've always heard that you have to get rid of it. I don't think we should risk eating any of it," Erin answered, looking grim. "I wish I knew what went wrong. The jars were sealed. Maybe we didn't keep the pressure in the canner up, or leave the jars in there long enough. I can tell you this: from now on, I'll be monitoring the process much more closely."

Angie joined them, still drying her hands on a towel. "Almost everyone is past the worst part of this. Do we have bleach in the cache cavern? I think we need to spray the floor of the cave and everything we've used needs to be disinfected. The sheets will need to be boiled or bleached, maybe both. Basically, anything that got any body fluids on it needs to be handled carefully and thoroughly sanitized. That may be overkill, but I think we need to do it."

"Will we ever be able to get the stench out of the cavern? It smells putrid in there." Tanner grimaced.

"We'll all need to sleep elsewhere for a while. I'm glad we have the new cavern, because I particularly do *not* want the smaller children or the older folks coming into the nasty cavern for a long time. Almost all of us were in the new cavern, asleep, when the vomiting started. Fortunately, nobody threw up in there. As soon as BJ and Sarah ran out of there retching, Erin woke everyone and told them if they felt sick at their stomachs, to move to the other cavern. She put several buckets in there, too. Then she called me on the radio and I came right over. Her quick thinking may have saved some lives, and certainly kept the new cavern from becoming contaminated."

"I believe it's time we moved some of us back into the lodge." Erin pushed a strand of auburn hair back from her face. "NERC probably won't send anyone back here, and according to what Mac heard on the radio yesterday evening, that little organization is falling apart. I doubt that we need to worry about them anymore. What do you think, Tanner?"

"I think you're right. We know that at least four of the guards from Stigler are, uh, *missing* and that has to make them shorthanded. Let's move the healthy folks to the lodge, and as the sick people improve enough, we'll move them back to the new cavern, where it'll be cleaner and smell better.

"I also have a solution to the guard shortage. We've been sending two humans and one dog to each entrance. How about we sent one human and two dogs? Moxie's still little, so we'll put her with Blitz and continue her training, but we can put two mutts on each of the three cave entrances."

"That's a great idea. With the alarm system, it should work out okay. And Angie, I never did answer your question. Uncle Ernie stored crystalized bleach, like you'd use in a swimming pool. It stores a lot longer than liquid bleach. I also have a couple of garden sprayers that we can use."

Angie nodded. "We'll have to wait until we can move everyone out of there. They don't need to breathe that chlorine. Tanner, there's something else. I'm very concerned about your grandmother. At her age, and being generally frail, she doesn't seem to be improving as much as I'd like. I've done everything I know to do, and right now, that consists of trying to keep her hydrated. She hasn't vomited in a few hours, but she still has diarrhea, and she's very weak."

"Does Grandfather know?"

"Yes. I let him come in once we knew it wasn't a virus. He hasn't left her side. Val brought him a chair so he could sit with her. He's holding her hand and talking to her, but I think…well, I think that you should spend some time with them. Rose and Dana are improving and were sitting up when I left the cavern. I would say that all of you should visit her."

***

Julia's skin looked almost gray as she lay on a mattress on the floor of the cavern. Her already prominent cheekbones jutted out over sunken cheeks, and for the first time that Tanner could remember, her brown eyes were not sparkling. They seemed to have settled back into her head, and dark circles ringed them.

He'd brought in more chairs, so Rose and Dana could sit with her. Both of them were too weak to stand for long, but they wanted to be with their grandmother. John stood behind Dana's chair, his hands resting gently on her shoulders.

At Dana's request, Tanner brought the older grandsons for a visit. Zeke and Tucker stayed, quietly sitting at the side of the mattress Julia lay on, while Isabelle, Gina, and little Wyatt were better, but still too weak to get up. John had decided that the older boys could handle the truth, and he quietly told them that there was a possibility that Nana, as they called her, might not survive the illness.

Talako slid off the chair and lowered himself to the floor of the cavern, still holding his wife's hand, even when she whispered, "I'm tired," and closed her eyes. Angie checked on her as often as she could while still caring for her other patients, and

235

told them to talk to her. Erin stood with Tanner, her arm around him as they waited through the long hours.

Surrounded by family, Julia lay quietly, then briefly opened her eyes as though seeing something in the distance, smiled, and slipped away.

They buried the frail old lady in a clearing on the McNeil property. Talako said that he believed she'd want that. Gus and Mac carved a beautiful wooden cross to mark the spot, and to show their respect for her and the family.

Talako seemed to have aged as the day went on, but he spoke at the graveside in spite of his grief.

"She was a wise woman, a good and kind soul, who loved us all with every fiber of her being. She was my *chunkash anli*[1], and I will miss her, but her time here is over and I know we will meet again."

---

[1] Choctaw for "true heart"

Chapter Thirty – November 26 and 27

The Martin brothers raced toward Rian and Bree, their sibling rivalry popping up to give them added speed. Price won by twenty yards, due to David's injury. The two breathless young men jolted to a halt beside their friends.

"What happened? We heard shots," David huffed, trying to breathe and holding an arm across his abdomen.

Bree looked down at the blood on her shirt. "It was two guys from the bridge in Bixby, the one who questioned us and another one I don't remember seeing. They grabbed me, tied me up and gagged me, and took both the canoes, but Rian shot them. They said they wanted to get away from Tulsa, but their leader refused to let anyone leave."

"Well, we're glad you're okay. You wanna borrow my shirt again, maybe rinse that bloody one in the river?" Price asked.

"Yeah, maybe I can get enough dirt on it from the water to dye it so the stain doesn't show so much," Bree sighed. " Man, I hope that guy didn't have any blood-borne diseases. I sure wish I'd taken some clothes with me when I left for my brother's. I already had jeans and shirts at his place, but I didn't know the house had burned. This is the only top I brought, and I should have been better prepared."

"We need to get our packs, then we'll get you into something slightly cleaner," Price assured her. "And we thought that the biggest dangers were at bridges. Who would have guessed that we'd run into trouble way out here?"

***

Bree spread the formerly beige shirt over her pack in the bottom of the canoe. It had soaked up the color of the river, a pale rusty-brownish color, with a darker splotch on the front, but at least the majority of the blood had washed out. Rian touched the sleeve, and nodded.

"The dirt here isn't so red as it was out west, but I see what they mean by 'dirt shirt.' It really does stain the cloth, doesn't it?"

"Cotton takes the color best. Synthetics, not so much," Bree replied.

"We need to make a couple of decisions, and I'd prefer to make them before we go much further," Rian suggested. "Do we want to go through the populated areas around Muskogee, and do we want to cross another lake?"

"You're right. We need to decide well before we get there," David replied. "We got lucky at Keystone dam. If those idiots had been sober or had guns, we'd have had a bad day. We can't count on our luck holding forever."

"Let's look at the map again," Bree urged.

Rian got the map unfolded, and pointed to the river. "I think we're right here. There's that sharp curve to the northeast that we went through, and here's the oxbow I think we're on right now. The river is going to turn south soon, after a town called Haskell. Looks like we'll need to go under about six bridges before we get to the Kerr Reservoir."

"What's that?" Bree pointed at a spot on the map. "It's hard to read that tiny print upside down."

"That's Webbers Falls Reservoir, and that means another dam. Guys, we've come a long way on the water, but frankly, I'm not so sure it's wise to continue. It's fairly fast, and easy on our feet, but where there's water, there's going to be people, and that's two bodies of water in our way. I don't want to cross another lake," David insisted.

"I don't, either, but on foot, it might take a lot longer, and we'll still have some bridges to cross," Price argued. "We'll have to go around the lakes, won't we?"

"Not if we get off the river soon enough. If we get off before Muskogee, there's only one bridge shown on the map," Rian scratched his head. "Look, there are hazards no matter what we decide, and there's really no way to know which would be better, because the variables are too numerous. We can't possibly know what's around the next corner or on the next bridge. We have no way to predict any of this. It's just that, on the water, we're exposed and there's nowhere to hide. On land, we can at least take cover."

Bree held her hand up to stop the argument. "I say we stay on the river until we're almost to Muskogee, then we take off on foot. We stay alert, try to stay off roads and away from populated areas, and we keep moving. I think we could be there in a couple of days, if we push ourselves. I lost count of what day it is a while back, but it must be nearly December, and I don't like the idea of being without shelter. The days are getting shorter, too, and we need to get where we're going."

"I say we stay on the water until we get to the Kerr Reservoir's south end, then go on foot," Price shot back.

"I'm with Bree," Rian stated flatly.

"Sorry, bro. So am I," David added.

Price shook his head in disgust and stepped into the canoe. "Then, let's go. I think it's a mistake, but we don't need to waste any more time talking about it."

***

Without rain for the past several days, the river was lower than it had been at any point so far in their journey. It became a challenge to avoid sandbars and stretches where the water was only a few inches deep. Finally, Rian signaled for them to pull up on the south side of the river.

"This is it, I'm afraid. Muskogee is just a short distance away, and it looks like, from the number of roads on the map, if we go any further, when we leave the river we'll be walking into populated areas."

"Okay. Let's put the canoes up on the bank, and hide them a little, just in case we need them for a hasty retreat," Price suggested. "I guess the river being so low makes all of you right and me wrong, anyway."

"Price, we didn't know the river would drop like that. It's just that the rain stopped, and I'm glad it did. It would be miserable to have to make this trip wet and cold," Bree said. "It isn't a matter of who's right and who's wrong. It's a matter of practicality. Even if we had all voted to go the whole way by canoe, it's not working out for us. Do you still think we should go by water even though it's too shallow for the canoes?"

"No. I guess not. Well, we've been sitting around on our butts long enough. Let's get some exercise. I'll take point. We all need to keep our eyes moving and be aware of our surroundings."

Price led the way, trying to stay in wooded areas as much as possible, but sometimes, they had no choice but to cross open fields. They saw only a very few people. Those few watched them until they were out of sight, but nobody shot at them or tried to stop them.

"What's that?" David asked, pointing to the east. "Looks like a racetrack."

Rian raised his rifle and peered through the scope. "Yeah, it does. I think that's a training or breeding facility for racehorses. I sure wish we had horses right now."

"If wishes were horses...we'd be there already," Price added. "Let's move a little toward the west, and stay further back in the trees. There may be people around here who object to trespassers."

Price set a fast pace in spite of the need to be watchful. By the time the sun began to sink in the west, they had covered a few miles, and were almost ready to look for a place to stay the night. Their food supply was running very low, and they were all hungry and worried about what they would do when it ran out completely.

Eventually, they spotted a neighborhood of large, luxurious-looking homes, some with swimming pools. Staying in the woods had been easy until then, but they had to swing even more to the west to avoid walking right out across un-mowed yards. There was a winding creek, curving and twisting like a snake through the forest, and crossing it proved to be a challenge.

"We're well hidden here, so why don't we make camp and worry about getting across the stream in the morning. Surely there's a way to get to the other side without getting soaked," Bree suggested.

"Sounds like a plan," Rian replied. He'd been quiet most of the afternoon. Obviously, something was on his mind.

"Rian, what's bugging you, man? You seem to be a million miles away," David murmured as they searched for a spot where they could bed down.

"I'm just a little worried. What if your sister's friend says I can't stay? They'll probably take Bree, since she's a doctor, but they may not need me."

"You, me, and Price will go stay in town, on our own, but I don't think that'll be necessary. Erin's really nice, and our sister is her best friend. Erin took our parents in, so I have no doubt she'll take us and you, since you're a big part of the reason we got this far. She's like an extra big sis to us, and I'm almost positive she'll let you stay."

"Okay. I hope you're right. Anyway, I suppose worrying won't help the situation. How far do you think we are from Kanichi Springs?"

"I'm hoping we'll be there by day after tomorrow, but to tell the truth, I really don't know how long it'll take. The terrain here has a lot more hills, and I know there are some other creeks and a river we'll have to cross. Really, my answer is mostly just wishful thinking."

At Bree's suggestion, they split two MREs, using the unsanitary, but necessary, method of one person eating half the entrée, then passing it to another to finish off. Their sleep that night was miserable. A cold breeze blew across the area, scattering leaves and causing faint rustling noises, but at least the ground was dry where they stopped.

Early the next morning, they each got a few bites of one MRE. As they finished refilling the water reservoirs in their backpacks, the quiet was shattered by shouts and gunshots.

"Stay low! It sounds like it's coming from that last house we passed. Let's take a peek and see if we can tell what's going on," Rian urged.

The four friends grabbed their packs and crouched behind trees, only the tops of their heads visible over the slight rise. The shooting stopped for a minute or two, then started again. They could see that several men were shooting toward the big house, and whoever was in the house was returning fire from the upstairs windows.

"We've got to help those people!" Bree insisted.

"Which people? How do we know which side is the good guys?" Rian looked at her, watching as she realized that just because people were in the house didn't mean that they had the *right* to be there.

"I see what you mean. Which side is the side of the angels? The people outside may be the rightful owners, trying to retake their own home," Bree sighed. "This is sure a messed up world we live in these days."

"Yes, it is, and as much as I would like to help whoever the good guys are, we have to move on. This is not our fight, and we don't know enough about what's going on to risk our lives. I say we move on before someone decides to retreat in our direction." Rian started inching back down the slope.

"Too late, buddy. Looks like the guys in the house have won the day, and all the outside shooters are headed right toward us. We need to hide, and quick!" David called as he headed toward the creek.

"No, David! We need to move perpendicular to their path. C'mon!" Rian led the group west, further into the trees. They ran about a hundred yards, and found a suitable spot to hunker down.

"Well, that was interesting. Unfortunately, from the sound of it, they continued south," Rian moaned.

"And *we're* headed south. We'll have to be really careful, more than ever before; the last thing we want to do is run up on them or have them see us." Bree ran a hand through her hair. "Man, I wish I had a way to wash this mop. I hate having dirty hair."

"I could cut it for you. I have a dull pocketknife," Price quipped.

Bree rolled her eyes, but smiled, then turned to Rian and David. "Is Kanichi Springs due south?"

Rian checked to make sure the group of men was out of sight, and pulled out the map. "Looks like it's southeast a little. Maybe if we go east, then turn south, we can avoid running into those guys."

242

"Well, we need to move out. We aren't getting anywhere by hiding." David adjusted his pack. "Let's go. Our food will run out today, and the longer we take to get there, the hungrier we're gonna be."

"We need to be careful not to go too far east," Rian commented, running his finger southeast on the map. "If we do, we'll start getting into areas that are a little more populated. We'll be crossing Highway 69 at some point, and I-40, and then the Canadian River and Highway 2.

"Looks like Highway 2 crosses the Canadian just north of Whitefield. I think I'd rather find another way to get on the other side of that river. I've had my fill of bridges. The contour markings on the map show that the terrain gets steeper the further we go."

"Yes. We're entering what I guess you'd call the foothills of the Kiamichis." David looked around. "This is beautiful country."

Rian refolded the map and stuck it into a pocket of his cargo pants. 'Okay. Let's go. Those guys are probably far enough away now. I'll take point."

Rian set a grueling pace, but stopped occasionally to survey the area. He led them past farms and ranches, and soon, they approached Highway 69. Staying in the trees as much as possible, they moved slightly southwest, parallel to the highway, until they came to a spot where they could cross out of sight of any houses.

"I'll go first, then cover you. One at a time, fast, and keep your eyes and ears on full alert." And with that, Rian took a quick look around and darted across the highway.

Bree followed, then Price, and David came across last. Rian gestured for them to move out, and continued leading them, turning toward the east again.

***

That afternoon, the four exhausted travelers collapsed on the ground in a tiny clearing in the woods. They had made considerable progress, the urgency of getting to their destination growing due to the lack of food supplies.

243

"We've eaten all the dried fruit we had, and all but one MRE. We need to fish or trap or *something*, and soon, or we'll be too weak to continue," Bree said calmly.

"I have a makeshift fishing kit in my pack," Rian said. "The map shows a lot of creeks in this area. If we knew exactly where we are, we could find one and go fishing."

"We crossed two creeks earlier. Does the map say what their names were?" David asked.

"Let me look." Rian got the map out. "Yeah. Butler Creek and Dirty Creek. It's a good thing they were shallow. I bet a couple of weeks ago, we wouldn't have been able to get across. I think we must be getting really close to Highway 64. If we turn south, it looks as though we might be able to skirt around the Rattlesnake Mountains, but it'll put us awfully close to a little town called Warner."

"There's a college there. That's about all I know about Warner," Price offered.

"Well," Rian drawled, "if we parallel the highway for a while, we'll come to another creek, just past the town. I can't find a name on that one, but maybe we could find a good fishing spot. If we don't get there before dark, we can fish some in the morning, I guess."

"Can we rest for just a few more minutes? My legs feel like they're made out of jelly," Bree moaned. "I just need to be off them for a bit."

"Okay, but let's listen to our surroundings and not talk," Rian suggested.

At his friends' nods, he stood, and left the clearing, making a circuit of the area. When he returned, he sat for about ten minutes, then jumped up again.

"That's long enough, if we want to eat tonight. If we can find a place deep enough in the woods to have a fire, we can cook up a mess of fish and eat fresh food for a change, but we need to go."

The groans and dirty looks he got only made him smile. He knew he was pushing them, and he planned to continue. They could only live on fish for so long, and shooting wild game wasn't on the agenda. The sound of a shot might be their downfall.

David took the lead, heading east, and within just a few minutes, they found the highway. He waited until the others caught up, then pointed through the trees.

"Hey, we've come further than I thought," Rian said, looking surprised. "Let's turn south now; we should probably veer a little west, too, to avoid Warner."

"Why don't we go around Warner on the east side?" Price asked. "I hate backtracking."

"Okay, let me look," Rian muttered as he pulled the fraying map out yet again. "Looks like if we do that, we'll miss the branch of the creek I mentioned earlier, and it'll be about three more miles before we get to another one. What do you think?"

Bree bent down and touched her toes, arching her back, then straightened. "I'm good for a few more miles, unless you *guys* wanna wimp out."

That earned her a light punch in the arm from Price. "That'll be the day. Let's cross the highway and try for that other creek."

Chapter Thirty-One – November 27
Southeastern Oklahoma

Jen stepped slowly through the cache cavern, reading labels on the plastic tubs that held their supplies. As she moved around the stack of buckets and canisters, an arm wrapped around her waist, lifting her off her feet and pulling her against a hard, masculine body.

"Shane Ramsey, I'm going to learn enough kenpo to kick your butt if you don't stop sneaking up on me!" Jen threatened.

He let her down slowly, and when her feet touched the floor, turned her and wrapped her up in his arms for a long kiss.

"You can try, anytime you want."

"Do that again," she whispered, and he did.

"Now, when are we going to tie the knot, sweet Jen? I'm ready for you to be my wife. Do you want a fancy wedding -- well, as fancy as it *can* be under the circumstances, or will it be simple? I'll do whatever you want, as long as it's *soon*."

"I'd like to dress nicely, but not necessarily be formal. We don't need a lot of fuss. How about one attendant each, and keep it simple?" She kissed him before he could answer.

"Simple is fine. I'll ask Tanner, of course, to be best man, and I assume you'll want Erin. Will there be hurt feelings if you don't ask Sarah and Val?"

"No, I don't think so. They understand the reality of the situation, and they'll be fine with it. Too bad there aren't any flowers this time of year."

"Please don't say you want to wait until spring," Shane begged. "Can you do without flowers?"

"Of course. It's just a wish, but I know it's unrealistic, and I'd rather have no flowers at all than wait. Hmmm. I think I can be ready in four days. Mom's still a little weak from being sick, and I want to give her time to get better. Is that soon enough?" she teased.

"No, but it'll have to do." Shane held her gently. "I love you so much, Jennifer Martin. I've never felt anything like this before. I'm the luckiest man in the world."

***

Frances was initially shocked by Jen's insistence that the wedding would take place in such a short time, but after Jen explained that she didn't want an extravagant event, Frances swallowed her disappointment, since having a big fancy wedding was impossible anyway. Like most mothers, she had envisioned a lovely wedding, with a rehearsal dinner, several bridesmaids, a church decked out with thousands of flowers and candles, and a reception dinner and dance at the country club afterwards.

Those dreams, she realized, were not going to come true, and perhaps *shouldn't* come true, since Jen had never truly shared them. Her daughter was a straightforward, modern young woman who wasn't really into fancy, over-the-top celebrations.

"What will you wear? And what will *I* wear?" Frances asked. "I didn't pack any dressy clothes, knowing that we'd be living in the country."

"You're about the same size as Lydia, and I know she has some nice dresses. I'm sure she'll let you borrow something. I don't know what possessed me to pack it, but I have a very nice dress that I bought to wear to church. I've only worn it once. It's ivory, and it'll be perfect. We aren't going to be formal, or even semi-formal, just what you used to call 'Sunday dress'."

Jen thought for a moment, and added, "Shane already has a suit, and so does Tanner. The guests will have to be more casual. That can't be helped. But Mom, I'm so happy to be marrying Shane, it doesn't matter what we wear."

"He's a fine young man, and we think the world of him. Your father is especially pleased that you'll have someone who can protect you in this crazy world. We're happy for you, sweetie, and we'll welcome Shane into the family without reservation."

"Thanks, Mom. Now, Erin said that we can have a nice dinner after, and I was wondering…do you think you could manage a cake? Now that we're using the lodge kitchen again, we'd *really* like to have cake."

"I'll be glad to do that, honey. It'll be my pleasure."

"Shane went to town with Vince today to take supplies, and he's going to ask Ken and Terri to come. Tanner said he and Ian would drive in and get them. There's a risk to using the truck, but he and Erin insisted."

Their discussion was interrupted by Mac and Gus, who burst into the lodge living room with huge smiles on their faces.

"What's got you two so cheerful?" Jen asked.

"Give us a sec to round up some of the others, and we'll tell you." Mac's grin grew even wider.

Several minutes later, those who were able to come gathered in the lodge. A few people were still feeling the effects of food poisoning, and three were on duty in the caves, but the rest were curious to know what news Mac had heard on the radio.

"There was an official announcement – they're repeating it every twenty minutes," Gus said breathlessly. "They said that OPEC has lifted the embargo effective immediately, and FEMA announced that people in the camps who want to leave will be allowed to go, but those who want to stay can help grow food and they'll be paid for it. Also, the state governments are being asked to concentrate on rounding up any escapees from prisons, and to start hiring, or rehiring as the case may be, police and firefighters. The National Guard has been activated to secure all the major cities that are still under gang control, and they're going to start distributing food and supplies."

Mac stopped to catch his breath, and Gus took over. "Their priorities are to get the bad guys off the streets, get the grid going again, make sure the Internet is up and running, and distribute food. There's a new organization, too, staffed by volunteer docs, nurses, and dentists. They're setting up offices in each state and planning to focus on getting hospitals and clinics reestablished.

"We know it's going to take a long time for things to get back to anything resembling normal, but we can start again. We can gradually rebuild this country."

"And there's a serious note to all this, too, I'm afraid," Mac interjected. "The people who poisoned our troops in Afghanistan have been tried by an international tribunal and executed, along with those who attacked our bases. I'm sure they didn't get them all, but they got a lot of them. The two American pilots were court-martialed and sentenced to life without parole in Leavenworth. They said on the radio that the sentence was what turned things around. OPEC could tell that we were serious about punishing those pilots, and they even admitted that the Afghans got a fair trial, probably because the US let other nations prosecute them under international law."

Chapter Thirty-Two – November 28-29
Eastern and Southeastern Oklahoma

Birdsong woke Bree early, and she lay on the ground, staring up through the tree limbs, watching the sky change colors. She thought of her parents, and how much she would miss them. She remembered her brother, who had been her best friend growing up. So much loss, and yet, she was alive and had new friends who had proven that they would stick by her.

Her medical career was on hold indefinitely, but she had used her knowledge to help her companions, and would continue to offer aid when needed. Sadness mingled with hope as she wondered what they would find in Kanichi Springs.

The day before, they had continued their trek until they reached the creek Rian had seen on the map. Ever since they'd left the canoes behind, they'd crossed numerous secondary roads, mostly paved, but some that were dirt. Those didn't seem to cause as much anxiety as the major highways, although they knew that trouble could come from anywhere.

With about an hour of daylight left, Rian had gotten out his little homemade fishing kit, which consisted of line and three hooks wrapped in aluminum foil and placed inside a baggie. He cut the line and tied pieces of it onto tree limbs that David cut and trimmed.

Bree dug up some worms for bait, and they soon discovered that the fish were biting. Three of them dangled baited hooks in the creek while Price dug a Dakota hole and started a fire. He then wove slender green sticks into a makeshift grate on which to cook the fish.

Rian and David cleaned them, and Bree cooked what seemed like a feast. After eating their fill, Bree took first watch. They were all very tired, but having full stomachs helped a lot.

David had last watch, and as Bree began to stir that morning, she looked for him, but didn't see him anywhere. She needed to empty her bladder, so she got up, stretched, and walked toward a cluster of trees that would give her a little privacy.

As she stepped around behind the trees, already unzipping her jeans, she saw David, sprawled on the ground and bleeding from a small gash on his head. She knelt and checked his pulse. It was strong, and he was breathing, but out cold.

She noticed that Rian was getting up, and hissed his name, urgently gesturing for him to come. He grabbed his rifle and ran to her, taking in the situation at a glance.

"He has a knot on his head. I think someone hit him, but why?" She stayed relatively calm, turning David over to check for other injuries.

There were none. He had a purplish goose egg beneath the gash on the left side of his forehead, but no other injuries. He groaned, and opened his eyes, squinting at the light that shone through the leaves.

"Wha…what happened?" he murmured.

"You've been hit in the head with something. Rian, go get a flashlight so I can check his pupils."

Rian ran to get the light out of his pack, but the camo bag wasn't where he had left it the night before, and neither was David's. The packs belonging to Price and Bree were on the other side of the clearing. His and David's had been together, next to a tree, but they were gone.

"Price, wake up!" Rian shook him, and Price groggily sat up.

"Is it my watch?" he asked.

"No, you already stood watch. Wake up! Shake yourself or slap yourself, but *wake up!*"

Price stood up and shook off the profound sleep that seemed to have taken over his brain. "What's going on? Where's David? And Bree?" he asked, looking around their tiny camp.

"David's hurt. Do you have a flashlight in your pack?"

"Yeah. What do you need a light for? It's daytime."

"Just get it, okay?" Rian's patience was wearing thin.

Price dug around in his pack and got out his flashlight. Rian grabbed it and ran over to hand it to Bree.

She checked David's pupils, which responded appropriately, then raised her hand and asked him how many fingers she was holding up. He jokingly said "Six," and she knew he'd be okay.

"C'mon," Rian urged. "Let's get you back to camp."

Bree cleared her throat. "If you'll excuse me, I'll be there in a few minutes. And no peeking!"

Rian helped David up and Price got on the other side to assist.

As soon as Bree got back, Rian broke the bad news to them. "Our packs, mine and David's, are gone. Whoever hit David must have stolen them."

"Do you think it was just one person?" Bree asked.

"Yeah. If there had been more, they would have taken all the packs, and all the rifles. As it is, they only took two packs and one rifle. That sounds like maybe it was all one person could carry."

David put his hand to his head. "Man, I've got a terrible headache."

"Don't get dirt in that cut. I need to clean it up and bandage it. Do we have any first aid supplies left?" Bree stood and retrieved Price's pack, tossing it to him.

He dug through the little that was left and found a baggie with a small roll of gauze and some tape. Bree used a little of their clean water to sponge off the dried blood, and covered the small wound with gauze.

"We've got problems, people." Rian looked worried.

"What? More than we already had?" Price asked, appalled.

"Yeah, 'fraid so. The Sawyer water filtration stuff was in my pack. The water we have in the two packs is all we have to drink. It's a good thing we got into the habit of filling the reservoirs every night."

David started to shake his head, but decided that wasn't a good idea when pain shot through his skull. "Price should have a LifeStraw in his pack."

Price started digging again, and came up with the precious piece of survival equipment. "Yep. Still got it."

David had been sitting with his back against a tree, but lay down suddenly, obviously dizzy. "I don't know if I can handle a hike like we had yesterday," he moaned.

"We should move, though. Whoever did this might come back," Rian warned.

"Please let me rest a little first. My head has a drumline marching through it." David looked pale.

"Okay, buddy. Rest a bit. Bree, I have an idea. Come with me to the creek," Rian got up and offered his hand to help Bree up.

He hadn't put his fishing kit back into his pack the night before, leaving it lying on the ground nearby. He picked up the baggie and led Bree to the stream, where he filled the baggie halfway full of the cold water.

"We don't have any ice, but would this substitute for an ice pack to reduce the swelling?" he asked.

"Rian, that's good thinking. I think it'll help with the pain, too."

***

David kept the improvised cold pack on his bump for quite a while, then announced that he was ready to move. He was shaky and slow, so progress wasn't nearly as good as the previous day. By early afternoon, he said his head hurt too much to continue. They found a secluded spot to rest, and David quickly fell asleep.

He woke three hours later, feeling much better, and urged them to move out again. Within thirty minutes, they came to Highway 64. Rian checked the map, and mentioned that I-40 was only about a mile further.

"How you doing, David? Can you keep going?" Bree asked.

"Yeah. I'm fine."

"Now there's a tall tale if I ever heard one," Price chimed in. "Don't try to be a hero, brother. If you need to stop, say so."

"Let's see if we can find another creek. That fish last night was good," David replied softly.

Rian looked doubtful, but decided to go with that plan. "We can head straight south and catch a creek in about six miles, or we

253

can go southeast and hit one in four or five miles. If you feel up to it, David, I think the Canadian River is only about ten miles. It's up to you; you're setting the pace."

"How about we go until I can't go anymore?" David offered.

"Okay, but don't totally wear yourself out," Bree advised.

***

Just keep putting one foot in front of the other. I can do this, David told himself over and over as he plodded along between Bree and Price. Rian had once again taken the point, and other than the pain in his head, which had dulled from a blinding throb to a constant ache, David felt like he should be able to continue indefinitely.

It hadn't occurred to him that due to his injury, Rian had slowed the pace considerably. They knew they were getting close to Kanichi Springs, maybe less than twenty miles, but Rian refused to hurry, in spite of their eagerness to reach their destination.

They were short one rifle, David's, but he had a handgun and that would have to do. As he walked, he envisioned the reunion with their parents and Jen. He knew it would be wonderful to see them, to be with them again. Their family had always been close, and David had missed the joking and teasing that was their way of showing affection.

Price brought up the rear, hiking through the woods and across an occasional field, but stopping frequently to study the forest all around them. Rian had taken him aside while David rested earlier that day, and they had decided that there was a slight possibility that whoever had attacked David might follow them and attempt to steal their other packs.

Almost hoping that the culprit would be that stupid, Price was ready to repay him for hurting his brother. Somehow, in his mind, Price had decided that the attacker was a man, a loner who preyed on anyone who wandered through the forest.

David hurried forward to catch up to Rian. "I'm better now, and I wish you'd pick up the pace a little. I just realized that you're taking it easy. If it's because of me, it's not necessary. I'm fine, and I'm going to have this headache walking or sitting or asleep, so let's get a move on."

Rian grinned at him. "I wondered when you'd notice. Are you sure you're okay?"

"Yeah, I'm sure. I want to cover some ground. I think it's finally soaking in that Price and I are going to be back with our family soon. It hasn't seemed real until now, because I was too focused on the trip itself."

All four friends dived for cover as a shot rang out. It seemed to come from the northwest. Price had lagged behind, some instinct alerting him to another presence in the woods. He had flopped to his stomach on the ground right before the shot, having caught a hint of movement out of the corner of his eye.

He fired, and heard a cry as the shooter fell. Rian approached, darting from tree to tree, until he was could see that Price was alright. He scanned the forest and saw the figure on the ground, grasping his leg and moaning.

Price signaled for Rian to circle around to the left, while he went right. They crept cautiously toward the figure, rifles pointed at him, until they saw that it wasn't a *him* at all.

The shooter was a young woman, maybe eighteen or nineteen years old, wearing camo pants and a shirt several sizes too big. She was dirty, with stringy strawberry blond hair partially hidden by an old watch cap.

"Why the hell did you shoot me?" she demanded.

"Because you shot at us," Rian answered.

"No, I did not! I didn't even notice you. I was concentrating on the rabbit."

"What rabbit?" Price looked at her with suspicion.

"The one I shot, dummy. Why would I waste a bullet on you? You don't look very appetizing," she sneered.

Bree ran up, and knelt beside the girl. "I need to take a look at that leg."

"Get away from me! I don't need your help."

Bree looked her in the eye. "I'm Bree, and I'm a doctor. You're bleeding, and I need to see how bad it is. I just want to help."

"Okay, but only if those two move way back. One of them shot me, and I don't trust any of you."

Rian and Price joined David, who was sitting on a rock nearby. Bree helped the girl pull her pants down, and saw that the bullet had grazed her, high on the outside of the thigh.

"You're lucky. I don't have to dig it out, but I do need to stop the bleeding and clean it. Are you alone out here?"

"Why do you want to know? It's not your business."

"Well, since you are going to need to stay off that leg for a few days, I thought it might be good if you had someone to help you." Bree gave her a stern look. "We thought you were shooting at us. We've been shot at before, and maybe we're a little jumpy, but it was an honest mistake."

"I hit a rabbit. If you don't believe me, go look. Should be right over there." She pointed, then looked at the wound. "That doesn't look too bad. Hurts like the dickens, but I'll heal."

"Only if it's kept clean and the bandages are changed every day, preferably twice a day for a day or two. You're like the rest of us, not able to bathe very often, so the biggest risk is infection."

Bree cleaned the wound with water from her pack's reservoir, and opened a little packet of ointment, which she smeared across the red gash. Then she bandaged it, and signaled for Rian and Price to come over.

"If she'll tell us where, you need to carry her home. Walking will almost certainly cause more bleeding." She turned to the girl. "Where do you need us to take you?"

Looking defeated, the young woman finally gave in to the fact that she needed help. "Not far. I have a little cabin just east of here. But please, I need that rabbit."

Bree glanced back at David. "Hey, would you get the rabbit for us? We're going to take this young lady home."

Rian scooped her up. She was extremely thin, as were most people lately, but he could tell, if she was cleaned up a little and her hair was combed, she'd be a pretty girl.

"What's your name?" he asked. "I'm Rian, and the other guys are Price and David."

"I'm Zoe. I live with my little brother, Ethan. He can take care of me."

Price came up and walked beside them for a few minutes, looking like he had something on his mind. Finally, he seemed to make his mind up what to say. He looked at Zoe, his eyes haunted.

"I'm truly sorry. I should have made certain that I was shooting at an enemy, not just someone trying to find food."

Zoe stared at him. "I guess I saw you guys, but it really didn't register. We needed food, and I just didn't stop to think."

Price looked relieved. "Please understand that I'm not usually so impulsive. Sometime before daylight this morning, someone hit my brother in the head and stole his rifle and two of our packs. My first thought when you shot was that whoever it was had followed us, and was using David's rifle against us. I was angry at whoever hurt him, and saw an opportunity to get even."

Zoe looked thoughtful. "I think I might know who did it. There's a mean old coot who lives not far from us. He's probably in his early forties, and he's been told to stay off our property or we'll shoot on sight. I know he's been stealing stuff, and what happened to you sounds just like him. He can move around the forest without making a sound, and sometimes he'll go several miles, looking for something to steal."

"Will you be safe? I hate to leave you here if he's a danger to you," Price said worriedly.

"I don't think he'll bother us, but if he does, he'll be sorry. My little brother is almost fifteen, and he shot competitively. My parents were negotiating with a company that makes guns. They wanted to feature him in commercials and on a couple of hunting programs."

"Parents?" Rian interrupted. "What happened?"

"They left us here and tried to get to our house in McAlester, but never came back. We don't know what happened, but they've been gone for a couple of months."

"So, why did they do that?" Price asked, puzzled.

"We had some supplies there. They had a full tank of gas, but we were here when things got bad, and we just stayed, at least, we did until we ran out of everything. They thought they could drive in and get a load of stuff from the house, then we'd planned to just stay here until things settle down. How bad is it out there? We haven't had any news in a long time."

"It's bad, Zoe. I'm sorry to have to tell you how bad. Anyone with food, a car with gas in it, supplies of any kind...well, they're in danger of having those things taken from them by force. The government was rounding people up and putting them in camps, too. Maybe that's where your parents are. I hope so, anyway," Price explained.

"There's our cabin," she said. "My brother is supposed to be inside with the door locked. When either one of us is alone there, we stay in until the other one comes back."

The door of the little log cabin opened, and a gangly teenager stepped out, holding a rifle, but not pointing it at them.

"Sis, what happened?" the kid asked.

"I got shot. Don't worry. It's not serious, just a graze, and it was an accident. It'll teach me to pay better attention to my surroundings from now on."

The boy looked at the stranger who carried his sister, then at the others, studying their faces. Whatever he saw seemed to reassure him, and he stepped back so Rian could carry Zoe inside.

Bree stepped up to the young man. "I'm Bree, and I was about to start my medical residency when the collapse started. Your sister has a wound on her thigh, and you'll need to keep her off that leg for a few days and change the bandage at least once a day."

"I can do that. I took a first aid class at survival camp last year." He gave Bree a searching look, then added, "Thank you."

David handed the boy the rabbit. "She got dinner while she was out. Is there anything we can do for you before we leave?"

"No, I can't think of anything. Where are y'all headed?"

"A little town called Kanichi Springs," Price said, breaking their rule of never telling anyone their real destination.

"Cool. I know some people from there. We met at survival camp. Paul, Quinn, and Amaya Foster are their names. Quinn was my best friend at camp, and...well...his sister sure is pretty," the boy stammered, blushing.

258

"We'll tell them we met you, if they're still around," Bree promised, smiling. "Are you sure you want to stay here alone?"

Ethan looked at Zoe, who was sitting on the sofa, her injured leg propped up on a small coffee table. Zoe shrugged.

"Yes, we're sure. If our parents are still alive, they'll come back here. If we leave, they won't know where to find us."

"Well, if you have to leave at some point, come to Kanichi Springs and we'll help you all we can," David promised.

"We need to go," Rian reminded his friends. "Zoe, Ethan, take care."

The four friends had just started toward the door when they heard a male voice yelling.

"C'mon outta there, purty gal. Ah'm tarred o' waitin' fer ya. Ah mean to have ya, or Ah'm gonna kill that there boy!"

Rian turned to stare at Zoe. "Your friendly neighbor? Is that the guy you suspect of stealing our packs?"

"Yes. He's drunk again, I guess. He has a still in his barn and makes moonshine."

"You sort of neglected to tell us that pervert has designs on you," Bree scolded.

"He only does that when he's drunk. We just stay in and wait until he passes out. He'll sleep it off, then do it again in a day or two."

Ethan sat down beside his sister. "Zoe, he's getting worse and you know it. It's just a matter of time until one of us goes out to hunt and he's out there waiting for us. He's crazy, and he wants you."

"You want us to run him off for you?" David asked.

"Not your problem, but thanks," Zoe said. "We've been handling it for weeks, and we'll be fine."

"Zoe, we need to leave, and he's out there with a rifle. If we try to leave, and he so much as thinks about raising that barrel toward one of us, we'll put *him* out of *your* misery…permanently. There's no need for you to have to live in fear." Bree looked intently into the younger girl's eyes. "I promise you, problems like that man don't just fade away."

Bree turned to look at her friends. "Guys, take the windows, and one of you come with me." She wore her best "no nonsense" look. "We're going to stop this right now."

David and Price each picked one of the front windows, and Rian followed Bree out onto the porch, both with rifles held at the low ready position.

A middle-aged man stood in the yard, carrying a rifle that looked very familiar. He stared at Bree, almost slobbering in lust.

"Wahl, now. Ain't that a hot piece of wummin? Whar'd ya come from, missy? Ah b'lieve Ah like ya even better than that there other gal."

Bree raised her rifle, pointing it directly at the man's face. Her eyes narrowed, and she spoke with a terrifying softness.

"Try to take me, you piece of filth. I dare you."

The man glanced at Rian, jerking his rifle up and firing before he took time to aim properly. Bree shot him right between the eyes. The man's shot hit one of the landscaping blocks that bordered an empty flower bed in front of the porch.

"Let's drag that nasty excuse for a man out of here so he won't stink up the place," Bree said coldly.

"Remind me not to ever make you mad," Rian muttered.

Ethan ran out to see what had happened. "You shot him," he said, looking at Rian.

"Nope. Bree shot him. I wish I could see you two compete against each other. She's the best shot I've ever seen, but I hear you're pretty good, too." Rian patted the boy's shoulder.

"Yeah, but I've never shot anybody, and that guy shot back. She's really brave, isn't she?"

"Yeah, she is."

Rian and Price dragged the body away, rolling it into a ravine where it would hopefully be washed away in the next heavy rain. While they were doing that, Bree went back inside to talk to Zoe.

"Where did that guy live, sweetie?"

"Just a little way south of here," Zoe answered, eyes wide with disbelief that their main threat had been removed.

"We're going to his cabin and get our packs back. It was David's rifle the scumbag had, so it's a good bet that he's the one who pulled that little stunt this morning. As far as I'm concerned, anything left in that cabin is yours and Ethan's. Your neighbor won't be needing it anymore."

Zoe swallowed, then whispered, "Thank you. God bless you with safe travels for the rest of your trip. We'll never forget you."

Chapter Thirty-Three – Nov. 29-Dec. 1
Southeastern Oklahoma

Lydia smiled as she watched Frances model yet another dress. It was fun to see her friend enjoying the selection of clothing that was much nicer than anything she had worn in months. Living in blue jeans with a tee and a hoodie had made most of them forget the feminine pleasure of dressing up, but Frances was rediscovering that joy as she prepared for her daughter's wedding.

"This one. I love it, Lydia. It's just right: not too fancy, not too plain."

"I agree. That plum color is good on you, too," Lydia commented, noticing how Frances's beautiful blue eyes sparkled.

"Mom, that's the one, except you're liable to outshine me at my own wedding!" Jen teased.

"That will never happen, dear, but thank you. You know, I've often wondered how you could look so much like me, yet be so tiny. I'm just a bit more than average height, and you're petite, yet our features and coloring are just alike. Do you know what Shane calls you?"

"Uh, no. Do I want to?" Jen joked.

"I think so. He says you're 'fun-sized' and he lists that when he talks about all your good qualities, so I'm pretty sure he likes it. You two make such a cute couple." Frances turned so Jen could reach the zipper. "Lydia, thank you so much for loaning me this dress. You're such a sweet friend."

"I'm very glad to help. Is there anything else I can do for either of you? I have shoes that go with that, if you'd like to try them."

"Lydia," Jen interrupted, "I think Tanner's going to drive the Explorer to pick up Ken and Terri. There'll be plenty of room for you, and we would love for you to come."

"I'd be happy to. Thank you for inviting me. I believe you said the guests would be more casual?"

"Yes, but you can wear whatever you want. We aren't being at all picky about clothes."

"Great. I'll be there. It'll be good to see everyone again."
I've been seriously considering coming back, anyway. I think I'm ready, and it will be one less mouth to feed here in town. I can do a lot more to help there than I can here."

***

David set a brisk pace as they left the trashy cabin that had belonged to his attacker. *That man lived worse than an animal. There was literally trash and moldy dishes everywhere. How disgusting!* They had recovered their packs and David carried his rifle again, and all of them were hopeful that this would be the next-to-last day of their journey.

All of their various wounds were healing nicely, and Rian was walking on his injured leg without even a twinge of pain. They had much to be thankful for, and David hoped with all his heart that they would arrive at their destination without further encounters with anyone who wanted to hurt, steal, or kill.

They had decided, after a brief study of the map, that they could probably stay in the woods until they reached Whitefield, only emerging to cross minor roads. The river still lay ahead, and the only ways to cross it without going many miles out of the way were the bridge north of Whitefield, or wading across.

Zoe told them that they were about two miles south of the halfway point between Porum and Whitefield, so they had traveled further than they had thought. She also told them to take at least a day's worth of food when they picked up their packs from her neighbor's cabin. They hadn't done it, choosing instead to leave the food for Zoe and Ethan. All of it was probably stolen from travelers such as themselves, and they knew that Zoe wouldn't be able to get out to hunt for a while, and Ethan would need to stay close by to help her for a few days.

Their recent experiences had taught them to be more alert than ever. Price knew that had his shot gone higher, or hit an artery, he might have killed Zoe. His assumption that anyone in the woods was an enemy had caused injury to a young woman who wasn't doing anything wrong. Guilt wracked his conscience, even after she forgave him.

Avoiding other people had become part of life for them, even though they had met many good and generous folks along the way. There was danger all around them, and they each had their own demons to fight in that regard.

Bree had learned that women were particularly vulnerable in a society where there were few protections against rape. She longed to be in a safer environment where she didn't have to fear strangers. She knew that without weapons or special training, a woman was at the mercy of any man who got his hands on her. She was glad to have three men to protect her, but worried that other women didn't have anyone.

David's abdominal wound had given him the worst pain he had ever experienced. The ambush had made him hyper-vigilant, and his eyes seldom rested on anything for more than a few seconds. He had trouble sleeping, too, knowing that attackers could sneak up on them. He had a bruise on his forehead to prove it.

Price had become a guardian, overprotective of his brother and their friends. It made him a trifle reckless with his own safety and totally fearless in any fight to keep his companions from harm. His anger at those who had hurt his older brother had surprised him. He'd never felt the need for vengeance before, but in his mind, that was tempered with the need to protect others from the villains they encountered. He found his justification for the violence he was ready to commit in the belief that it was for the good of innocent people.

Rian was less affected than the others. His military service had prepared him for a world without law, and he was accustomed to danger, but the depth of his friendship with these three people had grown beyond even what he had felt for his closest buddies in the Army. These young adults were his family, and he thought of them as his brothers and sister. In fact, as close as he was to his own siblings, he loved these three just as much. They had been through a lot together, and he trusted them to watch his back.

However, ever since he'd been sent to the Middle East, Rian had become cynical about most people, and now that he was back, he had lost faith in his fellow Americans after seeing what they were capable of doing. It was almost as bad as being in Afghanistan; there was no way to be sure who would help or who would try to kill him. He found himself fighting an urge to close people out, to keep them at a distance so they couldn't betray him. The only ones he knew he could trust were David, Price, and Bree.

He was even apprehensive about living at the lodge, where he might be tempted to let his guard down. He wasn't ready to let himself relax around strangers, and that's what the people at the lodge were, yet he knew that he needed to accept help from them. That didn't sit well with his current state of mind.

They found the river after walking for a couple of hours, and followed it to the highway. There was nobody on the bridge, but they crossed it one at a time, covering each other with more caution than ever before. Somehow, being so close to their destination made them doubly aware of all the things that could go wrong.

When all four were on the south side of the river, they turned immediately toward the east in an effort to avoid the town of Whitefield. They knew very little about it, but didn't want to take the risk of going through any town on foot.

Rian carried the map in his hand now, folded to show the area around Kanichi Springs. They were so close that he feared passing the tiny community without realizing it.

David's hand went up, signaling a stop. He'd seen movement in the distance. Two men, both carrying rifles, strode through the trees at an angle that would take them out of sight in a few minutes. When he was sure it was safe, David gestured for them to continue.

They walked up and down hills, crossing roads and bypassing residences, and found a deep pool in a small creek, where they caught enough fish to fill their bellies. They camped, but decided that after David's head injury, whoever was on guard would stay close to the others, and not walk around the perimeter of the camp anymore.

The next morning, they set out again. They were quieter than they'd ever been on this trip, each of them lost in private thoughts and worries. Stopping at midday near yet another stream, they took the time to catch and cook a few fish. Since they hadn't had breakfast, all of them were feeling the effects of hunger.

After their lunch, they set out once again, this time with Rian in the lead. The terrain was becoming much more steep, yet there were acres of flat meadows as well. They saw a doe running from a buck, and knew that the rut was on. They found scat, and wondered what kind of animal had left it, not realizing that there were bears in the area.

Late in the afternoon, they came to a paved road. They could see a sign far to the east, too far away to read, so they stayed in the edge of the forest and headed that way. When they got closer, they saw that it was exactly the sign they had all hoped it was. The road led to Kanichi Springs.

Energized by hope, they walked faster and faster, until Bree got a stitch in her side and asked them to slow down a little. Soon, they saw the old grocery store, and passed shops that had been damaged by the tornado. They wandered around the town, looking for someone, anyone, who could help them find the lodge.

Ken watched from behind a bush as the four strangers sat down on the steps of the courthouse. He crept closer, trying to hear what they were saying.

"Where is everyone?" the young woman asked. "I thought there would be people here who knew Erin."

"Well, Dad told us on the radio that they had friends in town. I don't know where they are, but if we don't find someone, we'll have to start looking for the lodge ourselves. It's north of town somewhere." The speaker was a thin young man who greatly resembled another young man in the group, and Ken had the strangest feeling that he should know who those two were..

"Let's find a place to make camp for the night. It'll be hard to sleep with Price's stomach growling so much, but we need to get some rest." This time the speaker looked a little older, a little more mature than the others. His posture made Ken think that he'd been in the military at some point.

"Yeah, you're right. Meeting your parents and sister, and all the others at the lodge will have to wait."

Ken's brain finally clicked: the two young men resembled BJ Martin! He stepped out and cleared his throat.

Bree spun around, gasping, and Ken suddenly saw four rifles pointed at him. He showed his hands, and spoke softly.

"Welcome to Kanichi Springs. I'm Ken Abbott. Is there anything I can do to help you?"

The four stared at him, unsure what to say, so Ken continued. "I overheard you talking. Who are you looking for? Maybe I know them."

The four rifle barrels dropped. "We want to locate Erin Miller and our parents, BJ and Frances Martin. Our sister, Jen, too." David eyed the emaciated-looking man. "Do you know them?"

"Please tell me your names, and prove to me that you truly are Jen's brothers," Ken replied, looking back and forth between David and Price. "Surely you can understand the need for caution. We don't just direct strangers to our friends' homes."

Price chuckled. "Oh, we do understand. Trust me, we really, *really* understand. I'm Price, and that's my brother, David. We were conscripted into NERC, but we escaped from the camp in Pueblo. We need to find Jen, and her friends, Erin, Sarah, and Valerie."

He gestured toward the other two young people. "These two are our friends, Bree and Rian. We never would have made it without their help. What else can I tell you as proof?"

"What was your nickname as a boy? Where did you go to college? Where did Jen work? What did your dad do for a living?" Ken shot back.

"David and I were known as the Martin Menaces because we liked to play practical jokes on people. We were both students at NSU, and Jen worked at Bob Hurley Ford in Tulsa. Dad worked as a geologist. Anything else?"

"Yes. How did Erin get the lodge, what did she do for a living, and what does Jen look like?"

David stepped up. "Erin inherited the lodge when her uncle, Ernie Miller, died of cancer in the spring. She edited his books about 'the end of the world as we know it' and his survival manuals, too. Jen looks like our mom, blonde and very pretty, with blue eyes, but Mom is taller and more, uh, filled out. Jen is a little bitty ball of fire."

"As I said, welcome to Kanichi Springs. If you'll come with me, our friends will feed you and give you a chance to clean up a little, then we'll talk more."

Price looked at David, then at the others, who shrugged. "Okay, but where are we going?" Price asked.

Ken chuckled. "To Ernie's house. It's not far. Please, forgive me for questioning you so thoroughly, but we've had some people cause trouble, and I was just protecting my group."

He led them down the street and around to the home that Erin had so generously allowed them to use. Ken spent the time explaining how so many townspeople came to be living there.

***

Jen stared at the lovely woman in the mirror. She studied her reflection: tiny and well-proportioned, and looking as close to perfect as she ever had in her life. Erin had styled her hair in a simple French twist, which showed off Jen's slender neck and strong cheekbones. She was stunningly beautiful.

They were in one of the downstairs bedrooms in the lodge, one that Erin planned for the newlyweds to use with almost complete privacy for the next week. Only the kitchen and the stairs would be used by others, giving the newlyweds as much of a honeymoon as possible at the present time.

"Oh, Erin! Thank you for doing my hair. It's perfect – not too fancy, but still elegant. And Mom, thank you for taking up the dress. I didn't realize that my weight loss would make it hang like a sack on me. You did a wonderful job altering it."

Tanner tapped on the door, a secretive smile on his face. "You ladies ready? Everyone's waiting."

Jen checked her reflection one last time, and smiled at her mother and friends, just as another knock sounded.

Frances opened it, and BJ stood there, wearing the biggest grin that anyone had ever seen on his face. "Honey, Jen – we have extra guests for the wedding."

"What? Dad, what in the world are you talking about?" Jen demanded, looking puzzled.

"May they come in and say hello?" BJ asked, teasingly.

Jen and Frances glanced at each other, wondering if he had lost his mind.

"Sure, I guess," Jen murmured hesitantly.

"Boys," BJ called.

David and Price stepped into the room. Frances paled, her big blue eyes rapidly filling with tears. She was immediately wrapped up in a huge bear hug from both her sons at once. Jen joined them, then BJ, and the Martin family was together again for the first time in months.

Frances began to bombard the boys with questions about when and how they got there, but BJ shushed her.

"Honey, there'll be plenty of time later for them to tell us every detail of what they've been doing since they were taken from us, and for you to meet the two friends they brought with them, but right now, there's a young man in the living room waiting for their sister to become his bride. Poor Shane is so nervous; let's not keep him waiting any longer."

He turned to Jen, who was drying the tears from her eyes. "Are you ready, sweetie?" he said as he offered her his arm.

Author's Note

Thank you for reading *Kiamichi Journey*. If you enjoyed it, please write a review on amazon.com. It will help sales, which will help make my car payment!

I love hearing from readers, so if you have comments, suggestions, or just want to say hello, you can find me on Facebook or email me at chenryauthor@yahoo.com.

None of the incidents described in any of my books is intended to reflect poorly on individuals, cities, towns, or organizations. I will confess, however, that I was planning a vicious attack on our intrepid travelers when they passed through Guthrie, Oklahoma. I went to Guthrie to get a feel for the terrain where the fight was to take place, and drove around town for a while. Then I stopped to grab a bite to eat. That's when I began to have second thoughts. Everyone I encountered in Guthrie was friendly. I had doors opened for me, hats tipped, and greetings expressed. There I was, a stranger, and so many people were nice to me at Missy's, which has The Best Donuts Around, that I changed my mind. I decided that good things would happen in Guthrie, because it's a nice town. I'm planning a trip there with a friend this summer, so we can explore all the quaint shops downtown that I didn't have time to check out when I was there.

On another note, in *Kiamichi Storm: Book Two of the Kiamichi Survival Series*, I included an inventory list of what Uncle Ernie had stored in his supply caches. That list proved to be very popular with readers, so this time, I included a list of books that Uncle Ernie left in the cavern for Erin. If you want some great advice, detailed manuals, or just want to read a good tale, take a look.

Uncle Ernie's Survival Library

Survival in a Collapse Scenario

Absolute Anarchy: Interactive Guide to Surviving the Coming Collapse by Johnny Jacks. If you can only afford one book, this is it.

Handbook to Practical Disaster Preparedness for the Family by Arthur T. Bradley, Ph.D.

Prepper's Instruction Manual: 50 Steps to Prepare for Any Disaster by Arthur T. Bradley, Ph.D.

The Prepper's Workbook: Checklists, Worksheets, and Home Projects to Protect Your Family from Any Disaster by Scott B. Williams and Scott Finazzo.

When Disaster Strikes: A Comprehensive Guide for Emergency Planning and Crisis Survival by Matthew Stein.

The Modern Survival Manual: Surviving the Economic Collapse by Fernando "Ferfal" Aguirre.

Just in Case: How to Be Self-Sufficient When the Unexpected Happens by Kathy Harrison.

SHTF Medicine

The Survival Medicine Handbook: A Guide for When Medical Help is NOT on the Way by Joseph Alton, M.D. and Amy Alton, A.R.N.P. Again, if you can only afford one, this is the one.

Medicine for the Outdoors: The Essential Guide to First Aid and Medical Emergencies by Paul S. Auerbach, M.D.

Surviving When Modern Medicine Fails: A Definitive Guide to Essential Oils That Could Save Your Life During a Crisis by Dr. Scott A. Johnson.

Fortifying Your Property

Barbed Wire, Barricades, and Bunkers: The Free Citizens Guide to Fortifying the Home Retreat by F. J. Bohan.

Holding Your Ground: Preparing for Defense When It All Falls Apart by Joe Nobody.

Food Storage and Preparation

The Forager's Harvest: A Guide to Identifying, Harvesting, and Preparing Edible Wild Plants by Samuel Thayer.

The Prepper's Pantry: Building and Thriving with Food Storage by Anne Lang.

Emergency Food Storage & Survival Handbook: Everything You Need to Know to Keep Your Family Safe in a Crisis by Peggy Layton.

The Prepper's Cookbook: 300 Recipes to Turn Your Emergency Food into Nutritious, Delicious, Life-Saving Meals by Tess Pennington.

Better Than Store-Bought: A Cookbook by Helen Witty and Elizabeth Schneider Colchie.

Ball Complete Book of Home Preserving edited by Judi Kingry and Lauren Devine.

The Homemade Pantry: 101 Foods You Can Stop Buying and Start Making by Alana Chernila.

Food Storage: Preserving Meat, Dairy, and Eggs by Susan Gregerson and David Armstrong.

Food Storage: Preserving Fruits, Nuts, and Seeds by Susan Gregerson and David Armstrong.

Making it Yourself

Homemade: How to Make Hundreds of Everyday Products Fast, Fresh, and More Naturally from Reader's Digest.

Making It: Radical Home Ec for a Post-Consumer World by Kelly Coyne and Erik Knutzen.

Gardening

The New Self-Sufficient Gardener: The Complete Illustrated Guide to Planning, Growing, Storing, and Preserving Your Own Garden Produce by John Seymour.

Gardening When It Counts: Growing Food in Hard Times by Steve Solomon.

Post-Apocalyptic Fiction

The New Homefront Series by Steven Bird.

Society Lost Series by Steven Bird.

Canine Plague: Life Will Never Be the Same by Burt Walker.

Into the Darkness and its sequel, *Fade to Black* by Doug Kelly. *Into the Darkness* won the Best EMP Book of the Year Award.

The Survivalist Series by A. American.

EMP Survival Series by Chris Pike.

The World Burns Series by Boyd Craven.

299 Days Series by Glen Tate.

Stranded Series by Theresa Shaver.

Lucifer's Hammer by Larry Niven and Jerry Pournelle.

Apocalypse Law Series by John Grit.